I0636111

Billionaire Scandal

Billionaire Series

J.L. Ryan

Published by J.L. Ryan, 2018.

This is a work of fiction. Similarities to real people, places, or events are entirely coincidental.

BILLIONAIRE SCANDAL

First edition. June 1, 2018.

Copyright © 2018 J.L. Ryan.

ISBN: 978-1393626930

Written by J.L. Ryan.

Baby For The Billionaire

The Billionaire Boss

There had to be something she could do, but what? Rachel Greene looked at her surroundings and sighed. She jumped at the chance to live on her own, and now, well she was in over her head. She had always been the one who wanted out. Out of the family, out of the drama, out of everything, and now she was stuck in a tiny apartment in the worst neighborhood in D.C., with no hope of changing it. She put her head in her hands and sighed. On the computer screen in front of her was her budget for the next six months. No matter which way she plotted and planned, she only had about two months before it all fell apart. She leaned back in her seat, glancing at her reflection in the mirror on her desk.

She wasn't gorgeous by any means, at least not in her opinion. She was studious and bookwormy, if anything. At least that's what her brother used to call her. She had long chestnut hair and brown eyes, fringed with long lashes, something her grandmother said was a wonderful asset. She wore glasses most of the time, unless she had some special occasion, then she popped in her contacts. She was thin but still curvy, something else her grandmother said was a good thing. Not that it mattered, at 24 she had been to school most of her life and still, there was nothing to show for it. Sure, she could go home if things got too bad. The problem was, she would rather live in her car first.

She loved her family, there was no denying that. She was the oldest with a younger brother who was 20. He decided to start his adult life much earlier and was married with a three year old daughter, and a baby on the way. He also lived at home with their parents and grandmother, and his wife. When Tim started his new life, Rachel started hers. At first, her mother was sad she was moving out, but it was only a week before they moved the kids into her old room. There was something co-dependent about her family that made her want out. Everything they did, they did as one cohesive unit, no opinions required. Everything was about survival and scraping along, something Rachel was fine doing, but she would just as soon do it alone, without the heavy responsibility of six other people.

She looked back down at the screen. It wasn't doing much good right now, living her own life. She graduated from the local community college with a degree in Office Management. Somehow, her family talked her into getting student loans along the way so that she could "help out" with the extra money. Now she was in debt, with payments that were ridiculous and despite her efforts, she couldn't seem to find a job anywhere. If she'd only been able to keep her job at the hospital none of this would be happening! Even thinking about it made her skin crawl. She was good at her job there, always on time, and working harder than most. She wasn't tooting her own horn so to speak, it simply was the fact of the matter. One would think her dedication to the job would be something to applaud, but in truth it did nothing more but put her in a vulnerable situation where dirty old men could hit on her. Not just any dirty old man either. Dr. Peter Evans was her superior, she would even say that initially she liked him. It wasn't until he cornered her in a supply room groping at her that she felt disgust more than anything.

He was old enough to be her father yet he claimed that she was giving him mixed signals, which she strongly denied. He begged her not to say anything, and she didn't. If for any other reason than the fact that his career would be over if she did, and part of her believed he truly though she was into him. Every point he made was true. She came early and stayed late. She always turned in things to him personally. In her mind this was the action of a good employee, not someone looking for a good time from her boss. Either way, she now was very careful about what she did and how.

The problem was after she left the hospital, she couldn't find work anywhere. At first she told herself it would just take a little longer. But now, three weeks later, she was concerned. She leaned back in the chair and bit her thumbnail lost in thought. She didn't want to wreak havoc on her family, she certainly didn't want to sleep on a couch while paying for storage. She leaned forward again and jumped into a new job search, hopeful something would happen.

Byron Blakemore was tired and aching. He spent the early morning hours at the gym, hoping to relieve some of the stress he was carrying around, but looking across his desk he felt the familiar tension rise up. Some days he wondered what the hell he was paying these people for at all. He buzzed in Linda, who scurried in, pen and pad in hand.

> "Yes Mr. Blakemore?" She was a small lady. Probably no more than 4'9 and pushing 60. He knew she was struggling more and more to do her job, but he didn't have the heart to let her go.

> "Linda, can you set up a meeting with Carlisle please? Also, I need something purchased for my mother's birthday, I thought you might like the task." He saw her light up and he smiled to himself, Shopping seemed to be a skill most women mastered at, and retained an entire lifetime.

> "Yes, Mr. Blakemore." She scurried towards his door.

> "Oh Linda, one more thing can you send Alice in HR up for me. We need to discuss something."

At her nod, he dove back into his paperwork. There was always something that needed his attention, but this was too much. He leaned back once more rethinking the board of directors. There was no fire from any of them to make this business grow. He would be lying if he said he didn't enjoy the money, he did. He'd grown accustom to a certain kind of lifestyle and he wasn't about to give it up. He knew he had a reputation of being a stone-faced ass, but he preferred it that way, less drama. The only person who really knew him was his mother. She was a sweet woman and anyone who thought otherwise was a fool. He was worried about her, she was frail now and needed more than just he could provide. He heard the knock at his door.

"Yes, come in." It was Alice.

She walked into the room and pushed the door shut quietly locking it, before she walked over to his desk. She gave him a smile and he stood up, buttoning his jacket as he went. He walked towards her and tucked an arm around her waist, pulling her to him in a crushing kiss. She was the kind of tension relief he needed. He nibbled at her neck.

"I'm glad you're here today Alice, I'd hate to have to write you up for being absent again." He growled into her neck as she tilted back her head, enjoying his every move.

"You know very well why I was late on Monday, Mr. Blakemore." She moved to pull off her top and he gingerly kissed the tops of her breasts when his phone rang. He decided to ignore it and continue on until they were both naked.

She moved with precision as she worked her way down his body. There was something nice about how she took charge, not making him work for it. It was a mutual understanding the two of them shared. Both needing something, and eager to help the other.

Even now as she moved her mouth down his body he relaxed. He always enjoyed the talent she had at making things happen quickly and today was no different. He stopped her, pulling her up the length of him and moving to lay her on the desk. She smiled up at him greedily licking her lips as he pushed into her, filling her and owning her in that moment. It was over quickly, both finding a need fulfilled and both happy with the arrangement. Alice, after all, had a husband she didn't love, who consistently cheated on her with numerous woman in the building. He was actually working in accounting upstairs, clueless to the fact that his wife had not only found out his secrets, but was taking some pleasure out of life herself. It was how they started up, he told her about her husband. Not intentionally, but in passing, not knowing she was his wife at first. When she demanded to know more he showed her the footage caught on surveillance. Normally not talked to with any sort of demanding tone she amused him, and so the affair began.

Neither of them had any thoughts about it leading to anything. She was far too uncaring about the world, or the business. She amused him and met his needs sexually, but nothing more. Never having one serious conversation together before it was clear this was a temporary thing for them both. She was something to play with and he made sure she enjoyed it. He watched her button and fix her blouse in an effort to appear normal once more. Even that made him smile, he knew she would be reliving it for hours.

She turned to look at him. "Linda said you need me." All business now she sat across from him waiting to hear what he needed her to do.

"Yes, I need you to look into finding someone for me, for my mother actually. She is independent enough, but I worry for her. Someone not necessarily a nurse who wants to do everything for her, more of a companion."

"I can look into a few places, sure." She stood to leave. "When do you want them?"

"Let' shoot for next week, set up some interviews, I want to have a direct hand in finding the right person." He gave her a smile as he went back to work. "Have a good day Alice." He watched a smile cross her face and her exit.

A week later, Rachel found herself in the lobby of the Blakemore. She was surprised, she actually had been one of the people called in to interview for a position she wasn't even remotely qualified for. Blakemore was a large corporation and one she was always reading about or hearing on the news. She looked down at her hands nervously, she could only hope she wouldn't get thrown out right away. Why would someone looking for a companion be interviewing at Blakemore? Whatever the reason she was happy to be there. She looked around her at the other people waiting. Some in scrubs some in designer jackets. She pulled on her skirt, self-conscious about herself more now than before. It was obvious she didn't fit in, but this was her only chance to stay put, in her own place. Somehow she was going to march into the office and explain why they needed her here at Blakemore. It was a long shot, she knew it, but it was the only hand she had.

After a grueling hour she was finally next. The cute little blond who was directing everyone seemed to enjoy working here. She made her way over to look down at Rachel and she felt herself being judged, not something she ever enjoyed.

"You must be Miss Greene?" At her nod she told her to come along and follow her.

She made her way down a long corridor and finally to an office separated from the rest of the building. It was in a half moon shaped and separated by double doors which went from the secretarial area to what must be his office. She was escorted to the door where the blond pushed them open and allowed her to walk inside.

"Mr. Blakemore will be right back, just have a seat, please." The blond left, closing one of the doors behind her, leaving Rachel to look around the room.

At first she made an effort to sit down, but as she looked at the city below she couldn't help but walk over to the windows. There were only two walls in the entire office, both of those attached to the double doors facing inward. The rest of the office was in a half circle facing the city and the walls were floor to ceiling windows looking out. From where she stood it almost felt like flying. It was beautiful, she always loved the city, and although living as close as a child in Virginia she rarely made it to D.C. to see the sights. Once she went to a field trip with school and she was overwhelmed by the history, as well as the things you could see in the museums. Even now she smiled as she got as close to the edge of the window as possible and looked down.

"Be careful, if you do that too long it can make you sick."
She jumped back the voice scaring her.

She spun around and saw him there. He was dressed impeccably, as if the suit was molded to him. He was tall, and his face was defined by a strong jawline and the sharp planes of his face. His hair was jet blacked and slightly longer on top, but brushed back off of his forehead. Despite all of this it was his eyes that held her the longest. They were a deep blue, and piercing. It felt as though he was looking into her soul.

"I'm so sorry, its just such a beautiful view." She smiled at him and gave her a one over. He moved to sit behind his desk and she scrambled to sit back in her chair. She watched how he moved with grace and she felt nervous now about being here under false pretenses. She took a deep breath and swallowed.

"I see you have a degree in Office Management? Is that right Miss Greene?" He looked at her, there was something slightly amusing in his tone and she cleared her throat.

"Ye... yes I do. To be honest, I was thinking the ad may have been a misprint or something?" She shrugged slightly. "When I saw the company name I thought it would be a good idea to come in, and see if perhaps it... ah well to see if it was... a misprint." She looked away and blushed. She was rambling like an idiot.

"So, you decided to come to this job interview for a position you aren't qualified for because you assumed someone was inept at posting the ad? I'm not sure if insulting the business is such a good start, Miss Greene."

"Oh no, that's not it at all, I simply wanted to come in and... will see." His voice was rising now and she felt the heat rushing to her face. This guy was obviously an ass, and rude to boot. She felt his eyes on her again looking her over.

"Tell me, Miss Greene what are you good at?" He leaned back in his chair slightly, obviously enjoying the game they were playing.

She gulped. "As you mentioned, I have a degree in Office Management. I am also good at being organized, being on time and I am a stickler for having a very determined personality."

"Very determined? Well then, that's something we have in common." He smiled as he leaned forward. "Unfortunately, the ad was correct, I am looking for a caregiver for my mother. That being said, I appreciate the time you took to come in, and I have enjoyed our discussion." He stood, buttoning his jacket.

"Well, thank you Mr.....?" She shook the hand he held out to her.

"Blakemore." He held her hand just a second longer than normal and she moved to make her way to the door. "Miss Greene..." he called out to her.

"Yes."

"If anything opens up I'll call you myself." He gave her a flash of a smiled before he sat down dismissing her.

She shut the door behind her with a slight slam. She could still feel the heat in her cheeks and she was frustrated. What a jerk, it was the only thing she could come up with off the top of her head. More importantly, what the hell was wrong with her, she usually could handle herself with some self-control and he had gotten under the skin. He would call her directly? As if somehow she should feel special. As much as she wanted to scream her frustration about the charismatic billionaire, Blakemore, she really just wanted to cry. It took a lot to bring her spirits down, and she was nearing her breaking point. She climbed into her car and sighed. At least she tried. Now, she would make the trip into

Virginia for lunch with her mother, who would drill her for information about her life, or lack thereof.

Byron sighed. Finding someone who would suit his mother was proving to be a difficult challenge. Three days later and still he looked down at the stack of resumes on his desk and started sorting them one by one. Near the end he found Rachel Greene and he smiled. She was fire and ice that one. She was beautiful too, but he had a sneaking suspicion she didn't know it. She walked into his office and with a simplistic beauty looked out over the city and even then he wanted her. There was a part of him that was attracted to her innocence, the simple joy that crossed her face in those moments. Then, as the conversation began, he knew the precise moment when he frustrated her and made her angry. The crystal clear blue eyes shot daggers at him across the desk. She amused him, and excited him. He put her into the "no" pile and went on. Soon he narrowed it down to three people, all capable and seemingly nice. His mother could choose who she liked best. He buzzed Linda.

She came in with a smile and he noticed she was walking a little slower than she had that morning. He really should find her an assistant of some kind. He may very well be an ass to most, but he had a soft spot for Linda and knew her paycheck was important to her.

"Linda, I know you're busy. I wanted to ask you something, your opinion really." He walked over and sat on the corner of his desk. Linda smiled at him and sat down in the chair across from him.

"Yes Mr. Blakemore what is it, I'm happy to help however I can." She gave him a big smile and reminded him so much of his own mother he patted her arm.

"I am thinking of promoting you, to something more detailed. The problem is you will have to spend less time working with me and more time doing paperwork and such."

"Oh Mr. Blakemore, I know you let me stay because you're so sweet. I couldn't possibly get a promotion." She waved a hand at him.

"On the contrary Linda, you would be doing me a great service being in charge of some important clients. Helping me with meetings and the like. Plus, it comes with an assistant." He glanced down and removed an imaginary something from his pant leg.

"I've never had an assistant before." She gave him a wide smile. "Whatever you think is best Mr. Blakemore." She made her way back out to her desk.

After she was gone, he glanced down at the files on his desk. He knew exactly the right candidate for the new open position. He smiled to himself. He did tell her he would call her directly. She more than likely found another position by now, but the banter would be fun in and of itself. He dialed and she answered on the third ring,

"Hello!" She was noticeably out of breath making him wonder what she had been doing... or better yet, who she was doing it with.

"Miss Greene, how are you?"

"I'm fine, who is this please?" She was obviously moving something around.

"This is Mr. Blakemore... we met last week." There was a pause before she responded.

"Yes, Mr. Blakemore, how could I forget?" She said it sweetly, but he could detect a hint of sarcasm there. He smiled, he really did enjoy this.

"I was calling you about a position we have open, but if you're busy..."

"No! No, I'm not busy at all Mr. Blakemore, please, please go on." He felt it then, the tightness of his slacks. There was something about the way she pleaded with him that made him want her.

"I have an opening, it's a secretarial position... decent starting pay, benefits, etc. I know you mentioned you were looking."

"Yes, I am looking. I'd like to come in and discuss it, if that's ok?" She did her very best to sound nonchalant about the situation.

"Great, let's shoot for tomorrow 9 am?"

"That sounds fine with me, I don't think I have anything going on tomorrow at all." She did her very best to sound as though she may need to check.

She didn't want to appear desperate. She hung up the phone and sat down in the chair, maybe this was it but then who knew? He seemed to be genuine. She looked around the room at the boxes she was currently packing. As much as she tried to deny it, there was no way she would miss that meeting. She had very little time before she was out on the street. She sorted through her things to find a dress she only wore on special occasions. It was tight and black. Perhaps if she tried really hard it would show, and he would be inclined to ask her to stay. She held it up in front of her and frowned. He had such an effect on her it would be hard to ignore him, but she would do her best. She fired up her computer again rearranging her numbers with her new projected income... yes, it would certainly be a blessing in disguise. She snapped it shut and went back to packing, there was a good chance she would say the wrong thing, he got under her skin and she was quick to snap at him. Something she rarely ever did. He had this uncanny way of bringing out the worst in her. She worked late, managing to eat a heated can of ravioli for dinner along the way.

The next morning came bright and sunny. She smiled as she remembered that today could change her life. She jumped out of bed and ran into the shower. It took her longer than usual to dress and apply some slight makeup before heading downtown. There was a hustle and bustle in the air as she rode along, mindful of the people in the crosswalks and those begging for loose change. This was home and she loved it. She pulled into the parking garage and crossed her fingers that he would validate her parking ticket. She didn't even have enough money to get out of here if he didn't. She took a deep breath as the elevator took her to the top floor. When the doors opened, she made her way to the front desk and waited. Soon a short smiling lady who resembled her grandmother came to get her.

"You must be Rachel, come on dear, let me show you around." She was slightly hunched over and moving at a slow pace and Rachel loved her instantly. "Mr. Blakemore wants to meet with you for lunch, but until then I'm going to show you around a bit. He says he is "promoting" me." She gave the bunny ears as she explained. "The truth is I am old and need to retire but I would be lost all alone at home, and he knows it. So he is hiring my replacement, with the title of being my assistant." She gave a chuckle and they moved towards her office.

Although she had been through these rooms before, and back to his private office, she wasn't prepared for the size of the actual space she would be working in. Directly in front of his double doors was a lounge area, for meetings and to one side a fully stocked guest kitchen, the other entire wall was made for his assistant. She hadn't expected it to be quite so beautiful, really. She refused to get her hopes up, but she knew it would be difficult. Linda, she learned, was showing her where her desk was, as well as her private office behind it. At her confused look Linda explained.

"Sometimes, Mr. Blakemore has guests come over and they will sit out there in the lounge drinking and talking. Sometimes about the most ridiculous of things, you know how men are. This office in the back is yours for your personal use really, When you can do extra paperwork, etc., away from the hubbub."

Linda pushed open the door to the office space and Rachel was stunned. It was bigger than her entire apartment and was complete with a small kitchen of its own, a bathroom and a small sitting area. It was decorated in hues of pink and white and had a window of its own also, floor to ceiling but not nearly as wide. The idea of not getting her hopes tossed out the window by now and she spun around to see Linda's smiling face.

"Wow, it certainly is something Miss Linda isn't it?" She gave her a smile.

"Yes, it is and you will enjoy it, I can assure you. Come sit down with me." Linda walked over to the intercom system and buzzed.

"Yes, this is Linda, can you have a switchboard redirect Mr. Blakemore's calls for the interim. I'll let you know when I am back. "After a pause, she added.' Thank you Mary." She hung up and made her way back to the small sofa in the room. She settled in and Rachel was amused at the say she kicked off her shoes and leaned back to relax.

"I am most certainly getting old, my dear. Now let's talk turkey. Off of that main kitchen across the way there is another office much like this one but a little smaller. It's not connected to Mr. Blakemore's office like this one." She pointed to a seam in the door that she hadn't seen before. "I plan on setting up myself over there. I don't need as much space since I'll be passing off the bigger things to you. As a matter of fact, I've already moved over there and have yet to tell Byron." She gave her a smile.

"Byron?" Rachel was doing her best to follow along, but it was proving difficult.

"Mr. Blakemore, I used to call him Byron, but... well people thought since we were close he was showing favoritism, which he was, but then I'm old." She giggled.

Suddenly the seam in the door moved open and he was there. He gave her a once over and then smiled widely at Linda.

"I trust you have shown Rachel around some?" He offered her a hand as she tried to get up from the seat.

"I did, and she and I had an opportunity to chat some. By the way I've decided to move into the spare office behind the kitchen." She held up her hand at him. "Before you even start I did it because it suits me more, and its sound proof to all the man stuff going on in the lobby with your friends. Besides, I am thinking of cutting it down to three days a week and I don't need this much space." She said it with such finality he accepted her words without a fight.

Rachel was smiling at Linda and the match up with Byron...err...Mr. Blakemore. The two of them were like family in their banter and reminded her of her own. She watched as he delicately helped her make her way out of the room and she reevaluated her opinion of him. Maybe he wasn't a total ass after all. She waited for him to come back in and smoothed down her dress subconsciously. When she saw his shadow she stood up. He walked into the room with a smiled. He was in black today, all black and he was dashing as always. She moved her eyes back up and caught him watching her. She felt the blush rush to her face.

"Please, Miss Greene have a seat." He gestured and she did so waiting. "I hope you like what you see... of the office of course." He gave her a half smile and she felt her face turning red.

"It's lovely, very nice actually." She clasped her hands together in her lap. There was something about him that made her nervous, anxious even. Whatever it was would ultimately create a problem.

"SO you will take it, then?" He leaned forward towards her. "The job I mean." He watched her face intently.

"Don't I have to be interviewed or anything?" She frowned slightly.

"Miss Greene I think it's safe to say we have been through the interview already." He smiled at her and stood quickly, he walked over to her window.

She looked him over, him standing this way gave her a new view of him. His upper body was muscled and tight against the fabric of his suit, his body was sculpted and she knew he would be hard and muscular all over. She shook her head, trying to refocus on the task at hand.

"Then yes, I will." She stood to go, she hesitated just a moment to see what he would say next.

"We need to talk first, come in my office and shut the door behind you." He took the long strides to get there and she calmly walked behind him.

She shut the doors behind her and turned to face him. He was less than 6 inches from her. She could feel the warmth of his breath on her check and is eyes were an even deeper shade of blue. Her pulse was racing and she was both thrilled and terrified of what he would do next. She felt his hand tough her waist and the contact made her gasp slightly. He was watching her, waiting for her to move almost animalistic.

"I expect total honesty and realness between us at all times, do you understand? I also will not allow anything that goes on in this office, on any floor to be discussed outside of the office." He took a step towards her and she backed up.

"What do you mean exactly Mr. Blakemore?" She whispered the words waiting for his response.

"For example, if I have a woman here, it doesn't leave this office, if I have clients over here... nothing we talk about can be repeated. We often discuss business mergers that could make or break us."

"I understand." She swallowed hard. He was so close she could smell his aftershave and she was terrified to look into his face. She knew she would likely fall to the ground if she did the way her knees were shaking.

"Do you? What if I were to tell you that I want to kiss you. Would you feel like that is something you need to share?" He moved so that his lips were hovering just slightly above hers.

"No, not at all." She smiled at him, a new sense of confidence racing through her. He wanted to sleep with her. He didn't give one care about anything else. Just knowing it made her relax, she had dealt with co-worker issues like this before.

He watched the light flicker in her eyes and then dim. Something he said killed the kindling he was trying to ignite. He would have to figure that out, one day. "Good." He let her go and she walked towards the front door.

"Oh, and Miss Greene... I'll see you in the morning." He went back to the task at hand and she sprinted from his office.

All men were dogs, she thought. It was as simple as that, everyone she had ever met anyway. So her new boss wanted to have his way with her, big deal. Nine out of ten times it was too much time on their hands and not enough sense to put it all away, and keep it to themselves. Blakemore was a jerk just like the good doctor at the hospital. This time, however, she would call his bluff. She refused to lose her job over it this time and decided that if he did make a move, she would let it go long enough to give him enough rope to hang himself. He more than likely loved the chase the most so she wouldn't even give him one. She would be ready and willing to entertain his ideas and thoughts, but that's as far as she would let it go before putting a stop to the whole thing.

Byron sipped at the drink in his hand. What was he thinking, talking to her like that anyway? She looked like she was going to faint, and all he could think about was pushing her back on the desk and tasting her mouth. He always had some self-control and yet when she left, he'd been panting like a teenage school boy watching her leave. What was it that had her under his skin? She was beautiful, but in a nontraditional kind of way. She hadn't been prancing around the office in anything revealing like Alice typically did. It was her shyness, the way she turned away from him and refused to give in. Just thinking about her leaving and not giving in to him made her so much more challenging. His time with her would come, there was no doubt. She was like a little lamb though, he would have to be gentle with her... if he could only get himself under control.

The rest of the evening went by quickly for her as she prepared for her first day. She left her things packed, just in case. She would play this game with him, but she didn't want to lose, and she wanted to keep her job. Once she had him under her thumb she would be set, at least for a while. She could maybe get a nicer place. Plus, he did something crazy to her and she wanted to know why. Whatever happened, she would be as prepared as she could be. She moved her things around and put together a few nicer outfits. One day she would be out of this mess. She sighed as she heard the knob on her apartment door turning. Someone was always thinking this was A4. She was getting to a point where she didn't feel safe anymore. She simply had to get in good with Blakemore, then she could let him go.

The morning came and she was set to leave. She found the keys to her car and easily went out to go. In the mornings in her complex no one was awake until noon, so she was fairly safe. The evenings were something altogether different. One of her friends often told her to buy a gun, but she was absolutely against the idea. She made her way downtown and found HR, and the leggy blonde who had directed her to Blakemore's office a couple of weeks ago.

"SO Miss Greene, you must have left quite the impression on Blakemore." She looked her over and then shrugged. "Fill out all of this stuff, then you can go upstairs."

There was obviously something about this situation that pushed blondie in a bad direction. Whatever it was had nothing to do with her, but still she felt like she had disliked her immediately. She made her way through the mountain of paperwork and was finally finished around lunchtime. She made her way to her new office and only managed to get lost once, which was something of a personal accomplishment. She unloaded her things in the back office and made her way up front. Linda was nowhere to be found so she waited. Finally, he came in.

"Linda is out sick, come sit with me today. I can have you take some notes." He moved towards his office and she followed closely behind.

He turned and shed his jacket off and she watched his movements from hooded lashes. This was going to be harder than she thought. He rolled up his sleeves and finally sat down. He gathered up some paperwork and handed it to her, not really looking at her at all and she realized she may have been completely off in her assumption of what he wanted. She frowned, her plan would never work if she didn't at least attract him at all. She went over the paperwork in hand as he started going through the merger of two small companies that was on the horizon and she listened closely, learning the lingo about how he did things. Finally an hour later he seemed to relax some.

"Sorry, I tend to get overzealous when I'm talking shop." He gave her a lazy smile, which she returned and batted her eyelashes at him.

He felt something deep down, jump at her actions. She was openly flirting with him, a leap from yesterday's declaration. Perhaps she's had a change of heart, or she was playing with him. He smiled as he thought about it. Surely she knew better than to even try, he would have her naked and on all fours in an hour if he wanted too, but she didn't know him like that yet. He decided to test the water.

"DO you have a boyfriend, Rachel?" She watched his eyes moving over her as he talked. She took a deep breath in.

"No, do you?" She gave him a half smile and he chuckled.

"No, nor do I have a wife or a girlfriend. DO you have someone... close, someone who meets your needs?" He heard her gulp and inwardly he knew he had scored the first point.

"No, there is nothing I can't do better and more efficiently myself." She stared at him hard and saw his easy smile slip slightly. "What about you Mr. Blakemore?"

"Yes." He gritted the words out. She had planted the image of herself naked and alone and it was burned into his brain. She blushed at his response, some part of her expected him to lie.

"I see, she licked her lips slightly, suddenly feeling out of control of the conversation.

"Yes, I have someone, and yes, I think I could do it more efficiently." He watched her waiting for a reaction.

"I suppose that remains to be seen, doesn't it." She stood ready to make her way back out to her office. She knew he was there before she felt his hand on her arm spinning her around. He pressed her up against the wall of the office and leaned into her. She felt his mouth crush into hers in one fell swoop. It was a demanding kiss, pressing and pushing. His hands moved against her back, pulling her closer and moving upwards until his hands were in her hair cupping her head. He moved her mouth against his, nibbling and kissing until he was recklessly kissing her deeper again. Finally, they stopped and were both panting.

"I know this game Rachel, trust me, you won't win sweetheart." He whispered it in her earlobe nipping at the earlobe. She pushed him off and straightened her clothes.

"Perhaps, I guess that too remains to be seen. You certainly have a lot to live up to Blakemore."

She moved into her office, shutting the door firmly and locking it from her side. She made her way to the desk with shaky legs and practically fell into the seat. This was not at all going the way she had planned. She was going to be firm and alluring and yet here she was a shaky mess, having five minutes ago been ready to throw herself at him. She leaned forward, her head in her hands. She had certainly put herself in a unique situation this time. The rest of the day went quickly. She spent the remainder of the afternoon navigating the computer software system. She finally left as it was nearing 6. He's made no effort to bother her the rest of the day and she eventually relaxed. She pulled up to her apartment and sighed. This was the peak time for bad things around here. She saw a group of people, mostly men gathered around the step of her building. With careful and calculated steps she maneuvered around them, despite the calls and innuendos thrown at her. She slammed the door shut behind her and she cried. Life had to get better. She would be up the rest of the night, listening for someone to come to her door as they promised to do.

The first week went by smoothly, they would run into each other on occasion and there would always be something looming between them. He didn't try to kiss her again, but he was clear in telling her he wanted to. More than once he would have her come to his office and work with him on something and she knew he was watching her, testing her. With every remark he made to prove a point she would counter with one of her own setting him off into another flurry of tension. It was becoming an overwhelmingly charged game of cat and mouse with them.

The next morning was a Friday and she was happy to get out of her place. She was dragging and she did her very best to make herself look alive once she arrived. Linda fussed over her and immediately showed her how to use the email server and set up the new voicemail. They enjoyed much of the morning together and she took notes on everything. She didn't want to give him any excuse to let her go. He finally found them at lunch and offered to take them both out which Linda happily agreed to. She could find no excuse to say no and she felt a shot of heat course through her as he put his hand on the small of her back helping her into the car. Lunch was a fun affair. The place they went was so overpriced, she found it almost difficult to order anything at all. Once the food arrived, she fell in love with it and understood why he came there as often as he mentioned in the car. After Linda decided to go home since she was still not "100%." She watched as he helped her to her car and they watched her leave the garage.

"Get back in the car, I want to show you something." He slid back into the seat and she followed suit.

She frowned as they took off, she never even considered telling him no... or asking where they were going. She simply did as he asked. She made a mental note to be leery of that next time. She knew there would be a nest time, they both enjoyed the game too much, and she wanted the security of being with someone who could protect her. She was in a financial mess and afraid to go home at night. He needed to learn that you cannot simply take what you want without giving back. The car pulled up to a golden building, it looked like a restaurant or a hotel but she wasn't sure. He gave his key to the valet and took her hand as he moved gracefully through the building.

"Mr. Blakemore, where are we going?" She asked him quietly.

"Just be patient... you will like it." He smiled at her and she felt that same sense of excitement he always brought out in her.

They took the elevator and kept going until they reached the top. He moved out of the elevator and pulled her behind him until they stopped in front of a door. He slid the key in it and it opened, he held it, allowing her to go inside. The walls were silk and in shades of gold. The farthest wall away was glass looking down and out over the city, even higher than his building did. In front of the wall was a bed, huge and waiting. She spun around to look at him. She saw him smirk and shut and lock the door behind him. She crossed her arms and waited.

"Exactly what are we doing here, Blakemore?" She took a step back as he moved towards her.

"I don't play this game with you Rachel, you want me as much as I want you, and you've told me in more ways than one. Today I'm going to make love to you, thoroughly on that bed." He spoke every word softly and dangerously as he walked towards her. She felt her hands shaking as he moved in closer.

He moved her hair back off of her shoulders and kissed the side of her exposed neck. "I know a part of you wants to make up some excuse of why we can't do this, or why it's wrong. I also know there is a part of you who wants it and needs it." He moved his hand in her hair winding it in his fist as he moved his lips over hers.

There was something frantic about their actions as they undressed each other. She couldn't form the words to tell him to stop, she was far too gone now. She felt the air rush over her exposed skin as she crawled slowly into the bed and on her back waiting for him. He waited, watching her. Naked she was even more beautiful, her skin had a healthy glow and she was curvy right down to her thighs. She was perfectly shaped for him and he wanted her more than he ever remembered wanting anyone. He made his way over to the bed. She was taking shallow breaths as he kissed her from head to toe, stopping to drink his fill of her flesh along the way. He left no inch of skin untouched by his hands and mouth.

Finally, he moved to push into her and he lost all sense of control. She fit him like a glove and it was almost painful for her. He moved slowly, gradually moving more and more until with one final push he was buried deep. He looked at her then and started moving slowly, she arched up to meet his every thrust her fingers gripping his back, her legs wrapped around his hips pulling him forwards, and deeper still. She was lost in a haze of color, feeling his moving, his touch and his mouth. She lost control of everything and dug her nails into him as she felt the explosion inside her begin to climb higher and higher until it exploded into fragmented pieces in her mind. She opened her eyes as she did it and called his name which in turn pushed him forward as well and he followed close behind. He lay there still pressed into her for a few moments until finally they moved to untangle and he found his place behind her.

No one spoke for fear of shattering the fantasy world they were both in together. She couldn't feel any sense of victory in what happened, she had no control over any of it. She was simply there, and chose to do it. Her plans to make him want her or need her somehow until he had real feelings, ones that would make him want to protect her and help her. Now, he didn't even have to buy the cow before he took what he wanted. She had never experienced anything like this before, but she knew the game was over. Her plan had failed because she was weak. Now she would never get him to notice her for anything other than this. It occurred to her that she obviously felt something more for him for it to affect her this way. She turned to move away from him, but he simply said "no" and pulled her back in close to him. She knew she would not likely find herself in this situation again and she nestled in to enjoy it for now.

Byron was lost in thought. There was something special about her, something that meant more to him than just sex. Perhaps it was the game, or the way little things made her light up. She was different, and he liked it. He knew he had won the game they were playing, but he felt no happiness in that. She tried to move away and he had stopped her. He wasn't ready yet, to face whatever happened between them. She felt good like this, in his arms. He couldn't remember ever being with a woman that he wanted to hold after sex, someone who wasn't simply there to use or be used for a natural bodily function. There was never an emotional tie to the physical act and he didn't want to start now. She needed it more than he, and he would give her that. They both napped, sleeping deeply, having been equally satisfied and content. She was the first to stir and when she noticed the clock she started to panic. She jumped up and started throwing on clothes, and he watched her.

"Was it all really that bad, that you have to run?" He gave her a half smile which she failed to respond to. He knew something wasn't right. "Rachel... are you ok."

"What... oh yes, I'm fine, I just have to get home quickly... very quickly." She was still in her panties and bra and he was enjoying the show she gave him. It wasn't long before she finally dressed the rest of the way. He stood and slid into his boxers. He watched her looking for her keys.

"Rachel... stop... your car isn't even here, calm down." He put a hand on each shoulder to calm her. He moved the hair out of her face and she looked up at him. He was standing there his bare chest, smooth under her touch and she relaxed. "Stay here with me tonight. It's already 8:30, we can have dinner and... eventually sleep." He gave her a wide smile and she smiled back.

"I don't want to be that girl... who stays too long." She screwed up her face, and he laughed.

"You're not that girl, we are just having an extended Friday afternoon that's all, nothing more."

He watched her visible slump back onto the bed. "Why do you have to get home so fast anyway?"

She swallowed, thinking of the best response. "I just like to be in before it gets too dark that's all." She smiled at him.

He frowned, he knew there was something more there, but it wasn't any of his business so he decided to let it go. He picked up the phone and ordered room service and she smiled as she looked out over the city. No matter what happened, this would be a night she would never forget.

The next day he took her to her car. She finally climbed into her bed at home at 1 in the afternoon. Part of her wanted to be happy and content with what she had been through. Another part of her wanted to cry. If she were being honest with herself, she had just been part of the most elegant and elaborate booty call ever. She should feel bad about that, but amidst all of the lovemaking they talked about life, and family. He shared his vision and hopes for the future and she, given him some version of hers. Monday she would go back to work and pretend none of it ever happened. For now she could pretend. She fell into a deep sleep, recovering from the sleep she missed the night before.

Byron was having a similar discussion with himself, he followed her home trying to see what had made her want to get back there so badly the night before. He looked up at the apartment building she entered and swore to himself. She lived here? He frowned as he looked over the streets and the neighborhood. He felt something about her situation, he wanted to get her out of here and way from the people who loitered the area. This entire block was notorious for crime and violence. He knew it was too soon to storm in there and drag her back out and into his car. He made the trek home lost in thought. He finally made his way into his penthouse, still concerned about her. What was wrong with him? He had always enjoyed his bachelor life, the solitude was a strength for him. He hated people around all of the time, except for his mother. Now, she was in his head and offering her opinions about everything. On top of that he was worried about her, he didn't like that feeling, that connection it could only be dangerous. This whole thing was supposed to be about sex, even that went beyond what could be labeled as normal. She was both giver and taker and it had been the best experience of his life to date. He had a lot to think about and she made up most of it. He decided to do a little digging and find out more about her. It was probably crossing a line, but it would give him some piece of mind.

Monday came and the two of them went to work with very different missions in mind. She was determined to put the whole thing behind her and work hard. She was able to pay rent this month and could continue on that way, but if she moved to her parents house for a few months she could find something nicer, better, and less scary. She needed this to work, she had no other choices. She spent Sunday moving boxes into storage near her parents' house and all that was left were a few things she would need to survive for the next couple of weeks. She made her way to her desk and started logging into various sites. It was Linda's idea to start the day off that way. She glanced at his door, but made no move to bother him.

Byron was angry, and insulted. She used him. He could argue that he had used her too, but somewhere down deep he felt like he really connected to her. He made his way into the office passing her desk without saying a word. It would be hard to exist like this, her working for him. But if he fired her, she could stir up one hell of a lawsuit. He ran his hands through his hair, she was more than broke. She was in debt up to her ears and he even found where she tried to take out a number of loans but been denied. The final straw was finding an email where she detailed finding a solution to her problem, it was a note to herself really, but she had been looking for a solution. He would be damned if it would be him. He rubbed his eyes. He could feel a headache coming on, he would have to face her sooner or later. He buzzed her in. She came in professionally and sat across from him waiting for him to say something. He didn't even look up at her for the longest time. Finally, he did. She looked different somehow, she wore contacts today and let her silky hair flow down her shoulders just aching him to touch it. He shook his head.

"Miss Greene, there are some new events on the horizon for the company and there is a good chance you will be moving to a different department. I wanted to be the first to tell you, so that there was no confusion." He watched her eyes shooting at him like daggers as she crossed her arms over her chest.

"Really now, how convenient." She was angry and hurt, but mostly hurt. He used her and was now casting her off to a different department.

"It's completely out of my hands." He gave her a hard look.

"I bet it is. I can't believe I trusted you." She stood up and stomped her way back into her office.

She slammed the door shut behind her. It was just as well. Then she wouldn't have to deal with him all day, which would suit her just fine. Still, it hurt. Her plan to seduce him and make her life easier had been more like something she told herself to make being with him easier. She never stood a chance of telling him no. She was really to blame for the whole situation. She went in that room, she stayed the night... she opened up to him. She looked around the desk. This would never work, not really. She put her head in her hands just as she heard him storm in.

"I can't believe you would say anything to me about trust, Miss Greene." His eyes were staring down at her hard.

"What are you talking about Blakemore, I was there... you led me to that room." She felt the tears welling up but she refused to let them fall.

"Oh no sweetheart, I take responsibility for that one. I'm talking about your plan, to "snare a good man" to help you with all of your problems. You're in debt up to your eyeballs." He was seething and she stood to defend herself.

"SO what, who cares if I am in debt, why is that your problem and how is it any of your business. Oh wait... you can't believe you had sex with someone who's not rich like you, is that it?" She felt as though someone kicked her in the stomach, she was humiliated.

He grabbed her arm and pulled her to him. "I don't care if I found you penniless on the street in rags, I would have still seen you, still made love to you" he let her go "still wanted you." He sighed running a hand through his hair. "My issue is not that you're poor Rachel, it's that you set a goal in mind. O,ne to catch me, and make me fix all your problems."

She stared at him a moment before the realization of what he'd done became apparent.

"What did you do Blakemore?" her eyes were on fire as she looked him over. "Did you do research on me or something? What was it a background check.... Credit check? I'm sure the list goes on and on doesn't it." She waited. "Not going to admit to it, I guess, what makes you think I wanted or needed you to rescue me, Mr. Blakemore?" She stood with her arms crossed over her chest.

He had the decency to look guilty before he told her. "I read your emails, I needed to know more about you."

She blushed, humiliated.

"You tell me the truth now Rachel, was that your plan all along? Suck me in and use me to feel safe, to be secure?"

She took a deep breath before she answered. "I wrote that as a note to myself, yes at first when you said those things to me the first day I was here, I did. I thought I'd beat you at your own game." She faced the window as she spoke, letting the tears fall now. "I thought, somehow I would show you I can be just like you. But I didn't, the minute I was in that room with you I lost the game. We both knew it and I accepted it. I cared about you, you can't just use someone you care about, it doesn't work that way." She wiped at her face and spun back around to face him. "But it is clear that you play dirty too, researching me like I'm one of your corporate mergers or something. Like I'm not real, and here, you don't trust anyone or anything and one day it will leave you cold and alone." She grabbed her purse and jacket. "Obviously this won't work, I'm sorry if you felt used... but then that's exactly how I feel too." She left quickly making her way to the elevator and then to her car.

She sat in the garage for a moment, letting it all sink in. Just a few short hours ago, she had been on cloud nine, developed something real. She was going to take back her life, she had new feelings for someone and job security. Now, it was all gone, all at once. At least it was early, she could go home and be depressed alone. She made her way to the apartment amazed at the transformation. The days were so peaceful, the nights were right out of a horror novel. She fell into her bed and finally let go. Her body wracked with sobs as she cried out her pain, her loss and for Blakemore.

Byron tried to work, he focused his thoughts solely on the project at hand, yet he realized he reread started the same page about 6 times. He pushed the papers away from him and sighed. The entire situation with Rachel was a mess. He knew she was sincere, she had started out with a plan, but once they were in that room, she let it go and chose him in that moment. He regretted it now, demanding an explanation and hurting her. She had been crying by the window, he wanted to pull her close, but he couldn't move. Nothing in his life had been like this and he wasn't sure how to act. On top of all that he was out an assistant, again. He called down to HR and asked Alice to come up. He was still lost in thought when she opened the door. She sashayed into the room and made her way over to him, running her hands down his chest. He suddenly realized what she was doing and stopped her hands.

"Not today Alice, I need a new assistant. Can you start making some calls please?" He looked up at her and they knew it was done. Looking at her now he felt nothing, no excitement.

"So the little bookworm fled the scene did she? Fine, I'll hire you a new assistant." She started to leave.

"Alice." She stopped but didn't turn around. "This between us... its done." She turned and gave him a smile.

"I knew that the minute you hired her yourself Byron, I just had to try." She left the room.

He frowned. It seemed as though everyone knew him better that he knew himself. He had work to do, but he couldn't think straight. Fortunately, he had a few meetings at least that would take his mind off of her. She was right, it was better this way. They couldn't work together, not when every time he saw her he wanted to touch her. He glanced up at the clock and made his way to the conference hall.

The day went by slowly, Rachel felt every minute of it. She was hungry and yet she didn't want to move. She was always the strong one, always rolled with the punches, but something about Byron Blakemore left her shattered. She knew she was going to move, she'd lost her job and by the weekend she would be on her mother's couch amid the hugs and "I'm sorry's" she would likely receive from them all. Just that alone was enough, but admitting she was in love with Blakemore was the culprit of her current state. He was an ass, he was also kind and sweet and horribly romantic. She knew there was a connection from day one and instead of walking away from it... she dove in with both feet... right into a golden love nest practically on top of the world. She knew that at the very least, she would have that night, with him. She must have fallen asleep finally, because the next thing she knew there was a huge noise coming from down the hall. She jumped out of bed and hearing the yelling she made her way to the door. She heard men fighting, loudly and she immediately braced the door with a chair and hid in her closet. She dialed 911 and waited.

Byron was exhausted. He made his way into his lavish house and found his mother sitting in the living room watching television. If there was anyone who knew him, really knew, him it was her. She glanced up at him and he gave her a smile. His entire life she had been a constant for him. Always there no matter what. When he was little she always managed to scrape it together so that they had food and a place to sleep. Sometimes nicer places than others. He would always take care of her no matter what.

"Momma, how was your day? Did the new lady come?" He slumped down beside her.

"Oh yes, she was delightful she brought some cards and I beat her every time." She glanced at him and chuckled loudly.

"Good Mom, I'm glad, I feel better knowing someone is around while I'm not." He sighed and she turned the volume down on the television.

"Ok son spill it, what's wrong?" He looked over at her and shook his head. "You can try and tell me nothing but it will just put off this conversation longer. Talk to me boy." She gave him a nudge with her elbow and he smiled at her.

"It's about a woman." He saw her sit up quickly.

"A woman, well, I'd say it's about time then." She gave him a pat. "Go on what's wrong."

"I met her and then hired her, things got... involved." He gave her a look and she rolled her eyes.

"It always does. Keep going."

"Well, she had a plan, initially, to somehow make me fall for her or something and then get her out of her problems. So I called her out on it after I found out."

"How did you find this out son?" She looked at him thoughtfully.

He blushed. "I did a bunch of background checks and emails and stuff." He looked away.

"I see. Go on."

"Well, I confronted her and she got upset and quit and told me she was trying to get me back to playing games with her." He looked over at her, she was smiling.

"I like this girl already." She laughed lightly. "I'm sorry son, you can hardly be mad at someone for getting you back. Were you playing a game?"

"I don't think so, I mean I just like things a certain way. I don't want to get too involved, I've seen how relationships can be."

She took a deep breath before she answered. "Byron your daddy was a silly man who didn't care about anyone. He took what he wanted and left the world behind, including you and me." He nudged him again to get his attention. "Love wasn't the problem, or relationships honey, it was being afraid of them that drove him away and made him run like the devil. What you're trying to avoid, feeling something, loving someone... that was what made him the way he was." She took his face in her hands." I am getting old Byron baby, I need me some grandkids before I'm gone, don't stop your heart from feeling or you will be just like the man you detest." She let him go.

He sat thinking, then he noticed the flashes on the television. He only watched for a second before he felt his heart stop and his body go cold. That was Rachel's apartment building.

"Mom turn it up." She saw him freeze and she did so quickly.

They watched together, the news was covering a shooting that had happened in the building leaving some of the tenants either dead or injured. The entire building was considered a crime scene upon discovering a meth lab in the basement as the police raided and finally caught the shooter.

"Son, what is it?" She touched his arm concerned.

"That's her building, that's where Rachel lives. I have to go mom, I'll be back, I love you." He grabbed his coat and ran from the penthouse.

He knew he was speeding as he made his way to her building. The police were still there and people were everywhere. He combed the area looking for her hoping to see her. He needed to tell her, needed to protect her. He should have never let go in there in the first place. The day after their overnight at the hotel he should have stormed in there and pulled her back out with him. He was frantic as he raked his hand through his hair. If anything happened to her...

"Blakemore, what the hell are you doing here?" He spun around at the voice and she stood there draped in a blanket.

He didn't say a word he simply grabbed her and pulled her to him. He looked her over checking for signs that she was hurt. He kissed her then not giving her a chance to speak or move. It was a quick and hard kiss, something to prove that she was real, and she was ok.

"You're not hurt." It was more of a statement than anything.

"No, I'm fine, what are you doing here?" She stood there waiting for an answer he heart beating erratically from the kiss.

"I saw the news, I was worried about you. I came as soon as I found out. You're sure you're ok?" He held her head in his hands.

"I said I'm fine, Byron. Why did you come? You think I'm awful, yet you're here, and kissing me?"

"I love you." He said it simply.

"You what? Don't be ridiculous, Byron. Just this morning you were ready to kill me." She turned to go but he grabbed her arm.

"I am an idiot Rachel, I was so angry, because, I am in love with you. When I thought you didn't feel anything for me and I was just a means to an end it hurt, and I equated that to anger."

She was crying, he said he loved her but did he mean it? She looked at him in his designer suit, ruined with dirt and she'd never seen him look so disheveled. She looked at his eyes as he gazed down on her full of love.

"I love you too, Byron." She gave him a half smile. He scooped her up and spun her around.

"First things first, you are not living here anymore." He said it very matter-of-factly.

She felt her temper rise, he was already bossing her around. They started walking towards his car.

"Wait, how did you even know I lived here?" He kept walking.

"I followed you the day after the hotel." She stopped.

"You what!" He pulled her along to the car.

"I know I'm horrible, let's just go home." Before she could protest about his snooping, she felt the warmth of his lips on hers and she knew that home was exactly where she was.

****

The Billionaire's Bargain

"Tallulah! Less dreaming, more working!" my beloved Grammie Marigold cries out from the kitchen.

It was time to help with lunch.

"Coming Grammie!" I call back, reluctantly closing my Vogue magazine.

"There you are child, bless your heart you look a sort" Grammie chuckles, looking me up and down.

Ok so I look a little messy right now. Faded old skinny jeans, tank top and my hair up in a messy bun. No make up. Grammie likes to think a Southern Lady should always be well turned out.

I grin at Grammie, "Oh Grammie, I am just at home! It is only the two of us here. Why would I need to dress up?"

Grammie frowns at me, "Child, you should always look your best, you never know when someone special might pop by. And a lady is always well groomed."

I groan with faux desperation, "Grammie no one ever comes to visit us. We haven't had a visitor since I left college to care for you. Unless you count the nurse and the one time Doctor Peters came by. And Doctor Peters is about forty years too old to be a potential beau."

Grammie smiles at me sadly and draws me in for a hug, depositing a special Grammie kiss on my forehead,

"Tallulah I know it has been hard for you, I feel a heart load of guilt over you having to put your dreams aside to care for me. I don't want to see you let go of yourself or your dreams, things are just on hold, not over. Taking care of your outside shows you haven't given up on the inside," Grammie says sadly.

I lean into the hug, enjoying that special Grammie scent that reminds me of knitting and cookies.

"Thank you Grammie. I haven't given up. I still have my dreams and I know I will return to college. One day I will run my own non-profit and save the world," I smile to show I understand this career goal is a little naïve...although secretly I do believe I can make a difference, some day some how.

Grammie grabs me by the shoulders and looks at my firmly, "Now young lady, believe in yourself. I KNOW you will make a difference. Your Daddy felt the same way, he would be so proud of you."

I fall silent at the mention of Daddy. My father died when I was eight. He was a soldier killed in action. The military had been his way of making a difference. With my mom passing away from an illness not long after I was born it had just been Grammie Marigold and me for a long time.

I shake my head to clear old thoughts of Daddy.

"Grammie, one day I will change the world and I will make Hunter, South Carolina famous for having produced me!" I laugh and give Grammie a little twirl around the kitchen.

"I don't doubt it," I think I hear Grammie murmur as I set out making our soup and sandwiches.

———————————————————-

"And then your Grandfather said, 'Marigold, I need a wife and you'll do!'" Grammie chuckles, as we eat our lunch.

I laugh in return. I love hearing stories of my grandparents romance. I pretend to be fine waiting for the right man, but secretly I long to meet the man of my dreams.

At my age Grammie was married with two babies. Many of my friends from high school are married, and those who are not are at college.

The doorbell interrupts these depressing thoughts.

"Now there you go Tully," exclaims Grammie, "visitors!"

I get up from my chair and head to the front door, "probably just Mormon's Grammie, they are very dedicated and just won't give up on this die hard Baptist neighborhood!"

Yanking open the door with a distinct lack of grace I discover two men standing on the doorstep in suits. One youngish, maybe thirty, and an older man in his fifties.

Mormons. Well I am a good Southern Lady and even though I am Southern Christian to the core I *am* polite.

"Hello, thank you for visiting, however, we are happy in our religion and not looking to convert," I politely state with a firm 'thank-you-but-go-away' smile.

The two men look at each other puzzled. The younger one grins at me. I notice he has adorable ears that stick out. He also looks vaguely familiar.

"Ah well, Miss Tallulah, I too am a God fearing man, or try to be, however, my business here today is not conversion," the young man looks at me amused.

I feel rather foolish. Who else wears a suit in Hunter? Even the Mayor wears tan slacks, not a suit.

"Well then Gentlemen, what can I do for you today?" I say, recovering my poise slightly.

I suddenly wish I had followed Grammie's advice and dressed properly. She is always right!

"I'm here on some rather delicate business. We have mutual friends, through your father's military service. I too was in the army. A friend quietly mentioned you might be in need of some income. I have a business proposal for you," the young man watches closely for my reaction.

Income...? How did this man know our business? Grammie's illness has drained our resources, and our insurance has rejected our claim. Things have been a little difficult. If this man knew of my father though, perhaps this was legitimate?

"Well...perhaps, Gentleman you would like to formally introduce yourself and come in for some tea," I respond, realizing I didn't even know their names.

The young man smiles broadly. "My apologies Miss Tallulah, where are my manners, please do forgive me. This is my colleague, attorney Thompson Thompson. My name is Alexander Carlyle, a pleasure to meet you."

I stare back at him. Alexander Carlyle? Suddenly the vague familiarity becomes very clear. *The* Alexander Carlyle. He is the reluctant heir to America's first family, the dynastic Carlyle's. The 'family behind the families'. Tabloid heartthrob.

Alexander is the grandson of Alexander Senior, legendary businessman. Alexander's father was the heir apparent in the family but was sadly killed in a tragic bombing when working in the Middle East. It is well known no one else in the family but Alexander the younger is up to the task of succeeding Alexander Senior.

Which leaves America's future most powerful man standing on my doorstep.

————————-

Gathered around the dining table in the 'formal' room, Grammie, Alexander, Thompson and I sit in awkward silence as Thompson ever so slowly unpacks documents from his briefcase.

"Now then," announces Thompson, "I represent Mr. Carlyle and his business proposition for you."

I tilted my head to the side anxiously. Grammie folds and refolds her hands in her lap.

"Now then..." Thompson starts again.

Alexander interrupts, "I should handle this Thompson, thank you," he states firmly.

I see the steely glint in his eye that hints at why he is the new heir apparent to the mantle of head of the Carlyle family.

"Tallulah, may I call you that?" Alexander asks me, looking directly into my eyes. His eyes are slate blue and highly intelligent.

I manage to gasp out a response, "my friends call me Tully."

Alexander smiles with the charm that reputedly draws supermodels. "Tully. Lovely. Tully I have a unique proposal for you. I hope it doesn't offend you, or your Grandmother. I think it could be a good solution for both of us. Your problem is financing your Grandmother's treatment. My problem is, well..." Alexander looks embarrassed and not in control for the first time since we met. "Well I need a fiancé," he finally finishes.

A pause. Grammie Marigold speaks first, "a fiancé! Explain yourself young man."

Alexander shifts his attention to Grammie. "Well, Mrs. Marigold, you see I am the heir to running our family business. My Grandfather is eighty soon and as he gets on in his life he would like to be assured the family line is secured. He has set a deadline for me to produce a fiancé by his eightieth birthday, in three month's time. If I don't there will be consequences for me. My plan is to buy myself some time with a stand in fiancé while I work on an alternative plan."

My jaw drops. This is crazy! And not exactly the romantic moment I had in mind when I imagined meeting my first beau.

I am about to speak and ask the two gentlemen to leave when Grammie beats me to it.

"Well now that is indeed an interesting proposal. Tully you should accept," Grammie orders.

Furious, I turn to Grammie, "Grammie! This is a crazy idea! I am not going to go off with some man I don't know, even if he is famous and rich. We are not that hard up."

Grammie looked at me sagely. "Sweetheart, back in my day men and women courted a little differently to today. In times of war and hardship marriages were often practical decisions. Like Grandfather and I. And look how that turned out, a great love affair."

"We are not courting, it's business" Alexander and I announce at the same time. I looked at Alex witheringly as he attempts a conspiratorial smile at me.

Grammie smiles innocently. "Of course. Forgive an old lady, I get confused as to what is going on."

Grammie appears lost in thought then speaks firmly, "Tully I want you do to this. If not for my health then for yourself, you can top up your college fund."

"But who will look after you!" I cry out.

"Grammie will be taken care of during the engagement by the best nurses and doctors," adds in Thompson.

What could I say to that? And indeed Alexander and Thompson did have it all worked out.

In what seemed liked no time at all I found myself boarding a private jet for New York. I had barely even flown before.

I look over my seat on the jet to where Alexander and Thompson appear to be going over some very serious and heavy work. I debate whether to say something. Alexander and I have barely spoken since we left my house for the private airstrip. I feel awkward surrounded by such luxury on the jet.

I take a deep breath. Grammie would want me to be polite. "Alexander?" I say tentatively.

Alexander looks up, "Please, call me Alex. Alexander is my Grandfather"

I find my voice again, "I just wanted to thank you for this opportunity, and it is very kind."

Alexander, Alex, looks at me emotionless. "This is not kindness Tallulah. It is a business deal. I don't consider kindness when I am doing business. But you are welcome."

We continue the rest of the flight in silence.

Alex and I are travelling into the New York in a sleek black limousine with a chauffeur. This is a whole level above a Town Car, I think to myself, recalling reading of glamorous magazine editors travelling around New York in such cars.

Alex laughs next to me, God does that man have to have a perfect laugh too!

I take my nose of the glass window and turn to him questioningly.

"Are you enjoying the view of the city?" Alex says with a chuckle.

I blush furiously, feeling the sting of being a hick from out of town. I draw myself up haughtily, in my best Grammie Marigold Southern Lady way.

"Actually, Mr. Carlyle, I am, thank you." I turn back to my window, making a point of pressing my nose right up against the tinted glass. Is that the Empire State Building in the distance...?

Alex shifts from his seat to the middle one, next to me. I turn back to him, startled.

Alex takes my hand in his. It's like a shot of electricity through my body. His touch does something to me I cannot explain. I feel heat in private places. His hand is large and manly. I feel small and girlish, my hand in his.

"Tallulah," Alex says gently. I have noticed he has taken to calling me Tallulah when he something serious to say.

"I am sorry if I upset you. I find your enthusiasm for the city very beautiful. Having grown up here I forget how amazing New York can appear. I will never make you feel unsophisticated."

I look down at our hands. My nails are slightly chipped. The nail color is from the drug store. I was pleased with it when I put it on. Now it just looks cheap.

I look up at Alex, "But you did," I say softly.

Alex gazes at me thoughtfully. The silence and my hurt hang in the air.

"I apologize, it won't happen again," Alex replies stiffly, dropping my hand and moving back over to the other window seat. He looks out his window.

I watch him for a moment, puzzled. I cannot get a read on this man. Sometimes he shows kindness and understanding, other times I am firmly a business proposition.

I sigh and try to spot more landmarks out my window. If this is how it is going to be it may be a long three months.

Despite my hurt I can't help but think that Alex did not mean to hurt my feelings. Perhaps Alex is finding business is a little trickier when you apply it to your personal life.

———————————————————————————

The limousine pulls up in front of stunning Deco apartment building. Two uniformed doormen dressed in smart red spring forward and begin opening doors and trunks. Luggage is stacked efficiently on trolleys.

I am barely out of the car and a little overwhelmed already. This whole scene feels like everyone in it knows his or her role except for me.

Alex seems re-energized at arriving home, after we finished our car trip in another awkward silence.

He takes my arm and walks me into the large airy lobby. I gaze up in awe at a stunning chandelier that appears to take up the entire roof space.

"Welcome to The Deco, Tully, "Alex says cheerfully.

This is *the* The Deco. The famous 1920's Deco building, the last one designed by a celebrated architect.

In the 1930's depression a famous actress drowned in the bath in her apartment.

She had become addicted to pills after her lover, legendary newspaper magnate Marshall Archer, took his own life after losing his fortune in the 1929 stock market crash. Legend held that the actress still haunted the halls

I stare around the lobby, gawking unashamedly as details come into focus. Overstuffed sofa's take up on corner of the room, with an assortment of newspapers and magazines laid out neatly. I note the newspapers are arranged in alphabetical order.

Bronze sculptures are dotted around the room. Looking closer I see they are animals. One particularly engaging piece is of an owl whose expression manages to appear genuinely wise.

Alex notes my interest and draws me over to the Owl. "I call him Owlie. I consider him a friend. That's foolish isn't it?"

I smile with warmth at Alex. This is the first human moment I've seen from him. He looks a little embarrassed, like he shared something he hadn't meant to.

"When I was child my friend was a teddy bear. I called him Mr. Bear. Very original!" I laugh.

Alex and I share a laugh. As laughter dies away we find our eyes locked. After a moment just too long we break away awkwardly.

"Well then," says Alex, "let's see you settled in. Given you are meant to be my fiancé we will be living together, although as explained you will have your own room."

Alex and I head up to his apartment. I am not surprised it is the penthouse. I would expect nothing less of a Carlyle.

"How long have you lived here," I ask, as we travel up in the gorgeous heritage elevator, trying to make conversation to cover how nervous I feel.

Alex shifts from foot to foot. "Well, actually this apartment was a gift for my fifth birthday. Have you heard of Marshall Archer?" I nod.

"Marshall Archer owned the penthouse as well as a few other apartments in the building where he housed his mistresses. When he went bankrupt the debt was ultimately to my family's bank. The apartment passed into our hands and we have had ever since. My Aunt Prinny lived here with one of her husband's for a while and eventually it become mine." Alex's finishes.

I try to think of what to say. Inheriting famous apartments at five is a little outside of my experience.

"That's nice," I say lamely.

The doors ping open and we enter into another lobby, even more amazing than the ground floor one. *Three* perfect chandeliers line the roof. Art lines the walls. Some of it looks familiar, perhaps from high school art studies.

Heavy doors swing open to reveal an enormous apartment and a sweeping view of Central Park. I gasp. Alex appears perfectly comfortable and strides into the room, casually throwing his suit jacket over an elegant couch.

I tip toe into the room. I am worried my shoes might have something on them that will damage the dazzling rug that covers the polished wood floors.

Alex is pulling his tie off and heading over to a drinks shelf. "Relax Tully," he calls out to me. "This is home, it is a private place here."

I follow his lead and take me shoes off and wonder what next. Normally one would take in belongings and get settled, but that is being done for me. I carefully put my handbag down and head to check out the view that is drawing me.

Central Park is spread out in front of me like a green carpet beneath the sky. Wow, I whisper quietly to myself.

Alex coughs for my attention. "So Tully, before you go rest perhaps we should get the kiss practice out of the way?"

———————————————————-

Oh yes. The Kiss. Well, in love couples engaged to marry do kiss. It was in the contract that on occasion Alex and I would be required to kiss. The problem was that I had actually never kissed anyone.

It wasn't that I was some do-gooder virgin. More that Grammie had raised me not to do that sort of thing until I was in love, and I haven't found love yet.

A contract kiss is not exactly the grand moment of my dreams, but Grammie was supportive and it is getting to the point I just want kissing to be over. I'm twenty-one after all.

"Right then," says Alex, suddenly all business and putting down his scotch. "Let's get this out of the way."

"Oh great, kissing is a chore! How romantic," I say sarcastically.

Alex has me in his arms before I even knew it. He grasps me firmly in his arms and presses his mouth on me insistently. Even with his lips closed I can feel the warmth of the scotch he just drank.

Despite myself I relax in his arms and my mouth parts open a little. Private parts stir.

Alex's breaks away and my eyes open, questioningly. "This is a business deal, Tallulah," he says softly and intently. "There is no romance."

I regain my poise. Holding my head high I lock eyes with him. "Well then, let us do that again so we get the business right."

Alex smiles a half smile and holds out his hand, inviting me to pull myself into him. With a confidence I don't really have I initiate a kiss with America's most sought after bachelor.

"Not bad, Miss South," Alex grins as we break apart.

"I've been practicing on Mr. Bear," I respond, deadpan.

Alex laughs. I enjoy making him laugh, given he often seems oh so serious.

"When two people in love kiss, Tully, they kiss in a variety of ways," Alex's pulls me gently into his arms.

"This is the 'hi honey' kiss" Alex kisses me gently on the check and whispers in my ear "Hi honey". I flush at the light touch of his lips on my cheek.

"And this is the brush kiss," Alex gently brushed his lips across mine.

My head is spinning.

"And this," he continues, "Is a passionate kiss," Alex kisses me full on the mouth, easing my mouth open with his. His tongue moves smoothly into mine. My tongue naturally begins to move with his. The kiss seems to go forever.

Finally breaking the kiss we look into each other's eyes. I am speechless. So this was what everyone keeps going on about when they talk about kissing.

I think I see something in Alex's eyes before he becomes all business.

"I have to go out Tallulah," Alex says briskly. "Don't wait up for me I have a lot to attend to having been out of town."

I nodded dumbly. Of course. He is Alex Carlyle, Very Important Man.

"I have arranged for my assistant Bee to come by and take you shopping," I perk up at that news.

"Now Tully," Alex says seriously, holding my attention, "I don't have any problem with how you dress, but you do need to dress the part of my fiancé."

Alex's sensitivity in that comment shows he hasn't forgotten the limousine incident.

"Of course Alex," I reply, professional myself. "This is a business deal after all."

Alex and I looked at each other in silence for a moment.

"Good," is all he says as he turns on his heel and leaves.

—————

Bee turns out to be a lovely and efficient woman. Aged in her fifties she has extensive knowledge of New York and where to shop.

Shopping with Bee is delightful. There are no snooty looks when we enter the high-end boutiques. Indeed, we seem to be expected.

"A society lady needs to have a number of little black dresses," opines Bee as sales women fuss around me.

"A classic black dress is essential for charity lunches and low level functions," Bee continues.

"If a very expensive little black dress is what I wear to lunch what on earth do I wear to a ball?" I ask in confusion.

Bee simply sighs at my fashion ignorance and doesn't respond.

"And we also need some suits," Bee addresses to the sales ladies.

Bee looks me up and down; "The suits will look good on you with a lovely hat."

"I don't think I've ever worn a hat," I reply, unsure.

"Well dear you will need to start as you simply cannot attend the Polo Classic without a darling hat," Bee says with firmness.

"Yes Ma'am," I respond. Ma'am seems appropriate for Bee.

Shopping as a Carlyle is a very new experience. We don't carry our bags to the next store; our driver appears and discreetly whisks them away.

Arriving at another boutique, I discovered what I am to wear to balls. Glittering sequined dresses hung on the racks like works of art. Ribbons decorate some pieces. After seeing so much black fabric in other stores, this boutique is a revelation of a rainbow of colors, from the softest lavender to buttercup yellow.

An army of sales people put dress after dress on me. I leave the store in a sequin daze with a number of stunning gowns.

"Now that red gown is a show stopper for the Winter Ball, a very good winter color," comments Bee.

Everyone knows what the Winter Ball is. Every winter the Carlyle family holds their annual ball at their main estate, Carrington, in Connecticut. Legend holds that the ball is held in Winter as a power move, as most guests have left the city for the winter.

Guests are forced to fly back to the states from places like St. Barts for just a few days to attend the ball. Not to go is unheard of. The Carlyle's demonstrate their power by the lengths people will go to to attend.

"Oh look, it's Duckie," whispers Bee as we stepped out onto the sidewalk. "Look sharp."

"Alexander's great aunt?" I whisper back.

I have been provided with a chart of Alex's family tree. It is populated with women with nicknames like 'Duckie', 'Muffy' and 'Bunny.'

"Beatrice, Alex's little secretary, nice to see you," announces the well-dressed older woman grandly.

Duckie is a legend in New York society. She heads her own family dynasty from her marriage to Colbert Caldwell, head of a pesticides business. An unglamorous business, but the money in the billions certainly is not. Her grandson Duke is Alex's best friend.

Duckie turns her attention to me and looks me up and down. I wilt under her laser light beam and generations of society breeding.

"You must be the fiancé," Duckie drawls.

I square my shoulders and dig deep. "Yes, I am. How do you do Mrs. Caldwell," I say politely.

Duckie doesn't respond.

Duckie then turns on her heel and simply walks off down the street, presumably towards her favorite lunch spot Le Sandwich. A place that of course doesn't 'do' bread.

"Don't mind her, some of the Carlyle's can be a bit...difficult," says Bee sympathetically.

What kind of family have I gotten tangled up in? Thankfully it is only for three months.

The big family dinner introduction is tonight. Standing in front of the elegant mirror in my spacious room I try to calm my nerves.

"Looking good brings confidence," I say to myself. Tonight I am relying on Grammie's mantra.

I head out to the living room where Alex is waiting. I catch my breath as I walk in. He looks so handsome in a blue and white striped open necked shirt and pressed slacks. The blue in the shirt picks out his eyes.

Alex stares at me. I feel worried. Do I look bad?

"Tallulah, you look incredible," Alex says breaking into a grin.

Relieved, I smile back. "Thank you. Bee said a classic little black dress never fails."

I am wearing a simple chic dress from our shopping trip. I have accessorized simply with shining pearl earrings, necklace and bracelet. I readily admit I take my New York style inspiration from my favorite actresses.

My feet are getting used to their first pair of 4 inch heels.

"Well then, Sir," I say in my best Southern Belle voice, "shall we?"

We drive out to Connecticut to the family's main estate, the legendary 'Carrington.' It is nice to drive with Alex behind the wheel of his own Mercedes, not a chauffeur. We chat easily and I entertain Alex with the story of my encounter with Duckie.

"Duckie isn't so bad," says Alex with a laugh. "She plays the Imperial Queen but she can be warm if she decides she likes you. If she approves of you, you can be her acolyte."

"Lucky me!" I cry, "Does being Duckie's follower involve bread-less lunches at Le Sandwich and doing the heavy lifting for charity events?"

Alex slaps his thigh in laughter. "Oh Tully, you sure catch on fast!"

I grow quiet as we pull into the drive of Carrington. Huge shady trees line the drive along with discreet lighting. The drive seems endless.

The estate appears to stretch to endless ends. I wonder if Carrington is bigger than all of downtown Hunter. The car purrs to a stop in front of the house.

Alex throws me a glance. "Are you ready for this?"

I meet his eyes. "I am ready. This is business, right?"

Alex says nothing for a moment. "Perhaps we should practice that kiss again?"

But before I can respond he is out of the car and striding to the door where a butler has appeared.

What is he playing at, I think furiously as I follow.

———————————

Entering into the cocktails room I ignore the butterflies in my stomach and remained determined to hold my own.

A small group of adults are milling around. I quickly glance at the women and feel relieved I am dressed well. Thank you, Bee, I say in a silent prayer.

"Alexander!" A smiling woman dressed in teal blue notices our arrival.

"Hello, Aunt Daisy," Alex says with genuine enthusiasm.

"And this must be your lovely bride!" Daisy cries.

Kisses are planted on my cheeks, my hands grasped and a beaming smile bestowed upon me. Automatically I feel I like this woman.

"Tallulah, this is my Aunt Daisy, my Uncle's Jock's wife." I nod and smile and try to keep my family tree straight.

Daisy is the wife of Jock, the charming yet defensive 'family relationships' manager. Whatever that job is.

"Alexander, how very naughty you are hiding your girlfriend away until engagement," chastises a very, very thin and very uptight seeming woman.

"Miranda, how lovely to see you this evening," Alex says with a distinctly cooler tone than Daisy receives.

Ah, Miranda 'Miri' Carlyle. Wife of a presidential hopeful whose family wishes he had stayed behind the scenes, but whose ego wouldn't let him.

"Miranda, this is my fiancé Tallulah," Alex introduces me.

Miranda compresses her lips together into something resembling a smile. "Well Tallulah, Carrington must be quite a change from the trailer park!"

I choke my champagne. "Excuse me," I splutter ungracefully. Alex looks stunned.

"Well Alex found you in a trailer park didn't he?" Miranda looks innocently at us. Butter wouldn't melt in her mouth.

"No, Miri," Alex says grimly, "We met when I was visiting South Carolina on business and Tully was my waitress." Ah yes, our rather dull how-we-met story.

"Oh yes, silly me. You've dated so many women Alex I can't keep up," trills Miri as she moves away to greet another family member.

Thinking of Duckie I wonder if they teach Carlyle women the insult drop and heel turn.

Alex leans in and kisses me softly on the cheek. My spine tingles. "Don't mind her," he murmurs, "she's just jealous you look so beautiful tonight."

I grab his hand and squeeze it gratefully. I've only met three family members so far, if you can count Duckie as an introduction, and I am beginning to see why the price tag for this job was sky high.

Male family members descend on en masse. The familiar faces of billionaires take me aback. Hearty greetings are exchanged between Jock, Hartford and Alex. Looking at Hartford I can see what is meant by 'Presidential'.

Pembrey, Alex's cousin and Hartford and Miri's son, thrusts forward a hand,

"Pembrey Carlyle, a pleasure to meet the woman who has captured my cousin's heart," he says with a seemingly forced grin.

Pembrey. The failed businessman and failed heir. Given Alex's reluctance to take up the mantle Pembrey had a shot at running the family business. That experiment ended badly when Pembrey sent an important subsidiary of the family bank into bankruptcy, costing thousands of jobs, a big drop in the share price and acres of bad press.

Pembrey is now relegated to 'special projects', which seems to involve investing in vague tech start-ups.

"Thank you, it is a pleasure to be here," I respond.

Pembrey keeps holding my hand, "Well don't overstay your welcome, we do have hounds!" Pembrey laughs as if his joke is tremendously funny.

I withdraw my hand, confused.

"Oh Pembrey," fake laughs another very thin woman. "Alinda, wife darling, please my sense of humor is legendary in this family," protests Pembrey.

The smile on my face is beginning to hurt.

"Tallulah we are so happy to have you join the family," says Alinda with all the sincerity of a used car salesman.

"Hopefully the pitter patter of tiny feet soon?" Alinda asks enquiringly. "The more heirs the better," jokes Pembrey, taking a big slug of his drink.

I suddenly click. They are considering that the trust structure of the Carlyle family changes when a child is born into the family. It is a case of the fewer children in each generation the bigger the pool for each child.

My having heirs to Alex, which is not going to happen of course, would reduce the pool for their own children, three children Alex described simply as 'truly awful kids.'

"Ah not yet," I respond distractedly as a stylish woman swoops in to kiss me on the cheek.

"Darling! SO lovely to meet you, I've heard all about you," beams the woman.

"No you haven't," I hear Pembrey mutter.

Alex, who has remained quiet during the exchange with Pembrey and Alinda, brightens. "Hello Prinny," he says dropping a kiss on her cheek.

"Tully this is my darling Aunt Prinny, Princess of the Carlyle's," Alex says with a naughty grin.

"Oh you," laughs Prinny, "so bad."

This must be Victoria Carlyle, only daughter of Alexander Senior. Four husbands to date, multiple rehabs and one amazing wardrobe and sense of style that sees her regularly photographed for fashion magazines. Only while doing her charity work, of course.

We chat about our outfits and I begin to relax a little. Prinny tells me she is called Prinny as short for "Princess, because that is what I am." I nod understandingly.

And then Alexander Senior walks into the room and I suddenly realize where Alex inherits his sense of presence. It is like the room suddenly stands still and looks a little sharper and at the ready.

"Well now, enough chat, let us have dinner. Tallulah you will sit next to me." With that Alexander Senior is gone; perhaps that is where the women inherited their ability to drop a comment and walk away without waiting for a response.

I try not to down my drink from nerves, take a deep breath and prepare for the worst. Cocktails with these people have been enough to convince me this is not where I belong.

———————————————————-

"So tell us about your family, Tully," asks Daisy encouragingly.

So far I have been sitting quietly next to Alexander Senior who holds, of course, the head of the table. Alex is across from me on Alexander's other side.

"Well," I begin, "My father was in the military. He was killed in conflict. My mother passed away when I was born. Grandmother, who was a dressmaker, raised me. My grandfather worked on the railroads and was a justice of the peace." I am proud of my loving, hard working family.

Miri speaks up, "Oh railroads, how interesting. The Carlyle family funded a very prominent man's foray into railroads. We do have quite an interest in it."

Alinda chimed in, "Wouldn't it be amazing if Tully's family had worked on one of our funded railroads back in the day? That's like working for us. From working for us to sitting with us, how amazing."

I look over at Alex trying not to roll my eyes. Alex seems so down to earth how could he have this family? Maybe his time in the army helped keep him on the level.

Alex grimaces and shakes his head slightly.

"That is an interesting idea, Alinda," comments Alexander Senior. Everyone sits a little straighter at the patriarch speaking.

"That would be much like how the Carlyle's owned most of the mid-west at one point. From your ancestors living on our land to you sitting here, how amazing," Alexander finishes drily.

Alinda looks furious but keeps her mouth shut. I smile my best smile at her. I think I like Alexander Senior; he seems to have a handle on the people at this table.

"Alex you must be excited to be getting married. This has come as quite a surprise to us, but we are all looking forward to the wedding," Jock, the good-natured man of the family, steers the conversation to safer ground.

I try to look in love as Alex chats with easy confidence about our upcoming marriage. I manage a contribution on planning to go to Paris for a couture dress. Like I just naturally go to Paris for couture.

The conversation moves easily back to business.

Pembrey is discussing some improbably vague tech venture he is investing in. "And then the app will tell you what you want to eat," Pembrey drones on.

"Barclay will be furious when he sees what I've made in tech this year," Pembrey boasts.

Barclay? My ears pick up at the name Barclay Carlyle. While Alexander Senior is a famous name the rest of the Carlyle's are a little less high profile - except for Barclay. Barclay is not much older Alex however he is Alexander Senior's nephew and cousin to Hartford and Jock.

There is famous bad blood between Barclay and the rest of the Carlyle's. Barclay's father was Alexander Senior's twin. The two ran the business together as would be heirs, until their father, the legendarily brutal businessman William, declared them too soft.

He declared only one of them could be head of the family - and they must fight it out.

The story goes that Alexander Senior promised his twin they would walk away from the family together rather than accept the deal, but then double crossed him and grabbed the mantle.

Barclay's father was furious and spent the rest of his life as a playboy. Barclay got his revenge on Alexander Senior's branch of the family by becoming a renegade and eccentric billionaire in his own right, creating cyber security software. He is always in and out of the news.

"You need to focus more on your own successes and less on what Barclay is doing. That man is out to get us," Hartford reprimanded his son.

I see the presidential mask slip a little in Hartford's frustrated expression. Interesting.

I glance over at Alexander and Alex. They are just watching, cool as anything. I give up on trying to work out the family under currents at this table.

Pembrey catches my eye and delivers a beaming smile, "Now Tallulah, do you think you will be in shape in time for the wedding?"

The comment cuts all the deeper for it's normal easy delivery.

I push my chair back. "That's it!" I announce to the room. "I have had enough of this family's insults. I apologize for not being good enough for you all."

With that I take off my massive sparkling engagement ring and storm out of the room, to go and find a corner of the garden to cry in.

———————

"Tully! Tully! Where are you?" I hear Alex calling as I sit in a small private rose garden trying to recover my dignity.

"There you are!" Alex cries as he comes across me.

Alex sits down on the garden seat and wraps his arms around me. Despite my anger at his lack of support at diner I can't help but lean into his reassuring embrace.

"Oh Tully, I'm so sorry. They can be dreadful people when they feel their positions are threatened," he hushes my crying.

I pull away from him angrily. "They're dreadful? You are dreadful! Why didn't you stand up for me? I am supposed to be your fiancé! Is this how you would treat your real fiancé?' I demand.

Alex sighs and runs his hand through his thick hair. "No, Tallulah, it's not. It seems I am always seeking your forgiveness," he says ruefully.

I cross my arms and glare at him.

Alex explains, "I had always wondered how my family would treat a fiancé of mine. So I let them run on with it and didn't cut them off by standing up for you. I'm sorry."

I consider this information. "Well Alex, this is a business deal after all. I'm glad you are getting out of this what you need. For myself however no amount of money is worth this level of humiliation. I'm done."

I stand to leave. Alex jumps up and pulls me into a fierce embrace. "No, Tallulah, you are not done."

And then he begins to kiss me, deeply, passionately and almost aggressively. I try to push him away but he holds me tight to him. His mouth hungrily seeks mine. I weaken under his desire and begin to kiss him back.

My stiff body relaxes into his and we become one. Our mouths are seeking each other over and over. Our tongues say a thousand silent things to each other.

Finally, exhausted we break apart. We stare into each other eyes as the twinkly fairy lights of the rose garden cast a glow over us.

"What are we doing, Tallulah," Alex whispers softly.

"I wish I knew, Alex," I whisper back.

———————————-

Back at The Deco apartment things have shifted between Alex and I since the garden kiss. Alex has convinced me to keep on with our arrangement.

There is a veneer of politeness in our interactions that is appropriate for our business relationship, but also an underlying sexual tension that confuses and excites me.

Living together is torture. I catch Alex in the kitchen in a towel. His muscular body and hairy chest and wet hair do things to me I have pushed away.

He walks in on me changing for one of the endless events we are attending as a 'couple'. I shriek as he catches me in my lacy white underwear, about to slip into a chic little outfit.

"Oh gosh, Tully I'm so sorry, I thought you heard me knock," Alex apologizes.

Yet his gaze lingers on my body a little longer than necessary.

And then there is the kissing...

Without even discussing what has happened to our relationship Alex and I have taken to kissing silently and suddenly. He will grab me in the kitchen and suddenly brush his lips across mine, before walking away without a word.

I sneak up on Alex at his downtown office at Carlyle Center while he is on a business call and begin kissing him lightly all over his face.

"I have to go, urgent call on the other line from Tokyo," Alex snaps into the receiver.

He takes my chin in his hand and holds my face and returns the kisses in all the same places I had kissed him. His memory amazes me.

He picks me up and parks me on his wide oak desk. Either he is incredibly fit or Pembrey was wrong to criticize my weight, because Alex makes me feel as light as a ballerina.

I wrap my arms around his neck and we kiss hungrily. Alex begins to undo the gold buttons of my white and navy designer suit.

"Alex, stop," I say, tearing my mouth away from his.

"I...I'm not ready for this," I manage.

Kissing is one thing, but other things? I don't know if this man is my boyfriend or my boss.

Alex looks at me with restrained desire. He straightens up and brushes imaginary lint of his suit pants.

"Of course. This is business not pleasure," Alex says coolly.

I tilt my head and look at him.

"Yes," I reply slowly, hopping off the desk with surprising grace. "All business. It's why I am in my suit."

With that remark I saunter off towards the door.

As I close the door I hear Alex laughing. I grin to myself. I still am taking a childish pride in making the very serious and very important Heir to the Carlyle Throne laugh.

And focusing on jokes helps me avoid the big question - do I want Alex to be my boss...or my boyfriend?

The trouble is I don't know.

Everything I see of Alex's world convinces me that boyfriend is a bad, bad idea. I keep having a fantasy where Alex comes back to Hunter and gets a job on the railroad, but the problem is Alex wouldn't be who he is outside of living his Carlyle life.

And I love who is.

Oh dear. Did I just say I love him?

————————-

"Now ladies, let's all put our best caring faces on and welcome the chair of the committee, New York's most charitable woman, Mrs. Duckie Carlyle Caldwell!

Rapturous applause rings out around the Plaza ballroom from a group of women who all aspire to rule New York instead of Duckie.

"Thank you, thank you," Duckie quiets the crowd with her dulcet tones and the wave of a bejeweled hand.

Duckie wears a simple neat navy day dress. Her only accessories are her enormous wedding rings and a sparkling bird brooch. In simplicity, Duckie outshines the overdressed women in the room.

I tune out as Duckie launches into a speech. When the speech over, I start working the room.

"Tully! So great to see you!" Choruses a gaggle of blonde and gorgeous young women, friends of mine.

"Hi girls," I say with happiness at the sight of the famous Carlyle Quads.

The quadruplet daughters of Jock and Daisy, the four girls have been the only friends I've made in this cutthroat social world. Genuinely nice, albeit very spoiled.

Prinny's nose is rather out of joint at the rise and fall of the girls, who are always featured in the gossip columns. Unfortunately Prinny's social Princess star is a little tarnished these days given all the husbands and rehab trips.

"We must get a selfies with you!" shrieks Camile.

Celine chimes in, "Oh yes! Everyone is so keen for pictures of the mysterious future Mrs. Alex."

Claudia and Candy nod in unison.

I grimace at the reminder of my role of fiancé. I feel guilty about lying to the quads, which have been so kind.

Celine hands her phone to one of the two assistants who trail after them, who snap away as we strike a variety of poses. The second assistant takes notes on our outfits to add to the copy.

"They are calling you America's Duchess!" giggles Camile.

I give a startled laugh. A Duchess, I am not.

"It is very fitting given we are descended from an English Duke," says Candy.

Our conversation is cut off as Duckie swans in. "Girls, really that social media is so tacky," she reprimands the quads, but I can see her affection for them.

"And how are you holding up dear?" Duckie says, turning to me.

"How very clever of you to keep the wedding details secret to build interest, we all await the details with unseemly eagerness," Duckie looks at me as if she knows all my secrets.

Here's the thing about our 'secret' wedding details. There are none. That is because this is a business deal that ends very soon.

I exchange pleasantries with Duckie and I think I manage quite well. In these situations I've taken to pretending I am the ultimate socialite. It helps.

Duckie floats away to greet more of her subjects and I find myself face to face with CeCe Bartrand. CeCe is one of the aspiring queens to Duckie's social throne.

CeCe attempts to smile but her face won't move.

"Well Tallulah, how nice to see you. I was just saying to Alex the other night when he was over that we really should be introduced," CeCe looks at me triumphantly.

The other women around us shift awkwardly.

"Oh...Alex.... the other night?" I say bewildered.

"Oh yes, didn't you know Alex stops by? We are very close. We went out for some time. It is hard to let go of a connection that strong, even if his family commitments pull him in another more.... conventional direction," CeCe finishes with a knowing look to the women around us.

CeCe clearly means to humiliate me in front of all New York society. But I've learned a thing or two in my months moving through this pool of sharks. Unlike that disastrous first Carlyle dinner I am not about to run off crying.

"Well CeCe, Alex must have been comforting you over your latest plastic surgery procedure gone wrong."

The bug eyed social X-rays cannot contain their gleeful laughter. While they may profess to be friends with CeCe, one lady's fall is another lady's gain in this world.

With that excellent snarky comment I make like a Carlyle and turn on my heel and stalk away.

I make myself stay the whole event and up the ante. My socializing skills are amazing. I even think Duckie is impressed.

And I then I head home to confront my man. Because that is what I had decided he is. As Grammie had said when I called for advice, if a man kisses a lady then she is his lady.

———-

"How dare you!" I yell at Alex, throwing a crystal tumbler from his drinks tray at the wall above his head.

I have stormed into his office and am causing something of a scene. This is sure to end up in the tabloids, reported by his employees who saw me at it.

"Hey, what's all this Tull-Tull," Alex said, throwing his hands up in the air.

"Don't you Tull-Tull me," I yell furiously, even angrier now at Alex using a nickname he has given me.

Some 'boss', having a pet name for the employee he is kissing.

"I know you have been seeing that CeCe while coming home and kissing me everywhere from the butler's pantry to the maid's room," I glare at him.

Alex throws back his head and laughs, "Oh CeCe up to her old tricks is she!"

I grab another tumbler and get ready to throw it. If there is one thing I hate it is not being taken seriously when mad.

"Come here," Alex commands. Reluctantly I go and sit on his lap.

"CeCe is an old girlfriend, and a troubled one. I know she can seem awful but she's actually sweet and vulnerable. I stopped by her place to see her because her dog had died and she was pretty down. Nothing happened and it was just the once," Alex explains.

"Oh Alex, now I feel awful! I didn't say nice things," I bury my head in his shoulder.

"Don't worry about it, she probably did deserve it," Alex playfully tousles my hair and draws me in for a kiss.

"Tonight when I get home from work let's have a good talk about us. I'm falling in love you," Alex says simply.

I beam at him. He loves me!

"Me too," I say shyly.

We gaze at each other and I want this moment to go forever and ever.

Leaving Alex's office I skip out to the car. Even the paparazzi don't bother me today. I am a woman in love.

Sliding into the back of the limousine, I park my large handbag on the seat beside me and notice the driver has changed since I pulled up.

The man, who introduces himself as Peter, says the other driver has gone on a break. We chat easily. I don't even notice we don't appear to be going home.

Suddenly we pull into a nondescript underground parking lot and it occurs to me things are very, very wrong.

———————————

"Please, please," I say tearfully into the camera. "Please help me." I begin crying.

It has been three days since I was kidnapped. Three days of a concrete room, mattress on the floor and a shameful lack of privacy.

The kidnappers haven't hurt me badly, but I am a little battered and bruised from resisting them in the parking garage. My right arm really hurts.

Why hasn't Alex come for me, I think desperately. He loves me. He said so. He wouldn't leave me like. I try to stay positive.

As the days wear on with no sign of rescue I can't stop thinking of who would do this to me. Was it Barclay? The renegade billionaire is well known for his hated of Alex's branch of the family, and his questionable morals. Maybe I haven't been rescued because this isn't about money, but revenge.

I give up thinking about why and who, and curl into a ball and cry myself to sleep, imagining Alex's strong arms around me making everything better.

——————————————————————————-

"Nobody move or we'll shoot!" I wake up suddenly to the sound of shouting and gunfire. Rescue! Alex!

The door to my prison room flung open and Alex, dressed in dark combat gear like the solider he once was, storms in. I throw myself into his arms and start sobbing.

"Oh Alex!" I cry.

"Baby we have to get out of here," Alex put his arm around me and helps me move to the door and the nightmare is over.

When the endless interviews with the police are over Alex takes me to the family's country estate in rural Virginia.

A visit was made to South Carolina to visit Grammie and reassure her. I pretended Alex and I were still all business but I think she knew otherwise.

At the Virginia estate under Alex's tender care I begin to recover my strength and my bruises are healing.

"How are you feeling tonight," Alex says to me as we rest in front of the fire.

"Good," I respond, "My arm doesn't hurt anymore."

"And emotionally," Alex enquires, scrutinizing me. "Still a little shaky," I reply.

The police and the Carlyle family have determined a distant English Carlyle cousin, Lord Richard, had orchestrated my kidnapping.

"It makes me so angry," Alex says, gripping his glass tighter.

"A title and estate is not worth kidnapping someone over. The English laws may be unfair that when someone dies without an heir the title goes to a distant male cousin, but just because grandfather was ahead of Lord Richard in the distant line that doesn't justify what Richard did," Alex looks furious.

I nod and stare off into space. In the space of nearly three months I had gone from living a quiet life in Hunter and planning to go back to college to being kidnapped by an insane English Lord.

Romances with billionaires are far from dull.

"I'll never let anyone hurt you again," Alex says softly, kissing me.

We begin to kiss gently, then urgently. After all this time we haven't even made love. Right when we were about to sort out our relationship I had been kidnapped. This was our first chance with me well and time alone.

"I love you," he whispers into my ear as he drops kisses all over my face in the way I love.

"I love you too," I respond.

Alex scoops me up and carries me to our bedroom. The four-poster bed looks inviting with deep pillows and soft white linen. Glowing lamps cast a gentle light and keep the shadows away.

Alex sets me down on the bed carefully, like I am a porcelain doll that will break. Since the kidnapping I am less funny tough girlfriend and more of a precious jewel.

He sits down beside me and we kiss, we kiss for a long, long time. Unlike the playful kisses in the apartment these kisses feel less like a flirtation and more like the kisses between a loving couple.

Alex moves to tug off my sweater. Unlike when we were in his office, I don't stop him. This feels right, I feel ready.

We make love all night. It is everything I had hoped it would be. Alex makes me feel safe and loved. We talk quietly as the sunlight filters in through the window as dawn approaches.

"When did you know you were falling in love with me?" I ask Alex, as I prop myself up on an elbow to study his face.

"Before I even met you," Alex grins.

"Really?" I say, sitting up.

"Yes. I thought the whole idea was harebrained but Thompson insisted it would buy me time to develop an alternative plan to Grandfather's ruling. When he showed me your picture and I read your college admissions essay on wanting to make a difference I knew I had to meet you," Alex confesses.

"I told myself it was strictly business, but maybe it never was," he continues.

I am startled by this revelation. And embarrassed Alex had read my very earnest college admissions essay.

"I fell in love with you told me Owlie was your friend, when we were in the lobby," I confess back.

It was Alex's turn to look surprised. "Owlie? Why did that capture your heart?"

I smile and blush. "Well it was so sweet, and it made me wonder if maybe you needed a friend if you friend was a sculpture in the lobby. I sensed that despite your wealth you might be a little lonely."

Alex looks moody. "It can be difficult to be in such a serious position, and to be so wealthy. People treat me differently. Even my own family as I am the heir of the family."

Alex pulls me down under the covers for a cuddle. "But now I have you."

I snuggle in close, "And I have you."

We arrive back in New York as the first chill hit that air, signaling the approaching winter. I was quite glad to leave the upheaval of autumn behind.

Grammie moves to New York to live with us.

"I never thought anything or anyone could persuade you to move from the South, Grammie," I tease as she settled into her suite.

Grammie is all better now after first rate treatment funded by Alex as part of our deal.

"Oh child you should know by now the lord has many plans for us," Grammie replies.

"Why did you encourage me to be with Alex anyway," I ask her curiously.

It has always struck me as a little un-Grammie like to sell me off to a strange billionaire.

"God spoke to me," Grammie says mysteriously.

———————————-

"You will be hosting the Winter Ball next year," comments Alex as we snuggle in bed together.

"The Aunts have this year's one firmly in their grasp but next year it will be your time to shine, you will be able to raise huge funds for veterans," Alex continues.

One of the upsides of marrying a billionaire was not spending their money on shoes and designer outfits but on causes I really care about.

I was determined to bring a great deal to my charity work. Charity to me is not about having an excuse to get dressed up, but to really make a difference.

"Coming to grips with the Carlyle Foundation is going to take some time," I say to Alex. "I'm just going to focus on my work with veterans for now."

Alex pulled me in for a kiss. "I'm sure your Daddy would be so proud of you."

I lay my hand on his. "I hope so," I reply.

Alex pulls away and sighs. "But before we can consider balls and weddings I need to sort out my family."

I sigh with him. Alex's family had been a source of tension between us.

"I love how loyal you are Alex, but if I am to have to spend time around those people then the more difficult members need to drop it and the rest, while nice, need to show me more respect. I may not be American royalty but I matter," I state with conviction.

Alex's supportive smile melts my firm stance.

"Of course Tull-Tull," Alex agrees. "That is what I love about you. You won't compromise or apologise for being an everyday girl. You have self respect and confidence in spades."

"Maybe I will give Duckie a challenge to the Queen of New York role," I laugh.

"Oh I have no doubt you will, no doubt at all," mused Alex.

————————

Alex's Grandfather has remained a remote figure throughout our courtship. Aside from that awful dinner I have not seen him.

"He's moved into his reclusive phase," Alex explains to me when I ask.

Alex however, is in constant contact with his grandfather as they prepared for his succession to head of the family bank and investment portfolio.

Finally, after what seems like endless meetings, Alexander is officially anointed head of Carlyle Holdings, including the bank and all diversified investments.

"It won't take much," Alex comments as he straightens his tie ahead of a family meeting of aunt's, uncles and cousins. "I'm in charge now and they will play ball."

Striding into the oak paneled boardroom of Carlyle Holdings at the family headquarters, Carlyle Center, one could almost be forgiven for thinking the meeting was about to be chaired by a young Alexander Senior.

There was that presence I had fallen for. That is what separate outs dating a billionaire from a regular guy. Having control and responsibility for a wealth portfolio that can change the economy of an entire country gives a man a devastating presence.

"Thank you everyone for coming," Alex says briskly. "This quarterly family meeting is to discuss a range of financial account issues, trusts and personal family business."

"Forgive me Alex," starts Jock with easy charm, "I do like your fiancé but family meetings are for family. You are not yet married to Tallulah. It says so in the family charter, family meetings are for family only as declared by marriage"

Hartford nods furiously and Pembrey is about to open his mouth when Alex silences everyone.

"Enough," Alex declares.

"I am in charge now and if I want to change the charter I will. Tully is to be my wife very soon and I want her by my side," Alex cast a glare around the room, daring anyone to challenge.

Miri looks like she wants to say something but thinks better of it. Prinny strokes her little dog and doesn't dare request fiancé number five be invited to the meeting.

"We are going to pull together as a team, drop the catty comments and infighting and work towards some common goals. Namely streamlining the business which has become a little unwieldy, and building on our contributions to the community. In this time of inequality as a prime topic we need to be seen to be doing our bit," Alex finishes.

The room breaks out in applause. Seated to Alex's side I put my hand over his. We had gone over and over preparing for this meeting and I know how important it was to him his family come on board with his direction.

"We are with you Alex," declares Jock firmly. The charming Jock always knows where his best interests lie.

Hartford nods. He may be thinking only of funding for his presidential campaign but whatever his motives his support for Alex is welcome.

"Thank you," said Alex, showing no signs of the relief he must be feeling. He appears unruffled and in control.

"I am glad you are all on board with me. Sometimes family's need new blood. Tallulah is not the only person joining the family," Alex says.

Looks of surprise cross everyone's faces. Alinda looks calculating. Probably wondering if the new person has children who will reduce her children's inheritance pool.

"Barclay Carlyle is a man of extraordinary vision, talent and commitment. I am pleased to welcome him back into the fold of his family. I'm excited for his contributions. Barclay is not the villain of our family. All he ever wanted was recognition for the role his father played in building our fortune," as Alex speaks Barclay quietly enters the room.

The handsome renegade tech billionaire slips into a seat and listens to Alex continue.

"I also owe Barclay a debt of gratitude. It was Barclay's cyber software that helped us track Lord Richard. When we were blackmailed by the kidnapping into sending paperwork refusing the Dukedom, Barclay installed a tracker that helped us discover where Tully was," Alex looks at Barclay with gratitude as he speaks with heart.

"You owe me nothing," said Barclay. "Tully is family."

A pause settles over the room. This is a new Carlyle era, one where Barclay and I are now part of the family.

———————————

"Three days until the wedding!" I cry joyfully jumping onto of Alex as we settle into bed for the night.

Alex kisses me deeply. I never tire of his kisses.

"I cannot wait to see your dress," Alex says, sprinkling me with kisses on my nose.

I scrunch my face up. "That tickles!"

We make love tenderly and drift off to sleep in each other's arms. Around two am the phone rudely awakens.

"Alexander speaking," Alex growls into the phone. I sit up in my lacy negligee and watch him worriedly.

Alex listens for what seems like an eternity.

"I see," Alex says finally. "This can be fixed. I'll be in the office in twenty minutes. Assemble the team."

"What is going on Alex," I enquire.

Alex gives a deep groan like I have never heard.

"Pembrey has crashed the Euro. We have extensive currency holdings. While we make a profit on these we also have a community inspired motive and we use our holdings to keep the main currencies, like the Euro, the US dollar and pound, stable. Solid economies benefit us in the long run," Alex explains.

I listen intently as Alex continues; "Pembrey has sold off our holdings in the Euro. Such massive currency moves are rare.

"What will you do?" I ask, trying to find some kind of term of reference for helping your fiancé deal with an international financial crisis.

"You and I are going into the office and we are going to fix this," Alex speaks with grim determination as he begins to dress.

"We?" I reply meekly. "Yes, we," says Alex.

We head to the office and I spend very long days fetching endless rounds of coffee and pastries for the hard working men and women who work tirelessly to undo Pembry's work.

I quietly drop coffee on people's desk as they hurry to buy up available Euro's and raise the value again.

"We cannot let this crisis spread to America because it would push us into depression," Alex's says accepting a coffee from me.

"And that rat Pembrey is nowhere to be found," adds Alex with anger.

In the late evening on the day before our wedding the crisis draws to a close as the currency markets and finance ministers respond to Alex's moves.

The financial press hails Alex's white knuckled grip and steely hold on the situation.

The crisis though does claim a victim. Devastated by the shame brought on the family by Pembrey, Alexander Senior suffers a fatal heart attack.

Despite being rather reclusive for near the past decade the media hails him and extensive coverage is devoted to his passing.

"What do we now honey?" I question Alex when the news comes through about Alexander Senior, in the middle of the currency crisis.

Alex pulls me into a hug. "We are going ahead with the wedding, but smaller. I've already emailed our planner to scale things back.

Grandfather always wanted us to get married, so we will. We had already decided to go ahead when we started dating for real, instead of giving it time. Why stop now."

I nod and snuggle in close. "It can be a celebration for Alexander Senior. Tasteful."

Alex nods and hugs me back. "I couldn't have got through this crisis without you. The press are hailing me as a leader but we all know behind every great man is a great woman."

I smile into his chest. I don't think I will ever get sick of being Alexander's great woman.

———————————————————-

"Are you ready dear," Grammie smiles at me.

"As ready as I will ever be," I reply shakily. Even though we had quickly toned down the wedding I was still about to walk into a room of people who were famous, infamous or very important.

"Grammie, the Carlyle version of toning down a wedding involves politely asking the President not to come so there is less fuss," I try to joke to cover my raging nerves.

Grammie takes my arm and leads me towards the door to the main part of the Church. "You belong here," she says simply and her loving confidence carries me down in the aisle and into the arms of the man I love.

"Speeches, speeches!" cries Duke Caldwell, Alex's best man, as the reception is in full swing.

Everyone eventually settles into his or her seats and Thompson Thompson, Alex's lawyer, steps up to the microphone. I notice Grammie standing beside him and wonder when they became friends.

"During my time as a military lawyer I learned what was important in life. So too did my client Alexander Senior, who towards the end of his life came to see love mattered more than business," Thompson says.

What is going on, I mouth to Alex. He shrugs and looks as puzzled as I am.

Grammie takes the microphone. "When my son's military colleague Thompson told me of Alexander Senior's despair that his grandson refused to consider love, and I shared my worry over my singleton granddaughter, we realized we might be able to help each other out.

Thompson took to the microphone again. "We both knew neither stubborn party would go on a blind date. Tully would need a lot to persuade her to leave Grammie and only for Grammie's benefit, and Alex was so set on being a bachelor that we had to come up with something quite creative."

The penny drops. We've been set up. Alex jaw drops as he turns to look to me. The man the press are calling The Economic

Depression Savior completely missed his own life being set up for him.

"We won't go into the little trick we played on Tully and Alex," said Grammie, "but let me just say to this audience you have no idea what it took to get these two down the aisle to happily ever after."

Filled with bubbles of laughter I start giggling until I am almost crying. Alex gives in to my infectious giggles and we both laugh and look at each other.

"Well Duchess, it looks like we've been had," grins Alex.

"Duchess?" I enquire.

Alex pulls me in for a kiss. "Ah this is why I love you Tully. It never occurred to you that the line for the Dukedom that has fallen into the family's lap now passed to me, making you a Duchess."

I laugh and kiss my husband back, "never a dull moment as a billionaire's wife!"

******

The Billionaire's Gift

April's mind still reeled from the news. It was all anyone in her sorority house talked about, and all that she saw on the news. Lewis Edwards had been arrested and charged with securities fraud. It turned out that the investment scheme he was running truly was a scheme – a Ponzi scheme. He was bringing in new investors, most of them hardworking middle class looking to build retirement funds, and using the money to pay his high net worth investors. It all came crashing down on him, and in an attempt to pay back as much of the money as they could, the Feds seized all of Edwards' assets.

The problem for April was that Lewis Edwards was her father.

April would never have considered herself rich, but she was wealthy. They had enough money that she never worried about anything. She never even questioned why her mother left her father five years ago – though she suspected now that her mother got wise to his scheme and decided to leave. April felt badly now for insisting to stay with him. She had alienated her mother, and right now, she could have used a sympathetic shoulder to cry on.

Everyone had abandoned her. Her boyfriend of two years broke up with her. Her friends turned their backs on her. April was alone and miserable. As the spring semester wrapped up, April somehow managed to make it through her finals and wondered what would happen next. Would she be able to come back to school? Would she even have a place to live? The home she had known her whole life was locked up and taped. It and everything inside was to be auctioned off this summer.

April sat on the bed of her dorm room and looked out the window. Her roommate Sylvia had already left. Sylvia had hardly said a word to her since the news about her father came out. Of all of her friends, April thought Sylvia had the best reason. Her father had been one of the investors in the Edwards Fund, and he very likely lost a great deal of money.

The day outside was bright, far brighter than April felt. She let out a long sigh. She had held off on calling her mother. She knew that her mother would not turn her away, but she was also not sure how she was going to get to her. She was across the country now, in California. While she had managed to pick up her life, April doubted that she would be able to spring for a plane ticket at the last minute.

"You're still here," a light voice said from April's doorway.

April turned to see her sorority sister Chloe standing there. She was holding a suitcase in one hand and a box under her other arm.

"Yeah, I'm not in any hurry to get nowhere," April said.

Chloe set her things down at the doorway and walked over to Sylvia's old bed. She sat down and looked at April, measuring her carefully. April was not sure what to make of it. She and Chloe were never close. Chloe was a year her senior and a sweet girl, but the two of them had almost nothing in common.

"It's been hard on you the last few weeks," Chloe said at last. "Do you know where you're going?"

April shrugged her shoulders. "I'll probably call my mom out in California and see if I can join her out there."

Chloe frowned. "That's a long way to go for an 'if you can.'"

April appreciated Chloe's ability to quickly understand a situation; even she did not understand all of the details behind it. It did not help her though, and April let out another deep sigh before looking out the window again.

"You know," Chloe said, "I might have a solution for you."

April turned back to face Chloe. A solution was just what she needed. "What's that?"

"My dad owns a resort upstate. He always needs extra help for the summer, and it pays really well. You also get to stay at the resort free, though you're staying in the servants quarters. It's not too bad, as long as you don't mind spending your summer in a room about the size of this dorm room."

April never had to work a summer job. She was aware of the concept, but the practice itself was alien to her. Still, the idea of getting a job had a certain appeal. It meant that she did not have to depend on her mother, and if her mother saw her trying to make an effort to get past everything and be better for it, it might help the two of them repair their relationship. If her mother could help, she might even be willing to do it on more even terms than April having to move somewhere strange.

"Will it be a problem, to get me a job I mean?" April asked.

Chloe shook her head. "My dad's opinion is that anyone who can't ask a few simple questions about an investment probably deserves to lose their money." Chloe paused and gave April an apologetic look. "It's a harsh opinion. But it means that he's not going to have anything against helping you. Besides, nothing that happened had anything to do with you. It was all your father."

April gave Chloe the first real smile that she felt in weeks. "Thank you so much. Whatever he needs me to do, I don't care. I'll even wash toilets."

Chloe laughed. "It won't be that bad. It'll be hard work, but the resort is beautiful, and staff always get two days off during the week, so you'll even get to enjoy some of it."

April did not care about getting to enjoy the resort. For the first time since the investigation into her father started, April was starting to see the light at the end of a very dark tunnel.

She even thought it might not be a train.

****

April had never had the opportunity to visit Stuart Estates before. It was far more upscale than anything her family would have afforded, though she knew many of her father's clients probably frequented this resort. She wished she had gotten to see and enjoy it without having to be an employee. Set in a mountain valley, it featured a large manor house that hosted any number of events, from conferences to weddings and family reunions. Some of the upstairs rooms were still held as private rooms for guests, though a majority of guest accommodations were in "cabins," buildings that had once served as guest houses or were built later when the original property was converted.

Still, April thought that she would enjoy working here. The air was crisp and clear. She was surrounded by beauty. It was tranquil, even if her supervisor Henry Graven did promise that she would be far too busy to take notice of what was around them.

Mr. Graven was a cold man, tall with pale skin and dark hair. April recognized the name right away, and did her best not to cringe. He was one of the people who lost their retirement money to her father's scheme. She could tell by the way that he looked at her; he knew who she was. He would not be able to do anything overt, but if she gave him any reason to fire her, he would not hesitate to take it.

Her first day was mostly a learning curve, of going from being the person waited on to doing the waiting. Mr. Graven was grudgingly patient as she learned, and she found the rest of the staff to be kind and understanding. She did not think any of them knew about her circumstances, and she was thankful for that. It was still a stressful day, and she was happy to retire in the evening to her room.

Her "room" was one-half of a small cabin that April thought had probably been a campground cabin at some point. Now it was fitted with lighting and a small window unit to control heat and air. A bathroom had also been built onto it, to be shared between the two units. It was small, smaller than her dorm room had been, but it was comfortable, brightly decorated, and most of all private.

April lay on her bed and thought about her day. It has been busy. Mr. Graven was right. She had barely had time to notice the beautiful scenery around her. She decided she would change that. She would give herself a few days to get used to the job, and after that, she would take brief moments in her day to just appreciate where she was.

****

April knelt down to wipe up the spilled coffee and gather up the shards of china cups that were now scattered about the floor. She was still getting used to carrying trays and keeping them balanced. Something had brushed her thigh over her skirt – it was not a something, it was a man's hand, she was certain of that – and caused her to lose her balance. Now, she was mortified as guests watched her fumbling with the glass shards and spilt coffee, trying hard not to cut herself.

When the last piece was gathered and the last of the coffee sopped up, April stood, careful not to tip her tray and spill any of the shards. As she walked past a table, she felt a hand brush the top of her knee. She glanced back to see an older man with short, thick grey hair give her a wink. She quickly turned, trying to control her blush and pushed through the swinging doors back into the kitchen galley.

"Are you okay?" Leah, one of the other girls on staff asked her as she set down her tray of broken cups.

"A guest is getting grabby," April said. She let out a sigh as she began to move the shards into the collection bin set up for broken wares. "It just caught me off guard, that's all."

"You should be more careful with your tray Miss Edwards." Mr. Graven paused as he walked past her. "You are lucky that you did not burn anyone."

"I'm sorry. I'll be more careful next time," April said.

She did not look up to see Mr. Graven's look, but she was sure it was one of contempt. He walked on and she finished depositing the shards and took her tray to be washed. Another tray of coffee was set up, which Leah picked up to take out. April was relieved. She did not want to have to go back out into the dining room right now, not right on the heels of something so embarrassing.

The rest of the noon day brunch went by smoothly, and when April did have to go back out, she was glad to see that guests paid her no more attention than they did to any other member of staff. Slowly the guests filed out of the dining hall and out to the veranda.

It was still raining lightly outside, but it would clear soon. The guests would enjoy any number of outdoor festivities while the staff prepared the indoor rooms for evening festivities.

April moved to her area of the dining room and began cleaning the tables. Someone else would come behind to vacuum, but she wanted to make sure that the floor was cleared of any large debris. As with everything else, she was still getting accustomed to cleaning, and the rest of the staff were done and cleared away as she still worked, her mind turning over bits of half-remembered lyrics to keep her moving at a steady pace.

A hand moved over the small of April's back and along her buttock. She jumped up, pushing into the bulk of someone behind her. April had not even heard anyone come up on her. When she turned, she saw the same man with the grabby hands from brunch.

"You're like a little rabbit." His voice was smooth as he spoke. His eyes were even and demanding. April gripped the table and tried to put space between them, only to have him close it again. "I do like hunting rabbits."

"I need to finish my work." April could not think of anything else to say. The man's hands moved to her waist and slowly up her sides to cup her breasts.

Everything happened at once then. The swinging door from the kitchen galley opened. Mr. Graven walked out, followed by two other staff members. The door from the veranda opened and an older woman walked in, followed by two young men. April's hand collided with the face of the man accosting her with a loud slap propelled by the swing of her arm. It resounded through the dining hall before the woman began to scream shrilly.

April tried to wrestle control of her situation, but she could not. Mr. Graven was upon the scene immediately, asking the man – Henry Worthington as it turned out to April's surprise and horror – if he were okay. The woman screamed about a trollop hitting her husband. Mr. Worthington began his explanation of how she had come onto him. April tried to speak up, to give her side of the story, only to be hushed by Mr. Graven or Mrs. Worthington screaming about lies. The noise brought more guests from the veranda into the dining room.

Mr. Graven finally took hold of April's arm, squeezing tightly and leading her away. She tried to protest over his assurances to Mr. Worthington that he would take care of the situation. He led her out into the hall and spun her around hard, slamming her back against the wall and knocking the air from her. Further down, guests poured out of the dining room and into the hall, not wanting to miss the end of the drama.

"I have been very patient with you, but I will not have you accosting our guests," Mr. Graven kept his voice stern and even.

"I didn't do anything wrong," April said.

"You slapped one of the resorts most honored guests. You will go up to him and you will apologize."

"I will not. The man is a pig!" April said louder than she meant to.

Mr. Graven pulled back his hand and aware of the crowd stopped himself. He lowered his voice and leaned in closer to April. "You are fired, do you understand? You will go to your cabin and pack your belongings. I expect to see you gone from here within the hour."

April could not say anything else. She turned and ran down the hall as tears began to stream from her eyes, burning her cheeks in her shame and embarrassment.

****

Nigel Conroy knew two things very well. Henry Worthington was a misogynist and a womanizer and the staff of Stuart would happily kiss the ground that he walked on. He was certain that

Worthington could have murdered the poor girl and the staff supervisor would still have found a way to claim she had fallen upon his knife or gun herself.

He also had a very good idea of who the girl was. He face was familiar, one he knew he had seen recently on the news. If he was right, she had been through enough. Being fired in front of all of the guests here was the last thing she needed. As the crowd began to slowly disperse, he took hold of the arm of another staff, a cute young woman with short blonde hair.

"I'm sorry, but I wanted to ask you something before you had a chance to go away," Nigel said, releasing her.

"It's alright sir," the young woman said. "How can I help you?"

"The girl that just ran down the hall, what was her name?"

The young woman narrowed her eyes, and Nigel did not blame her. He sensed protectiveness and found himself very much liking this young woman.

"I don't mean any harm, but she didn't deserve what happened, and I think you know it. I'm pretty sure I've seen you here for a few seasons, so I think you know what really happened. I just want to make sure she'll be okay."

The young woman continued to eye him warily. Nigel did his best to project his sincerity and she finally relaxed. "April Edwards. I can take you to see her. We share the same cabin."

Nigel nodded his head. "Thank you. If anyone says anything, just tell them I pulled you aside to help me with an errand. I'll vouch for you, I promise."

The young woman did not say anything else. She simply turned and Nigel understood he was expected to follow her. She led him through a side door of the main estate house. The morning rain was now stopped, and the humidity of the afternoon was quickly setting in. She kept a brisk pace as she led him to the servant's cabins and to what he presumed to be her own.

Nigel stepped in to a small living area with a couch, chair, and television and three doors that along the two adjacent and one opposite walls.

The young woman turned to the left door and knocked gently. "April sweetie, it's Leah."

"Please go away, Leah. I don't want to talk to anyone," April's muffled voice came through the door, thick with her tears.

Leah looked back at Nigel but he nodded, waving his hand to urge her to continue.

"April, there's a man here to see you," Leah said.

The door swung open and April appeared, her face streaked with tears and fire in her eyes. Nigel felt a great deal of respect for her suddenly, and felt very badly for anyone that earned that ire. He thought she could have a fiery temper, one she might not even be aware of.

"I'll gouge out that bastard's eyes if it's him," April said before her eyes had a chance to survey the room. When they fell on Nigel, some of the fire pulled back, though he noticed it did not withdraw completely. "Who is that?"

"He's one of the guests," Leah said. "He wanted to make sure you were okay."

April stood there and studied Nigel before turning back to her friend. "Tell him I'll be fine."

"Can I speak to you for a few minutes?" Nigel took a step forward.

Leah looked from Nigel to April, and he could see the helplessness in her eyes. She had duties to attend to and could not be playing referee between them.

April sighed and placed a hand on Leah's shoulder. "It's fine. You get back up before you get into trouble too."

Leah hesitated, looked between the two of them again. She finally nodded. "You find me before you go, okay?"

"I will. Thank you." April gave Leah a hug. She released her and Leah walked past Nigel, giving him a careful look that he read very well. April had a bad enough day, and he did not need to make it worse.

As Leah walked out of the cabin, Nigel turned his attention to the young woman before him as she stepped out of her room. She wore only the simple black dress common to all of the staff. The white apron had been discarded somewhere, either in her room or thrown aside as she fled the shameful scene.

"You have a good friend. Have the two of you known each other a long time?" Nigel was curious about this young woman. The media had painted her as the aloof princess of a sinister financial king, carefully keeping herself out of the direct light of the media. He was not seeing that here. He was seeing something vastly different.

"Just a few days. Leah is a real gem, though." April tilted her head to one side. "What are you doing here?"

Nigel gave a small laugh. "You're not going to ask who I am?"

April shook her head. "I know who you are. Your face shows up in almost every magazine, usually some story about a broken-hearted girl or a large playboy party."

Nigel brought his hand up to his chest and feigned injury. "You wound me. But that's fair enough. I won't lie. I know who you are too."

April frowned deeply. "Here to gloat then?"

A sharp pain stabbed through Nigel's chest and he was surprised to feel it. He was not sure why he felt so much sympathy for this young woman. She was attractive. Her dark hair and bright, blue eyes would be enough to captivate any man. Something else had drawn him in, however. He just wished that he could put his finger on what it was.

"No," Nigel said simply. "I really did want to make sure you were okay. Do you know what you're going to do?"

April shook her head. "I can't go back down to New York. My face is still all over the television. I guess I get to hope that the few days of pay I have here is enough to fly me out to Los Angeles."

"You don't have anyone that can help you out?" Nigel felt very badly for her now. He knew from the news reports that her father's assets had all been seized. He never imagined that it would leave her destitute. He wondered if anyone had bothered to care about that.

"I talked to my mother. She's working as a waitress and trying to get into acting. She barely has enough money to pay her bills." April paused. "Why am I tell you this?"

Why am I about to do what I'm about to do? Nigel was glad to see that at least both of them were behaving in ways they did not understand. She had an excuse. She was under duress. He had no idea what his excuse was, but he knew he would not be able to stop himself now.

"Would you like to spend the rest of the week here with me, as my guest?" Nigel asked.

April's look of shock made him smile. "What?"

Nigel took in a deep breath and let it out. "I'm not sure why your supervisor was so hard on you, but I'm sure that you did not have it coming. A few broken cups is not worth risking a sexual harassment lawsuit. You don't have anywhere else to go right now. So, take a few days to figure it out. Maybe you and your mother will be able to work out something. In the meantime, enjoy the resort as a guest where your old boss can't touch you. As for Mr. Worthington, have the best revenge you can have on him."

April crossed her arms. "What's that?"

"Show him that it had no ill effect on you. Show him that you're over it and moved on. People who do things like that; they thrive on knowing the chaos they've caused."

Nigel watched April carefully as she considered his proposal. She was wary, and he did not blame her. He knew how quickly people in his own circles could turn if the sensed weakness or unattractive controversy. He did not expect that people in hers would be any different.

She finally uncrossed her arms and gave him a square look, setting her shoulders even. "What's the catch?"

Nigel shook his head. "No catch. You'll have to stay with me, but I have one of the luxury cabins, so you'll have your own room. No expectations, except that you'll accompany me and keep me company. That's all."

April continued to study him carefully. Finally, her stance relaxed. "Okay. I'll accept your invitation."

Nigel nodded. "Good. Do you have street clothes?"

April laughed. "Nothing worthy of a place like this."

"Then I'll add one more caveat to this deal. Allow me to take you into town for a shopping trip."

April nodded. Nigel sat down to wait for her to gather her things. This was a quaint and small cabin. He wondered if she had a chance to see the luxury guest cabins yet, and what she would make of them.

****

April held her shopping bags in her hand as she followed Nigel up the walkway to the large cabin. Large picture windows dominated the façade, glowing through their translucent white shades. He carried her suitcase and occasionally made as though to be bearing too heavy of a weight. She could only laugh at that.

Nigel Conroy the man was nothing like the man in so many magazine articles that she and her sorority sisters would read. She thought he could have his arrogant side, and occasionally as he took her through the shops in town, she saw it, typically, when he put down a dress or outfit because he felt the price tag was too low. Mostly, he was normal, if somewhat impulsive in taking her on as his guest.

He opened the door to the cabin and held it for her to walk in. It opened immediately to the main room, open with a vaulted ceiling. A large fireplace dominated it with a couch and two oversized chairs set in front of it. A wide high definition television hung above the fireplace and a full entertainment system sat to the left side. Along the left wall stood a bar and to her right the room opened to a dining room and a kitchen. April wondered if it saw use at all and wondered at its inclusion.

A stairway led up in front of her, dividing the mysterious kitchen from the rest of the downstairs. Nigel closed the door behind them and led her up the stairs. To her right another large living area was set up with balcony rails do that it looked down below them. Beyond it was a hall with three doors. Nigel guided her to one and invited her to set down her things. A double bed sat in this room and a elegant dresser. She set her bags down beside the door as Nigel set her suitcase down by the dresser.

"There's a bathroom right across the hall from you. If you don't like this bed, you can try the one in the room next to you. My room is at the end of the hall. I don't know if you do your own laundry. If you do, the French doors in the hall have a small washer and dryer behind them. You can also set your laundry in the bins outside for staff to pick up. It's your choice, but I do my own laundry."

April blinked her eyes. "You do your own laundry?" She tried to imagine this man measuring out detergent and could not imagine it.

"My housekeeper at home taught me after I ruined my own clothes at another resort. I've had bad luck with staff losing my things."

April wondered if his items were lost or taken. Most of the staff here were honest and hardworking, but she supposed that anyone could be tempted to take something that belonged to someone famous. "I suppose you cook too."

Nigel shook his head. "No, that's never a pretty sight. I hoped you did, actually."

April laughed and shook her head. "My cooking is part of our sorority's hazing ritual." She watched as he gave her a dubious look, tilting his head to one side. "I'm serious. I once boiled the coating out of a pan."

Nigel leaned against the doorframe, his look becoming quickly serious and contemplative. "It's not fair, you know."

"I know. I have to be more careful with pots." April wanted the levity. The look in his eyes unsettled her.

"I'm serious. It's fine that the Feds want to make sure your father pays back the money that he's taken. That's good. They can't take away his ability to care for the people he's responsible for. That punishes you for something you didn't do."

April swallowed hard. She did not like the look in Nigel's eyes right now. It made her want to probe and want to understand the depth of empathy that he had in this moment. She did not want to do that. He was being nice to do this for her, but she did not want to complicate things any more than they were already complicated for her.

"Right," Nigel pushed himself from the doorframe. "You've had a busy day, so I'll let you rest. I'll wake you up in the morning and we can go and enjoy brunch and some horseback riding if you like."

"Horseback riding would be nice," April said. "Thank you again."

Nigel smiled as he turned to the hall. "Thank you for accepting my invitation."

****

The young boy stood in front of the blazing fire, his eyes picking up the orange flames, reflecting them back to the world. Tears streamed down his soot-covered face and when he coughed, he sounded congested and full of smoke. Inside, in the flames, was everything he ever knew and understood to be love, compassion, and order. He could not understand what was happening, or why Nana uttered apologies as she tried to clean the soot from his face.

April sat up in bed and took in a deep breath. Vivid dreams did not come on often, but when they did, they always left her feeling strange, as though she were coming back into her own body. It was, she thought, the effect of her mind moving from its dream reality back into the real world.

The dream bothered her, and as her day played back in her mind and she remembered where she was, she understood why.

She had found the story by chance. Her ex-boyfriend had a playboy magazine sitting on his bed, and she flipped through to the life story of Nigel Conroy, as promised on the cover, while he played on his game console. When Nigel was five years old, his mother had set fire to their home. She had drugged her husband and her son's nanny. She spread kerosene through the house, then over herself and her husband, lighting the both of them on fire. As the fire spread, Nigel's cries somehow managed to wake the groggy nanny, who stumbled out of the inferno, holding the crying child.

The image in her dream was an image from the magazine article, a picture that had been taken of the boy as he stood watching the inferno that had been his home. He said in the interview for the article that he did not really remember the day, but it still influenced his life. His mother suffered from mental illness, untreated because both her family and his father had considered the idea of mental illness to be shameful, something that others faced, not them. Nigel had inherited his father's fortune, and when he was old enough to decide a direction for it, created a foundation to encourage the treatment and de-stigmatization of mental illness.

How could she have forgotten such a terrible, tragic story? April put her head in her hands and began crying.

****

April followed Nigel up to the main estate house, where brunch waited for them. She wondered what Mr. Graven would make of her being there, or Leah for that matter. She thought about Chloe, who had gotten her the job to begin with. She hoped that Chloe was not told about what had happened. She hated to think that she would be made to regret helping her.

Brunch was a pleasant affair, full of conversation. They sat at a large table with other resort guests and engaged in polite conversation. A few of the people at her table knew who April was, but none of them seemed to think her situation warranted more than a passing acknowledgement. She was happy for that. She noticed a glare from Mr. Graven. When he attempted to come to the table, Nigel rose and pulled him aside quickly. April did not know what was said exactly, only that it began with, "before you embarrass yourself."

After brunch, they followed the other guests out to the veranda. There was no rain today, and the early afternoon was quickly growing warm. April followed Nigel through the crowd of people as he walked the direction of the stables.

Mr. Worthington backed up, separating her from Nigel and almost causing April to run into him. He turned, startled, and gave her a kindly smile. "My apologies miss. My son was just clowning around as boys are want to do."

"That's okay, Mr. Worthington," April said carefully.

Mr. Worthington blinked his eyes and gave April a broader smile. "Well, I'm afraid you have me at a loss. You know me, but I don't know you."

April smiled, feeling strange and light. After the huge scene the day before, he did not even recognize her face. She supposed that in the world Mr. Worthington inhabited, it was impossible that a woman who was a servant the day before could be a guest today.

She supposed he had never seen Cinderella.

"I'm afraid I'll have to leave it that way," April said. She glided past Mr. Worthington before he could stay anything else. Nigel had stopped and turned. He was now waiting on her, his look quickly becoming confused as she walked up to him.

"What happened?" he asked.

"I just bumped into Mr. Worthington," April said and decided to laugh. "He didn't even recognize me."

Nigel blinked his eyes and tilted his head. April continued on to the steps that led down from the veranda. The stables were ahead, and she wanted to smell the fresh hay and the horses. Mr. Worthington did not think enough of the day to even realize she and the servant he tried to molest were the same person.

If he could not be bothered, she supposed she did not need to either. The thought of putting the incident behind her lightened her step. After weeks of being remembered, a single moment of being forgotten was bliss.

****

Nigel's horse bucked and he pulled up on the reigns to gain control again, watching the young woman who laughed, carefree on the back of her own. She pulled up on the reigns and turned her horse so that she could twist in her saddle to look at him. This time yesterday, she was in tears. Now, she could have been a completely different person. Nigel supposed in a way, she was. All she needed was a glass slipper and they could have been a prince and princess in a fairy tale.

"You shouldn't look so serious," April said. "Horseback riding is supposed to be fun."

"There's fun, and then there's slapping my horse's rump and startling him," Nigel said, but he found her smile to be infectious.

April shrugged her shoulders. "You were riding like an old man. I just wanted to see if you really knew how to ride."

Nigel took in a breath and nodded his head, recognizing the challenge. "I know how to ride, my dear. I took my first lesson at ten years old."

"Seven," April gave him a smug look.

"I still have you on years riding," Nigel said. He was only about six years older than April was, but his pride was wounded now.

They continued their ride along the forest trail and up the mountain. It was beautiful here, and being out here among the natural beauty seemed to have a good effect on April. Nigel was not sure that he understood why her encounter with Mr. Worthington had left her in such a good mood, but it was nice to see that the forest around them was keeping it in place.

They reached the water trough for the horses and dismounted, tying their reigns off on the poles there so the horses could drink and relax. This stop in the ride was along the ridge of the mountain that the horse trail wound. It offered a nice view of the valley and the estate below, and Nigel was happy to see that few others were taking advantage of the stables today. Most were heading out to the cricket grounds or down to the lake.

Nigel turned to look at April, and saw that she was watching him. The look in her eyes was deep and sympathetic. He wondered at it, but was not sure what to ask her. Perhaps she was feeling badly about spooking his horse.

"This is really nice," April said. She turned and looked back over the valley below them. "I really do appreciate you doing this for me."

Nigel stepped up to her and took her hand in his. She did not pull away, and he held it tighter. As they looked over the valley, she talked about horseback riding in the boroughs outside of New York City and spending her entire weekend learning how to care for the horses. It was, she admitted to him, the only chore she ever learned to do, and one that she always loved.

With her face in profile to him, Nigel could see that she was deeper in her thoughts than her words expressed. Was she remembering the good times with her father and mother, or was it just her father? He realized he had no idea how long her mother had been in Los Angeles. It could have been weeks or years. He had the feeling from how she had talked about her prospects of getting there that they two of them were not very close.

April turned to face him, and Nigel found himself caught by her eyes. They were deep and contemplative while bright, catching the sky above them. Nigel brought his hand up to her face, cupping her cheek. He did not think about what he was doing. He simply leaned forward to kiss her.

****

Nigel's kiss was soft and careful, and it moved through April's body quickly, drawing her free hand up to his shoulders. Between her legs, she felt warm and alive. Nigel released her hand and moved his arm around her body, pressing her body closer to him. She could feel him hard against her and her own desire flared, surprising, and delighting her.

He broke away and looked down into her eyes. April wanted his kiss again, and with a flush realized that she wanted more. She imagined their bodies entwined together here along the mountain ridge, where other riders could come upon them at any moment. The idea tingling and warmth between her legs grow and she reached up to kiss him again, finding him responsive and welcoming.

Nigel brought his hand down from her face to her breast and cupped it gently. April wrapped her arms around his neck, running her fingers through Nigel's brown hair and lacing it through her fingers. He squeezed her breast and held her firm against him. April wanted him. She wanted to feel his hands caress her body, to feel him deep inside her. Her body ached and screamed its want, and as the pounding of hooves came up the mountain trail, she could not pull away from him.

They broke their kiss as another pair of riders came up to the trough. April flushed again and looked from Nigel to the newcomers.

"That must be some view," the woman said as she dismounted her horse. She tied it off next to Nigel's own and looked at her partner. "Do you think we can take a look over the ridge too?"

April stifled her laugh and took Nigel's hand, guiding him back to the horses. As they untied theirs from the trough, the new couple moved over to the ridge, sitting on the stone bench. April mounted her horse and waited for Nigel to join her. She considered heading back, but she wanted to push up the mountain. Yes, she wanted Nigel, and she thought if she told him she wanted to go back to his cabin now that he would. She also understood that part of that want came from moments like this, riding together and enjoying each other's company.

She could let it build.

They continued up the mountain trail, passing the new couple as the man put his arm around his companion. April supposed that the view really was romantic. She hoped there would be other such views on their way up.

They rode for another hour, and April could feel the heat of the day working into her body. A stream snaked along the slope of the mountain, coming close to the trail and skirting away from time to time. She thought about the hour, and how nice it would be to have a shower before they went up to the estate house for dinner. When she made the suggestion to Nigel that they head back, he was reluctant at first, until she mentioned showers. The look in his eye brought a new tingle between April's thighs.

As they made their way back down the mountain, they passed the couple that had come up to the water trough. They exchanged waves and continued on, stopping only briefly at the trough to allow the horses to get water. April's mind kept turning to the shower waiting for them, and she did not want to stop any longer than necessary. She thought of water on her skin and Nigel caressing her body and grew impatient to be back.

When they made it back down to the stables, the hands there took the horses from them, removing their tack and rubbing them down gently. They made their way across the estate grounds to the guest cabins, and April looked at Nigel. She could tell that he had something on his mind, and she wanted to be through it before they reached the cabin.

"Is something the matter?" April asked. She could not think of any other way to get conversation starting.

Nigel looked at her and gave her a gentle smile. "It was a beautiful ride, but I'm afraid I was a bit," he paused and looked up to find the words he needed, "presumptuous."

April took in a deep breath and nodded her head. Oh, to get him to see how much she wanted that kiss. She did not want to come across as someone easy, or who was trying to get something from him, but she knew exactly what she wanted from the rest of her evening.

"I told you I wasn't going to make any demands, and here I am crossing that line." Nigel placed his hands in his pockets. "It's not fair to you."

April twisted up her lips in thought and nodded again. "It's not." When he snapped his head to her, she gave him a smile. "Well, it wouldn't be if I weren't receptive to it."

Nigel narrowed his eyes and gave her a smile. He took her hand and picked up his pace. When they reached his cabin, he opened the door and she walked inside. When he closed the door behind them, his arms were around her body, pulling her back against him. April sighed and eased her stance so that she could feel his hardness pressing against her.

"I want you so badly I can taste it," Nigel whispered into her ear. He nibbled the lobe gently.

April turned around in his arms and brought her hands up to his shoulders. He pulled her tighter against him and April rose up to kiss him again. His tongue moved between her lips and danced with hers. She could taste his desire in his breath and wanted to drown in it. She brought her hands around to the collar of his shirt and slowly worked her way down his buttons.

When he broke the kiss, Nigel lifted April's shirt above her head, discarding it to the side and shedding his own. He moved his hands down to her waist and unbuttoned her shorts, pushing them down her body. He started to kneel, and a panic filled April.

"I'm sweaty from the ride," April said. She wanted what his kneeling offered, but she wanted it to be perfect.

Nigel stood. "Then let's have that shower."

He pushed down her shorts and underwear in one motion. April slipped out of her shoes and her clothing, releasing the catch of her bra behind her back and dropping that as well. She was naked before Nigel, and as his eyes took in her body, she shuddered, nervous. Would he find her pleasing?

"You are beautiful." Nigel placed his hands at her waist and pulled her to him again. He kissed her deeply and then released her, gesturing her to walk up the stairs. He guided her back to his bedroom with its oversized king bed dominating the room, and then to the bathroom beyond.

A large garden tub stood at one end of the bathroom. Next to it was a double size shower with stone tiling. April stepped up to it, and twisted the knobs on either side to start the water. Nigel stepped up behind her and she could feel him, naked now, pressing against her. She stepped into the shower and he followed.

Nigel took a large sponge and poured soap on it, lathering it in the stream of water that sprinkled over them. He brought it to April's body and caressed, leaving the soapy lather behind to be quickly washed away by the water. He moved along her chest, her arms, and her torso before moving down between and down her legs. When he finished, his lips were there, at her sex taking it in. April gasped and pressed her hands to the wall to support herself. His mouth was magic there, drawing her desire out of her and building it into a wave to crash over her body. She shivered as her body counted every bead of water that struck her.

When he stood, April took the sponge from him, lathering it again, and running it across his shoulders, down his torso, and up his back. She brought it down to clean his manhood carefully and knelt, kissing what was now clean and hard softly before washing his legs, stroking down and then up along them gently. When she was through, she wanted to take him into her mouth, but he took hold of her arms and pulled her up. He kissed her and brought her leg up, pressing himself between her thighs.

She welcomed the feel of him hard and firm as he penetrated her. April wanted to feel him deeper, and when he brought her other leg up, she wrapped them around his body. He held her thighs and trust deeper into her and she felt alive and desirous. She kissed him passionately as he pressed her against the wall, seeking the depth of her, joining with her in their shared passion. When he pulsed into her, April took hold of his hair, gripping it between her fingers, reveling as he pushed still deeper into her.

When he was spent, he lowered her legs gently. April found them wobbly and weak, and stood under the warmth of the water, letting it pour energy back into them. Nigel kissed her again and pulled away, smiling as he dipped his head under the stream of water to wash his hair.

"I like showers," April said. She brought her own head under the showerhead and hoped that the water would mask her embarrassment over saying something so silly.

Nigel looked at her. "They can be very nice, when the company is."

A playfulness moved through April and she tilted her head to one side as she reached for shampoo. "I tried to be very nice and you stopped me."

Nigel laughed. "I didn't think that good girls were supposed to do that."

April's mind turned and spun at his teasing. "I'm in a shower with a man I just met yesterday. How good of a girl can I be?"

April's breath caught at the look in Nigel's eyes. It was both dark and desirous, and empathetic and sincere. She had no way to respond to it, and no word for the feeling it drew up inside her. She wanted to throw her arms around him and run away screaming at the same time. Overcome by her fear and desire, she could only stand there, her hands at her head, ready to massage shampoo into her scalp.

"You can be as good as you want to be," Nigel said.

He brought shampoo up to his own head and closed his eyes as he worked it through his hair. April swallowed hard and washed her own as well. When he opened his eyes again, the depth of emotion had passed. April suppressed a shiver and wondered once again at this man. He was a playboy. This week and this affair was one of many he had, one of many that he would have.

Some small part of her mind tried to challenge that, and April quashed it quickly as she rinsed her hair and turned off her side of the shower.

This was just an affair, just like any other Nigel Conroy had. He was taking a young woman he saw in distress and helping her through it the only way he knew how to. She bore him no ill will for that. In fact, April thought the world could use a few more Nigels.

****

The dining hall was lit brightly tonight, and a string quartet played Vivaldi as guests entered. Nigel led April to a table for two and they sat down, waiting patiently for a server to come by. Evening meals were meant to be more intimate, but the menu was still a general fare for all guests, a choice of steak, chicken, or fish, with either rice or potatoes and summer vegetables. April decided that she would have the fish and rice while Nigel ordered a steak and requested a bottle of wine to be brought out to them.

April spotted Leah among the servers and gave her a small wave. She did not want to embarrass Nigel, and while she thought he would understand her wanting to say hello to her friend, she knew that the other guests would consider the gesture to be gauche at best. Leah gave her a small and excited wave, looking from April to Nigel and back. She mouthed, "wow" as she poured water for another table, and moved to another. April gave an innocent shrug and smiled.

Nigel looked over his shoulder and back to April, smiling. "I think you've inspired new dreams in the female staff."

April laughed. "If only it were that easy for romance." She paused and thought about her last two days. "I'm not even sure how this happened."

Nigel reached under the table and brushed April's knee lightly. She could see he wanted to say something, but before he could, a man walked up to the table. Nigel withdrew his hand casually and looked up at the newcomer.

It took April a moment to register who the man was, and panic filled her. This was Chloe's father, and she could imagine the story told to him, and the reprimand her friend received. April had never met Michael Stuart, when she was hired on, she only worked with Mr. Graven, but she understood him to be a shrewd and clever businessman.

"Mr. Conroy, it is always a pleasure to have you here at the Estate." Mr. Stuart turned his attention to April and gave her a broad smile. "Ms. Edwards, it is good to see that you're enjoying your stay with Mr. Conroy. My daughter sends her regards."

April relaxed at the tone in Mr. Stuart's voice. Whatever story had gotten to his ears, it was either not believed, or countered, perhaps by Chloe herself. April made a note to herself. If she could not find her friend this summer, she would do so during the school year – assuming she was able to get back down to New York City to attend the university. "Thank you. Please tell Chloe I said hello."

Mr. Stuart nodded his head. "I will. She's enjoying a nice trip in Europe right now. She's spending the summer studying there as part of a fellowship. I will be sure to let her know when I talk to her. The both of you enjoy your evening."

He walked away from the table and over to another. April looked to Nigel to see him smiling wisely.

"What?" she asked.

"You looked like a deer caught in headlights for a moment there," Nigel said.

"The whole reason that I had a job here is because Chloe convinced her father to hire me. I was afraid that the worst of what happened reached him."

Nigel shook his head. The server brought their wine and poured a glass for each of them. When she left, leaving the bottle on the table between them, Nigel spoke. "I doubt anyone would have dared saying anything to him. The whole situation would have had him asking too many questions and probably getting other people not you fired. He probably wouldn't do anything to Worthington, though he should, but there are limits to what even Mr. Stuart can do."

April sipped her wine. She had not thought about just how precarious of a position that Mr. Graven really was in with how he had fired her and why. It occurred to her that she could file a complaint, but she realized she did not want to. Mr. Graven seemed to really care about his staff. His attitude toward her did not mask that. She doubted the scene would have played out quite the same way if it had been anyone else. The situation may have been hushed. The girl may even have been reassigned to other duties while Mr. Worthington was here. She thought that other things aggravated the situation, and while it was not right for Mr. Graven to hold her accountable for her father's actions; it was not worth him losing his job over.

"You're a good person," Nigel said.

April blushed, wondering if he read her mind, or if he just understood the situation itself. "Thank you."

"I mean it, you are." Nigel sipped his wine. "Anyway, I'm glad that you accepted my invitation."

"I am too."

They enjoyed their dinner together, using time to chat and get to know each other a little better. That tiny voice April's head tried to ask her if that was the kind of conversation that playboys engaged in, and she refused to answer. Her life was complicated, very complicated. She did not need to complicate someone else's as well.

After dinner, they wandered the estate house, seeing what festivities were taking place tonight. A company was holding an important shareholder meeting in one of the conference rooms. Both of them thought that was too boring to enjoy. Staff cleared the dining hall and the string quartet continued playing music. Guests who were not taking part in the shareholder meeting or any of the other smaller events filled up the dining hall, dancing to baroque music and enjoying the evening on the veranda.

April and Nigel joined in this. Nigel showed April a few simple steps for ballroom dancing, and they moved together to the music. With his arm around her waist, leading her in steps, April felt her desire swell up through her body again. She wanted to kiss him and knew that would not be proper here. They spotted the couple from the trail and exchanged smiles. As they danced past, April caught a snippet of their conversation and realized they were enjoying their anniversary here together.

"This is a magical place," April said as Nigel guided her off the dancefloor and over to a table where drinks were set out for guests.

"Oh?" Nigel handed her a glass of punch and looked at her curiously.

"The couple on the trail today, they're enjoying their anniversary here."

Nigel glanced out to the floor. "Is that so?"

"Apparently. I wonder how many other people are here for special occasions."

Nigel paused as he brought his glass to his lips and considered the people out on the dance floor. "I've never thought about it. I always just come up here and enjoy the mountains and the lake. I don't really think about what is going on with the rest of the guests unless I know them personally."

"I wonder about people sometimes," April said. "When I was a child, I would watch people on the street and wonder where they were going to and coming from. When we would be in a restaurant, I would imagine what conversations people were having at other tables. I always found my life to be easy and boring, so it was a fun way to make things interesting."

"Oh for things to be easy and boring."

April looked and saw Nigel's eyes turn dark with thought again. She supposed that for him, a boring life would have been ideal. She could not imagine what it would have been like for him. Did he have grandparents battle for custody of him, or did servants and lawyers raise him. He did not talk about that in the Playboy interview. April found herself curious again, and wondered if she would have the chance to explore that deep into him.

They danced for a few more songs before walking out onto the veranda and back up to Nigel's cabin. They held hands as they walked, taking in the view of the stars above them. April concentrated on trying to remember the names of any of the stars and constellations she saw and was ashamed that she could not. She should know them. She had learned about them in high school.

She never applied herself, and that knowledge drove home her precarious situation. She always assumed that he father's money would be there to take care of her. She would just move from that security to the security of a man. Now, that option was not open to her. She was not marriageable material. She was fine for a fling, but she did not want to live her life being the naughty fling of rich men.

She was going to have to decide on a direction for herself. She realized that depending on her mother was not the answer either. She was an adult. It was time that she acted it, and took on the responsibilities that brought.

Nigel let her into the cabin and followed her inside. He walked to the fireplace and turned on the gas starter. The logs, April realized, were only for show, to create a simulated fireplace. It was still beautiful, however, and she found herself pushing aside her thoughts and worries for another day.

She walked over to the couch and sat down. Nigel joined her and when he leaned close to her, April welcomed his kiss and his arms around her waist. She thought of making love to him in front of the fireplace and her excitement grew.

He broke the kiss and brought his hand up to April's cheek. She looked into Nigel's eyes and wondered at what thoughts were behind them. His eyes still looked contemplative and serious.

"I want you to stay with me," Nigel said.

April smiled. "I can sleep in your room if you'd like." She knew that was not what he meant, even as she said the words. She did not want to have the conversation that was coming. She realized that she had been running from it since their shower today and she thought she understood why now.

"That will be nice, but that's not what I mean," Nigel said.

April put her finger on his lips. He took her hand and kissed the back of it, bringing it back down to her lap.

"It is not fair," he said. "You're going through something you should not have to go through. Nothing that happened is your fault, but you're suffering for it."

"Lots of people suffer for things that aren't there fault." April suspected that Nigel suffered a lot. What was it actually like, growing up the son of a woman who killed herself and her husband? How many years did he spend wondering if that would happen to him? How many people treated him as if it would?

Nigel let out a sigh. "They do. I would help every single one of them if I could. We can't. We can only help those we can." He paused and sat back. "Do you know about what happened when I was a child?"

April nodded her head. "I read an interview where you talked some about it."

"The woman who took me out of the fire, she was my nanny. She was a kind woman. She was stern, and I grew up thinking she was mean sometimes. She took care of me. She did not have to stay with me. She could have let my family's lawyers find someone else. She was burned very badly in the fire. I lied when I told the interviewer I didn't remember the night very well. I did, but I didn't want to talk about it. She refused to let the paramedics treat her or take her to the hospital until she knew I was okay. She ended up being scarred very badly because of that, but it was the kind of woman she was. She stayed because I was the person she could help."

April took in a deep breath and squeezed Nigel's hand tightly.

"I want to help you. You were not working here because you wanted to. You were here because you had to be. No one should have to work like that. I don't want you to have to work like that."

April felt her heart filling and breaking at the same time. She cared about Nigel, more deeply and more quickly than she thought she would ever care about anyone. She could see herself easily falling in love with him, if she were not there already. She appreciated what he wanted to do, and she thought she understood what it meant to him.

That did not mean she could just accept it.

"Did you know I couldn't name a single constellation in the sky tonight?" April asked.

Nigel gave a small laugh. "I think I know the Big Dipper and Little Dipper. Not everyone knows the constellations."

"No, but people can point to the things they do know," April said. "I can't. My whole life I have depending on other people. I depended on my father to put me through school. I knew I just had to wait to get married and have another man to depend on for my livelihood. If it didn't work out, I would be able to get a nice alimony settlement and probably more money from Daddy again.

"I can't do that anymore. It doesn't matter that it's not fair. It matters that it life now. If I go back to school, I can get a real degree. I can figure out what I want to do with my life and do it, and not have to depend on anyone else."

Nigel brought his hand up to her cheek again. "It's a hard place, I know. The most important person in your life let you down, and depending on another person after that is scary. What happens if I let you down?"

April felt her heart break. She did not want to look at Nigel that way, but he was right. That was exactly what she was scared of. It was more than that, though. She could not expect him to pick up where others left off in taking care of her. It was not just a matter of what he might do anymore. It was what she had to do.

"You're such a wonderful person," April said. She leaned against the back cushion of the couch and let herself gaze into Nigel's eyes. "From most of the stories I've read about you, you're this carefree playboy who does philanthropy and just enjoys his money. You really are so much more than that. It's not that I think you would hurt me. I'm scared of it, but I know better. It's also what I have to do for me."

Nigel leaned his head against the back cushion and looked at her, silent in whatever contemplation he was in.

"I have no idea how I'm going to do this. A lot of people work their way through college. Some of them take student loans. I can do that too if I have to. If I talk to the financial counselors, they'll help me find a job and work out a schedule that I can pay for. I can always change schools if I need to. People do it every day. I'm no one special; I just thought I was for a long time."

Nigel let out a deep breath. She could see understanding and acceptance in his eyes.

"I could see you with a career. I think if you find something that you're passionate about, you could really put yourself into it and do something amazing," he said. "I would like to see that."

April smiled. "Thank you."

"Can I pay for school?" Nigel sat up again.

April was stunned and unsure how to answer his question. He had turned this around somehow and she felt as though she had been flipped on her head. "Pay for school?"

Nigel nodded. "I see the people who work their way through college. Sometimes they can pursue what they want. Sometimes they have to compromise. I want you to find and pursue whatever you want. I can pay for your school. You can stay on campus or with me, which ever you want. I won't pressure you there, though I would like to keep seeing you after this week."

April's mind was still trying to catch up to this strange change in their conversation. She tried to find words, and could not get anything to make sense from her mind to her mouth.

"You can say yes," Nigel said. "I would really like that."

April let out a laugh and sat up. She shook her head and looked down, trying to let her mind finish playing catch up. Nigel was serious about helping her. She did not think it was just some passing fancy of his. His understanding and his persistence told her how intent he was on this. She looked up and smiled at him. "Okay. But I get to pay you back for my school, even if I'm just donating it to your foundation. I appreciate it, but I want to be able to give something back to you."

Nigel returned her smile and broadened it. "I can accept that. You will have to apply yourself, though. I fully expect you to find a career that you can follow through on."

April moved closer to him on the couch. "I promise. I'll think about it this summer and decide." She paused before kissing him and pulled back. "What do I do during the summers?"

Nigel put his arms around her waist and pulled her down to him. "I'm sure we can negotiate something."

He kissed her. April welcomed his tongue through her lips. She thought again of making love to him in front of the fireplace and moved her hands up to unbutton his shirt.

It was a good place to start.

*****

Bonus Books

The Billionaire's Caregiver

People often think a new beginning is something that happens when there is a tragedy. Shelby Watson, on the other hand, disagrees entirely. Sometimes, a new beginning can simply happen to someone, and not be some epiphany out of the ashes of what was once a mess.

Simply put, life happens, but starting over is never easy. Shelby sighed and stretched out her legs on the sofa. Tomorrow, she would start again. Never one to be defeated, she knew she could pull herself out of this "new mess" she was in.

There was something about the way her big toe poked through the worn socks that made her rethink that idea entirely.

"You and me, Dobbs...she scooped up her puppy who had buried its head under the thick blanket. "All we really need is each other." Dobbs was a Chihuahua mix. Shelby found him by the door of her apartment one day, and when she opened her apartment door, he ran right in, in front of her.

He had been there since. It may have been the forlorn look he had about him that Shelby found endearing, or just the fact that he was standing there soaked to the bone. Whatever it was, Shelby knew she couldn't leave him out there, so let him stay.

The sound of banging caused Shelby to wince slightly. The pipes in this old building were always making some awful noise whenever someone was taking a shower. Shelby looked around at her efficiency apartment.

Clean and tidy it, was her home. She lived in the 3rd block of town. The lower the number indicated the worse sections of town. This was no exception. Her neighbors all consisted of drug dealers and prostitutes, though none unfriendly. Shelby would work early mornings and try to be home before dark. As long as she kept to herself nothing bad would happen to her...well less likely to, anyway.

All of the details of her life had changed now. The part-time morning job she had been able to find, she had lost. Nothing of her doing, simply a cut in positions at the senior home she was working at. They had pulled her aside that morning and given her the bad news.

"Shelby, your work here has always been wonderful. I hope you realize this is not a reflection on the quality of your work. It's simply based on the financial needs of the company." Dr. Brenner sighed and looked over at her as he delivered the news.

"Many of the seniors are moving into better equipped facilities and they...well they already have staff there. He ran his thin bony fingers through is even thinner hair.

It was obvious to Shelby this wasn't something he enjoyed doing and decided to help take the pressure off.

"I understand Dr. Brenner. I really do. I just don't know how I'm going to make it now." Life had always been a series of ups and downs for Shelby, and this was just one more set back. She stood to stand and extended her hand to Dr. Brenner.

"Thank you for helping me get things going here Dr. Brenner. The last three years have been wonderful. I hope you will let me use you for a reference." He stood and methodically pumped her hand, covering the hands with his other one.

"I really am sorry, Shelby."

There was a sense of helplessness that Shelby felt when she headed home. Now, she and her pup gracefully sat on the old worn sofa she had gotten from the thrift store down the street. Shelby decided it was time to start sorting the factors of her life out. She jumped up and grabbed her notebook from the counter.

Determined, she created her spreadsheet, lists of bills, things to do, what not to do, etc. Balancing her checkbook, Shelby calculated that she was ok for the next three weeks, but when the rent was due, she would be in trouble. She walked into her kitchen and pulled some canned spaghetti from the cupboard, methodically putting them in a bowl and then the microwave.

This is not where she envisioned herself a few years ago. She had big plans to go back to college to get her graduate degree in nursing. She was barely scraping by, but she knew that her resilience was powerful and that she would make it through. The one thing she was sure of was that she would not cry about it but would just keep moving on.

The next day things seemed bleak. Shelby walked to the corner store and bought a newspaper and began sifting through the want ads looking for a job. She wasn't above doing anything and would do whatever necessary to keep things going. Sitting on her foot, she took notice of anything related to her field first.

Under the dark header she saw an ad for a home health nurse. Perfect. She picked up the phone and called, but was greeted by a nasty voice.

"Kayla I told you I can't do this with you right now. You will just have to trust me. It's better this way." Shelby winced at the explosion.

"I'm sorry Sir. I think I may have the wrong number, I was calling about an ad." As she began to cradle the phone back into the receiver, she heard him yell.

"Wait yes, Oh God I'm an idiot. Miss...Miss?" He was obviously flustered.

"I'm here."

"Good. I'm terribly sorry. Your number was just like someone else's, and well... Ok, so yes, can you come out today? I need to wrap this up before I leave this weekend, and I have only gotten a few responses."

Encouraged, Shelby shot up out of her chair. "Yes, of course I can, what time?"

"Um, let me think." She heard shuffling on the other end. "How about now?"

"Now?" Shelby looked around mentally, figuring out what to wear." Sure now is good. I just need an address."

After getting all the necessary information, Shelby changed into a light grey dress and black boots. Shelby pulled her hair back and gathered up all of her references. As she started to walk out, she grabbed her purse and said a silent prayer.

"Wish me luck Dobbs, this is for dinner tonight."

Maneuvering her car down the highway was easy. Shelby loved road trips and had been into the town of Fauquier many times. Often considered the "rich" area, she never had much opportunity or reason to come this far out before.

Today was different. She had an interview, and hoped it would fix this mess she was in. Pulling down the long winding road into the countryside, Shelby admired the houses as she passed them. Most of them were old, and laced with gingerbread latticework. They looked warm and cozy. At the end of one street in particular, Shelby found the house she was looking for.

All she could do was stop the car and look up in awe. There is no way, she thought to herself. The magnificent mansion was on top of a ridge high above the roadway. There was a winding back entrance that was gated, and the front lawn was landscaped perfectly. Shelby glanced over at her car with it's rusted out fenders, and wondered if she really knew what she was doing.

With a sigh, she pushed her glasses back up and drove up the driveway. She pulled off to one side, straightening her dress as she stood and shut the door. She mentally prepared herself for whatever was on the other side of the door, took a deep breath, and knocked.

Billionaire, Michael had never been more frustrated in his life. He was handling the merger of two companies, trying to line up a meeting with his partner, and simultaneously trying to find someone who could come sit with his grandmother. At 40, Michael was all business with dark hair and eyes and didn't have time for anything frivolous. His grandmother was his only soft spot. She had raised him, and her encouragement is what created the man he was now.

Suddenly ill, the doctors believed she had a stroke, and now she was in bed and unwilling to do anything. He glanced over at the clock. Where was this girl anyway? She seemed interested, but was probably another "no show." He started gathering up some paperwork just as there was a knock at the door.

Shelby waited patiently. When the door finally did open, she found herself stunned for a moment as she looked at the most handsome man she had ever met. Tall and dark, he was almost like a sculpture. Trying not to stare, she attempted to recover quickly.

"Hello, I'm Shelby. We spoke on the phone." She held out her hand to him.

Michael took her hand, shaking it lightly. He was not without his own reaction to her. Small and petite, she had hair piled on top of her head. It was dark brown and a wonderful accent to her almond-colored eyes. She wore little makeup, and was a natural beauty.

"I'm glad you're here, though I thought you would have been here sooner." Shelby frowned at the gruffness in his voice. He wasn't as pleasant as she had hoped.

"I'm sorry, I was coming from Manassas." She tried not to take offense, as he was obviously very busy.

"I see. I am looking for someone to care for my grandmother. Full-time and an occasional Saturday. I try to be here on weekends as often as I can, and she has another nurse as well. I need someone who can try to get her to do more, or at least want to. She had a stroke a month ago and the doctors think she should be fine to get out again, but she is simply laying there." He paused to look her over.

"You're very small. Are you sure this is something you'd be interested in?"

Shelby felt the anger rise. "Mr. Jameson, I can assure you that I am very capable, despite your opinion of my small stature. Would it be possible for me to meet your grandmother? I think it's always important to see how well I click with someone."

"Sure that's fine. She knows you're coming. We can head upstairs in just a few moments. I'd like to ask a few more questions first, if that's ok?"

"Certainly." Shelby relaxed slightly. The fact that this guy was an ass made the fact that he was gorgeous much easier to look past.

"Ok so I see you are working with Everest Healthcare. Do you plan to continue to do that as well?"

"If so, this may be a bad idea. I really need 100% attention for this. My grandmother is very important to me, and multitasking is something most people think they are good at, but sadly..." he looked her over once again, "are not."

Fuming, Shelby responded in clipped tones. "No, I am no longer there. I was let go recently." Before she could elaborate, Michael interjected quickly.

"Why? Was there some sort of horseplay or something? I won't tolerate any of that at all, Miss Watson. I simply won't. You do seem rather young, and I can understand if this is something that you don't feel you can handle."

He stood up as if he was dismissing her entirely.

Panic set in but even that wasn't enough to calm her anger. "Mr. Jameson, I have been working at this for a long time. I am not young, as you so nicely put it, and as a matter of fact, I'm 33. I love this type of work, and the reason I was let go was for budget cuts, not horseplay. Perhaps if you allowed people to answer your questions without simply writing them off, you would have more candidates for this position."

Shelby stood to leave.

Fire and ice. That was all he could think of. She was absolutely adorable when she was mad. He could see how her nose slightly turned red as she had been giving him a piece of her mind and although not used to being talked to like that, he gained a new kind of respect for her.

"Point taken, Miss Watson. Shall we go meet my grandmother?" He held the door to the hallway for her and allowed her to pass as he made his way up the stairs motioning for her to follow. Shelby was surprised she had even gotten this far. He was a real piece of work, this guy. Money did that to people, she thought, and could only assume that was it. Along the hallway there was artwork. Some bright, some dull, and some muted. It was a lot to take in. As they rounded the top of the stairs, Shelby looked down and couldn't help but think that her meager apartment would fit in the foyer below.

Nancy Jameson was in good spirits. She wanted to do more, but her body just wouldn't allow her to. Besides, when she is here like this, Michael comes around more. He was her only grandson and always had been her favorite.

She had three granddaughters, but they all had their own families, and were too busy to ever visit. Michael had always been special. He had dark coloring like his grandfather and was just as stubborn. She smiled warmly as Michael entered the room with a petite brunette in tow.

Nancy didn't miss the sparks that flew from the young lady's eyes as Michael made some comment on how he could show her how to use the elevator if need be.

"Grandmother this is ...I'm sorry what your name was again?" He did look guilty so Shelby took pity on him and extended her hand to Nancy.

"Hello my name is Shelby, how are you?"

"Well I'm in this bed deary so not very good, I suppose." She winked at Shelby and smiled wide.

"My grandson feels like he needs to find someone to watch over me and make me do things I am not ready to do. I suppose that's why you're here my dear. Come over here and let me get a look at you."

Having taken an immediate liking to Grandmother Nancy, Shelby complied and walked over towards the bed. Nancy noticed how her grandson followed Shelby's every move. This was interesting indeed and was exactly the distraction she needed!

After a while of discussion and rules, Shelby stood to leave. "It was very nice to meet you Miss Jameson."

"Now Dear, if you're going to be here with me all the time, I insist you call me Nancy or Grandmother, whatever suits you."

"Grandmother, no one has offered Miss Watson a job yet. I hardly think she needs to start calling you Grandmother." Michael chuckled.

"Michael Dear, it is my money is it not?" Grandmother smiled up at him lovingly and patted his hand on the bed. "So, I say she is hired."

"Shelby that is if you will take the job of course."

Never a person to have nothing to say, it took everything Shelby had not to laugh at the interplay. It would seem that Grandmother Nancy was the only one to bring Michael down a peg or two. If for that reason alone, Shelby would take the job.

"I would love to Nancy." Shelby smiled up at Nancy and then at Michael.

There was some mix of being irritated by his grandmother's words and being floored by the smile that Shelby gave him. He didn't know what to say. After clearing his throat, he kissed his grandmother on the head and turned to leave.

"Miss Watson, if you will kindly follow me back down stairs, we can go over pay and hours, and so on."

Shelby said her goodbyes again and followed Michael down the stairs. He even smelled good, like leather and soap. What was most adorable was the way his hair curled in the back of his neck just slightly. What in the world was wrong with her?

Never suckered in by the connection between men and women, she usually had a fairly good grasp on self-control. Sure she had met a few nice guys and done her share of dating, but that was a long time ago and there had been no one in at least three years. Maybe that was it, she needed to get out more.

Offering her a chair, Michael detailed the terms and pay of the job. More money than she could imagine, Shelby sat stunned while he rambled on.

"Miss Watson is that acceptable?" She glanced up at him sharply. Oh no, what had she missed.

"Yes of course, that's more than fair."

"When can you start?" He watched her closely. He could almost watch the play of emotions she was thinking and feeling.

"Anytime is fine. I don't live far, even if I was late today. So I am free anytime."

"I'm not sure if you realize that this job is more than just being here from one time to another. Obviously, you will have to move in here, as that is part of the deal." He moved to gather up his things and glanced at his watch. He was already late and was starting to get irritated, as this matter should have been handled over an hour ago.

"Oh no, I can't do that Mr. Jameson, I have my own place. I'll stay there." He was surprised. He had seen the worn shoes she was wearing, and heard the racket her poor car made as it climbed the hill to the house. He just assumed that she would be more than happy to move in.

"Suit yourself, but I may need you sleep over on occasion. Is that fair?" He caught her eye again and reached out to shake her hand.

He was all business and it suited him. She reached out and felt the warmth as he took her hand in his. She felt like he lingered perhaps just a second longer than normal; but it was probably just her imagination. There was something powerful about the way he carried himself. Like right now, just staring at her. Closing her eyes for a moment, she managed to get out "Of course."

After saying their goodbyes, Shelby made her way to the car and headed home. What was it about Michael Jameson that made her crazy? He was arrogant, stubborn and bossy. He was also handsome, loving to his grandmother, and made her feel safe. All of that from one visit. Thankfully, he didn't live in the house year round, or she would be in trouble for sure.

The next few months were a flurry of activity. Shelby commuted every day to her job with Nancy which she loved, and had enough money to pay up her rent for a while. Michael and she spoke on the phone almost every day discussing Grandmother's day and how things were going. He typically had a joke to tell, but on some days, he was distant and moody.

Either way, they had come a long way and she considered him a friend. Gone was the canned spaghetti, and Shelby was actually able to cook food for herself. Even Dobbs was happier. She had just settled down to watch TV for a bit before turning in when the phone rang. It was a frantic Michael.

"Watson, my grandmother seems to have had a heart situation of some kind. I am in town and headed to the hospital and she has asked to see you." He was obviously in pain as he choked it out. Despite their differences, Michael had been nothing but nice with her and she didn't want to see him hurt. Worry was a motivator for Shelby and she immediately started to change clothes as he talked.

"..wanted to know if she had been acting differently lately or anything?"

"NO no she's been fine, and we have actually been walking a few times and..."

He cut her off immediately. "You had her walking? What in the world, Watson were you thinking? She wasn't ready for that. Just come to the hospital as soon as you can." He hung up leaving Shelby stunned.

She was frustrated herself wondering if he was right. She gathered up her purse and headed downstairs. Trying to avoid the people in the halls, she made it to her car safely and let out a deep sigh. Unfortunately, it was not meant to be. As she turned the key nothing happened. Slowly, she laid her head on the steering wheel. What now? She jumped out to look under the hood. Apparently, sometime during the night, someone had stolen her battery... now she was stuck. Knowing she could never forgive herself if she didn't see Nancy, Shelby made her way back to her apartment and called him.

"Yes What!" He yelled into the phone.

"Michael, please don't yell at me."

"Oh it's you. I'm sorry, Watson. The number thing again. Yes what's up?"

After much explaining, it was settled that Michael would come by and pick Shelby up on his way. She wasn't too far from the hospital herself but at night it was better to ride with someone. A few minutes later Shelby heard the knock on her door and opened it to a disheveled Michael. He was a mess, worry etched on his face, but handsome as ever.

Michael took in the apartment, if that's what you call it. Small but tidy, he imagined she could do just about everything. His issue was with her neighbors.

"This..is where you live, Shelby?" He gestured to the occupants sitting in the halls and the loud music.

"Yes why?" Shelby had her pride. This was her place and it wouldn't sit well if he was insulting.

"I'm terrified for my safety out there. I can't imagine how you've made it all this time. You're so small and there are at least 20 people just hanging outside."

"I am not so small and I am just fine. Let's go." She crammed her gloves into her purse and yanked open the door leaving it open so he could follow.

In the car Michael looked over at her. She had her signature bun in place and there was a pained look on her face. Obviously, he had hurt her feelings.

"Look Watson, I'm sorry. I didn't mean anything by it. I just worry. I mean grandmother worries about you is all." She had noticed the slip he made and smiled inwardly. He cared.

They arrived at the hospital and Nancy looked tired, but was noticeably happy to see her two favorite people. These two sure move slowly and I'm not getting any younger, she thought. She smiled at them both. What a striking couple they make. This little heart "issue" was just what was needed to bring them together for a while.

"Oh my dears, I'm so happy to see you both. They say I'm ok but are keeping me for a few days for observation. Can you imagine two whole days? I'll be bored out of my mind." Truthfully, she was glad. She had been feeling uncomfortable today but she knew Michael was coming to town and wanted he and Shelby to spend some time together.

"I'm just glad you're ok." Shelby was concerned at how pale she was. "This is my fault. We shouldn't have been walking this week."

"Oh pish posh. It's probably just gas or something." Michael rolled his eyes at his grandmother.

It was at that time that the nurse came in.

"I'm sorry, but you'll both have to get going Mrs. Jameson need to rest..."

They said their goodbyes and headed out front. Michael was very quiet, brooding again over some business merger gone wrong or something. She glanced over at him and he was caught up in thought, so she let the ride continue on in silence.

They pulled into her apartment complex and Shelby began to open the door.

"Wait, Watson I'm going up with you. I need to make sure you get in there in one piece."

"You don't have to do that Michael, I'm fine." She started walking and he followed anyway.

As they reached the top stairs of the building, a man reached over and touched Shelby on her leg making her jump. Michael immediately jumped.

"Don't touch her!" he moved between Shelby and the man.

"Michael it's fine. He is harmless." Secretly, she was touched that he jumped to her rescue.

Opening the door, they went inside. Michael was again impressed by the simple charm of her place. He sat down on the sofa and was greeted by a flying ball of fur. "Oh my, what is this?" He scruffed the dog on the back of the head and it bounced off.

"You once told me you had a dog but I hardly think that little thing qualifies, Watson." He smiled up at her.

Shelby had moved to the other end of the couch. "He is something, that's for sure." She giggled as they watched him get into a fight with a dog toy.

"You should just move into the house with us, Shelby." Hearing these words, Shelby caught her breath. She even noticed he had used her first name.

"Why would I do that? I'm perfectly fine here." What she didn't say was that she couldn't handle watching him with the various women he dated. She cared too much about Grandmother Nancy to ruin her relationship by being too close to him."

At that moment there was an obvious gunshot. Michael jumped up, and in his demanding voice she had grown to love he simply stated, "Get some things, Watson you're going with me."

The ride to the house was uneventful. Shelby knew he was mad, but to be honest, she wasn't sure why. He parked his car in front of the house and they went inside together. "You can have the room down here. I'll sleep upstairs and you know your way around. I'm getting a drink, I certainly need it."

She could use one herself, she thought as she went into the spare room downstairs. Changing into pajamas, letting her hair down, and tucking Dobbs into the bed, Shelby decided to go into the den where Michael was and get that drink. If, for any other reason but to calm her nerves. Knowing they were here alone was setting her on edge.

He was sitting in the leather-bound chair by the fireplace. He already had a drink, or was it two? Nothing could prepare him for her entrance. It felt like someone had punched him in the stomach. She was in all pink and her hair was flowing down her back. This casual image of her was one he had played out in his mind during one of their conversations on the phone. He had thought about it ...and now here it was.

He watched her walk over to the bar, pour a drink for herself, and tip it back. Impressive he thought. He stood up and moved closer to her. He could see all the shades of auburn in her hair when he was up close like this, she smelled like honeysuckle.

"You're moving in here, Watson." He said it with a finality that only made her angry.

"You can't tell me what to do, Michael. I work for you, but you don't own me." She was flushed with anger as he turned towards her.

"You could be killed, Watson. That place is dangerous, men groping you in the halls and gunshot...real actual gunshot, Watson." He ran his hand though his hair.

"My grandmother would kill me if anything happened to you and I didn't try and stop it." She couldn't help but feel some disappointment at the words. She had hoped he would say something about how he cared.

"I'm not moving in Michael. Let it go." She put her glass down and turned to leave. He grabbed her left arm and spun her around. It could have been the alcohol or the stress of the day, but something made him lose himself in that moment.

He gripped her wrist tighter than he meant to and put his right hand into the waves of her hair, pulling her towards him. The kiss had meant to be angry. He needed her to listen to reason but what started out hard, became softer, deeper, and more meaningful. Slowly, he dropped her other wrist and cupped her face in his hands, nipping at her lips and taking in the smell of her skin. When the kiss broke, he looked up at her.

"Watson, you're driving me crazy." He dropped his hands back down and watched the emotions play out on her face. Rocked to her core, Shelby could only stand and wait. Wait for the fluttering to subside, wait for her heart to stop racing, and wait for him to stop looking at her so intently. Not knowing what to say, she turned and walked stiffly back into her room. He followed her.

"Talk to me Watson. Why are you running from me? I know you feel this craziness just like I do."

"Yes I do Michael and that's why I won't live here." She turned to look at him. "I am a mess inside and I need you to go and leave me be so I can think straight." She saw the pained look on his face but heard him leave the room.

Shelby laid in bed thinking about that kiss. His kiss only intensified the connection they had. It wasn't all her. That was comforting, but what wasn't, was that she couldn't stop the fluttering she felt deep down. The way he moved towards her and the way he kissed deeply and without thought.

Laying here was obviously not going to figure it all out. She decided to go get a drink of water. They came from such different worlds. He always had someone worldly on his arm, some debutante. She had even met a few of them when he was there and she had been working.

The one thing they all had in common was that they were beautiful. Always regal and gorgeous, she always found something to do to keep away from them. After they would leave, Grandmother Nancy always had some snide comment about each one that made Shelby giggle.

"He will never find the right one unless he shops from a different field," she would say. Smiling now, Shelby opened the refrigerator door and started sifting through things until she found exactly what she wanted. Cake, it was the best cake around and had been left over from a party Grandmother Nancy had earlier that week. She stood there eating quietly, not hearing him until he spoke.

"You have quite the "strictly business" thing going on here, Watson."

She slammed the door shut on impulse, having been caught red handed.

"Yeah I try." She smiled slightly. He walked over to her and with one finger, wiped the chocolate off her bottom lip.

Feeling the heat begin to creep up again, Shelby took a step back.

"We need to talk Watson, and now." He walked until she had backed up to the bar. He moved his face closer to hers.

"I think it's obvious that I want you. I don't know how else to put it." The bluntness of the statement made Shelby gasp.

"The only way I'm going to stop trying is if you tell me you don't feel the same way." She was pinned between him and the bar and he was watching her face.

"Michael let me go," she tried to squirm but it was no use. She was stuck.

"Just tell me you don't want me to touch you and I'll leave you alone Watson. Just say it."

Knowing full well she felt the same way he did she, Shelby did the only thing she thought was right. She looked up at him and ran her finger down the right side of his face.

"I can't tell you any of that, Michael because I want the same thing." Before she could finish the words, he crushed his mouth to hers. He put his hands in her hair tilting her head back more. She kissed him back more fervently, having let go now. He lifted her up off the floor and put her on the bar top. Running his hands along her legs, all the while teasing and nipping her bottom lip.

"We should stop Michael." It was more of a pant than a statement.

"You're right, Watson, we should, but I can't. Not anymore." Pulling her to him, he lifted and carried her into the bedroom and kicked the door shut behind him. Sitting her down, she stood motionless, watching him take his shirt off and move towards her. She was frozen to the spot she stood on, not knowing what to do next.

He walked to her and started slowly unbuttoning the front of her pajamas. Each button exposed new skin that he had to kiss. He loved the way she smelled of sunshine and honeysuckle. He looked up at her.

Needing no words, she walked backwards towards the bed, pulling him with her as they went. Sliding back onto the comforter, he followed, pressing the length of him against her body. He looked down and knew in that moment, he was lost. Her hair spilled across the pillow, her lips were parted slightly from being thoroughly kissed, and her eyes were shining up at him. He could tell she was scared and excited. He ran his finger along her bottom lip.

"I need to hear you say it, Shelby. I need us to be real in this moment and together."

He gazed at her. "I can stop if you want, but you need to tell me now before I can't anymore." His honestly made her want him even more. She slowly pulled her shirt off and tossed it to the floor.

"I want you Michael, I always have." Needing no further encouragement, Michael stood and took off the rest of his clothes looking down. He stood back for a moment, letting himself take in her naked form. She was perfect.

Once, he thought her tiny, but looking at her now, he could see every curve she was given. Almost scared to touch her, she made the move first.

"I'm getting a little self-conscious Michael. What's wrong with me?" She started to cover up again.

"No don't "...he grabbed her hand. "You're beautiful, Watson, absolutely beautiful." He laid down on the bed again, taking a moment to calm his racing heart. He was acting like a teenage school boy, wondering why in the world was so nervous.

This was different. He knew it and probably always had, but he needed her to feel loved, wanted, and cherished.

The night progressed, and the two made love into the early hours of dawn. Before falling asleep, the last thing she heard was him saying her name and draping one arm across her body. Sometime during the night, Shelby got cold, having been woken up by something, only to find herself naked as the day she was born. She tried to keep from moving, but right before she almost fell asleep, she felt Michael's arm grasp her stomach and pull her into him. He kissed her ear and they drifted back to sleep for a few more hours.

Never a late sleeper, Michael woke up to greet the day with a smile on his face. Shelby was amazing. She was not just beautiful, she was the type of woman men dream of. She gave as much as she received, and never held back. This was something Michael couldn't help but admire. He looked at her lying among the sheets as he headed upstairs to shower and get ready for the day. He just didn't have the heart to wake her up.

Shelby woke up to the smells of coffee and the clink of pans. She rolled over to snuggle in more and her eyes flew open as she remembered...everything. Oh wow she had never been so careless in her life. She scrambled to jump in the shower before he found her. Before she was soaped up she heard him come into the bathroom.

"Watson, I see you're joining me today finally." He chuckled.

"Michael really, I am in the shower, I'll be right out." She could only smile as she heard him hum a tune as he left.

What would she do now? It had happened and there was no going back, but she could stop it now. Now that they had gotten it out of their system, she could put Michael Jameson out of her mind altogether.

She entered the kitchen, dressed for the day and ready to go to the hospital. Michael was cheery and leaned towards her as if to get a kiss. She managed to avoid it discretely.

Frowning, Michael went back to cooking. Something was wrong. Breakfast passed with no mishaps and they set off for the hospital.

Grandmother was overjoyed to see them. They each took a side and listened to her tell them about how awful the night had been and the bed situation. She moved on to complain about the food and how happy she would be at home. She could tell something was amiss between the couple, but it would sort itself out.

Michael was having a hard time understanding what Shelby was thinking. The night had been something people only dream about and yet when he got close to her, she ran. Something wasn't right, but he would find out soon enough.

The doctors came in and discussed the grandmother's situation. They equated it to a chemical reaction to something she ate, at which grandmother smiled. They passed the morning laughing with her, planning the next event. At lunch, the doctors ordered them out, saying she needed her rest, so the couple decided to go to a nearby restaurant for something to eat.

It was a beautiful café, overlooking a pond and situated amongst lush landscaping. They dined on wine and oysters, which were new to Shelby. Michael was about to broach the subject plaguing him, when a woman came up to the table.

"Michael darling, where have you been?" The woman was like something from the cover of a magazine. She had on long flowing pants and a silk shirt complete with a huge brimmed hat.

"Baby, I have missed you so much. How nice of you to bring the maid to lunch." She smiled over at Shelby, who immediately excused herself and went outside.

Angry Michael pushed the woman back away from him. "I told you to leave me alone. Why are you here? Stop calling me and stop following me."

Without waiting for an answer, he stormed out onto the street and to his car. Shelby was standing by the passenger side and he opened the door, then went to his side and got in.

"I'm sorry, Watson that was ...the number..." at her confused look he added "remember when you would call and I thought it was her?"

"Aha, that is her." Shelby still felt awful about the exchange and self-conscious as well. The maid, really?

When they arrived at the house, Shelby went to her room. Thinking she would have some time to think, she was surprised when Michael stormed in behind her.

"What the hell Shelby, after last night I thought,"

"What...you thought we would just act like nothing happened? You think I would go away? Well I'm not. I love Grandmother Nancy and I'm not going anywhere."

"What are you talking about Shelby? I don't want you to go anywhere. I want you here. With me." He said it with such finality, Shelby could do no more than look up at him.

"What?"

"I love you Shelby. I have since the day we met and you came here. But when I was at your place and heard that gunshot it was all I could do to not kidnap you myself and tie you up here so I could keep you safe."

"But I'm not like you Michael. She called me "the maid" for goodness sake." She looked down for a moment.

"Shelby do you really think I care one moment about what people think?" I want you and I choose you."

Tears were flowing freely now as Shelby looked up at him.

"Well," He asked impatiently.

"Well what? " She was confused.

"Damn it Shelby, you're killing me. Do you or do you not feel anything for me?"

Laughing, she ran into his arms and kissed him. "Michael I have loved you from the moment you opened that door."

He let out an audible sigh. Happy and content, he pulled her close to him and kissed her deeply.

Hand in hand they headed back to the hospital. Grandmother had taken a nap and was refreshed as she looked out the windows to the parking lot. Seeing Michael, she smiled. He really was a good boy. But what made her happiest was seeing him hand in hand with Shelby.

Perhaps her plan to become a grandmother had worked after all, and if she played it just right, she could somehow start planning a Fall wedding at the house. She may be getting old, but this was enough to keep her busy for at least a good many years to come.

The Billionaire's Wish

Braden Davenport was on cloud nine. Even now, as he pulled off his helmet, he felt great. He was on a streak and this was going to be his best season yet. He brushed his hand through his jet black hair and smiled at the people around him. It was nice having fans. They were the only constant in his life, always there to cheer him on. The problem was, they didn't really know him.

That's not to say that it isn't great doing what you love for a living. He was able to buy his first house at the age of 23, and at 29, he owned three. He liked to have a nice place to stay whenever he was in his favorite places. Racing was a dangerous sport, but it was in his blood, a part of him. Being here in Austin for the MotoGP race had been a fluke, but a happy one. He was a last minute add in and he was happy he said yes.

He would always rather be racing than home alone or out with some nameless girl that didn't know him very well. For now, he was home in Texas, at least for the next two months. It was the place where this all began and he was happy to be there. He loved the dry air and the open grounds in the hill country, and the city life in Austin. His next race was in Vegas and he was happy for the break. The win today would put enough money in the bank that he could live off forever, but it was never enough. Having lived such a hard life growing up, he liked the better, secure, lifestyle he had now.

He basically lived his life in an orphanage. He never knew his father, who left his mother soon after he was born. His mother was heartbroken and soon became an addict. He still remembered what it was like finding her there when he was 7. She made the wrong person mad, and they gave her some bad stuff. He found her unresponsive, lying on the living room floor. They didn't have a phone, but fortunately he was able to run to a neighbor and they called the police for him. He still carried around the guilt because he couldn't save her. He eventually left the orphanage and made a few friends. He had a difficult time trusting people, getting close to anyone.

He got his first job at the thrift store in town. He learned the hard way that life was about making the right choices or you end up with nothing. Over time, he managed to secure a room, and that's when he met Gerald and Abbie Smith. Older, they were frequent shoppers where he worked, and they always amused him. At 80, Gerald was a big bear of a man. Abbie was a tiny little thing at 77. Abbie would tell Braden he looked too thin, and Gerald would pull him aside and talk cars with him, something he always loved. After a year or so, they invited him to dinner. At 19, he still seemed like a kid to Abbie. She was always fussing over him and making sure he actually ate when he came over.

Gerald was the person who taught Braden to race. He owned many bikes, he was a collector of sorts, and the moment Braden rode one, his life changed. He maneuvered them like a pro. After some help from Gerald's contacts, he quickly became successful and was able to secure himself a lucrative future in racing. When Braden was 21, Gerald passed away, and Abbie followed a year later. He moved in to help her after Gerald's passing, and held her hand when she died.

That was seven years ago now, and he could still remember it like it was yesterday. He shook his head, remembering, and smiled. He made sure his bike was always in tip top shape, and made frequent visits to his trusted mechanic and best friend, Mike's house. They met in his early years of racing, and had been friends ever since.

The most important thing that Gerald taught Braden was that the bike is your money and the only way you can ride it safely is if you have a hand in what goes on with it. The bike was his family, and he protected it as such. He finally set off for the hour drive to Marble Falls, where Mike lived.

Mike was always a party guy. One girl to the next and one disaster away from an addiction. What he did have was a nice house, and a serious garage behind it. It was the one thing he always took care of. His mother would come over once a month and clean up for him. As he pulled into the parking lot of the townhouses, Braden noticed the changes. The place next door was vacant the last time he was there, and he wondered if Mike even knew that someone had moved in.

He was taking the next few weeks to run off with his newest girlfriend and had given Braden the key so that he could drop some things off, and pick up some things for the bike. He noticed her the moment he pulled up. He watched amused as a woman was desperately trying to get her key to work in her door knob.

"Damn it."

She was angry and she was beautiful. She finally kicked the door and turned to go to her car. She stopped when she saw him watching her. She gave him a half smile before pushing her hair back and squaring her shoulder.

"I'm not usually so easily flustered. My key broke off in the door... now I am rambling sorry... so yeah, I should go." She turned to go again and he finally said something.

"I can probably get that out of there if you want me to try." He crossed his arms as she gave him a half smile.

"That would be... well... yes, please." She smiled at him again and he went to the truck.

Chloe closed her eyes and took a deep breath. She was standing here rambling like an idiot. It always happened when she met a guy, especially an attractive one. Attractive didn't even begin to describe this one. He was, by far, the most attractive guy she had seen in a long time. He had black hair and dark eyes and just enough stubble on his face to give him that mysterious look. She never even kissed a guy like that and she never would. It certainly didn't hurt to watch him though. He was all muscle, and it was obvious he worked out. She blushed as he came back towards her, hopefully he hadn't seen her looking him over like that.

He smiled as he worked on the door. She was looking him over and it made him smile. The fact that she blushed when he looked at her made him like her even more. He finally broke the broken key out and he turned to look at her again. It was her eyes that struck him first. Deep blue and full of life, they contrasted the abundance of red flowing hair. She was a big girl, he liked that about her. She had curves in all of the right placed and he wanted to touch every single one of them. He glanced at her hand and didn't see a ring, which was a good first step. He handed her the broken pieces of the key, and when his eyes met hers, he saw her blush again.

"It should be fine now, I had to put some lube in it." He gave her a half smile.

"What... oh thanks." She gathered the pieces up and headed towards the door. "Thanks again..."

"Braden... my name is Braden." He held his hand out to her and she shook it.

"I'm Chloe, nice to meet you."

"Perhaps I can get you to have dinner with me sometime, Chloe?" He watched the myriad of emotions cross her face.

"Sure, that sounds like fun." She turned to head back in again and he smiled.

"Chloe, can I get your number?"

"Oh, sorry." She wrote it down and turned to go again.

She was a flighty one, but that was part of the excitement for him. He watched her go inside and he left, heading for his place in the hills. She was timid, something he would remedy. Even now he thought about her curves and how they would feel under his fingers. He rarely ever lost at this and he didn't intend to start now.

Chloe shut the door with a thud. That was very sweet of him, offering to have dinner with him. It was typical of some guys, nicer ones anyway, to offer to take the big girl out. She didn't need to get paraded around and everyone's opinion of him go up because he did her a favor. Still, he seemed genuine. She made her way into the house and took a good long look at herself in the mirror. She had been working hard to lose weight, to be in better shape. She was down 20 pounds but she still hated the way she looked. Aside from her friends and her little brother, she was alone. In some ways it suited her. She'd had one serious relationship and that left her ready to just put the idea of love and romance behind her for good.

After, she made her way into her room to throw on pajamas and spent the rest of the afternoon cleaning until Charlie got out of school. At 12, he was more than a handful of energy. In a week, he would be gone with friends on vacation, and she would really be alone all summer. He had been living with her a year and a half now, but some days it seemed like only yesterday that he had moved in. She was 22 and ready to tackle the world when she got the call. Her parents and her little brother were in an accident.

Like most people, she didn't think anything could happen to her. She rushed to the hospital, but her parents were both gone, leaving Charlie, with her. It was a rough start, but they were good now. She'd be lying if she said she didn't get lonely sometimes though. He kept her busy, one activity to another. Motherhood at her age was not part of her plan, but she was lucky they had each other. That thought brought her back to Braden. She wondered if he had a family. He seemed like a nice guy.

She never had an opportunity to meet her neighbor. As far as she knew the little lady that came in and out on occasion was the only one who visited that house at all. She sighed, she had rambled on and on about nothing, he must have thought her a complete idiot. Finally, she sat down to calculate how to pull off everything this month.

She was a local teacher, well she was a substitute. She was still in school part-time but she was determined to finish. Most of the time she worked enough days to just barely pay the bills, but having a 12 year old with numerous after school activities put a dent in things. Not to mention the rent on this place was out outrageous. Since her parents were renting as well, their place was too much for her to take on.

They were always like the traveling circus, always moving and changing. Chloe didn't want that for her little brother. She lived that life and he needed stability. She would simply have to cut out some things, but first she would have to find what those things were.

Braden walked into his house, well Gerald's and Abbie's house. They left it for him in the will. No children of their own, they took him in and loved him as if he were theirs. He didn't live here, it didn't feel like he should, and to be honest, he didn't want to take over. He liked being able to walk in and see their things as they left it. It gave him a sense of peace. Deep down, he knew it wasn't healthy, he should sell it, but for now he couldn't let go.

He checked on things here and then headed to the place he lived in the hills. He called ahead the week before so that it could be opened up and aired out. He hadn't been here in months and knowing it would be ready was one of the many luxuries he enjoyed. He had a house manager and a housekeeper, both trustworthy friends, and he compensated them well for the work they did for him.

Once he was there, he made his way inside and he poured himself a drink, leisurely making his way to the large windows overlooking the city. He wanted her. The thought crossed his mind and he smiled. Chloe, there was something about her that struck a nerve, and he wanted to figure it out. He thought at first it had been her coy and shy personality, but he had played that game before and knew that wasn't it.

There was a depth to her, and he wanted to know more. Women were always around, throwing themselves at him and offering him their charms. It came with the business... and the money. It was rare he felt connected to someone who didn't know about either of those things. She felt the connection too, but she simply dismissed it, and he wanted to know why. He suddenly smiled as an idea came to mind. She had no clue who he was or the money he made. Even in her wildest dream, would she ever guess that he was a billionaire. He pulled out his phone and called Mike.

Braden pulled up to Mike's townhouse once more with a renewed spirit. Mike had given him the green light at least for the next few weeks. That would be plenty of time to figure Chloe out. He glanced over at her place before heading inside. Much like his penthouse, the place hadn't been lived in in months. Everything shined and gleamed. "Thank you Mrs. Anderson." He said under his breath.

She was a sweet woman, often quiet and reserved, but she could clean the hell out of this bachelor pad. He decided there was no time like the present to start pursuing his curvy neighbor. He made his way over to her door. It wasn't late, so he gave it a knock. She opened the door in a flurry, and as soon as she saw him, she looked shocked.

"Braden hello." She smiled at him and he felt the heat rising in him. Her hair was pulled up on top of her head and she was wearing a t-shirt and sweats. Casual and damn near the sexiest thing he had ever seen.

"Hello Chloe, thought I'd see if you were up for a chat? It's just that I've been out of town and it's hard to get resettled." He gave her a smile and gauged her reaction.

She was just a little intimidated. She assumed he would move on and let her be, but here he was, in his tight jeans and arms that looked ready to rip out of his shirt. She gulped slightly, what was wrong with her? She usually had more control over herself than this. She gave him a half smile.

"I wish I could. It's just that my little brother is here and is sleeping." There, that should put him off.

"Oh, I see. Maybe we could sit on the deck?" He shoved his hands in his pockets and she mechanically nodded a yes. He smiled at her again and she moved to let him in.

She must be completely out of her mind. What was she doing? She didn't even know him that well and she just let him walk right into her house. He could be a crazy person or something. She sighed.

"I'm not a killer or anything, if that's what you're worried about." They had made it to the sliding door and he leaned in behind her, whispering it in her ear.

She felt the heat of his breath on her ear and shivered. It had been a long time, very long, and she was just sensitive that's all. They moved out to the deck, and as she shut the door and turned towards him, he was directly in front of her.

"Are you married Chloe?" He leaned towards her as he said it, propping his arm against the sliding door beside her head.

"You're very forward aren't you?" "No, I'm not, said Braden, are you?" She ducked through his arm and made her way over to the wrought iron chairs on the deck. It was dark out there. Having forgotten the deck lights were blown, she silently cursed. She turned around again, and this time he walked over to the rail. She joined him there, waiting and suddenly he turned towards her.

"No, I'm not." He put an arm on either side of her and rested against the railing. As he did so he leaned into her breathing in the scent of jasmine.

She was lost in that moment, He was inches away from her and her only thought was that he must be really desperate to be here with her. More than anything else, she didn't want to look like a fool, it's happened before and she didn't want to go through that again. She dipped below his arm and faced the trees again. She could hear his chuckle, and she frowned.

"You are something else Chloe, you know I want to kiss you, but you keep running, why?"

She looked at him, surprised by his admission. "Why do you want to kiss me? I'm sure you have plenty of other women to kiss, besides, I don't even know you, Braden."

"What better way to get to know me, Chloe." He stood and gave her a smile.

There was something about the way he said it that left her wondering if he was serious or simply out of his mind. She shook her head and turned back around.

"Don't be ridiculous Braden."

She said it simply and he realized she meant it. He frowned as he thought about it. Maybe she wasn't attracted to him. There was only one way to find out. He slid over to the right and grasped her hand in his and pulled her towards him. He saw the look of surprise on her face as he put his hand against the back of her head, pulling her into his arms as his mouth crushed hers.

She was on fire and he did nothing but add fuel to it. She felt his mouth nip at her lips and then dive deeper. She opened her mouth to him, unconsciously meeting his kiss eagerly. As their tongues danced, she felt the fire inside begin to build and grow. It had been so long, and he was very good. She felt his hands then start to move. First, slowly he ran them down her back and over the curve of her hip, pulling her even closer to him. She felt his mouth slowly leave her lips and trail down her neck and he nipped her collarbone. He moved his hands up her hips and his mouth found her again. The kiss was passionate and full of promise. She felt his hand slip under her shirt and she panicked, pushing him away.

Braden stood frozen, what the hell was wrong with him. He planned on sweet talking... maybe steal a kiss, but this... He ran his hand through his hair and walked to the deck to calm himself. One thing was for sure. She wanted him just as badly as he wanted her, she couldn't deny that now. He looked over at her, she was stone-faced and looked almost sad. He frowned, that was not what he expected to happen, but why would it make her sad?

"Chloe, I'm sorry." I didn't mean to get so carried away."
She looked down and then back up at him, a smile now sitting on her face.

"I understand. Like you said, you haven't been home in months. I'm sure you're just tired." She moved to walk back to the door leading to the house. She whispered to herself "Plus it's dark out here, I'm sure that helps."

"Helps with what?" He was beside her, he was like a cat the way he moved.

"Nothing sorry, just rambling as always. I should get to bed, I have to be at work early." She smiled at him, but he knew something was wrong here.

"Sure, I understand." He turned to go and then spun back to look at her. "I like kissing you, Chloe. I won't lie about it, and in fact, I want much more than that. I wanted you to know I plan on trying to make sure you know that regularly." He walked down the front steps whistling. She stayed there until she heard his door shut. She leaned her back against the door to try and calm her racing heart.

The days went by quickly, they would often pass each other in the front yards or as they came home. Both of them caught up in work. He consistently asked her to come over for dinner, but she always had reason to say no. He never made any other move to kiss her or otherwise, and she relaxed more around him. They spent two different afternoons sitting out front talking about life, where each time she was sure they had an audience at all times. One afternoon she opened up more than she planned.

"So, Charlie?" Braden asked as Charlie was throwing a ball with a friend in the parking lot.

"My parents were killed in an accident, he was with them, but survived. That was almost two years ago now." She watched Charlie playing. "He is a good boy though."

"That has to be hard on you, suddenly having a 12 year old." Braden watched the expressions changing on her face.

"It took some adjusting, for all of us." She took a sip of water from her glass.

"Why aren't you married?" He asked it very matter of factly, but with a deeper tone to his voice. She turned to look at him.

"I almost was once, actually."

He sat up at her admission. So she had loved someone, being close to them. "You know you have to tell me now Chloe?"

"No, I don't Braden." She stood up, brushing off her skirt as she did and headed into her house. He stood and followed.

She noticed him standing in the doorway. "Really Braden, following me into my own home? Even for you that's a bit much." She started folding the towels on the table in the kitchen. He didn't say anything, but methodically started helping. She paused to look at him and he simply grinned at her. She rolled her eyes.

When they were done, he finally spoke. "Why don't you want to talk about it?"

She put her right hand on her hip. "Because it doesn't matter Braden, that's why." As she turned to go he grabbed her forearm and pulled her to him.

"It does matter Chloe, it certainly is part of why you are the way you are."

"What the hell does that mean "the way I am"?" She felt the sting then. She was different. Why did people always feel the need to point it out to her?

"Wait a minute Chloe what do you think I am talking about here?" He took another step closer, never letting go of her arm.

"Let me go Braden." Her eyes glittered dangerously.

"Not until you tell me."

"Fine." She yanked her arm free. "I was engaged, he seemed to accept me." She gave him a glance. "He was always sweet and kind and then when my parents died, he never made it to the funeral. He apologized, and I was stupid enough to believe him. When Charlie moved in, he tried to force me to send him away to a boarding school of some kind.

He said this was not the future he planned and that Charlie was not his problem. So I refused, and he slept with my friend. I caught them in my friend's house. The worst part was, it had been going on for a long time. She was one of those model-thin blondes. I should have known better." She looked over at him finally and he was in shock. He moved towards her again and she stepped back.

"I'm sorry that happened to you Chloe, he was an ass."

"Thanks."

Her voice was clipped and short now. He knew she was reliving it and it was his fault. He looked at her, she was sad and hurting and it had left something scarred in her. He felt that same feeling when he was put in that home. Like no one understood him or cared to. He didn't want that for her, for her to feel that way. He reached out and grabbed her again and pulled her to him. They stayed that way for a long time, just standing close with him pressed against her until Charlie came running in breaking the spell.

"Chloe, look what I found, a frog!" He happily made his way over to her and she shrieked backing up.

Charlie glanced at Braden, rolling his eyes. "Girls." Braden couldn't help but laugh at the scene before him.

"Well, I have to get going, Chloe. I expect to finish this conversation later." He ruffled his hand in Charlie's hair. "You be nice to your sister." He gave him a smile and he headed out. He had a tremendous amount of paperwork to sort through at his place.

The next week went by uneventfully. She would glance at his place when she went to work, subconsciously hoping to see him. He was a good friend of Charlie, and that was all. School would be out in two days. Finally, it was Saturday, and Charlie was leaving. She knew the Bakers were picking him up at 11 and she started helping him to move his things outside as they waited. He was smiling at her and she finally asked him why.

"You are gonna have a whole lot of time to spend with your new boyfriend next door when I am gone, Sis." He started laughing. She swatted at him.

"Charlie, that's not funny. Keep your voice down. He is not my boyfriend, he is our neighbor."

"Okay, so why is he always asking you out?" He looked up at her and started to laugh again.

"I don't know. Maybe he feels sorry for me because my little brother has such a big mouth." She pushed him as she made her way down the stairs.

"No, he likes you Chloe, I like girls at school... that's how he looks at you." He shrugged at her glare and went back to moving things.

"No, he doesn't, guys like him don't like girls... well like me. That's just the way the world is. It's up to younger guys like you to make the world better." She threw a pillow at him and he scrambled to catch it before it hit the ground. Finally, they noticed the Bakers coming up the side street, and after some time, he was loaded and leaving.

She waved at him, feeling a little sad at the prospect of spending so much time alone. Once it had been easy to fill her time, and now, she was like a mom, and without him, she wasn't sure what to do. She turned around and

Braden was there watching her. She gave him a wave and headed back to her house.

He watched her go. It was the longest week of his life and all he wanted to do was touch her. Between issues with the races, complaints from other drivers about a leak, and his manager trying to set him up on random surprise dates at dinner time, he just wanted something normal. He wanted her. He heard what she said and it made sense to him now. "Guys like him and girls like her." She had no idea what he wanted, but he was going to tell her. He took long strides to her door and rang the bell. He felt the anticipation curling up. When she opened the door, he practically fell through it.

"Braden hello..." He cut her off, pulling her to him and covering her mouth with his. He bruised her lips with his attack and she felt her defenses slip away. She thought of nothing but him for a week.

They moved together in the living room and she leaned back on the couch as he pushed her down. She felt the length of him against her and it was perfect. His hands were everywhere and as he unbuttoned her shirt he felt her freeze.

"Look at me Chloe. I want you, all of you just as you are. Stop fighting me." She was still frozen and he knew he had to convince her. He pinned both of her arms above her head with his left arm as he moved his right hand over her curves. She was rounded and smooth, and he loved it. She was aware of every nerve ending in her body, as his hands reached around and under each breast, lifting her bra slightly so that the nipples were exposed. He cupped each globe lovingly until he reached the pert nipple that had hardened under his touch. He pulled and tugged on them, creating a deep ache deep down, soon covering each one in succession with his mouth.

Chloe was lost in the sensation. No one had ever taken time with her like this, ever. His hands were lighting her on fire with every movement.

She was all fire, just like he knew she would be. He was almost in pain with the need to rip off her clothes and bury himself inside her, but he wanted to go slow, wanted it to be good for her too. She was laid out on the couch, her hair, a red flaming swirl around her head and yet he could still tell she was nervous. He moved lower to make a final step in making her his.

Her eyes flew open as she felt him slide his hand under her and lift her off the bed as he loved her with his mouth. She couldn't move, couldn't do anything but feel the way he felt against her. She felt the tension fade away and the mounting pleasure begin to spiral out of control. Her legs were shaking as she climbed that ultimate peak to release. She let go of her resolve and fears and put her hands in his hair and let go.

He felt her release, and the way her legs were trembling made him ache for her more. He moved above her and watched her face as he moved to push inside her. She was tight, and it took more than one pushed to fully envelope himself within her. With a final push, he was exactly where he needed to be. He pushed her knees up and over his shoulders as his movements became more frantic, more demanding. Soon, he stood back from her, one hand holding each knee as he pounded into her relentlessly. He heard her moans, and knew she was sharing in the intensity. Her hips moved with his, and the explosion was powerful as he pushed into her one last time and release came.

They both lay there, trying to breathe and trying to make sense of what just happened. For Chloe, it was unlike anything she ever experienced. She looked up at him and he was smiling down at her. He leaned in and kissed her lightly before he stood up. She once again marveled at his chiseled body. He saw her glance and smiled at her. Hopefully she knew that he found her sexy and he enjoyed touching her. He made his way to the kitchen and Chloe quickly redressed. What had she done? She felt the blush rising up her face. He had seen her, all of her. No one ever had. She made her way into the bathroom and then followed him in the kitchen.

His phone rang and she turned to look at him and he frowned as he listened.

"Chloe, I have to go. I'm sorry, something came up."

"Sure it's fine go ahead." She felt the same fear from before, he would leave now.

"Chloe look at me." She did. "I will be back, I promise. " He kissed her quickly on the head and left.

To say he was worried was an understatement. The twenty minute drive took him 12. He pulled into his lot and stared up at the flaming mess. His penthouse was on fire and all he could do was watch. He found the house staff and was happy they were okay. The three of them watched as the fire department did their best.

The next few days Braden spent sifting through what had once been his home. His home hadn't been saved and very little else had either. He had to meet with the investigator today and then the adjuster. The police assumed this was an accident, but he wasn't as sure. He was staying at a nearby hotel, trying to hold it all together, but barely. He made sure the staff had rooms and that they were well taken care of. Most of his time was spent on the phone or on conference to various media networks and the racing team. He thought about Chloe, her smile and her sweetness. He missed her. Everything he put into proving he liked her the way she was vanished the night he left, and hadn't come back. He promised, and now she would never trust him again.

Chloe knew she was a fool. She spent that entire night waiting for him, as if she believed in his story, or that he would come back. She waited, and the joke was on her. Life had, inevitably gone back to normal. As a teacher, she threw herself back into the work of planning for the next school year. She found that by journaling a lot, she was able to keep her heart from hurting too much.

The reality was she cared about Braden and what he thought of her. The times they spent talking was a big part of that. He was a kind and sweet guy, despite his obvious fetish for big girls. It wasn't that he never came back that night. The fact was he had never come back at all, until yesterday. She hadn't actually seen him, just that his lights were on and music was playing inside. How he could just ignore her now was the brunt of the pain.

She wished for a moment that she had the strength to march over there and demand an answer, but it was better off left alone.

She glanced at the clock and headed out to go grocery shopping. As she did, she heard the door open next door and she cringed. The last thing she wanted was a run in. She turned around and it was a woman, a very thin, very hot blonde woman. The blonde in question gave her a wave and she straightened her shoulders and left.

Braden had cancelled the rest of the afternoon and made the decision to try. He had to explain, and most importantly, he had to tell her the truth. He drove to her place and waited. He saw her car, he knew she was there, but for the first time since he was a child, he was scared. He was a nationally known bike racer and had been with more than a few women all over the world and this one woman had him questioning everything about himself. He felt the guilt like a punch in the stomach. Not just for leaving her like that, but for not telling her the truth about who he was. He finally got out of the car and went to the door.

She heard the knock and frantically made her way to the door. She found a solution to her financial woes and was moving in a roommate. To say the mess from what had once been storage was everywhere, would be putting it mildly. She climbed over the final boxes and pulled the door open. There he stood.

"What do you want Braden, I am really busy." She hoped the nonchalant way she talked to him would fool him.

"We need to talk Chloe, really talk." He sounded serious and she finally made eye contact. Still gorgeous, he looked rough. He looked tired and she knew something was wrong. She moved out of the way and he came inside.

He felt a sense of panic at the mess. "Are you moving?" He glanced around.

"No, I found a roommate. Nice guy, good job." She crossed her arms in front of her and waited. She would let him speak, but she wouldn't make it easy for him.

Braden felt a rush of anger. He would be damned if some "guy" was moving in here. "There are some things I need to tell you and explain. I need to know you will let me explain it all and then we will talk about this "guy" you think is moving in here."

He made his way to the living room and she followed. Her arms were crossed again and her eyes were flashing fire. Even now, he wanted her.

He turned the channel to ESPN and turned to look at her. "This is the best way I know how to explain."

She sat there stunned watching sports news, which she didn't even know existed. Some bike racer had a house that burned down and, wow, he was local. She suddenly felt sick. He was everywhere, pictures and stories and she knew. He turned it off.

"Oh my God Braden, are you ok?" She looked at him and touched his hand.

"I'm fine, my house is gone though. That's where I have been. That's why I didn't call."

"Why didn't you tell me you were famous? It would have made our fling that much more memorable for me." She gave him a half smile.

"Stop it Chloe, I don't look at you like that and I know you don't either. It's more than that and you damn well know it." She moved off the couch and towards the door. He caught her hand as she went by, standing up in the process. He kissed her forcefully, only letting go when they needed air. It was then he noticed her tears. He kissed her eyelids and wiped them away.

"Don't cry Chloe, please, I'm so sorry for everything." He pulled her into his arms and buried his head in her hair.

He kissed her face and then her mouth again. It started so simply, wanting to comfort each other, and soon they were lost in the moment. She pulled away from him and went up the stairs, and he followed. Once there, he took the lead, grabbing her hand and pulling her with him into the room. Their actions frantic now, they undressed each other. He turned her around to face away from him. She felt him unzip her dress and trail his fingers down her spine as the dress slipped to the floor. He reached around to cup her breasts, which overflowed in his hands. He pulled her back against him and she felt the hardness there.

"Don't ever question what you do to me Chloe, feel what you do."

She did just that, taking him into her hand and feeling the length of him. He pushed her over towards the bed and she climbed into it and he stopped her. She was half on and half off the bed when he moved behind her. He filled her suddenly and quickly, and she gasped at his entry. He moved his hand up to her hair, winding his fist in it and bracing himself as he plunged into her faster, and deeper. They moved together both seeking and searching for something. She was the first to reach her peak and she moaned out his name as she did so pushing him over the edge as well. He pulled her to him spooning behind her. She was his, and she always will be. Suddenly she stood.

"You should go Braden." She pulled her dress over her head and stood. He stood as well and she was once again reminded of how perfect he was.

"Chloe please."

"Braden this.... this was a mistake. You know it as well as I do."

"No, it's not a mistake, how can you even say that after what just happened?"

"We come from different worlds, Braden, you're... famous for God's sake and I am just some..."She trailed off. "You lied to me, Braden."

"I know, at first I just wanted you. I was driven by a need to be inside you, loving you. Then things changed."

"No, they didn't Braden... ...you should go... now."

He saw the firm set of her jaw and knew she was serious. He took one last look at her before he left. Chloe waited until she heard the front door shut and she locked it before crumbling to the floor and gave over to the tears.

Braden was not himself. His driving was awful and he couldn't connect with the course. He normally would love the flowing hills of Virginia, but he was officially not on a streak anymore. He angrily threw his helmet into the seat of the car and made his way to the crew. They all knew to avoid him when he was like this. Braden angry was a rare thing, but it usually had a quick turnaround. This time he was like this all day. He was angry, and worried. Chloe refused to respond to any messages he sent her and he missed her. She was so damn stubborn and it hurt that she didn't feel the same way.

Braden made his way into the hotel and caught a glimpse of himself in the mirror. He was dirty from the race, but he was changed now. He spent his entire adult life alone until this one woman came into it and now he was worried about someone else. He knew she had been struggling, in more ways than one. She shared her situation with him, told him her secrets, and he lied to her. He knew she was hurting, but couldn't she see how he felt? He frowned. How did he feel exactly? He got into the shower to wash away everything from the long day. He had to do something, and soon.

He met up with Mike for dinner that evening who put it all in perspective for him.

"You're in love with that chubby girl back home aren't you?" Braden stood and towered over him.

"Don't ever say that about her again, do you understand me?"
"Whoa, whoa buddy calm down. I didn't mean anything negative about it. I am just telling you man, you got it bad. The whole damn crew is afraid of you the way you're tearing things up all the time. Not to mention you lost your streak, you need to see her and make it right. Either let her go or marry the girl."

Braden sat back in his chair and thought about what he said. Marry her? The thought gave him a start of panic, but the idea of coming home to her, all the time was one he could love. He ran his hand through his hair. He hoped she and Charile were okay, if only she would answer his damn calls. He suddenly had an idea, one that might make her call him after all. He pitched his idea to Mike, who chuckled and started to make the call.

Chloe was frustrated. The roommate was an ass and he left his things all over her house. More importantly, he was indifferent to Charlie. Treating him like a bug in his way all of the time. Last night was the final straw. He came home drunk and groped her, and she was finished with it. She took a deep breath before knocking on his door. She had to do it repeatedly before he finally yelled something and stumbled to open it.

"What Chloe?" He moaned as she pushed the door open wider.

"You have to move, Josh. I can't have this kind of environment for Charlie."

"You can't just kick me out, Chloe. I have rights. Besides, you like it when I touch you, don't even try to lie." He took a step towards her and grabbed her again. This time she pushed at him and scratched his face. He gave her one blow to the face and she staggered backwards. She rushed to the living room calling for Charlie and the two of them made their way out to her car.

Mrs. Anderson watched the little car pull away with a shake of her head. That was a bad man in there, she saw her holding her face when they left. She pulled out her phone to call Mikey and tell him the plan couldn't work now. After Mike hung up the phone, it took him a minute to turn around. He knew once he told Braden, he would lose it. There was nothing he could do but to tell him.

"Well, what did she say?" Braden was eager to hear Chloe was ok.

"Seems like she is gone man, I mean she had a couple bags and she and Charlie left."

"What the hell do you mean they left?"

"Sit down man I'll tell you everything."

Braden did, only because he knew he wouldn't get any information otherwise.

Twenty minutes later, Braden called the airline and booked a flight to Texas. The sonofabitch was going to pay and he would be the one to do it. Mike tagged along, mainly because he didn't want

Braden to end up in jail. They took the direct flight and Braden was full of tension and ready to fight the entire time. Finally on the ground, they picked up a rental car and made their way into the city. He was practically out of the car before it even stopped. He made his way to her house and when the door opened, he let the first punch fly.

Mike glanced down at the man on the floor. The guy didn't even have a chance. Braden knocked him out with two hits. Braden made his way upstairs and checked to make sure she had yet to come back. He wasn't sure where she would go, she had a few friends, but no one she spoke about enough to give him any clear direction to head in. He walked back over to Mike's and sat in the chair by the window so he could watch and wait. He glanced up at Mike.

"Give me your phone."

"Why?"

"Just trust me, I'll give it right back."

He took the phone from Mike and sent a text to her from his number. He visibly relaxed when he got a response. It was wrong, but it had to work. She would be furious, but he would at least get to look at her and make sure she was ok.

Chloe was concerned. The message said that she needed to come home right away. She wasn't even sure who sent her the message, but she had to find out what was going on. She dropped Charlie off at a friend's house and made her way home quickly. She had so much to figure out and she was exhausted. She glanced at herself in the mirror. It had only been a number of hours, but her right eye was purple and bruised.

She couldn't go back in there. He was horrible. What had ever possessed her to let him move in in the first place? Money, always money. She wanted to keep Charlie in one place with his friends, something she never had, and this is what happened. She pulled into her parking lot and got out of the car. She would wait out here. She couldn't go in there alone ever again. It was then that the door next door opened and she saw him.

It was only a couple of months, but he was perfect. He took a few long strides to get to her and before she could say a word, he wrapped himself around her and picked her up. He literally picked her up. She heard him whisper her name and she closed her eyes against the emotional overflow she felt inside her. Why was he here? She pulled away and he stood back looking her over. When he looked at her face, he swore.

"That asshole." He started walking towards her place and she went after him.

"Braden wait." She went behind him and they made it to the door. She grabbed his arm. Suddenly there was another man there. He pulled Braden away.

"Calm down man." Braden turned towards her as the police pulled up out front.

"Oh no, Braden the police?" She walked towards the car again. She felt his hand on her arm.

> "Yes, the police Chloe. Look at your face and what he did to you." She tentatively touched her face with her fingertips. She saw the rage fill his face again and she touched him. "I'm fine Braden, really."

He watched her go speak to the police and he glanced at the front door as it slowly opened. Josh came staggering out and Mike once again grabbed Braden by the arm, preventing him from going to jail. The police made their way over to Josh and cuffed him. After they were gone, Braden turned to face her.

"We need to talk Chloe, now." He went inside and she soon followed, but not before Chloe saw the blond from before walking hand in hand with Mike. So she was never with Braden. Somehow that helped to make her feel a little better. At a wave from the two of them, she made her way inside where Braden was waiting.

"Braden, nothing has changed. I love that you came here to help me, I do, but we are still so different. Everything we do is..." She stopped as he kissed her. She closed her eyes, even if they couldn't be together, she could enjoy the way it felt when he kissed her, even just for another moment. She relaxed in his arms and he felt it. He pulled her even closer to him and ran his hands over her curves.

She was everything, and he wanted all of her. The kiss intensified and he undid the back of her dress pulling it to the floor. She was lost in him, his touch and felt the coolness of the air against her skin. She trusted him unlike she had ever trusted anyone else. He pulled her into the living room never stopping the kisses he trailed down her neck. When they made it there, she stopped him. She could be herself with him, for the moment. She walked around him and shed the rest of her clothes. She walked to the couch and laid back on it, fully unclothed and waiting. He watched her, his mouth hungry to touch her, but reveling in the way she was with him now.

She was no longer concerned about if he was attracted to her, or if he wanted her. She believed in him and how much he wanted to touch her. He finally moved towards her, gently moving his mouth down her chest, stopping to kiss and run his tongue over each crested peak. He buried his face in her breasts pulling on them and kissing every inch of them. She had her hands in his hair now pulling his head back up to kiss her deeply. He moved his hands along her curves and she arched up to meet them.

She moaned at the sensation and was aching for him with a need deep down. This is how he wanted her, how he needed her to be with him. He moved his fingers over her, working to a fevered state and he watched the expression on her face as she became more demanding of release. He wanted to give her more and he slid down, burying his face in her and tasting her.

He felt her hands in his hair as she grinded into him and finally he felt her reach that ultimate peak and he knew it was time. He raised above her, his excitement evident and she stood to touch him. Sliding her hands down his body over his chest and further until with a swift intake of breath, she held him in her hands. She slid to the floor, and when he saw her look up at him, it was almost too much. He pulled her up to him and kissed her deeply before pushing her to the couch again.

He mounted her swiftly, pushing into her depths. He reached the full hilt of himself and stopped. He wanted to just feel her surrounding him like this. He looked up at her face. She was flushed from her climax and eager for more, but he wanted to watch the expressions as he moved her. He moved slowly now stretching her to her limits and testing himself, his ability to prolong the inevitable.

He felt her hands on his chest as he looked down at her and he watched her curvy body move with his. He wanted her, always. He pulled out and slammed back into with a force that shook them both to the core. It had never been this good, this satisfying. The need was far too great and they both were aching to reach that final release. He moved faster now, steadily grinding into her and she was almost whimpering, and calling for him. He loved her like this, with abandon.

He increased his speed and was both grinding and pounding into her at the same time. It was good, too good. She called his name as her body moved on its own. She was no longer in charge of it and she felt the orgasm start low until it shuddered through her entire body, leaving her spent and breathless. Her explosion rocked him to the core and he couldn't hold back any longer. He slid his hands under her and lifted her off the bed slightly as he plunged into her again and again until he shared in her release. He buried himself inside her as far as he could. He wanted her to know he had given it all to her.

They lay there holding on to each other. Both afraid to speak, afraid to break the beauty of what they had shared. He knew she would run from him now, but he wouldn't let her. He was in love with her and he couldn't imagine life without her in it. She was the first to move, raising her head to look at him.

"Braden." She whispered and he gently kissed her lips. He held her that way, the two looking at each other waiting for the other to say something else. She was what he had been missing his entire life, she was family.

She raised up, suddenly self-conscious of her nakedness. He knew the person she was in the throes of passion was not who she was every day. It was a part of her she shared with only him, and he loved her all the more for it. He pulled her dress from the floor and helped her into it. He noticed she relaxed some and glanced at him sheepishly as she did it.

"Chloe, before you say anything, I need you to know something." He moved the strands of hair that had fallen into her face as she moved. She waited and looked up at him.

"I am in love with you." I know you don't know how this will work, but I know you have feelings for me too. I know you worry about everything, from yourself, to Charlie and money, and this house."

"Braden" she started, but he held up a hand to her...

"I'm not finished. The last few months have been the worst kind of hell for me. I found my mother dead on my living room floor when I was twelve, and aside from a loving couple who gave me a family for three years, I have been alone my whole life. I didn't even know what I was missing until you and Charlie. I love you.

Chloe. I want you with me... you and Charlie. I have more money than I can ever spend and I want to share everything with you."

"Braden... I love you too." He relaxed with her words and pulled her closer to him. She was worried about life with Braden, what she never considered was how awful life would be without him. She smiled up at him and asked.

"Will you miss all the models and thin girls? Can I really satisfy you, Braden?

"Chloe, what we have is better than anything I have ever done in my whole life. You are sexy and gorgeous, and ALL I want is you." She smiled and a giggle escaped.

"What's so funny?"

"Charlie said you liked me even before any of this. Now I have to tell him he was right."

"I love you Chloe."

He kissed her again, and for the first time in her life, she believed it.

The Billionaire's Secret

Amelia Randolph was fuming. Her grandmother was sick again, and it had to be the water. She paced the room in the hospital where she watched her grandmother sleeping. Nothing had been right in a long time, not since that ass, Jacob Montgomery had installed that new water filtration equipment.

She'd had her suspicions for a long time, but then they tested it, and she knew she had to be right. She had called, prodded and attacked everyone she could. It wasn't that she couldn't be a lady, she could. Her grandmother was the most important person to her and there was no way she could just stand idly by and wait for things to get worse.

Friday she would get her chance, until then she was doing her best to keep calm. If she went too crazy beforehand, she may not be able to state her case, and she had to. She looked over at the woman nestled into the bed that seemed to swallow her up in its massive size

"I'll, fix it Nana, I will." She whispered the words to herself. Her grandmother had been asleep for an hour now and a sounder sleeper you would never meet.

She caught a glimpse of herself in the mirror near the doorway. Her normally tamed head of hair was a jumbled mess. She was an average girl, at least she thought so. At 5'7 she was taller than many girls, she had dark green eyes and was in pretty good shape. She wasn't perfect by any means. She filled out her clothes nicely and was curvy. She was far from the model stick thin types most men preferred. Her hair was naturally curly and hung down past her shoulders.

There must have been 4 different shades of red mixed in there. Today what she needed most was some conditioner and a pony tail. She glanced over at the table where lunch had been placed and noticed a rubber band, it would have to do. With a shrug, she wrapped her hair in a severe bun and at least managed to contain the wild mess.

She took a seat by the large window in the room and opened a book. Reading calmed her and had always been a favorite pastime. There was something magical about being swept away into someone else's fantasy world. It made thing easier, especially when times got dark. She gave her Nana another look over. She had saved her life, literally. She owed her everything, and wouldn't stop short of giving her as much back. She would fix this mess, or die trying.

It had been twelve years since her life had changed for the better. At 26 there wasn't a day that went by that she didn't remember, and take time to appreciate the life she had now. Her mother had been an angry, bitter woman. That's pretty much all she could remember about her. She'd had Amelia young, they could have been sisters really. Her life had been hard and full of everything negative. Amelia could remember being hungry, and cold more often than not.

Her mother was always entertaining one man or another. Whatever money she made prostituting she would spend on drugs, throwing her son and daughter a crumb or two from time to time. When Amelia turned 10, things got even worse.

She felt the sadness well up in her, even now. Her brother's name was Evan. He was always a sweet boy, and often sick. He was younger by five years and Amelia tried her best to protect him. He never hurt anyone in his whole life and he could have been something wonderful. The day he disappeared was the longest day of her life.

Her mother was running late as always, and they were starving. She was only 10 years old, and she knew they could go to the neighbor's house and Miss Sinclair would help them. She was always giving them bread and candies. She had specifically told

Evan to stay at the house. She had tucked him into the cot in their corner of the room and told him to wait and she would get them some food.

He had smiled up at her and she hugged him before going. It was the last time she would ever see him. Miss Sinclair wasn't home, but on her way back to their house someone had seen her, had followed her. He was a big man, he smelled of whiskey and smoke.

He grabbed her by the arm and refused to let go despite her kicking and screaming. With a kick to the groin, she had finally broken free and she ran, probably faster than she ever would again in her life. She made it home, and Evan was gone. She frantically looked for him, but there was no sign of him.

When her mother made it home finally she told her, but was ignored. Her mother just told her he was probably off playing somewhere. She felt helpless and lost, and she never wanted to feel like that again. Her thoughts were always with Evan, even now. Not long after the county had come and taken her away. She couldn't save him, but she could do something about her Nana.

There was something special in the air the day Lenora Randolph came to Bakerstown Girls Home. It may have been because her birthday was the day before or it may have been the way it was supposed to snow that week, which rarely happened in South Carolina. Whatever it was, you could almost feel it. Amelia had lived there for 2 years, and in her mind it was wonderful.

She had her very own bed and clothes and they always had food. When the people had put her here she had been scared, but over time she realized that it was wonderful. She didn't sleep at night for a long time, but gradually she had stopped having nightmares and now she felt more like everyone else.

There were always people coming there, looking to adopt a girl to love as their very own, but she never thought much about it. Babies and young girls were always the ones chosen. That was something she has been just fine with. Out there you never know who will come around, who will hurt you. Here she was safe. She knew everyone who worked there and she also knew they locked the doors every night. Inside the girls home, she didn't have to worry. It was a shock to her when a nice lady had come around to greet all of the older girls in her wing.

It was a rare occurrence and while everyone was putting on their best clothes she just went about her normal routine. Eventually the lady had asked her what her name was and the conversation they had that day changed her life forever.

"What is your name young lady?" The lady smiled at her as she sat down on the bed beside her.

"Me? My name is Amelia. How do you do?" she had thrust her hand out like she saw them do on television and the lady shook it in return.

"How are you doing today? I hear there is snow in the forecast." The lady had leaned over and smiled at her as they talked. Amelia smiled back, she was nice and she smelled like cookies.

"I'm okay. I guess. Sure is getting colder that's for sure, but I like it. I used to hate it when I lived out there and I didn't have heat, boy it was no fun at all. Now I hope to get to see some snow real soon." She went back to making her bed.

"It sounds like you have done a lot of stuff in your life, Amelia."

"I guess so, you see how everyone is running around and trying so hard to be their best? I just don't understand that at all. I just want to be me all the time, so I don't make anyone sad when they find out who I really am. That's why I ain't dressed up in the Sunday clothes. I hate to be a pest Ma'am, but could you stand up? I just have to get this bed made so I can get to breakfast. I am always hungry and I sure like to eat."

Amelia had given her a grin as the lady had jumped up quickly. She made her bed and gave the lady a hug before she headed down to the lunch hall.

"You sure smell nice, lady." Amelia skipped her way out of the room and thought nothing more of the situation, and the lady she had left upstairs.

Later that day the nice lady had asked her if she wanted to come live with her and at first she had said no. The lady had sat back on the chair in the library and watched Amelia for a moment before asking her why.

"It's not you lady, you seem real nice, honest. The thing is, there are a lot of bad people out there. Here they lock up the doors real tight and it's safe that's all. I guess, I just don't know how you do things. I don't want to get hurt like I did before. I don't want them to take me like they did Evan."

"Who is Evan, dear?"

She had leaned over and whispered. "I'm not supposed to talk about Evan. No one believes me about him. He was my brother and one day someone took him."

The lady had frowned for a second and told her. "Amelia, I can assure you one thing. I lock my house up every night, just like they do here. I am all alone in there and sometimes I want someone to talk to. I had a nice man who I was married to his name was Harold but he died and he is in Heaven now. I can't promise you won't ever get hurt again, the world is full of hurt, but I can promise I'll be there with you to help you through it."

She had frowned as she thought over what the cookie lady had said. She had locks, and she was sad too. Plus, she would have someone to help her and it was nice to hear someone say that. She would miss her friends here, but maybe she should go, the lady seemed real sad and maybe she could help her.

She smiled her best smile and agreed to go. She gathered up her small bag of things and with a deep breath she had walked out of the children's home and into the arms of her loving Nana. Her life had changed for the better, and Nana was the reason. She owed her so much and it was killing her to see her sick like this. Everything that she had gone through Nana had made it better, even if it was just a hug when the boy at school was mean to her or helping her by sitting with her through a panic attack.

Even now she still had those, when she couldn't be in control. Either way, her Nana fixed everything for her, she would do the same for her now. She glanced up at the clock in the room and sighed. She needed to work, that always helped keep her mind occupied. After another glance at her Nana she left to get some work done.

Jacob Montgomery worked hard and he deserved the nicer things in life. He wasn't cocky or overly confident. He didn't think he was some gorgeous Brad Pitt all women wanted. He did, however, think he was a good man, and he tried hard to do the right thing. It was the reason the mess he was in was so difficult.

He looked down at the picture in his hand and sighed. Amelia Randolph was becoming a problem he didn't want or need. He put the picture of the plant back down and raked his hand through his dark hair. Ever since the water had tested positive for some abnormal chemical content she had been blowing up his office day and night.

It wasn't that he didn't care, in fact, he was just as concerned as she was. The problem was she was a screeching, loud, demanding woman and he wasn't relishing the idea of having a meeting with her at all. There were steps that had to take place and he was only part of the board.

For whatever reason, she felt like somehow, it was all his fault. He had tried to call her back, only to get her voicemail, which in turn, had led to the meeting they were having on Friday morning. He wanted to give her the good news, for her grandmother's well-being, and to get her to stop leaving long winded, potty mouthed voice mails on his phone at work. He glanced out the long window in his office. It had been a long and windy road to get to this place.

At age 31 he had achieved more success than any other Montgomery before him. His great-grandfather had started this business and since then it had grown leaps and bounds. It had passed down to each Montgomery until now it rested on him. He could remember as a child watching his father, work the phones, spend his evening planning and most importantly dress sharp.

There was something about a great suit that made a man. Having something tailored to you was one of the luxuries he enjoyed as the CEO. He didn't drink, or do drugs and he worked effortlessly putting in long hours to make the business a success, and well, he liked nice suits. It gave him that extra push to do well and added to the confidence of representing the company well. It had started with his grandfather and one day he would pass this entire empire down to his children. That is, If he ever got married.

Jessalyn crossed his mind and he smiled. She was a wildcat if there ever was one. The wealthy daughter of a fashion designer they crossed paths on occasion and he had been taken in right away. She was a leggy blonde, her features almost too perfect, most likely due to a random number of surgeries. Despite the insincerity of her looks he liked her inquisitive nature and they had enjoyed each other's company for the last two years.

More often than not he would call ahead when he would be in town and she would make time for him, and vice versa. She was often away for modeling shoots and he was away for some business deal or another. On the rare occasion that their calendars would sync up they would get together and try to be "normal." She knew his world, the demands of it and never complained.

They never took things any deeper than a mutual respect and a great sex life. The last time he had seen her had been three months ago, and everything had changed. Somewhere along the way she had fallen in love with a model named Brutus and she couldn't meet for a rendezvous anymore.

He tried to gauge his feelings on it. He was stuck somewhere between relieved and lonely. He didn't have time for anything serious, and yet he hated never having anyone to spend time with. One of the benefits of that was that he had more time to focus on the task at hand, the water treatment system his company had installed a few towns over that could be making people sick. That brought his thoughts back to Miss Randolph and he cringed. It was going to be a long week, and an even longer Friday.

The weather in South Carolina has been never predictable. The winters would range from snow and ice to a mild 50 degrees. There was no understanding it really. The winter would fade easily into spring without much distinction and until you looked at a calendar there was no telling what month you were in at any given moment. Today was one of those chilly days where you wanted to go outside and take the day off, all bundled up.

Sadly, it wasn't meant to be for Amelia. She loved her job that wasn't the issue. What she loved more was her Nana and truth be told she didn't feel like she was doing much good. She loved the freedom her job gave her. She was a guardian and legal consultant for D.S.S. She traveled all of the time. She would often spend her days in Charleston then to Myrtle Beach.

Sometimes she would have a chance to go north for a few days. Wherever her work needed her, she would go. She loved working on each case, and was always thrilled when she felt like she was really helping a family. So many children were always left scared and alone. She could never go back, but she could move forward with change.

Today she was in Myrtle Beach meeting with a family, two children and abusive parents. It never got any easier when she met them for the first time. It just certainly helped when they gave her a smile. She took a deep breath and went through the double doors to the lobby where she would meet the children and the attorneys. He felt like he was somehow responsible for the entire mess. Each board member was currently looking down their respective noses at him across the table.

"Look Jacob, we understand this is a ...um... situation, however we have to follow protocol. I've managed to get with the investigation team and they are looking into the mess. I've heard you have a meeting with the Randolph family and I think you need to reel that in for us."

The comment came from Brandon Workman. He had been there as long as his father had.

"Listen, Workman I get what you're saying, I'm just not sure why I am the only dealing with P.R. Do we not have a team for that? I have my own business issues to work out with the Landowe project." A few of the people at the table glanced at each other and then to the table.

"Well, I'll be honest with you Jake, you're the spokesperson for these types of situations. You're the charmer, the good-looking guy. A situation like this takes finesse and strategy." He had the decency to blush slightly.

"Let me get this straight, I am the CEO and I am also a part-time playboy schmoozes the ladies in my off time?" He sat back in a huff.

Workman looked around the table at the other members before settling on Jacob again. "Well, yes so to speak. Your father was the same way before you. You both have that ability to put people at ease." He smiled slightly, the noisy throat clearing around the room didn't go unnoticed either.

"You mean with the women." He gave Workman a half smile. He was the voice of reason around here after all. "Fine I'll go at it alone, but I need some real results from the testing site before I walk into whatever mess comes with the Randolph lady."

Amelia stared at herself in the mirror in her old room. Today was going to be a long day. She was certain of that, and not much else. She had taken great care to look nice. Her hair was twisted up on the back of her head, her make-up was subtle and effective and she wore a nice suit and skirt. It fit her just right. She wore pumps, something she rarely did and she had a firm set to her jaw. Today she would get some answers. She stood and squared her shoulders and took a few deep breaths.

It was just like going into a new home. She would listen, make her assessment and they would go from there. She made her way down to the car and drove into town. It was a 25 minute ride into Charleston, just long enough that she could take in some deep breaths along the way and try to stop her heart from beating out of her chest. It would serve no purpose if she lost her temper, no matter what she had to stay calm.

She climbed the front stairs of the building and looked up at the massive structure. She shook her head. Who needed that much space for anything? It was all too much really. She entered and gave her name to the guard who patted her down with a wink and she was finally in the elevator going up. She heard a shout and she noticed a man running towards her so she thrust her hand out to stop the elevator. He slid into the elevator and took a deep breath.

"Wow, I barely made it that time, thanks." He glanced over at her. She was beautiful, her hair was a jumble of colors wound up tightly with the appearance that it would break free at any moment.

"Sure, no problem." She tried not to stare at him. He was reeking of sexiness. He had dark hair slightly unruly and blue eyes that felt like they could look a hole right through you. He was tall, very tall and impeccably dressed. She self-consciously ran her hands down over her skirt. She could feel him watching her and she finally turned to look at him.

"Is there something on my face or something?" She noticed his surprise and then the grin that slid into its place. "No, not at all, you're just beautiful, that's all." It was his turn to get a rise out of her. He saw the blush creep up her neck and into her face. "Whatever." She rolled her eyes and stared back at the elevator, watching intently as it made its slow accent to the top floor. "You are, but I have to say it is refreshing."

He failed to elaborate as the doors opened and he stepped out. "I hope to see you again." He whistled as he strode away from the elevator, leaving her wondering what he was talking about.

Men were crazy, that much she was sure of. Finally the elevator climbed the last few floors and she exited it into a massive waiting area. There was a coffee bar on one end of the room which looked like a small café. She couldn't believe the excess that people used. She made her way to the receptionist desk and gave her name.

"Randolph, you said Miss?"

"Yes, that's right." She noticed the receptionist glance around a bit before buzzing back to Mr. Montgomery's office.

"Yes, ok, yes that's fine, I'll let her know." She had glanced up at Amelia a few times before hanging up.

"Mr. Montgomery is on his way here now and as soon as he arrives I'll send you back."

With a huff, Amelia made her way over to an overstuffed chair in the lobby. He wasn't even there yet. The whole thing was ridiculous. He was probably on some yacht somewhere while her grandmother was lying in a hospital sick. She felt the tension rising and she hoped he would get there soon before anything else happened.

Jacob made his way up the stairs to his office. She had been a real beauty that one. She was gorgeous, but in an unrefined way and she was direct, something many people never were in his life, it made him like her even more. He was kicking himself for not getting her name at the very least. For now he would just have to hope he would run into her again soon. She was in his building how hard could it be to find one woman?

He gathered up some paperwork from his desk and made his way over to the conference room. The receptionist had already called him ten minutes ago and told him, Amelia Randolph was there. He knew what kind of morning as ahead of him, but he had exited the elevator a couple of floors down so that he could sneak up the back way.

He didn't need to be attacked in his own lobby. He quickly scanned the paperwork in his hands regarding the water testing site and frowned. This was not going to be a good meeting. At least he had chosen a conference room in the corner of the floor where they wouldn't be bothered, or heard. Reluctantly, he buzzed up front and told the girl to bring her in.

It was ridiculous how long someone had to wait for a meeting. The lack of attendance only solidified her opinion of Jacob Montgomery. If he had been a real gentleman, if he cared, he would have at least been on time. Finally the blonde called her name and escorted her to a room at the far side of the building. When she entered, she simply stared at the blonde shut the door.

"You! Really? Did you know it was me or do you always say things like that to people in an elevator?" She crossed her arms and stared at him as he stood.Equally stunned, and a little disappointed he thrust his hand out to her. "No, I didn't know it was you Miss Randolph." He gestured for her to take a seat.

She was upset, she'd be lying is she said that the mystery guy from the elevator had made her feel that warm fuzzy feeling you get deep down. To find out he was that ass, Montgomery she had been dreading squashed any thoughts she'd had while waiting in the lobby. To think, she actually hoped to run into him again, so she could apologize for being so gruff and to figure out what he meant by those last words. Now she was sitting face to face with him.

It was difficult to think straight with her sitting there staring at him. She was all fire and ice at the same time and he was intrigued. There was simply no way the squawking shrill voice on the voicemails could belong to this woman. He shook his head and decided to get down to business.

"Miss Randolph I am glad we were able to get together finally. I understand you have concerns over the new water treatment plant we have put in and I assure you I am working hard to figure out where the problem is." He sat forward looking at her intently.

"Listen, I know you think your gonna just give me some BS about the plant and how great it is. I don't want to hear any of that. The fact of the matter is people are getting sick, or in the hospital. Something is wrong and I am just here to find out what you are going to do about it before I start asking people myself." She leaned up in her chair meeting him eye to eye.

He almost couldn't stand it. She was on fire, and beautiful. He would be amused watching her come to life if it were in any other situation. He was not used to women like this, so full of fire. Typically a woman would be a hellcat from time to time, but that was in the bedroom. If they started out like this he could only imagine... Damn, he was getting sidetracked.

"I don't think you need to start asking anyone else, Miss Randolph. The fact of the matter is we have men down there working on it now. The most recent tests I have right here." He pushed the papers over to her. "As you can see there is nothing showing that the mineral content is above average. Although the levels are normal at the plant I am still concerned about why this happened to you. I have no intention of letting it go until I am sure we have fixed the problem, if there is one."

"All I know is that my Nana was fine and then the day after the water was running through your plant she started getting sick. She had been in the hospital three times and each time it's after she goes home and starts using your water." She pointed her finger at him for emphasis.

"I understand, Miss Randolph and I assure you there is nothing I won't do to make this right, for you." His eyes glittered at her dangerously as he emphasized the "for you." She felt the heat rush through her as he watched her. She cleared her throat and glanced back down at the paperwork on the able.

"This paperwork can say whatever it wants, the truth of the matter is something is wrong and I intend to find out what it is." She stood now and he rose with her.

"Fine, meet me at the plant tomorrow morning." He wasn't even sure what possessed him to say it. He knew very little about the mechanics of the plant itself, but he did have a full knowledge of the filtration system.

"What." She crossed her arms over her chest as she looked up at him.

"Tomorrow, meet me at the plant. I'll go take a look around myself and if you're there you can see things as they develop." He crossed his arms and the two of them stood facing each other for a long moment.

The whole thing was dangerous. She knew before she agreed that this was going to go badly. Despite the anger she held at the company, she was attracted to him. She hated herself for it. He stood casually waiting for her to give him an answer. He was probably used to women throwing themselves at him all the time and she would be damned if she was one of them. He was off limits and she needed to turn off whatever attraction she had. He was just a stuffy suit running a business that hurt her Nana. With renewed spirit, she looked up at him.

"Fine, I'll meet you there, what time." She said it with a deadly calm. Almost as if she was someone else. He didn't like this side of her, it made him take a step back.

"9 sharp. Does that work for you?" He took a small step towards her and watched the blush start to creep back up again. She felt it too, he was sure of it. "Sure, that's fine." She turned to leave and opened the door to the room and stopped as he called her name. "Yes?""

"Don't be late." He grinned as she shut the door with a bang and made her way out of the office.

Jacob Montgomery was a jerk, a total and unmistakable jerk. Not only that, he was arrogant and self-serving, just thinking about the way he stood there arms crossed without a care in the world made her want to scream. She rammed the car into gear and pulled out and headed to the hospital. She was still angry when she arrived.

Who did he think he was giving her orders anyway? She was a grown woman, almost as tall as he was and he thought he could just tell her what to do. Her family was the victim here. He was a bully, yes, that was it. He was just like those kids at the children's home who would give her grief the first year especially. They threw their weight around, uncaring about anyone else. Yep! Jacob Montgomery was a no good bully! She walked into her Nana's room to find her sitting up and chatting happily with the nurse.

"Nana you look great!" Her anger was gone in an instant. The turnaround was almost unbelievable. Yesterday she had looked so sick still and in the two nights she had been here she had done a complete turnaround.

"Amelia sweetheart, come give me a hug." She raised her arms up and Amelia hugged her tightly. She was so scared, every time she got better and went home the next time it would be worse.

"You must feel better Nana, I'm so glad. Every time you go home it makes you sick. It's that damn water system and I am working on getting it taken care of."

"Now, now Amelia we don't know that for sure yet. " She patted Amelia's hand lovingly and leaned back into her pillows. "I may look better, but I am terribly weak still. What have you been up to today, dear you are all dressed up?" She snuggled back into her pillow and shut her eyes momentarily.

"I had a meeting that's all. I met with Montgomery, to hash out things about the plant." She whispered it, in hopes Nana wouldn't really hear everything she said.

Her Nana's eye fluttered open. "You what! Oh Amelia it won't do it you get yourself all worked up. You know as well as I do that if you push too far you're going to get into trouble. Plus, we all know what happens with that temper of yours." She closed her eyes again, but not before giving Amelia a "You know what I mean" look.

"Yes, Nana I know all about my temper. In my defense, though I don't really get too upset unless I have a real reason to." She humbly looked down and started fighting with a string on the comforter covering the bed.

"Amelia, sweetheart, don't misunderstand I love all your fire, but just last week you made the poor paperboy cry." She gave a slight giggle before folding her hands over her lap.

"He was throwing the paper in the rose bushes Nana, how on earth can you climb in there and get it!"

Nana simply opened her eyes and gave Amelia a knowing glance. "I know, dear." She patted her hand one last time and Amelia watched as she was soon fast asleep.

Amelia sighed, it wasn't a lie. Her temper often got in her way. She liked to think that she was just passionate about certain things. Her work, her Nana and what was right. Besides, most of the time she was loud, but not angry. There was such a lack of common sense in some people she simply couldn't help herself. She made her way across the room and opened her tablet to look at her schedule.

She had a new family to work with next week, but the rest of this week she was free. She hadn't broached the subject of Nana coming to stay with her in her apartment yet. She knew it would be a fight.

Nana loved her house. It was where she and Harold had lived right after they got married and she had never stayed away from there unless she was in the hospital or when she had come to see Amelia graduate college in Maryland. It wasn't that she didn't understand.

The house had been here over half of her life. It was where she had learned to love, learned to trust again. It would always be a part of her life. She had to have Nana closer so that she could watch her more, be there if she needed anything.

Besides, her apartment was on the city water system in Ridgeville, not on the new "system" purchased from Montgomery Enterprises in Daniel Island. She could keep her safe if she would move in. She folded up her table and rested her head against the chair. She let her mind unravel the day's events and found herself fuming once more over the words of Jacob Montgomery.

She decided to get a room in town for the next few nights. It might be a huge expense, but she needed to be there early tomorrow, and the water was still in question at her Nana's, where she had been staying. She said her goodnights to Nana and made her way to a small and efficient hotel along the water. She had always enjoyed Charleston.

Even as a child she had loved the water, even when there was such a chill in the air like tonight. It was only mid-November and yet with temperatures like this maybe they would get some snow this year. The thought made her smile and think back about the snow when she had moved into Nana's house so long ago.

It was a long ride. It must have taken hours to get to the little white house, she was standing in front of. She looked up at the nice lady beside her who had decided to take her home. She took her hand. She was scared, but she didn't want her to know. She had left the girls home and she hoped this was going to be ok.

The nice lady patted the hand in hers and they made their way up the steps. When the door opened, she took a deep breath in of cookies and warm air. She loved being warm and full, both things she knew the nice lady said she never had to worry about again. She watched and waited as the lady locked the door behind her. It was only then that she relaxed.

"I've decided that maybe you should call me Nana. I'm not your mother, but I hope to be there to help you grow up. How does that sound?"

"Nana... I like it." She gave her a toothy smile and walked over towards a big picture on the wall of a man. "Who is he?" She hooked a thumb in the direction of the picture. Nana made her way over to her.

"That was my dear Harold. He went to Heaven a few months ago." She gently touched the picture and then turned to Amelia. "Well, dear are you ready to see your room?"

"I get my own room?" Amelia had gaped at her and followed along behind Nana. When she opened the door, she could just stand there. The entire room was draped in pink and green. There were flowers on the large seat window and she had the softest pink blanket on her bed. There were pillows everywhere and Amelia rushed forward and immediately began to roll around the bed with them, giggling as she did. Nana laughed, pink may have been a bad choice this girl was not about to paint her nails all day she wanted to make a mess.

"The only thing left is to go buy you some clothes, we can do that tomorrow." Amelia ran to hug her close, happy for the first real time in her life. At some point that first night she had been overwhelmed by it all and snuck into Nana's room. She waited but a second before Nana pulled the blankets back. Without a word she had climbed in and snuggled down in the warmth of the blankets.

The snow came that weekend and the two of them played in the yard and built half of a snowman. She had laughed more in those two days than I her entire life combined. It's how her new life started and now that same chill was in the air tonight. She was still smiling when she put her bags on the floor of her room. She had a nice view and this would be a good way to make efficient use of the time she had. She locked and relocked the door.

A habit of sorts since she was a child. She let her thoughts stray to Evan. She had spent the better part of her career looking for him, some sign of him. She always came up empty. Every lead would bring some closure to another family, but never hers. She decided to take a shower and start prepping for her day tomorrow. There was no telling what Montgomery had up his sleeve.

So far all Jacob knew was that she wasn't married, and was adopted. He was scanning every piece of information about Amelia Randolph that he could. He needed to find something to connect them. To get her to relax some when he was around. She was 26, graduated from Maryland University. Worked at DSS on a flexible schedule.

She was practically broke, and had fairly good credit. He scanned her finances and noticed she spent a great deal of money looking for someone named Evan Hollinger. Whoever he was, she really wanted him found. Prior to age 12 there were no records for her. He sat back in his chair and spun to look out the window. Something about her fascinated him. Sure, she was beautiful, but that wasn't it.

He had been around beautiful women most of his life. Something wholesome about her made him want to know more. Whatever it was he was not giving up. He was used to getting and doing what he wanted and he wasn't going to start losing at the game now. She was all fire, and all talk. He would find a way to reach her and when he did, he would enjoy their time together. He smiled to himself before heading to take a shower.

The next morning was cold and gray. There was a bitter chill in the air that was hard to shake off. Amelia knew she needed to bundle up and she chose some casual clothes for the day. Denim and an oversized white sweater as well as her knee high leather boots. She put on her coat and hat, leaving her hair down for the extra layer of warmth. She glanced at the clock and swore. She was never late, ever. Why today of all days did she have to rush? She hastily grabbed her purse and made her way to her car. She didn't even have time for coffee that certainly added to her mood. She climbed in and turned the car over and nothing happened. She tried again.

"Really?" She said it out loud. The car had been giving her issues for a while now, but it was not the day. Of all days, not the day.

She jumped out of the car and shut her door with a bang. Now she would have to call someone and try and get the thing towed over to a garage. She hastily called Montgomery Enterprises.

After ten minutes of dealing with some snotty girl she passed on her message. He was probably laughing at her misfortune and happy she wouldn't be there to get in the way. She kicked the curb on her way back into her room and waited to hear from him.

Oh man, she was going to be angry, he smiled slightly thinking about her reaction. He wouldn't doubt it if she was kicking in the side of her car right now. He hung up his phone and looked around the penthouse for his coat. He decided to try and get on her good side and so he sent her a text asking where she was staying.

Perhaps there was some way he could put her back in a good mood before he arrived. He made his way downstairs and to his personal car. He liked to venture out on his own sometimes and today was the perfect day for it. He glanced up at the sky and frowned. It was probably going to snow later today. They weren't going to have much time if he didn't hurry. He pulled out onto the highway and made his way into town.

She was puzzled by his message, at least she assumed it was him. It wasn't like he had said "hey, it's Montgomery." She was frustrated by the whole situation and her lack of expertise when it came to cars. She needed to take a class or something. This was an awful situation to be in.

She saw him pull up before she even looked at who was driving. The red sports car was sleek and shiny and she knew it could only belong to Montgomery. She walked towards him from the lobby as he got out. He was handsome in black denim and a polo shirt. He had on a black coat and gloves, which he took off as he made his way over to her. He even had a sexy sway to his walk. She rolled her eyes, disgusted with herself.

He tried to gauge her mood as he made his way over to her. She had her arms crossed again, a sure sign she wasn't happy. Her jeans were tight, perfectly tight. She had rounded hips, he wanted to touch and her mane of hair flowed down past her shoulders. He wondered what it would feel like if he put his hands in it. Instead, he gave her a smile.

"I figured I could just pick you up and we go together. Saves time and gas."

"You could have told me you were coming. Or said who you were when you text me, you know?"

"Sorry, I was in a hurry." He frowned at her slightly. She really was always in a foul mood. "If you're coming I suggest we get going." He turned and headed towards his car.

She felt bad immediately. What was wrong with her, she was never this short tempered. She followed him to the car and slid into the seat, buckling up as he shut her door for her. She waited until she was inside before addressing the topic at hand.

"Listen Montgomery, I'm sorry. I don't know what's wrong with me. I'm just so concerned about Nana. This car situation just pushed me over. I appreciate the ride, really." She gave him a quick glance as he buckled up.

"My pleasure, and please call me Jacob. Using my last name reminds me of high school football. I don't want to revisit that." He grimaced slightly and she smiled.

They made their way to the water treatment plant near Daniel Island. It had been a huge undertaking for the company and he had overseen every aspect of the project. He had educated himself about the filtration process, but he wished now that he had learned more about the engineering of it. It was a gleaming metal unit attached on one side to the building that held the support offices and the staff who maintained it.

They made their way down and into the building. She had never been this close to it before and was in awe at the mechanics that went into running something of this magnitude. He asked for Benjamin Astren the manager of the plant and they were quickly greeted by a round man with a face as red as an apple. His happiness was almost infectious as he pumped both of their hands and led them into a control room. Most of what he said made no sense to her, but she took in every aspect of the system and how it worked.

"This channel here, do they lead strictly to Daniels Island or does it cover something else as well?" Both men turned her way and Benjamin answered.

"This filtration channel strictly runs to Daniels, more specifically the smaller end of Beresfor Creek. You can see the larger system pumps into the larger area of Beresford and then branches to Nowell Creek."

She looked over the system more before following them down towards the actual filtering controls. If the filtering channel ran strictly to Daniels Island than the issue would have to be central to that one run. She moved towards the huge pumping filters. They were massive and connected the water in the creeks into the system and then back into the holding tanks that would then pump water to the homes where they were directed. The whole set up was beautiful, even if it was making people sick.

"I have set up something for you both. I understand that there has been some concern on your part Miss Randolph about the water content. I have some instruments here, and if you would like to I'd be happy to allow you both to take your own samples and run them through the testing equipment. I think this could help with what you're looking for."

She smiled at him and readily agreed. They spent the next two hours moving and testing water both filtered and unfiltered. They talked about life in general, her work and his and she found that he really wasn't too bad to spend time around after all. He was still a rich snob, and a bully, but he wasn't as bad as she originally thought.

He was feeling the same way. She was a strong and smart woman and, unlike most women he knew, she didn't care that her clothes were wet and messy. She was on a mission and was all businesslike about it. She needed to know the truth. He loved the tinkling sound her laugh made when she wasn't trying so hard to be stern. He wanted to kiss her, right there with water spraying on them in the frigid air.

Even in these temperatures he was on fire thinking about it, about her. Eventually they were done and what they found left them both puzzled. There was no indication of any levels of negative or harmful properties in the water. What was being sent into Daniels Island was as pure as it could come.

What bothered him was the lack of an Hd5 filter he had specifically asked for on the system. It hadn't been put on the system and he had a pretty good idea why. The bored had fought him on the cost. They both left the plant lost in thought. After an audible sigh coming from her he glanced her way. She was upset and visibly so.

"I know you wanted, needed even, something to be there in that water. I had it tested over and over again. I also know, given your personality you wouldn't believe me unless you did the testing yourself."

"What do you mean my personality? Contrary to what you may think I am a very pleasant person to be around." He gave her a look with a half grin and she knew she was delivering him exactly what he had been referring to.

"Yeah, okay, I get it, I can be... difficult. It's just Nana, it doesn't make any sense at all Jacob. She is fine then goes home and then is sick again and everything they test at the hospital says it's in something she drinks. She only drinks water, I know that for a fact. That's all she has ever drank." She tapped her fingers on her lips in thought.

"I'm not sure what it is, but I'll continue to keep digging. I like it when you're not angry at me." He smiled at her again.

She felt the heat rising in her face. He had the most unusual ability to make her blush. She usually had a firm control on it. He turned left as they entered town and she frowned. This was not the way to the hotel. She felt the panic start building and she gripped the handle of the car door.

"Where are we going?" She gritted out the words. He turned to see her white faced and gripping the door. What was wrong?

"Hey, you ok? I was going to stop off for lunch, that's all. There is a diner right there see?" He pointed ahead and she could see the building. She relaxed and pulled her hand off the door handle.

"That's great, I'm starving." She gave him a weak smile and he frowned. Something was not right and he intended to find out what it was.

She excused herself to go to the bathroom once they were inside. She splashed some water on her face fighting the tears she didn't want to come. When would she ever stop being afraid? It wasn't often, but when the panic would set in, it was hard to shake off. Jacob wasn't going to hurt her, she knew that.

There was something about the day Evan had disappeared and the way the man had grabbed her. If he hadn't come along she might have made it home. She stood and used a paper towel to blot dry her face. She pushed her mass of hair back and pinched her cheeks for color. She frowned slightly. Was she really in here primping for Jacob Montgomery? She turned and made her way into the restaurant.

He noticed the color had returned to her face as she sat down. He continued to watch her as she ordered food and he gave her a smile once he had done the same. They made random small talk and he smiled again.

"What are you smiling at Jacob?" she leaned forward in the booth slightly.

"Nothing at all Amelia, I am appreciative of how you do things that's all."

She frowned again, that didn't sound very promising. "What do you mean how I do things?"

"I'm just used to women being a certain way that's all. I like you better." He flashed a smile at her again and she blushed.

"What's wrong with me that I'm not like other women?" The words were no sooner out of her mouth and the waitress delivered the food. She looked down at the massive meal before her. Chiliburger, fries, milkshake and cherry pie. She took a gulp and blushed as she looked up at him, "Point taken." His laughter was loud and she joined in with him.

"You are too much Amelia." He wiped at his eyes and started to attack the food on his side.

They hadn't been eating long when a leggy blond came into the diner. She gave a once over around the room until she found who she was looking for. Amelia knew trouble when she spotted it and this was definitely going to go badly.

The blond stopped at the table and made eye contact with Amelia. The two instantly disliked each other. The air surrounding the blond was enough to make you choke. She held her head up high and had a disgusted look on her face as she glanced around at the other patrons in the room.

"Jacob, darling." She said it sweetly and he gave a start as he glanced up at her.

"Jessalyn, wow, what are you doing here?" He stood up quickly and glanced over at Amelia.

"I called the office and they said you were stopping here on your way back, I had to see you darling, and something important has come up." She looked down her nose at Amelia before adding. "Darling, what are you doing in a place like this?"

He gritted his teeth and introduced the two. "Jessalyn this is Amelia, Amelia, Jessalyn."

"Nice to meet you." Amelia managed to get out. She received a half smile from her counterpart.

"Jessalyn, now is not a good time we are working on some business together and I'm driving."

"Really Jacob we need to talk, it looks like there is another person here with you, " she gestured at all the food on the table, "Can they not take her home, I really need to chat with you." She felt the sting of the words and noticed he had the decency to look angry.

Before he had a chance to make it worse, she decided to chime in. "Jacob its fine, I can find my way to the hotel, it's just around the corner. Go its fine." She leaned back in the chair, noticing the pained look on his face.

"No, it's not right here." He threw her his keys. "Drive it to your hotel and I'll come get it later. I'll just ride with her." Before she could turn him down he left and escorted blondie with him.

It wasn't really about what she said. It was really about how this woman was the type Jacob was obviously interested in. She never wanted to be like that. She would take her jeans and a chili burger every day of the week before she would show up and look down her nose at the world. She finished her lunch and decided to take the sports car for a ride to the hospital. The rest of the evening flew by for them both.

Jacob's head was reeling and he wasn't sure what he was going to do. Jessalyn had come back here just to tell him she may be pregnant. The last thing he needed was a baby with a woman he didn't love. It changed his entire thought process. If it was his of course he would be a good father. There was nothing more important than that. She was going to the doctor tomorrow and then he would know what was going on.

He looked over at his clock. 8 pm. Amelia was probably wondering when he was coming to get his car. He loved that car, he was still surprised he had given her the keys. He tried to call her but no answer. He smiled. She had been carefree and relaxed. He liked her that way. Whatever had caused her to panic in the car is what concerned him. Something wasn't right there and he decided to look into it. He sat forward and opened his computer.

Her back was killing her. All she could think of was the pain she was feeling and her eyes flew open to investigate the culprit. She was draped across the chair in Nans room and the blanket someone had draped over her had twisted itself into the nuisance currently digging into her back. She glanced at the clock and yawned. It was 10 o'clock. She needed to get back to the hotel.

She felt around the table for her keys and frowned at the weight of them. Suddenly her eyes opened wide. She still had his car. Damn. She jumped up carefully tiptoeing out of the room and rushed out to the car. She slipped into his cool leather seats. It was only then that she noticed the snow was falling. She grabbed around for her phone and noticed he had called. She decided to text him in case he was asleep.

"Fell asleep, sorry. Your car is at my hotel whenever you want it."

She carefully made her way through town with a smile on her face as the snow fell gently in waves. She had just pulled into a spot and jumped out when she heard something behind her. She stopped.

"Hey beautiful come hang out with me." He was drunk and walking towards her car. He was halfway between her and the hotel. She grabbed her purse and started to run past him. He reached out and grazed her arm and she went into a full panic. She sprinted past him and ran into something hard and warm. She looked up and Jacob was the last thing she saw before she fainted.

Warmth. She always loved it. She snuggled down into the blankets and sighed. She had been having the most wonderful dream about Jacob kissing her. Jacob! She sat up with a start. The last thing she remembered was looking up at him.

"Hey there sleepyhead." He was comfortably draped out in a chair beside her bed and reading through some paperwork. She looked over at the clock. It had only been an hour since she left the hospital.

"What happened? What happened to that man did he leave?" She was frantic now and shaking like a leaf. He walked towards her and wrapped her in a hug.

"He is gone, Amelia, I called the police and he is gone." He felt her relax in his arms. She smelled like lavender.

He wanted nothing more than to stay just like this. She raised her head to look at him and it was more than he could take. He crushed his mouth to hers. Tasting and exploring. He had wanted to kiss her since the elevator and it was better than he had expected. He felt her let go and he deepened the kiss. He slid both hands into her hair and pulled her head closer still. They fed on each other's lips until finally the kiss broke.

He stared at her, wanting her. He couldn't remember a time in his life where he wanted someone more. She was panting, having been as rocked by the kiss as he. Not like this, he wanted her but not because she was vulnerable. He stood and walked over to the window. The snow was falling and it was getting deeper by the moment. If he didn't leave now he would be stuck here.

"Jacob, are you going to leave? You don't have too, if you don't want to." She wasn't sure if she was motivated by fear or desire. She just didn't want him to leave.

"I don't want to leave, Amelia. I'm rarely one for doing the right thing, trust me." He glanced over at her. "You've had a rough night, I don't want to take advantage of you. When we make love

I want it to be because you want to." The last words he spoke as he looked at her.

She needed no other convincing. She wanted him. He had been there for her, and stayed to make sure she was ok. He had helped her try to find out the problem with the water. He had been there. She stood beside the bed and took off her pants as he watched her.

She climbed back onto the bed on her knees and pulled her shirt over the top of her head. She rid herself of the rest of her clothing quickly and he was afraid to move. She was perfect, if he moved he was afraid he would ruin it somehow. He managed to say her name through gritted teeth.

"Amelia, are you sure?" At her nod, he quickly made his way over to her. He covered her in kisses and so started a night they would never forget.

The sun was almost angry. That was the only thing she could think of at the intrusive way it beamed in on her. She glanced at the clock and was shocked it was 9 am. She never slept this late. She tried to sit up and felt the chill in the air. Suddenly the previous night flooded her memory. She looked around her. She was in a tangled mess of sheets, and she was alone. She wrapped one around her and made her way over to a note on the table.

"Be back soon, getting breakfast. Shower. We need to talk." J

She smiled as she made her way to the shower. Gone were the fears of the night before. She knew she would have to explain it all to him in time. She frowned, in time? She would be a fool to think this was anything more than a one time thing. Especially after meeting "blonde and leggy" yesterday.

This was just one of those things that happened. He probably thought she was some slut anyway since they had only met this week. She shrugged, she owned everything she did, good or bad. She showered and dressed quickly waiting for him to return.

A mile away Jacob was all smiles. Jessalyn was not pregnant, and he was falling for a red haired siren. He had gotten the call while waiting for the food to take back to the hotel and he was relieved. He really wanted to focus on where this was going with Amelia.

He had never felt so alive, so free. He made his way back to the hotel carrying the food when he noticed the men working on the pipes beside the diner they had visited just the day before. He stopped the car and a thought occurred to him. With a huge smile he made his way up to her room.

"Amelia... you in there?" He knocked on the door and pulled her into his arms as she opened it. He put the food on the table and grabbed her hand. "We have to go, come on." She was confused. What was he running all crazy about? He was on his way back out and noticed she was only half dressed and had a head full of wet hair. She noticed him taking in her appearance.

"Yeah, so I was thinking I could finish getting dressed first and then you can tell me what's got you so worked up." She moved to slide on her jeans and he watched her every move. He was fascinated by her.

"Sorry, I get excited sometimes. I think I have an answer for you, first let's eat. There is snow everywhere and you need to eat."

"Yeah, because I'm so skinny I may just float away." She said it with sarcasm and a smile.

"I don't like skinny, I like curves." He glanced at her and crossed his arms, "You'll do." She threw a pillow at him as she wound her hair up in a ponytail and sat down to eat a quick breakfast.

"So you have an answer about what?" She sipped her coffee and ate her food.

"Oh no, it's a surprise, just eat and we will go." He gave her a huge smile as she licked her fingers clean. She was adorable.

"What?" She shrugged. He handed her a coat and they made their way to the car.

As they rode along she thought it was a good time to bring up last night."Jacob listen. Last night was great. I don't want you to worry I will be expecting anything. I hope we can be friends and everything." She watched the trees fly by as she said it.

"What are you talking about? Expect anything? This isn't high school, Amelia.

"I'm just saying..."

"I know exactly what you're saying." He cut her off and she frowned. She had given him an out, and he was pissed. She glanced back out the window and frowned, they were headed to her Nana's house, she was sure of it. He made the final turn and pulled into the driveway of her childhood home."Jacob what are we doing here?" She got out and waited as he pulled a large bag out of the trunk.

"I was thinking, your Nana was getting sick when she was at home drinking, but the water tested fine at the plant. The only solution is the pumping system here at the house."

They made their way around the house to the old water cover and pump. She knew factually it hadn't been changed or looked at in at least 12 years. He pulled the cover off the system and turned on the water directly coming out of the pipe. He put some in a vial and put two drops of something in it and shook. It took less than a minute before theater turned a dark blue color.

"I knew it, the lead levels are through the roof. The problem is the system outside the house Amelia."

She took the vial from him in awe. All this time she had been coming after him and the problem was, literally, in the backyard. She made her way inside and he followed. She sat at the kitchen table and rested her head in her hands. Now she would get it fixed, and everything would go back to normal.

"How much does one of those things cost?" She glanced over at him as he looked around her old room. "It varies really, not too much." He smiled at her.

"Listen, I don't know what I said earlier, but I was trying to make it easy for you to walk away, you get that right?" She crossed her arms over her chest. Something she had done many times before.

"Amelia, I don't want to be let off the hook, I want you, I want to be there for you when it gets hard, I want to eat chili burgers together and be close if you panic again, and you don't have to be scared of anything ever again." He took a step towards her and she frowned.

"What are you talking about? Panic again or scared anymore?" She looked up at him and her face fell. "Did you look up information about me, Jacob?"

He looked scared before he answered. "Yes, but I wanted to get to know you that's all I didn't know about, everything you had been through."

"So you found out all about me and then slept with me? What was the reason, pity?" She was loud now, angry and crying.

"Amelia, no, it's not like that. He took a step towards her."

She stopped him, "Go Jacob, just go. NOW!"

Nothing left to say he made his way outside and spun his tires as he headed back to Charleston.

She had been back to work two weeks now. She tried to take on every case she could, to help take her mind off of things. Two weeks since she had seen him. He was still texting and calling and she refused to acknowledge any of it. He had betrayed her. She looked up from her desk.

Tonight she would go see her Nana and check on the new system she had purchased with a new credit card. It would take at least a year to pay it off, but it was worth it. She made her way to her car and set off for Daniel Island.

This had to work, he had tried everything else and yes, it was sneaky getting Nana in on it but she wouldn't respond to him. He was in love with her and she loved him too, if she would stop being so stubborn. He had hurt her, he knew that now, but he couldn't make it right if she avoided him.

He glanced over at Nana who was rocking happily in her chair. They had talked for hours about Amelia and she knew he loved Amelia very much. She had shared so much about Amelia he loved her even more than he had before. He stood when he heard the car pull up. She was going to be furious, and he knew it.

"She will only be mad for a moment son, she is always more bark than bite." Nana chuckled to herself.

The door opened and she came in with an armful of bags. "Nana what in the hell is that monstrosity out back? I didn't pay for that and I hope they don't think I'm going to. That model was $5,000 more dollars than the one I got you. Not that I don't want you to have the best but ..." She trailed off as she turned and saw him there.

"Don't get mad, don't say anything until I'm done Amelia." He glanced at Nana who gave him an encouraging nod. Amelia stood frozen to the spot. "I am in love with you Amelia Randolph and I probably was from the first day we met. I know what I did was wrong, I'm sorry if I hurt you. The truth is we belong together.

You help me be a better man and I'll force you to go to society balls and spend a lot of money on charities and things you will hate doing, but you will do it because you love me. I want to spend my life with you Amelia, and I want to face challenges together. I want to help you find Evan."

He looked over at her and the tears streaming down her face. Good or bad he wasn't sure yet. Nana, who always loved a good love story sat up on the edge of her seat and waited. With a sob Amelia threw herself into his arms and relished in the feel of him holding her. This was where she belonged. She looked up at him.

"That monstrosity out there I bought for Nana. She deserved the best. She brought us together, it was the least I could do." He gave Nana a grin and she just shooed him away. He hugged her close.

"Do you remember in the elevator that day, I said it was refreshing?" He smiled.

"Yes, what did you mean exactly?" She pulled away slightly.

"I meant it was refreshing to meet a woman who was beautiful and didn't even know it." He leaned in for a kiss.

Legal Affairs

Jennifer was ecstatic when she left her job interview because she knew she impressed Trevor, the charismatic, handsome lawyer with whom's firm she was seeking employment with.

"I see that you've worked as a paralegal for a couple years," Trevor commented after reading Jennifers's resume.

"Yes, I was hired right out of college by the law firm that represented my father when he owned some commercial property," Jennifer replied.

While she was trying to pay attention to his words, Jennifer was mesmerized by Trevor's striking blue eyes and dazzling smile. She also felt a twinge of excitement when she noticed that the debonair attorney wasn't wearing a wedding ring.

Trevor was brilliant, and even though he was a partner in a prestigious law firm, he was only 25 years old. He graduated college very early and finished law school before most of his classmates even completed high school.

"Where do you see yourself professionally in the next five years?" Jennifer was unprepared to answer this question, and while she tried her best to sound creative and profound, she worried that she came off silly and trite.

"I would like to be working for a well-established law firm where I could further my knowledge of the legal system as it pertains to corporate law and international economics," she sputtered.

Jennifer was so mortified by her reply that she could literally feel her face getting red and hot. She wished that she would have prepared for the interview more, but it was too late now, she thought.

Trevor seemed to be impressed with everything Jennifer had to say, and even more so with the tight, low-cut blouse she was wearing. Jennifer, or Jen, as she liked to be called, thought about dressing conservatively, but decided to be a bit more daring.

"Why should I hire you?" Again, Jen wasn't prepared to answer this question, but quickly came up with a clever answer that even she was impressed with. "This is my dream job.

Some of the other applicants might have more experience or better credentials than I do, but after a couple of months or so, I'll have those same credentials, and I'll also have the passion that those other applicants lack," Jen replied.

The rest of the interview went well and Trevor told Jennifer that he would be in touch. Jen's post-interview euphoria was short-lived because days went by with no phone call from the hunky legal eagle.

Finally, after about two weeks he called and left a message on her cell. "Hi, Jennifer, this is Trevor Parker from the law firm and I'm calling to see if you are still interested in the job, and if you are, please call me back."

Jennifer didn't want to seem desperate, so she waited a respectable 2 hours before she returned his phone call. She was so nervous, she could barely catch her breath, and for a minute, she thought about hanging up.

Trevor's secretary answered on the second ring and promptly transferred Jen over to his extension. "Trevor Parker speaking, may I help you?" Jennifer's heart skipped a beat but she managed to keep her cool. "Hello, Mr. Parker, this is Jennifer Adams returning your call."

Trevor responded, "Hey, Jennifer, thanks for calling back, and please, call me Trevor."

"Very well, Trevor!"

"Jennifer, I would like to offer you the paralegal position."

"Thank you, I accept," Jen replied.

"I'm a laid-back type of boss, so if you don't mind, why don't we discuss the details of the job over coffee at the corner cafe instead of at the office?"

Jen replied, "That would be great, I love that little cafe, it's so quaint."

Trevor responded, "Great, how does Thursday at 11:00 sound?"

"It sounds perfect," Jen said.

"Fantastic, I'll see you then!" replied Trevor.

Jennifer called everyone she knew to tell them about her new job. Actually it wasn't so much the job she was gushing over as it was her new boss, Trevor. She couldn't believe her good luck.

She never thought she would find a job this quick, and only in her wildest dream did she ever think that she would be working for someone who looked like Trevor. Not only was he gorgeous, he seemed very kind, easy to get along with and super funny.

Jen couldn't decide on what to wear for her meeting with Trevor, so she decided to buy something new. She really wasn't in a position to be buying new clothes, but this was a special occasion.

At the store, Jennifer tried on at least a dozen outfits but couldn't make up her mind. She finally decided on a tight-fitting black dress that was professional enough for a business meeting but seductive enough, she thought, to get Trevor's attention.

When Thursday finally rolled around, Jen was beside herself with excitement. She felt confident in how she looked, but she was so nervous that she forgot to put on lipstick.

Jen never goes out of the house without lipstick, but by the time she realized that she had forgotten to put it on, it was too late to turn back and go home. Instead, she ran into the closest drug store and bought a cheap tube.

Not only did she purchase the lipstick, she also purchased a box of condoms, just in case. Jen has never slept with someone after only meeting them once, but she had a feeling about how her meeting with Trevor was going to go.

Sure, this was a business meeting of sorts, but she felt such a connection to Trevor and she knew that it was reciprocated. She was very hot to trot for her new boss and wanted to be prepared in the event that things heated up after their meeting.

Trevor arrived early to the cafe and took the liberty of ordering two large coffees and a couple blueberry scones. Soon after, Jennifer arrived, confident in her appearance, thanks to her new lipstick purchase.

Trevor, the gallant gentlemen that he is, stood up and pulled out her chair. After exchanging pleasantries, they discussed the job.

Trevor offered Jen almost twice as much as she was making at her last job, and she wouldn't be working weekends or holidays either. "How does 4 weeks vacation sound?"

Jen's last job only allowed for a one week vacation after being on the job for a year, and having four weeks vacation was the icing on the cake. "It almost sounds too good to be true," she replied.

After Trevor and Jen were finished discussing the details of the job, their conversation quickly turned personal. They found out that they had mutual friends and that they once even worked for the same company.

After feeling more comfortable with one another, Trevor asked Jen if she would like to join him for dinner at his home.

He lived only a few blocks from the cafe, and because he was a gourmet cook, he was looking forward to preparing his new employee the best meal of her life. Feeding her, however, wasn't the only thing on his agenda.

Trevor was instantly attracted to Jennifer the moment he first saw her. The sexual chemistry was obvious, which is why Jen purchased the condoms at the drug store when she bought her lipstick.

"Your home is spectacular," Jen told Trevor.

"Thank you, Jen. I bought it from one of the partners of the law firm who retired to Florida about a year ago."

Before the couple made their way into the kitchen to start dinner, they started kissing as soon as they got into the house.

Jennifer vowed that if she ever "married rich," she would give her parents enough money so that their lives would change for the better.

She would pay all their bills, buy them a new home and make sure that they never worried about money again.

Trevor shook his head moving closer to her and putting his hands on her blouse. "We're being irrational. Just go for it. He ripped the shirt from her body and it fell to the floor. His lips went to her neck, while her hands went to his shirt, removing it from the confinement of his dress pants.

She started off tediously undoing button after button, but then knew that she needed to move the show on the road. She busted open his shirt, the way that he had busted open hers.

Her hands trailed down his chest, while he continued to kiss her neck. She arched her back, sighing against his kisses. His hands went behind her back, as he slowly removed her bra. Her breasts pressed hard against his bare chest.

Her hands went to his pants and she quickly removed them. They fell to the floor and he kicked them off. Then his hands went to his boxers and she drug them down his legs, while his hands caressed her nipples. She eyed his manhood, salivating at the sight.

His hands slowly slid down her stomach and then wrapped around her back. He undid the zipper to her skirt and it fell to the floor.

His hands went to her panties and he looped his fingers through them, tugging them off of her body. Before she had time to comprehend the next move, she felt him lifting her into his arms and laying her down on the floor.

Their lips met, his tongue dipping inside her mouth. As their tongues clashed together, his hands continued to massage her breasts, gently feeling each part of her sensitive skin.

As he was about to enter her, he pulled back. "Damn, I don't have a condom," he groaned, starting to regress.

"It's your lucky day, because I have one," Jen coyly replied. She had almost forgotten that she bought them earlier.

She wrapped her arms around him and pulled him closer to her. "Ugh..." she groaned, arching her back, but not breaking from the kiss.

As each thrust turned harder, she was forced to part from the kiss. "Ugh...Oh God...yes..." she whimpered, barely able to get the words out, it felt so good.

As one arm continued being wrapped around him, her other arm fell down to her side and she tried desperately to grab anything to hold onto, finally choosing for a leg to his chair. Her hips bucked against his.

He pressed up against her, with a hunger that she never endured. "Oh God...yes...yes..." he cried, pressing harder to her core.

"Wow..." she sighed, closing her eyes and just lying there. As she was focusing on her next move, she felt hands on her legs, parting her ever so softly.

Then it was over and she was fighting disappointment, until she felt something else. She tried to control her breathing, as she felt his tongue exploring every inch of her body.

She felt the smoothness of his moves and she sighed against his deep and masculine movements. "Hm...hmmm...hm..." she signed, her body gliding against the intensity.

As his tongue was seeking out each crevice that she could provide, she felt her body begin to shake with desire.

As his tongue slowly weaved its way out of her mouth, she dropped her hands from his head. She closed her eyes and took in deep and slow breaths. She felt him easing his way back up her. Her eyes opened and she stared at him. She only saw desire and nothing else.

He wrapped his hand around her neck and pulled her into a breathless kiss. His tongue circling around hers. He pulled from the kiss, bringing his mouth down to her flesh of her neck. She could barely keep up, as she was fighting exhaustion.

She closed her eyes and tried to focus on his intimate paths around her skin. Between kisses, she heard his words. "God, you're sexy!" She could relish in that forever.

When she felt him retracting, she heaved a sigh. He fell off of her and she could hear the restlessness that he felt. "Wow..." he mumbled, as they both just laid there and tried to catch their breath.

After their rendevous, Trevor led Jennifer into the kitchen while he prepared their dinner. Not only was Jennifer impressed by is sexual prowess, she was also floored by his cooking skills. "Where in the world did you learn how to cook like this?"

Trevor replied, "Believe it or not, I studied in Paris at the Cordon Bleu after graduating from law school." He went on to say, "I had dreams of owning my own restaurant for as long as I can remember."

The dinner was extraordinary, and Jennifer couldn't believe her good luck. What more could she ask for? She was just offered a great-paying job, her laywer boss was gorgeous and very interested in her, he was a great lover and an amazing cook.

Jennifer wouldn't starting her job at Trevor's law firm for two more weeks, and during this time, she was hoping that she would be able to spend more time with him to get to know him better.

After they finished dinner and chatted for a while longer, it was time for Jen to leave. Trevor was leaving for a business trip in the morning and would need to leave for the airport very early.

The couple kissed good-bye and Trevor assured Jen that he would call her when he settled into his hotel room the next day.

Jennifer couldn't think about anything but Trevor. He's the best lover she'd ever had, and even though they only knew each other for a day or so, she felt that she was falling in love with him.

Jen believed in love at first sight, and when she called her mother to tell her that she's met the man of her dreams, her mother was not as thrilled as Jen hoped she would be.

"What do you know about this guy?" Jen replied, "I know that he's a rich, gorgeous lawyer who makes a mean chateaubriand steak."

Jennifer's mother had an uneasy feeling about the whole thing, but she tried to sound happy and encouraging.

Jen waited for Trevor to call her when he got to the hotel the next day. When it got to be 10pm, she got concerned, not because she didn't think he would call, but because she feared that something may have happened to him. Since Jennifer didn't have Trevor's cellphone number, she was unable to call him to make sure he was alright.

Trevor never called that night, and in fact, Jen never heard from him at all. After two weeks went by, it was time for Jen to start her new job at Trevor's law firm.

When Jennifer arrived at the office, the receptionist let Trevor know that Jennifer was waiting to see him. When Trevor walked into the lobby, Jennifer could barely catch her breath.

She was expecting a robust welcome from her new boss in light of their wild night of passionate sex, but instead, he greeted her with a curt, "Good morning Ms. Adams. Welcome to the law firm." He barely looked at her.

Trevor acted like he didn't even know Jen, and because of this, she felt like walking out the door. She didn't even want to start her new job. How could he treat her like this, she wondered. She wondered if she'd said something to offend him or if he was turned off by her passion.

Jennifer asked Trevor how his business trip was and he replied with a cold, "Very well, thank you." Jen was shocked by his attitude and was even starting to feel a little scared.

Although she thought of quitting, she decided to make the best out of the job. It paid well, it was close to her home and the benefits were excellent. Jennifer was going to ask Trevor what his problem was and why he was treating her so poorly, but she decided to just let it go.

She was simply going to chalk up the experience with Trevor as a one-night stand. She's had them before where the guy never called her, so why should this time be any different. It was just weird because this time, the guy was going to be her new boss.

After a couple days, Jen was starting to settle into her new job, and despite all the drama with Trevor, she was actually starting to feel comfortable. She got along with the other lawyers and paralegals, and while Trevor still treated her like a stranger, he was very professional towards her.

It wasn't until about a month later that Jen found out that Trevor's great grandfather started the law firm many years ago and than his grandfather and father had also been partners. The firm was steeped in tradition and professionalism, and Trevor intended to keep it that way.

Jennifer also treated Trevor with respect and never held his icy attitude towards her against him. As time went by, Trevor started to warm up. One day, he asked Jennifer to come into his office.

She didn't think anything of it and assumed it was to talk about a case she was working on. Jen enjoyed working on this particular case because she got to know the client and his wife very well. They were extremely nice, and they even told Trevor how highly they thought of Jennifer. This is exactly what he needed to hear.

Trevor held his law firm in very high regard because it was so steeped in tradition. He only employed those who he considered loyal, and who wouldn't "crack" under the pressures of working for him.

Doing what he did to Jennifer was somewhat of a test to determine if she had what it took to still do her job despite extenuating circumstances. He fully expected her to quit or not even show up on the first day of her job because he failed to call her after their sexual encounter.

After Jen proved that she could maintain her professionalism and even excel at her job in spite of what happened, proved to Trevor that she was the type of employee that he wanted at his law firm.

Trevor finally decided that he had to come clean. "I had to do what I did to prove to myself that you were right for the law firm."

He also said, "You see, Jen, I just wanted to make sure that you would still be able to perform your job in spite of adverse circumstances."

Jennifer replied, "I actually cared for you, and for me, it was more than just a one night stand."

Trevor responded, "I had feelings for you as well and even though I wanted so badly to call you when I got to the hotel, I just couldn't."

Trevor further explained that the law firm was almost "sacred" to him and he had to do everything in his power to ensure that the employees were dedicated and that they would not quit just "because."

While Jennifer thought his tactics were unethical, in a way, she understood why he did what he did. A couple of paralegals and attorneys quit abruptly at her last job, leaving the clients in the lurch. Because they quit so suddenly, cases were delayed, which often caused financial hardships for the litigants.

Trevor and the other partners in the law firm always saw to it that their clients were treated with the utmost respect and that their legal cases were handled as quickly and efficiently as possible.

Trevor now knew that Jen was "true blue" and dedicated to the law firm. She had a strong work ethic and her legal skills were an asset to the company. Once Trevor explained the reason behind his behavior, the couple hugged. Jen said, "I'm so glad you finally explained yourself."

She further said, "I don't think what you did to me was right, but I'm hoping that maybe we can start over, now that I "proved" myself to you." Trevor sheepishly replied, "I would love it."

The couple took it slowly and were very discreet around the office. They didn't want anyone to know about their relationship. After a few months, Jen and Trevor declared their love for one another and decided to get engaged.

Jen eventually applied to law school and was accepted. When she graduates and passes the bar exam, she'll become a partner in the law firm that she almost stopped working for.

The Billionaire's Desire

Alexander Jacobs knew his life would be different from now on. Nothing could prepare him for the changes coming. Had he known, he would have done something differently, prepared somehow. He would have tried to make his father proud of him, and he would have loved his mother more.

He hung his head in his hands. There was nothing he could do now. His life was changed, and all he had left to focus on was tomorrow. His life was quiet now, too quiet.

His parents were both gone. They were killed by a drunk driver, he had no siblings, and only a few friends he could count on one hand, friends he could trust that is.

He sat back in the high backed chair and took a deep breath. Even the friends he did have were busy with their own lives. He was 23, still too young to know what he was doing most of the time, and now he was going to have to run a business that he hadn't much thought about before.

He enjoyed the fruits of the family business. He always had everything he needed or wanted. He was spoiled and selfish. He shook his head. Now he had to grow up.

Alex glanced up at the clock on the mantle. The meeting started at 2. That gave him ten minutes to get his head together. He started rifling through the ledger on his desk, trying to prepare for the day ahead.

His parents had been gone almost a week. The funeral was yesterday. They deserved more...deserved better. He would do his best to make them proud. He knew he would have to because there was no one else who could.

The only bright spot in his life yesterday at the funeral was Brienne. Brienne Warhol had been there. He remembered the day he first saw her in 4th grade. She was all elbows and freckles with her long red hair in braids. She was beautiful. They grew up on the same street, or close to it.

She was always a gangly tomboy, playing in the dirt and riding bikes with the boys while all the other girls were happy playing inside with Barbie and practicing with makeup and nail polish. He smiled thinking about the 6th grade dance.

He prepared to ask Brienne for weeks, but she never seemed to notice he was there. She was always busy with everything else. Most of the boys thought of her as one of them, but not Alex. He was very much aware of the fact that Brienne was a girl. He had it all planned out and walked up to her at lunchtime. She was sitting at a table with some of their friends all arm wrestling each other. He took a deep breath and simply said:

"Brienne, will you go to the dance with me?" He said it casually despite his racing heart and had taken his usual seat across from her while waiting on a response.

"Sure." She said it so quickly he had to look at her to catch her eye and make sure she was actually responding to him. She gave him a slight smile and set out to arm wrestle, and beat, Bobby Anderson on the next match.

His dad sent him in the company car to pick her up the night of the dance and he was terrified. She came down the stairs in a green dress and her hair all brushed out. It looked just like fluffy orange cotton. She was beautiful. He opened the door for her, and once they were inside, she started chattering away about school and how these girl shoes were so dumb.

He just let her talk. He liked the way she went on and on. He was always the quiet one and she didn't know how to be. It may have been because she had no mother, and her dad was doing the best he could with her. Whatever the reason, she always had a lot to say.

They pulled into the school parking lot and immediately their group of friends gathered around. It was just like any other school day. At some point she had braided her hair so it would stop "flying all over the place" as she put it. The rest of the night was spent with the group of friends. No dancing, and certainly not what he planned.

He shook his head and smiled as he was brought back to the present. She came to the funeral. She was there for him, and he loved her all the more for it. They were friends now, not as close, but still friendly enough.

She would send him emails from school and he would write back talking about whatever was going on in their sleepy town of Dale City Virginia, as well as what was happening to their friends and who was moving and who had come back.

He enjoyed the way she would write about her classes, which ones were easy, and which were harder for her, and the way men seemed to always want to ask her out and not ask her opinions. She had gone off to New York after high school. She always dreamed of going there, and since her goal was Columbia Law, she thought her best option was doing her undergraduate work there as well.

Brienne always worked hard to do well. Alex would frequently ask her if she needed anything and she always told him no. She was defiant and determined to succeed. He admired that in her. He went to college locally at Mary Washington and studied Business. He didn't have a clue what he wanted to do and his father told him it was a great back up for whenever he figured it out.

Today he was thankful for that. Seeing Brienne yesterday after such a long time felt good. Gone were the braids and freckles, and in their place, was a sophisticated woman. She was still as beautiful as the day he met her. He never even had a chance to speak with her though. She gave him a wave at one point, and he smiled back.

She was rarely in town, and when she was, he always tried to make time for her. They would usually eat Chinese take-out and laugh and listen to music from the year they graduated. The last time she visited was over two years ago. Even then, she hadn't strayed much from The Brienne of middle school. It was obvious something changed. Yesterday, he was surrounded by his parents' friends and business associates. By the time he was able to get a few moments alone, she disappeared.

It would be easy to find her. Still in the same house, her father lived down the street. They lived in the cul-de-sac of the neighborhood off the loop that led to his house.

Alex's parents were wealthy and enjoyed living in a mansion. They planned to have more children but it never come to pass. Brienne's house was part of the mill town and he knew he would find her there.

He had every intention of going to see her tonight. After this meeting of course. He stood and grabbed his paperwork, took a deep breath and headed down the corridor. He could do this.

Two hours later, Alex pulled forcefully on the tie at his throat. What a mess. The merger was two days away when his parents were killed. He wanted to go home and grieve but this paperwork had to be done before something, or someone, showed up to rock the proverbial boat.

He spent two hours being briefed about acquisitions and merger paperwork. The logistics of operations and the appointing of officers to manage the foreign accounts was making his head spin, but he had to learn every detail of the business.

The only person he trusted was Jameson, who was his father's trusted advisor and best friend. He was the one who prepped him for today and the one who would help him take the business to the next level. Alex would be fine, he had no other choice.

Alex headed home to organize the pieces of his life he could still control and to change and relax before tackling the next big thing that would inevitably come up. The driver pulled up to the gate and they moved on until they rounded the front of the house.

Not really one for the rules, Alex jumped out of the car as they stopped. He refused to wait for the chauffeur to open the door for him. He was capable and refused to follow all of the rules.

He bounced up the front stairs and opened the door to the main hall. He could smell his mother's perfume when he entered the house. He hoped it would always be that way, but sadly time erases everything. He made his way upstairs and changed into jeans and a t-shirt.

He was sure being seen in town like this was something frowned upon now that he was the head of the business. He was suddenly forced to become his father. The thought made him cringe as his father had been stern and fair, but not easily approachable. His mother was the nurturer and his father the businessman.

Alex ran a hand through his black hair and looked at his reflection for a moment. He had lines around his eyes. The stress was already taking a toll and it had been days. He had short black hair and blue eyes. Not unattractive he supposed.

He dated his fair share of women and enjoyed having fun and meeting new people. He would figure out his new life as he went. He shrugged and grabbed his jacket as he headed out. He decided to walk. The April air was crisp and clean, and it helped him to clear his head.

Brienne always had something to say that would make sense, make it better. She never indicated she was interested in Alex at all. Once upon a time he thought she was the one for him, but instead, become good friends. That was worth so much more than romance or sex. He walked the ¼ mile in silence thinking about his parents.

They loved each other very much. They were always together and the night of the accident had been no different.

His father had been hosting a dinner to raise funds for one of his business mergers. His mother accompanied with him, ever devoted to her husband. They said goodbye to Alex that night as he watched television in the den eating a snack. He yelled a hello and gave them a wave and a glance before they left. Why didn't he go say goodbye the right way, why hadn't he hugged his mother? The fact that he barely gave them a wave made his resolve that much stronger. He would make his parents proud.

He made his way up the drive of the house Brienne grew up in. It was small and quaint but clean. Even now, her ten speed bike was propped up against the side of the house. Untouched in years, it was a symbol of a childhood long gone. She opened the door before he even knocked.

"Alex." She smiled at him and opened the screen door and came out on the porch. She hugged him tightly. "I'm so sorry about your parents." She stood back and he took her in. She was more beautiful than he could remember. She finally tamed her hair and was dressed in a black dress. She was elegant and he was lost.

"My dad is getting his treatments so I thought I should come outside to you." She walked over to the swing on the porch. Her father was sick, he thought. She had such a hard life growing up but she was strong. They sat on the swing together for a few moments and chatted about the weather. She asked about work and he shared and she told him about school and how soon after she graduated she would be going to Columbia. She had been accepted.

"Hey brat you made it in?" He sat up quickly.

"Yes I did." She nearly sparkled with the excitement.

"Wow that's great Brie. You worked so hard and I know you're excited." He grabbed her hand and gave her a squeeze.

"Thanks, I am overwhelmed really. I have so much to do to get ready and...well there is a lot." She smiled at him.

"Well we have to go to dinner tonight and celebrate, my treat." He offered and she accepted.

"We never get to hang out anymore, like old times." She sighed. "It was so much easier when we were kids. No one was sick and we all had each other. We had our family and friends." She sighed.

"It certainly has changed, you're still a brat though." He looked at the tree across the street, thinking. He stood up to go. "I'll pick you up at 6, and wear something nice." He smiled at her as she stuck her tongue out at him. He made his way back up the hill towards the bend in the road which would lead back to his house.

Damn you Alex. She watched him leave. He was so handsome, and that was all she could think about. It made it hard for her to concentrate when he looked at her. She hated the way he called her brat. He'd done it since they were in middle school. She looked down at the slippers she was wearing.

They were so different, she and Alex. Once upon a time she thought he had a crush on her. It was probably at that horrible dance in 6th grade when she figured out he just wanted to be friends. He picked her up and she tried so hard to look pretty.

Her father enlisted help from the neighbor to help with "girl stuff." They did their best. No one knew about conditioner yet and her hair was always so unruly. He picked her up and they went to the dance. She talked him to death. It's what she did when she was nervous.

Everyone thought she was just one of the guys and in some ways, she was. She loved playing football and wrestling and she hated getting dressed up. But there was something about Alex that made her feel funny. Looking back she knew it was because he made her feel like a girl. Feeling like a girl was a new idea for her that was for sure. Once they arrived at the dance mean Mary

Jenkins pulled her aside in the bathroom and told her about the "bet".

The boys all bet that she would be "different" if she dressed like a girl. So she knew then they were testing her, fearful their friendship would be gone for good. So she braided her hair in the bathroom and went back to being one of the guys. She refused to allow her heart to hurt because she wanted Alex to like her. They were all friends and that was more important than anything else and they didn't want to lose her.

Even now she shook her head as she thought about it. The entire "group" was disbanded by now. Two of the group members left for the military. One was a teacher in town, one was killed in a boating accident, one was a police officer two towns over, and then there was she and Alex. It was funny that they were the only two who didn't have people in their lives. That alone made no sense. Alex was not only the most eligible bachelor in Dale City, he was gorgeous to boot. It made no sense at all.

She picked the pillow cushion on the seat as she swung lightly. She was no angel. She dated her fair share of men. Most of them where playboys and only wanting one thing from her. As she took her education more seriously, they took her less seriously. What she wanted was an equal, but who knew if that even existed. Alex was always out of her league anyway, he was rich, refined and charming, and she was all tomboy and barely had enough money to get through school.

Even today he in his designer jeans and she in her slippers with a hole in the big toe. She laughed lightly. They were on opposite ends of reality but they were friends and that was enough for her. She sighed, time to check on her father.

She made her way through the house and cringed. It was a mess. She hated leaving him alone for so long. She hadn't been home in two years. It was just too expensive to come home, she needed every penny for school. He said he understood but it was hard for him. He had gotten sick some time ago and it never seemed to go away.

He had breathing treatments and on the phone he always told her he was fine, being here now she knew he had been lying. The house was turned upside down. TV dinners and coffee seemed to be a staple for him and he had no one to come check on him. She found a clean spot on the couch in the living room and sat down to start planning her course of action and what she would tackle first.

A few hours later she looked around her. It was better than she had expected. She scrubbed every inch of the living room and kitchen. There wasn't a speck of dirt on anything and the four large trash bags on the front porch was a testament to her hard work. She was filthy. Her hair in braids and wearing jeans and a tank top, she was a visible mess.

Her father spent the afternoon resting and it wasn't until there was a knock on the front door that she even considered how long she had been at it.

She opened the front door to find Alex standing there. He was perfect. Blue suit and tie white shirt. His hair brushed back, he could have been on the cover of a magazine. She stood there for a moment before the realization set in that she had been working much longer than she realized. He smiled at her and it brought her back to reality quickly.

"Alex, I ...well see the thing is." She looked down at herself and he cut her off.

"I'm early brat, you have time to get ready unless you want to change the plan and do something more industrial?" She threw a rag at him and he chuckled. The truth was she was adorable. Hair in braids and cleaning, it was like he stepped back in time for a moment. He needed that moment. He felt normal even if for only a few moments. He settled onto a bar stool and watched her head upstairs to get ready.

"I'll hurry Alex, I promise." She called down the stairs to him.

"Just wash your hair, whatever you do, I think I saw a candy bar wrapper in there." He smiled.

He heard the bathroom door shut and the water come on. She always kept him amused if nothing else. He looked around the house. Her father was alone here and it was cozy. He much preferred a smaller space when being alone. It was nice - almost like the house was hugging you. Unlike the space Alex had at home. He was alone in a tremendous amount of space.

She bounded down the stairs and the transformation was astounding. She straightened her hair somehow and was wearing a dark blue dress with a square cut neckline and black pumps. Her face was alive with pink cheeks and some light gloss on her lips. Otherwise she was without make up.

"You gonna stare at me like I have two heads or are we going, Mr. Jacobs?" She put her hands on her hips and tapped her foot. He shook himself free of his thoughts and stood so they could go. The drive was pleasant and uneventful. He decided to drive them himself and made reservations in the town nearby.

They had reservations for 7, and he knew she was always multitasking so his early arrival was on purpose. They dined on oysters and salads, and he ordered steak for his main course. She had the fish. They chatted about the past and who was where. It was over dessert when a burly looking man came over to say hello.

"Alex and Brie...now if Junior and Jerry were here I'd be rich right now." He smiled and Alex stood and embraced his friend. Brie did the same and kissed Brandon on the cheek. He was part of the "group" and had managed to stay close by. He wasn't in uniform but Alex knew he become a cop a year or so ago. He was always the jokester of the group which made his profession that most interesting. He had always been the one to get them into trouble and now he was the one enforcing the rules.

"Just look at you two, how long has it been two three years?" Alex motioned for him to sit and he did so.

"My buddies and I are out celebrating a big bust we took down earlier today. I have to get back but after seeing "Red," over here." He hooked his thumb towards Brie. "I just had to come say hello."

Brie smiled at him. "You look great and congrats on the bust."

"I look the same, you on the other hand look great." He leaned towards her obviously flirting and joking at the same time.

"Sorry to hear about your folks Alex man, really. I was at the funeral but you were surrounded by people." He sobered for a moment.

"Thanks Bran that means a lot to me." Alex took a long drink. "So why would you be rich?"

"Oh yea that." He chuckled "A long time ago Jerry and Junior and I made a bet on who was going to marry Brie. They said Mason but not me, I said Alex. We all put two bucks in and buried it under the old cotton mill steps." He laughed and they joined in.

"Well we're not married so you'd still not be rich, besides that money was spent a long time ago." Alex smiled at the shocked look on his face.

"Well you two look married enough all fancy and laughing I just assumed..." he trailed off as Brie took a long drink of water. "Wait what do you mean that money was spent a long time ago?"

"Well the thing is Mason and I heard about your bet and we dug that money up and bought soda pop and chips one afternoon. We sat by the old mill and laughed at how we pulled one over on you all." Alex laughed at the look on his face.

"Well damn, and here I thought I had $6 in savings I could count on." He smiled at them and stood up. "I have to get going, y'all look real nice together so don't fight the love people." He sauntered off giving Brie a wink as he went.

"Well Bran has certainly not changed a bit." Brie changed the subject as to avoid and discussion about love.

"Have I told you you look beautiful tonight Brie? I'm slow so I doubt I have but I wanted you to know it."

He gave her a half smile and she blushed. What was wrong with him anyway, he was being awfully flirty. They wrapped up dinner and he headed back to her house. She had always been easy to talk to and having this time together was wonderful. She helped him feel more like himself than he had in a long time. They sat on the porch swing for a while. He wanted to enjoy laughing for a little while longer.

"When do you head back?" He glanced over at her on the swing.

"Tomorrow." She looked down at her hands. "I have registration Monday and classes start next week. I feel like I should turn it all down though. Dad, he is just not well and I worry about him."

"You can't turn it down Brie, you have to go. I can check in on him from time to time. You have worked too hard to quit now."

She looked over at him. "Really, you'll check on him? That's an awful lot to ask of you Alex, you have a company to run." She leaned back.

"Yes really, it will bring me back to reality from time to time." He smiled. He stood up from the swing. He knew if he stayed too long he'd make a fool of himself like he did long ago. She didn't think of him like "that" and he didn't want her to feel uncomfortable. He especially didn't want to ruin their friendship.

He gave her a hug and she leaned into it. If only he didn't think of her like a boy. She knew he didn't want to ruin their friendship, but it was hard not to want him to see who she was now. He was her best friend and that would have to be enough.

"I'll be back in June maybe we can do this again?" She smiled at him.

"Of course you know that." He was being polite in his words when what he wanted to do was kiss her.

They parted ways both thinking of the other. The night was long for them both. What they didn't realize is that life was about to change and it would be much longer than just June before they would see each other again.

Days turned into weeks and then months. Soon it had been a year since his parents had died. Alex was learning his new role proficiently. He had a hand in the last two accounts and things were looking up. He tried to do well and think like his father. It paid off.

He would get an email from Brie from time to time about classes and work but time between them grew wider and wider, she worked all the time it seemed. He checked in on Mr. Warhol every Sunday and he was doing remarkably well. He even had a lady friend that came around. He would leave voicemails for Brie occasionally and tell her about her father, but never heard back.

The months grew longer and the contact slowly grew more sporadic. He was busy with work and it consumed him. He dated a cute blonde from legal for a while a few months ago, but the drive to do better created some distance between the two of them.

He was alone. Once the solitude had frightened him but now he felt solace in numbers and accounting. One day he was reading the papers when he saw an article about a drug bust in Manassas. There on the page was Bran's ugly mug smiling happily like he hadn't a care in the world. He was promoted and Alex smiled. He deserved it. He read the article and was even more surprised that he was getting married as well.

"Well well well Brandon I can't believe you're taking the plunge." Alex grinned thinking about when he saw him last at the restaurant. He and Brie were having dinner. What was that a year ago now? He shook his head time was flowing by so fast. Brie...he hadn't thought about her in a while. He hoped she was doing well at school. Her curriculum was difficult, that much he knew. He decided to send her a quick email. He hadn't heard from her in 3 or 4 months now.

"Just checking in to say hello, hope your well. Your dad looks great and is happy with his new lady friend. Keep in touch.

A

He signed it with his initial as always. He went back to the proposition on his desk, there was always work to be done and this particular company had a lot of excess baggage that would have to be trimmed. He worked through lunch and finally raised his head after the sun went down. Dinner was a rush of snacks and coffee. He rarely had time for anything else.

"Alex, you need to take better care of yourself." Jameson had come into the office and was sitting on the edge of the couch.

"I know Jameson...so you tell me every other day." He said it quietly but with a smile on his face.

"I mean it Alex you need to get out and live, meet a nice girl ..." he trailed off.

"There is no time for all of that, Jameson and you well know it. So much time was lost in the early days when I was learning and now I have to make it right. When I do, I'll go out and have fun as you put it."

Jameson gave a huff as he stood to go. "Lady Alice is here to see you Alex perhaps she can keep you...ah...company for a while." He left and Alex scowled slightly as she came in. She was petite and blonde and liked to be serious. It may have been her education but she rarely laughed as it would make people think she was "a silly blonde" and not take her seriously.

"Hello Alex." She held up her had to stop him from saying anything. "I know we haven't seen each other in a while, but I was hoping we could go over a case I'm working on and at least share a meal. It's a lonely business and I don't have many people I trust. Besides you make me feel smart and pretty, I like that combination and quite frankly, I need some stress relief." She smiled at him.

He was never been one for settling down but she was right. It was a lonely existence when you're in this world. She was smart and she was pretty. He could use the distraction. Besides, she presented it as if their relationship could be some kind of business arrangement and, much like her career she was very determined to do things perfectly, their sex life had been no different. He smiled at her.

"Agreed Alice, agreed. I would love to work on it with you, I just can't give you more than you're asking for right this moment." He looked at her directly. He wanted to be honest up front.

"Once I thought I wanted marriage and family Alex, but I can see clearly now that work is a better path for me. I'm happy with friends, with some benefits. I'd rather have someone in my bed I trust than someone I love." She took off her gloves and settled into the sofa as Jameson came back in.

"Dinner?" He glanced towards Alex.

"Yes Jameson, can you order food for us and have one of the drivers pick it up. Miss Alice and I have some work we need to do." He never looked away from Alice, and Jameson smiled. At least this was a start. Time went on for a while and the mutual benefits to the relationship kept both Alex and Alice happy.

She was thriving at work and was looking for new work in a bigger firm. Alex couldn't have been happier at work. Things were thriving and he was content. Each night he went to bed alone which was when he would over think things and what he wanted. He was happy, he had money, and he had a beautiful lover. What was missing? He would go to bed each night wondering why he couldn't just be content. Even Mr. Warhol married his lady friend. Was there more out there?

Brienne was in very much the same position. She worked and worked and never had a moment's peace. The tuition depleted her savings and there was no hope for paying for her final two years unless she worked. She was working in the law library in the mornings, she had classes in the afternoon and evening, and was working in a bar after class at night.

Days seemed to fly by and with her strange hours, time was a relative thing. She needed to go see her father...or at least call him. He met someone and had a quick wedding. She was happy for him, after so long he deserved to be happy. Plus, she knew he was being taken care of. She received an email from Alex a few months ago.

She hadn't even found time to reply to that. She heard he was dating Alice Pope, it was a name that popped up in news articles she read about him. His business was doing well, extremely well from what she understood. She didn't want to bother him with stupid emails from an old friend. He was nice enough to send her a hello and for that she was thankful. She received an invitation to Brandon's wedding but she knew she couldn't make it.

If she missed one day it would only set her back even more. She met a nice guy at work but she had no time to date. His name was Blake and he would often come sit at the bar with her and walk her to her car. They made small talk and he was nice enough.

She knew he wanted more but was concerned about things progressing in a direction that was ultimately going to go badly. Tonight was no exception. He was sitting across the bar laughing with some guy about how the Cowboys were going to beat the Redskins on Monday night. He caught her eye and gave her a wink. He never missed a beat of the conversation and defended his

"Cowboy" honor to a fault. He really was nice. That night after the bar closed, he walked her out and this time he seemed different. He hugged her goodbye and when she turned to go, he pulled her in close for a kiss. She let it go on for a moment, it had been a long time since anyone kissed her. Before she knew it, one thing led to another and she found herself waking up the next day with him in her bed. She stood there now, towel wrapped around her watching him sleeping. It was a fun night, but the connection she was looking for wasn't there. She actually felt bad for letting things get out of hand. She tiptoed into the shower to get ready for the day, not wanting to wake him up and face where things stood now. She ate a quick breakfast, left a note for Blake and headed downtown to Kirby and Bates where she was working. They were prepping for a huge case and it was all hands on deck for sure. She sat in the conference room combing through files and let her mind drift for a second. She felt different somehow, yes she had a fun night but it was something else. Perhaps she just felt old. She smiled.

Alex would tell her she wasn't old, she just lived like it. Alex, he was so different from anyone else. Blake was not Alex....why she even thought it was bothersome enough. She spun around and got back to work. This stack of paperwork would not sort itself, that much was sure. She worked through her day excited about the fact that tomorrow was Saturday. The law firm was closed and she had no classes so she had the day free until work tomorrow night.

This was her day to run all of her errands and get all of her work done. She could also sleep in past 6:30 am. Her only indulgence was ice cream. Every Saturday afternoon she would get comfortable and eat ice cream and watch an old movie. Only one, she had to study and time was precious.

The day dragged on and after her classes she headed home for a quick bite and to get ready for work. At some point Blake left, and even the bed was made. She changed into her other clothes and headed out. Fridays were always crazy, there were people drinking and laughing, and most of the time there was a fight or two over some woman.

Blake wasn't there, which was odd, but he probably had things to do. Finally, as time went on, Brienne found herself looking at the clock more and more. One more hour, and she had almost a free day to herself. She wrapped things up and headed home. She was exhausted.

She was lucky only one year to go and she could take the bar exam and be done. She was 26 and still young enough where she could build a career and eventually be able to relax. She didn't want to be poor and struggle like she had done all of her childhood.

Her father did his best, but it was easier and cheaper to let her just dress and behave like a boy. She was fine with it, as it gave her friends. Besides, she had no idea what she was "supposed" to act like. Her father was her only role model. He worked long hours and she had to fend for herself a lot of the time.

They scraped by enough to keep the house, but food was rare, She went to bed hungry on more than one occasion and she decided she would never do that again. Her career was her foundation and it would make it so that she never went hungry again. She pulled into her lot and made her way to her apartment. It was a small efficiency on the campus. She did tutoring part time three times a week to allow herself the luxury of living alone.

She considered calling Blake but let the idea go. It was fun, but she didn't have time for all of the drama that comes with having a man in her life. Saturday came bright and sunny. She rolled over at it was 8:10. Even that simple thing...sleeping in made her happy. She started her day doing some shopping and settled in at noon for movie time. She frowned because nothing good was on television.

She sighed and turned it off all together and pulled her laptop into her lap. Maybe she could respond to some emails and some articles for her class. Not fun, but it was better than watching TV.

She opened her new emails. She really needed a system. She spent the next two hours replying and writing to professors and classmates, and her father until she finally cleaned the entire thing out. The next email in the list was the one from Alex now 6 months old. Should she? She shrugged.

A,

Life is busy, I hear business is doing well, I saw your article in the Times. She is pretty. I hope you're happy.

Yours,

B

She sat back and ate her ice cream, then gave her father a call to listen to all that was happening back home.

Life went on and on. Alex was now in charge of a corporation ranking number three on the stock exchange. He was secure and enjoying life as much as he could. Tomorrow his parents would have been gone three years. Three years ago he sat in the very chair he was in now.

He ran his hand over the cool leather. He not only carried on the business, he also become everything his father wanted him to be and he did it by working hard. Alice moved on and found a position with a firm in Washington. He was alone again. He let his mind drift to thoughts of Brie. She wrote him back and told him Alice was pretty. Why would she say that? Why did he focus on that? He shook his head. Nothing made sense as far as Brienne Warhol was concerned. She found a new life, one that didn't include him. He hadn't seen her in years and only heard from her from time to time.

He sorted through the stack of mail on his desk. He wasn't as overwhelmed now. Experience taught him to know the size of the correspondence and what was probably inside. He found a green postcard and pulled it from the stack. It was an invitation to a graduation. Probably some staff member or associate.

He turned it over and felt his heart race a little faster. It was for Brienne. She did it. She was graduating from Columbia and with honors, no less. He leaned back in his chair and smiled. She hadn't completely forgotten him, he thought to himself. May 15th. He had a little less than two weeks. He called Linda the secretary.

"Yes, Mr. Jacobs?"

"Linda clear my schedule for the weekend of May 14th. I'll be out of town for a few days."

"Yes, Mr. Jacobs. I'll take care of it."

"Thanks Linda, and plan the weekend off for you too, paid of course, you deserve it."

"Thank You, Mr. Jacobs!"

He hung up, thinking about the weekend he would be gone. He hadn't been this excited about something in a long time. He decided to stroll down to Mr. Warhol's and see what his plan was for graduation. He remembered the way he felt when he came down here to check on him.

He always felt like he was helping Brie somehow. She was far enough away to make it hard to see her father and she never had time to come home anymore. Now he was doing well and he felt like he wasn't needed anymore. He knocked on the door lightly and was greeted by a plump older woman who wore a huge smile.

"Alex, come on in...it's been so long. How have you been?" She enveloped him in a warm hug and shut the door behind him.

He blushed slightly. There was something overwhelmingly motherly about her. She was nothing like his mother in looks or stature but she carried the same warm love about her. Mr. Warhol walked into the room and smiled at Alex.

"Alex, we were just talking about you. Brienne called me a couple of weeks ago and asked about graduation and asked about you." He gave Alex a knowing look.

He swallowed hard. She asked about him? "How is she? I never hear from her, but I just assumed she had a lot of classes this final year."

"She is better than good, she is happy to quit one of her jobs and be able to focus on the bar exam for a while. After graduation I think I have her talked into coming home for a few months until she takes the exam. She needs the break because she works so hard." He sighed.

"What has she been doing exactly? I know she had a full course load and was tutoring, but that's all she really told me." He smiled up as Mrs. Warhol handed him a glass of iced tea.

"She never told you about...work?" Mr. Warhol cleared his throat. "I think maybe she was embarrassed about it or just too busy. I wish I was able to help her more. She deserved more from me." He turned somber.

"Mr. Warhol, do you remember when all the neighborhood kids would be playing softball in the field and how we broke Old Mr. Sampson's window?" He smiled remembering.

"Oh yes he was fit to be tied, ole Sampson." Mr. Warhol smiled.

"Do you remember when prom came and the car broke down and we were all stuck over the state line trying to buy beer?" Mr. Warhol busted into a fit of laughter at that one.

"You boys would have been in so much trouble." He grinned at Alex.

"Who saved us? Who paid for ole Sampson's window, who came and got us all and helped fix that car and get it home?" He looked at Mr. Warhol. "That is two of many examples I can give you, but you saved us all. We never even thought to go to any other parent because you were the "cool" parent. We are all thankful for you so don't ever think you didn't give us all something." He smiled over at Mr. Warhol who looked about to cry.

"Thanks for that son, I loved every one of you. You protected Brie, kept her from getting into too much trouble. I'm proud of all of you. Your father would be proud of who you've become. With Brie, I just worry. She's still a girl, she works three jobs, and always keeps a good face on, but I'm not sure how hard it's really been on her." He sighed.

"Well you can see when you go to graduation, and at least get an idea of what has been going on. Why is she working three jobs? I ask her every time I talk to her or hear from her if she needs anything. Of course I never hear from her." He raked his hand in his hair.

"Well she is stubborn our Brie." Mr. Warhol smiled at him. "You probably know that better than anyone else. As for graduation, I'm not sure about all of that just yet." He glances at his wife. "We will have to see."

"You are going aren't you?" Alex sat up. "She needs you there, it's important to her."

"We are going to try that's for certain." Mr. Warhol patted his hand and stood up to refill his drink.

Alex sat back lost in thought. He smiled at Mrs. Warhol who handed him some chocolate cake. He loved the way it felt here. The house that hugs you. He smiled and they went on talking about Brandon's new baby.

The next week and a half, Alex made all of the necessary preparations for the trip. Some of those preparations included securing seats to fly to New York for not only him, but Mr. Warhol and his wife. Money was the issue, though Mr. Warhol didn't want to discuss it. Alex didn't want to give him any reason to refuse his help. He had the tickets delivered to the house and when Mr. Warhol called to complain, he said they were free with his frequent flyer miles and they were also nonrefundable. He wouldn't want to waste them would he? He didn't think Mr. Warhol bought it, but he relented and was grateful.

They were all leaving in the morning and Alex had some work to complete before he could just leave town. He worked into the night with a sense of excitement. What was wrong with him. It was a graduation not a wedding? He smiled to himself. She was going to be surprised when she saw the three of them show up. They decided to surprise her. He knew she hated surprises, but it serves her right for never writing him back, he thought. He smiled and fell asleep.

The flight was on time and Alex could only grin as he heard Mr. Warhol fuss about first class and how it just "wasn't right." Mrs. Warhol, on the other hand was in awe, and was happily sampling all the food on the flight, much to Alex's' amusement. They settled in for the flight and he drifted off.

Nothing was going right! Brienne was furious. She was pacing for more than an hour waiting to get her final grade in one of her classes. This grade would determine her GPA and ultimately be a huge factor on her resume. Not only that, she had graduation today and she wasn't even sure if her father was coming at all. She called him all morning and nothing. Nothing! She glanced at the clock and hit refresh on the computer. There it was...A.

She did it. She completed law school at the top of her class. She was Valedictorian. She swallowed and sat down. She felt the stress of the last three years melt away. It was worth it. She stood and started to dance. No one could see her. She was in her own place, so why not. She bounced around some mix of the hula and the running man. She stopped in a huff and plopped into the chair. Today was the day. The day she could start to relax.

Her father asked her to come home for a while....Alex was there. She pushed him out of her mind. He was probably married to Alice by now. She stood and gathered her things to head to the graduation. She arrived at the stadium and was greeted by Professor Abrams who handed her the tassels to wear for the ceremony.

"Thank You." It's all she could get out. She hoped and prayed for this moment. She prepared a speech just in case. She knew the running was between her and one other person. The ceremony began. The usual lengthy pomp and circumstance, and she made a point of keeping her speech short and sweet. She focused on the importance of family and friends, and shared a story from her childhood. She felt the sweet relief of months of work as she walked across the stage and was handed her diploma.

That's when she saw him. As she walked down the aisle back to her seat, she saw his blue eyes and black hair. He was clapping for her as she walked by. He made eye contact and she felt her knees go weak. What was he doing here? She could think of nothing else as she waited for the ceremony to end. As people began to filter out, she was able to find him easily enough. He towered over most people. He had to be 6 ft. tall. His hair was still dark and slightly wavy on top now. He looked older and wiser somehow. She wasn't the only one to be taken back.

Alex stood rooted to the spot. She literally took his breath away. Gorgeous, her red flaming hair was artfully arranged around her shoulders, framing her face. She was wearing heels and a short black dress. She was older, more mature and ...perfect. He swallowed hard as she made her way over to him. She looked to his right and saw her father and his new wife.

"Daddy?" She ran to him and he engulfed her in a hug. It was obvious he was crying.

"I am so proud of you baby girl, you did it!!" He smiled widely and introduced her to his wife. They made small talk for a moment longer when Mr. Warhol cleared his throat and took his wife by the elbow.

"Dear let's make our way to the car, I believe we are going to dinner, Alex, we will meet you at the car." He gave Alex a wink and headed out.

"Hello brat." He smiled at her.

"You know I hate that Alex." She smiled at him anyway. "What are you doing here and how in the world did you find them?"

"I made them come with me on the plane, I don't like being alone. Your father doesn't take help lightly."

"No he doesn't. I tried to make some extra money to send, but he wouldn't hear of it. You can tell me how much Alex, and I'll get it back to you."

"Don't be ridiculous Brie, think of it as a graduation gift. I brought them here and I'll take them home. Almost like a role reversal from our younger years. I owe him that much. He got me out of so much trouble."

"Like Ole Sampson's window?" she glanced over at him and giggled.

"Exactly." He held the door for her leading outside to the car. He rented a car and driver and she was surprised by the limo that waited for them.

"Alex really?" she looked over at him.

"Happy graduation brat, even if you don't ever call me." He ushered her into the waiting car and they headed to dinner.

It was a happy occasion, everyone was chattering away about everything from graduation to life in Dale City. Brie told them about work and all of the cases she worked on. Eventually, Mr. Warhol announced that he was old and wanted to go back to the hotel. Not one to be disrespectful, Alex asked for the check, which he paid for, despite the protests of the dinner party. They made their way back to the hotel where Mr. and Mrs. Warhol said their goodbyes and made their way upstairs. Brienne looked at Alex. She was a little tipsy from the champagne at dinner but not so much that she wasn't aware of her surroundings.

"Want to go watch a movie in my room or something?" He asked it casually as though they were still in school, bored on a Friday night.

"Sure I don't have to go to work tonight." She giggled and Alex looked at her for a long moment. She was working in a bar of all places. She could have been hurt.

They made their way up to his room which had its own living room and she draped herself on the couch unceremoniously. He moved to make some coffee, watching her frustration with her dress being too tight to sit comfortably.

"Hey brat if you want, I have pajamas with me, you could wear them if you want to lose that dress." He froze the moment he said the words. "You know what I mean...they are on the sink in the bathroom."

Brienne made her way into the bathroom and changed. When she returned. She found him artfully arranging cups on a tray. She loved him her whole life and he never even knew she was there. She graduated today and wanted to do something crazy. She walked over to him. He was still in his suit but had lost the tie. She stood as close to him as she could and he braced himself and looked down at her.

She was too close. Something about her made all of the air in the room disappear. She had that mischievous look in her eye he knew so well. What was she up to? He turned to face her and try to figure it out but before he could ask, she threw her arms around him and pulled him down to her. She tasted like honey and champagne. He kissed her back, deeper longer. He pulled her closer to him and put his hands in her hair pulling her closer still.

She didn't know what she was feeling. He was kissing her back and her head was spinning. He was nipping at her mouth when the kiss finally broke. He looked at her with a sad look on his face.

What had she done? He was disappointed. She had crossed a line and would probably ruin their friendship. He just stood there looking at her.

"Alex, I'm so sorry. I just got carried away." She tried to sound reasonable.

"I understand Brie, you just had one too many drinks is all." He turned around to go back to making coffee. He dismissed her entirely. She had hoped...hoped for what? He would suddenly think of her as a girl and not one of his friends? She was a fool. She had to get out of here. She started for the door.

"Brie where are you going?" He saw her at the door. She wouldn't look at him.

"I can't stay Alex not now, I don't know if you can work through this or not but...I just don't know anything." She left the room and headed downstairs. Alex let her go. He called the driver and told him to take her wherever she wanted to go. What was he supposed to do? She never thought of him as anything other than a friend. Now he felt his heart all twisted up just like it had been 15 years ago. Why did she kiss him? Why now? He took a long drink of the coffee.

He sat down in the chair. Was it a game? It made no sense at all. The only thing he could do was try and figure it out.

An hour later he was still plagued with the reaction she caused in him. He buried that a long time ago and one kiss and she drags all of it back out again. It wasn't fair. He stood and grabbed his jacket and called his driver. He needed answers.

Her apartment was on the other side of town. He stood in front of her door and knocked. When she opened the door, he could only stare at her. Still in his pajamas, she braided her hair and washed her face. She looked just like she did years ago, all braids and freckles. She blinked and he shook his head.

"Listen brat I'm not 13 anymore. I don't know what's going on with you but we need to figure it out because I'm all twisted up all over again. He frowned because this was not what he planned to say.

"Thirteen, Alex? What are you talking about? At that age, I was following you around and you didn't even know I existed." She crossed her arms and continued. "I knew all about the bet at the dance and how you all planned to keep me from becoming a girl and all that, Mary Jenkins told me. It's ok, I understand. I've had the crush so long I just got overly excited and kissed you, that's all."

He stood there. Bet? What the hell was she talking about and she had a crush?

"First of all there was no bet, Mary Jenkins liked me and told you that to keep us apart. I was half in love with you already then and you just went into tomboy mode as soon as we got there."

He sat down on her couch and she followed. They both sat and thought about it for a while.

"You loved me then?" she whispered it.

"I have always loved you brat." He looked at her.

"I've loved you too Alex, I just wanted you to be happy and you deserved something, someone better." She shrugged.

"There is no one better Brie, this whole time I thought you just saw me as your friend, and I had no idea." He put his hand over hers.

"I thought the same thing Alex." She looked up at him and he smiled before leaning in for another kiss.

This time is was longer deeper and meant more, it held a promise of a future where they could both be less lonely and find happiness and peace. When they separated, Alex began to chuckle.

"What's so funny, mister?" She frowned.

"I think we owe Brandon 6 bucks." They both started laughing and he pulled her into his arms again, this time for good.

The Billionaire's Addiction

Marisa stared down at the eviction notice, reading it a second time as her eyes skimmed over the letter. "You are hereby ordered to leave the premises in one week," she read out loud. She could feel the tears stinging the back of her eyes.

She knew that it was only a matter of time, being two months behind rent and no sign of when she could catch up, she was just thankful that they waited this long. She put the letter in her purse and got out of the car. She could only hope that hours at her waitress job would begin to pick up.

She entered the restaurant, passing through the dining area to get to the time clock. She nodded to the occasional regular customer, giving them her best smile. She didn't want to show the outside world just how much she was struggling.

When she got in the break room, she headed to the table that always held the new schedule. She looked around and saw that her friend, Chad, was there. "Hey, Marisa, the schedule isn't out yet."

"Oh..." her face fell, then went to the hallway where her boss' door was wide open. "Is Frank in a good mood?" she asked, with a lighthearted laugh.

Chad shrugged, "Haven't really had to talk to him." He stood up from the table and smiled her way. "See ya around."

She nodded, "Bye, Chad."

She headed down the hallway and peeked inside to find that he was looking down at some papers and she wondered if it was the schedule. She knocked and he looked up briefly, then his head went back down. "Hello," he mumbled.

"Hello," she nervously looked around the office. "May I talk to you for just a minute?"

He seemed to groan, as he looked back up. "Sure."

"Well...I don't exactly know how to approach the subject."

He rolled his eyes, "Just say it."

She sat down in the chair that was facing him. His expectant stare was nerve wracking. "See, I was hoping that maybe next week I could have some extra hours, anything that you can give me." She was pleading, but she was desperate. She didn't want to tell him about the eviction notice, so she hoped that it wouldn't come to that."

He looked away from her. She saw a pained expression in his eyes. "Marisa, we need to talk." She didn't like the sound of that, but she just nodded. "I was going to tell everyone this in a couple of days, but there really is no reason dragging it on. You have been a valuable employee for the last five years and I owe you that much."

Her jaw dropped, it didn't sound like happy news that he was about to share. "What are you trying to say, Frank?"

His eyes feel to the stack of papers on his desk. He leaned forward, ruffling through the stack. When his hand landed on a paper, he removed it and handed it to her. She looked down at the pink slip. She skimmed through the notice stating that she was being fired. She looked up at him, but couldn't find the words. "I'm sorry, Marisa. If I had any other way...I would take it."

"You're firing me?"

"I'm closing the restaurant," he slowly spoke. "It hasn't been good for us. You know the lack of hours and I don't foresee it getting better."

"When?" she asked, hoping that the tears wouldn't start falling.

"The buyer wants us out in two weeks."

She covered her face. She was at a loss for words. "So, you have already sold it?"

He nodded, "I didn't want to spring it on you guys."

She stood up from the chair, angry that her world was spinning out of control. She couldn't fight back the tears much longer.

"Spring it on us? Frank, we all have to look for jobs. Did you think of that?"

"I know, but..."

She brushed away a tear that had fallen down her cheek. "I'm sorry, but you don't know." She looked away, "I have to clock in." She turned from him.

"Marisa, wait..." he began.

She just shook her head and glanced back toward him. "I need time to think."

"Please don't tell anyone."

She turned around and sighed heavily. "Really? You want the rest of the staff to be shocked by the news more than they already will be?"

"I need to tell them and I will tell them."

She nodded, "Fine. I'll give you twenty four hours," she headed out of the office and slid her badge through the time clock. She let out a slow breath, to calm down her nerves, before pushing through the break room door. She needed to figure out what she was going to do and she had no time to waste.

***

Marisa walked in her apartment and headed for the kitchen. She reached for the bottle of wine to pour herself a glass. She needed something to unwind with. When she poured the glass and lifted it to her lips, she found herself thinking about what she was going to do. She put the glass down and left the kitchen.

She went to her room and grabbed her laptop and then took it back to the kitchen. She took a drink and then turned the computer on.

She punched in a website to search for a job. As she narrowed it down to places that were based on location, she gradually looked down the list. She sipped her wine, taking in the positions. Many of the places she wasn't qualified for, but then her eyes fell on a few positions that were in search of secretaries, assistants, or receptionists.

She jotted down their information, then closed her laptop. She figured it was too late to do anything about the eviction, but she needed to find a job. She downed the rest of the wine and put the dish in the sink.

She headed upstairs and turned on the water in the bath, pouring in his some bubbles. She pulled her clothes off and got into the bath, sinking down so that the bubbles were covering her completely. She could feel the tears falling down her face and she sniffled.

She hated feeling this way. She was alone and losing everything that was important to her. As she wiped a tear from her eye, she heard her cellphone ringing. She grabbed a towel, wiping her arms off and then reached across to her pants, where she removed the phone. She saw on the caller ID that it was her mother. She groaned, but quickly answered the call. "Hey, Mom."

"How's it going?" She asked. Her voice was cheerful, causing Marisa to try to push away her worries.

"Oh...same ol' same ol'," she lied. "How have you guys been?"

"We have been good. We were hoping you would come home for the Independence Day Barbeque this year."

When she was living at home, she loved the barbeque. However, she was now twenty-five and had moved away nearly seven years ago. She only went home for the occasional Christmas when she didn't have to work. "I think I'll have to work that day and won't be able to come back." Again, she stated a lie.

There was a long pause on the other end, before her mother spoke up. "Please try. Your sister has some news and we would love to see you."

News? Marisa thought. "I'll see what I can do. I have two weeks to see if I can work it out."

"So, you are going to try?" Her mother sounded hopeful.

"I said I would, but I can't make any promises," she snapped, then felt bad that it came across that way. "I'm sorry Mom. It's just things have been busy."

"I understand," her mother replied and Marisa knew that she really had no idea. "We just really miss you."

"Yes, I know. I miss you guys, too." When she lived at home, her best friend was her sister, who just happened to be only five years younger than her. It was tough on all of them when she decided to take off right out of high school. "Hey, I better go. I hear the doorbell." She spoke, just wanting to get off the phone.

"Goodbye, Mom."

"Goodbye, Honey. I'll talk to you soon."

"Okay," she quickly hung up the call and pushed her phone away from her. She didn't have time to worry about her parents, too. She sighed, closing her eyes. She prayed that she would find a job quickly and all of this could be put behind her.

She stepped out of the tub and wrapped herself up in a thick, warm towel. She would get some much needed rest and then spend all day job searching, if necessary, until she had the perfect one.

***

She crossed off the second job on her list and glanced over the openings. She wasn't having the best luck, but she still had several positions open that she could apply for. She drove a few blocks and turned a corner, where a large law office stood in front of her. She parked the car and crossed her fingers, heading up to the door.

When she entered, she looked around until she saw a wall that had several names on it. She walked over and glanced down at the listing. "Martz, Tucker, and Bradley Law Firm," she whispered and then glanced up at the wall and noticed the name in gold letters.

She headed in the direction the arrow pointed, to where she was brought to a narrow hallway.

She saw the glass door with the name of the law firm and she went inside. She looked around to find a lot of bustling going on and people on the phone, talking over copy machines. She noticed a blonde woman, staring at her computer, but she didn't seem too distracted by other things going on. So, she approached her.

When she didn't look up, she cleared her throat. Finally the woman looked up, clearly annoyed. "May I help you?" She snapped.

"Uh..." Marisa looked down at her chicken scratch on the notepad. "I am interested in applying for the job."

The woman rolled her eyes, "You and every other teeny bopper."

"I'm not teeny bopper. I'm twenty-five and..." she began, but that made the woman appear even more annoyed.

"Yeah, did I ask?" She replied, rolling her eyes.

Marisa felt awkward in that moment, nearly stepping back, apologizing for wasting her time, and leaving. "Um, I—"

"Go through that door," she interrupted, "until you will find a large desk and you can ask about the position there. This is a mail room only and we don't handle such things. If you would have come through the other door, you would have clearly noticed that." She laughed with sarcasm and then went back to her work.

Marisa wanted to say, *did I ask?* However, she refrained from being sarcastic and headed toward the door. She opened the door to find a much more reserved area. She walked up to the desk and a middle-aged redhead looked up and smiled. "Hello, may I help you?"

"Yes, I would like to apply for the position that I saw online."

The girl nodded, "Of course. The way interviews are being handled is by being interviewed on the spot. It usually lasts about a half an hour. Are you free to stay?"

Marisa's eyes got big and she nodded, "Of course."

"Great. I will see if the boss is available. Please, have a seat over there," she pointed to the chairs and Marisa went and took a seat. She found herself extremely nervous, as she scrunched the paper in her hands and waited for a response. It was about five minutes later, when she was walking back to her. "You may follow me."

Marisa attempted several short breaths, to gain her composure. When they reached a door, she noted that she was still as nervous as ever. The woman opened the door, allowing her to walk into an office. The moment she got inside, she saw a tall, dark, and gorgeous guy sitting at his computer.

Her voice escaped her, as he looked up. He had the most magnetizing blue eyes, with brown wavy hair. His smile was charismatic and she was completely gone. "Hello. Please have a seat." He motioned to the chair in front of his desk.

She sat down, unable to function while looking at him. He smiled, cocking an eyebrow and giving her a peculiar look. "Why don't you start off with something about yourself."

She searched for the words, realizing that she had to say something. "Um...my name is Marisa Jamison."

"Ms. Jamison, it is a pleasure meeting you." Again he smiled and she was caught off guard. "My name is Jeffrey Bradley, one of the lawyers here." She smiled, still unable to speak. "Why don't you tell me about your experience."

She looked down at her hands, then slowly her eyes went back to him. "Well, I don't really have much experience. I currently work at a restaurant."

"For how long?" He asked, taking down notes.

"Five years," she replied, hoping to soon start breathing regularly again.

"It is true that this is different from a restaurant, but you have to have customer service skills."

"I definitely have that," she spoke, suddenly feeling a bit better.

He smiled, "Tell me why you would want to work in a place like this?"

"Well, the restaurant I work in is getting ready to close and a lot of positions that I was looking at require more experience. I think this would be an interesting job." She shrugged, "I am a quick learner."

He took down some more notes and then looked up. "Well, there have been several applicants. Some more qualified than others. The pay is competitive and we offer a strong benefits package. You would start at $55,000 a year."

She nearly fell off her chair. "Are...are you serious?"

He nodded, "Did I stutter?" His face was blank, like he had flipped a switch and joined the dark side, but then quietly laughed and she shook off the strange feeling she had.

"No, but just a bit taken aback."

He nodded, regaining his smile. He then stood up and she figured that the interview was over. She was bummed to realize that it was only about fifteen minutes and she figured that that was not a good sign. She stood up and shook his outstretched hand. "When can you start?"

Her jaw dropped, "I'm sorry?"

He shot another glare in her direction. "When....can...you...start? My assistant quit last minute and I need a replacement." He stated, slowly easing out the words.

"As soon as you need me." She conceded, knowing that she would have to work around her work schedule. She just was elated by the turn of events.

"Okay, then I will see you tomorrow." He sat down and went back to his computer.

She processed the words in her mind, but before leaving she glanced back in his direction. "Tomorrow is Saturday."

He nodded, "I'm aware, Ms. Jamison." She paused at his door, but he looked up. "Is working a Saturday not a possibility for you?"

She was worried that he would snatch the job away, so she quickly shook her head. "No, Saturday is great. Thank you!" She left his office and silently celebrated that things were looking up. Tomorrow was a new day and she wouldn't focus on everything she lost, but everything she was gaining.

***

It wasn't until she was home and in bed that she even thought about how she didn't know what time she should be there. She decided to just go in at eight o'clock and hope that that was fine with him. She dressed in her dressier clothes and headed to the office.

When she got there, there was another car in the parking lot. She parked and went up to the door. As she walked through the offices, she noticed that the once bustling of a mailroom, was deafly quiet. She glanced around the room and then went to the other part of the office.

She opened the door to find that it was also quiet. She casually walked down the hallway, the only sound was the clicking of her black high heels. She went to his door and saw him through the glass door, busy at his computer. She knocked softly. "Come in!" He called. She entered, but he didn't bother looking up. "You're late," he mumbled, continuing to type away.

"I'm really sorry. We didn't really..."

He put up his hand and looked at her, "Don't let it happen again."

"Yes, sir," she mumbled.

He stood up and walked around the desk, glancing over her outfit and causing her to feel awkward. "You also don't have to be so dressed up, unless we have a meeting." She glanced down at her outfit and frowned, but didn't say anything.

"Follow me," he ordered. They left the office and headed back down the hallway. He pushed a door open and they entered, bringing her into another office. "This is your office. You can decorate as you please, but don't get too caught up in it. You will do a lot of work in my office and be expected to do whatever I ask of you." He hesitated, a heated stare appeared. "Whatever I ask you. Understand?"

She took a step back from him. She felt a strange sensation as he spoke to her. It was like he was cutting to her core and she couldn't understand what was happening. "Yes, I understand," she spoke, but she wasn't sure if she really did.

"Perfect." He leaned over the phone and pressed a button. "When you need to talk to me, press this button. It will buzz and inform me that you are calling me.

When I call you, you will hear a buzz and you answer by pressing this button." He looked at her, shifting to stare into her eyes. "Do you need to take notes?"

She nearly laughed, then shook her head. "I think I have it, but thanks."

She couldn't help but notice how his demeanor was different from the interview. He was belittling and acting like he was better than her. She felt like a child he was training to ride a bike or use the restroom.

It was a different phase that she wasn't expecting. "Suit yourself." He shrugged, heading out the door. "Get comfortable with the office and I will get with you soon."

"Thank you," she mumbled, walking around the desk and sinking down in the chair. She felt out of her element and hoped that it was just nerves, because she was already hooked into the job.

The money would be more than enough to keep herself in the apartment. She started messing with the computer, getting a feel of the drawers in her desk, and swiveling in her chair, when she heard the phone buzzing at her.

She stopped what she was doing and stared at the phone. She pressed the button that he showed her. "Yes?"

"Jamison, come to my office," he ordered. His voice was almost gruff.

"Yes..." she started to say, but she heard a tone that signified he was no longer on the intercom.

She rolled her eyes and headed back to his office.

She went into his office and put on a smile. He stood up, with a pile of papers in his hand. He walked around and handed her the papers. She looked them over. "Follow me," he ordered.

She willingly did so, as he led her to another room. "Am I going to remember where everything is?" she asked, laughing lightly.

He turned around and his gaze was cold and distant. "Do I need to draw you a map?" He asked, with no sign of teasing. She shook her head and he turned back to the filing cabinets. "You are to file these forms by date that they were completed." He pointed to the date and then looked up at her, "Understand?"

She nodded. "Good!" He mumbled, heading out of the room and leaving her alone. She frowned, turning back to the filing cabinet. She didn't know why he had to be such a jerk, but she wasn't going to jeopardize it by questioning his actions. He was the boss and that was what she would keep telling herself, because it was going to pay the bills and that was what mattered most.

**

Marisa woke up to the knock on her apartment door. She glanced at the clock and frowned, "Six o'clock?" She mumbled, putting on her robe and stumbling to the door. The knock happened again. "Coming!" she called, hoping it didn't across as gruff. She opened the door to see that Jeffrey Bradley was at her door.

She quickly pulled the strap tighter around her robe. She was not used to awkwardly standing in front of her boss, wearing just a nightie and a robe. "What are you doing here?" She asked, realizing how rude it came across. She didn't care; she figured that it still wasn't as rude as he had been the past three days.

"I told you we had meetings today." He brushed into the apartment. When she turned around, she saw that his eyes were casually washing over her body. "Are you going to be dressed like that for every meeting we have?"

She looked down at her outfit and then glared at him. "Smart..." she finally said. "If I would have known that you were going to be here at the early light of dawn, I would have been sure to put on a formal gown."

For the first time, since he hired her, she noticed a smile on his face. She had to take a step back, because she didn't expect for a simple smile to melt her heart. "I apologize. You are most correct. I didn't tell you about the fact that I like to prepare for the meetings. Since the first one is at eight o'clock, I was just trying to get a head start. I can come back."

As he was passing her, she reached out and grabbed his arm. He turned to look at her and she shrugged, "You're here now...you might as well make the best of the time. Have a seat at the kitchen table and I will hurry and take a shower, get dressed, and be back before you know it."

"If you insist."

She rolled her eyes. She didn't really feel like she had much choice. "I do." She left him standing there and hurried into her bedroom, where she grabbed a change of clothes and then went into the bathroom. She would make it a quick shower and then be out there and ready to start the day.

She barely had time to think, before she was turning the shower off and getting dressed. She threw her hair back in a ponytail and went out to the kitchen.

He looked up, "That didn't take long," he muttered.

"Told you I would be fast," She replied, sitting down across from him.

"Indeed you did," he replied, pushing the paperwork in front of her. "We are meeting with Troy Houser. He is suing his ex for full custody of his two children."

"That seems harsh," she mumbled.

"Excuse me?" He asked, looking intently at her.

"I just mean that she's their mother. Why would he do that?" She shook her head, leafing through the papers.

He opened another folder and pushed it toward her. She looked down to see a picture of a little girl, a bruise on her arm.

She looked up at him, "Is there proof that the mother did this?"

He shook his head, "No, but that's why I'm here...to find proof."

Marisa snickered, "Whatever makes you sleep at night." She put the folder down and closed it up.

"What do you mean by that?" He asked, clearly angered by her attitude.

"You may be looking for proof to prove something that isn't there. Maybe you are defending the wrong person. Ever think of that?"

"Why are you so convinced that he's in the wrong? You know nothing about this case."

"Maybe not, but I'm just saying that you shouldn't just believe him because he's your client." She spoke, crossing her arms and staring at him.

"Duly noted, Jamison, but I don't recall hiring you to be a lawyer. This is my case and my job is to prove that he is the better option for those two kids."

"Even if he's not?" She asked, calmly.

"It's the price a lawyer pays. You don't always get the innocent one." He pulled the papers back toward him and continued to leaf through the files. She watched him, but she felt a feeling of dread inside of her. She heard a knock at her door. Their eyes met, as she got up and went to the door.

She opened the door to find her landlord on her step. She glanced back to her boss and then pushed her way out the door. "What do you want, Harry?" She asked.

"Have you thought about that letter I gave you? You only have three days to make your move...either pay up or get out. What will it be?"

She could feel the tears at the back of her eyes, but she begged for them not to fall. "I know. I'm working on it."

"Friday...that's your last day. I don't want to lose you as a tenant, but I have a business to run."

He turned away and headed to the stairs, "Goodbye!" she mumbled.

She went back into her apartment and saw that he was watching the door. She didn't respond about the visitor, but he did speak. "Friend?" He asked, casually.

"More like enemy," she replied with a laugh. She shrugged, "Back to this case. I will step back and let you do your job."

"Thank you!" He removed a couple of pictures from the file and held them up. "We do have proof that she had been having an affair with this guy, while she was still married."

She nodded, *still doesn't make her an abuser,* she thought. She pushed the thought from her mind and reached out for the picture. She looked down and saw this woman dancing with this man. They looked like they were in love. She gave the picture back to him and shrugged. "Nice picture," she mumbled.

"For a cheater," he replied, shaking his head. "I guess that's it. I am sorry that I interrupted your morning."

"No worries."

"I'll see you in the office in about an hour."

She nodded, watching him leave her apartment. She sunk down at the kitchen table and covered her face with her hands. She didn't want him to know what was bothering her, so she had to hold it in. Yet, she had no idea what she was going to do.

***

Jeffrey buzzed in on her phone at eight o'clock sharp. "Yes?" She asked.

"The client is here. Come to my office first."

"Yes, Mr. Bradley," she spoke, picking up a pad of paper and pen and heading out of her office. She walked down the hallway and entered his office.

He looked up and then stood to his feet. "I just wanted to make sure we were on the same page about today's meeting."

"Meaning?" she asked.

"I don't want you speaking your mind. I get that you aren't convinced, but it's not my job to convince you. It's my job to convince the judge and I don't want you getting in that way." He moved to the door and held it open for her. "Understand?"

"Loudly," she spoke, brushing past him. She turned around and put up her finger. "For the record...I would never get in the way of YOU doing your job." She turned on her heels and walked down the hallway to the boardroom. She stopped and turned around to see that he was lagging behind.

He held out his hand to show that he was welcoming her in first. She nodded and entered the room. She smiled as she took a seat. "Hello, Mr. Houser," she shook his hand.

She saw that Jeffrey was doing the same, as he took his seat. He put the paperwork in front of him and then looked up. "Tell me your story, Mr. Houser."

She watched, as he seemed hesitant. However, then he finally spoke. "I am suing for full custody, because my wife isn't suitable."

"You mean your ex?" He asked.

He nodded, "Yeah...yeah, my ex. She isn't suitable. She drinks and has abusive tendencies."

Marisa jotted down the information, as he stated them. "Tell me about her abusive tendencies."

"Well...when Valarie was two she ended up with a broken arm."

Marisa looked up at him and saw that he was sweating profusely. "Your ex beat her so bad that she broke her arm?" He asked, making notes of his own.

He nodded, but then paused. "They said that she fell off the Merry Go Round, but I never bought that. I know my ex."

"When did you get divorced? How old were the children?" Jeffrey asked.

"Hm..." he looked up to the ceiling. "I think that Valarie was four years old and Trey was two."

"So, you divorced her two years after the suspected abuse started?"

"Yes, so?" He asked, defensively. "I loved her and I didn't want to believe that she could be a maniac, but the truth had to come out."

"How old are the children now?" He asked, barely making eye contact.

"That was two years ago." He spoke, carefully looking between the two people sitting opposite him.

"So, it was about four years ago that Valarie broke her arm?" Marisa glanced at Jeffrey. She could tell where he was going with it, but she wondered if he was questioning him because of her or because of him.

"What does that matter?" Troy asked, again defensively.

"Nothing. I just want to see how you handle the questions that you are going to be fired. What I am asking is only the breaking point. If you don't answer them with ease, you'll be perceived as hiding something. Are you hiding something?"

Again I turned my focus on my boss. He was good and not batting an eye. For a moment it made sense why he was arrogant. It was the only way he knew how to be. "Nothing. She deserves to suffer, because those kids belong with me."

"Okay," Jeffrey replied, taking some more notes. "Do you have anything else to add?"

He shook his head, "Nope. I have said my peace." He replied.

For the first time since entering the room, Jeffrey turned to Marisa. She couldn't read what was in his mind, but she wondered if it was doubt. He stood up and turned back to Troy.

"Thank you for stopping by and I will let you know when you go before the judge." They all shook hands again and Troy left the room.

Jeffrey followed after him, not saying a word to Marisa as he headed back to his office. Marisa looked down at her notes and noticed what she had written. Most of it was about his attributes. He was shaking, nervous, sweating, and defensive. He didn't act like something that believed what he was saying and somehow she wanted to prove that.

***

Marisa sat at her desk, tapping her pencil loudly against her computer. Her thoughts roamed to the landlord and the meeting with their client. She finally took a deep breath and headed out of her office. She made her way down to see him. She noticed the door was open, but she knocked anyway. He looked up,

"Come in, Jamison." There was something about the way that he called her by her last name. She loved it. His eyes remained on hers. "Well, are you going to stand all day gawking, or do you have a question?"

She felt her face flush, as she looked away. She didn't know how he could do that. When she finally regained control, she looked back in his direction. "What did you think of the meeting?" She asked. It wasn't exactly why she came in there, but she figured it would buy her some time.

He shrugged, "Okay, I guess. Why? I suppose you have an opinion." He snarled.

She shrugged, "Maybe, but I won't say a word. I'm a woman of my word."

He laughed, glancing down at the papers. "Well, if you do decide to voice your opinion...I'll listen." She was surprised to hear him say that. He looked up and she thought she even noticed a smile. "Doesn't mean I'll take your side. It just means I'll listen."

"Right," she shook her head. She glanced down at the picture on his desk. For the first time, really noticing it. "Is that your family?" She asked, staring at a picture of a brunette woman, holding a toddler in her hands. His hand was on her shoulder.

She glanced at his hand and noticed that he wasn't wearing a wedding ring. She had figured she would have seen it before, if he had been.

He nodded, "Yes," he replied, but the word came out quiet.

"Good looking family," she replied, then turned to leave, but when she reached the door she decided to just say what was on her mind. "I guess I do have something to ask you."

He looked up, "About the case?"

"Well...not exactly."

He put down his papers and nodded, "Go on."

She felt panic welling up inside of her. She then tried to breathe and think of how she could possibly approach the subject with someone that she barely knew. "You see...I was kind of hoping that possibly you could give me an advance on my first paycheck?"

If there was once a smile playing on his face, it was now gone. "I don't do charity." He replied, looking down at the papers.

Her jaw dropped, "Charity?"

"Yes. I believe in working your way from the bottom and knowing that it will all work out in the end. I don't give handouts."

She couldn't believe her ears. She believed that you should fight to get ahead, but she also believed in doing something for the good of the cause. Yet, this had nothing to do with charity.

"It would ultimately be my money. I'm not understanding the problem." She replied, feeling a sense of urgency.

He rolled his eyes, "Yes, but if I do it for you this one time then you are going to expect every time. That's the way things work."

"You're wrong. I just need some extra money this week. I didn't make a lot at the waitressing job and things got behind. I really could just use a jumpstart."

He shook his head, glancing down at his desk. "I can't do that. You may see yourself out."

She felt her face turning red, but this time in anger. "You know what you are?" She fired out.

He looked up, eyes wide, "No...what am I?"

She stared him down, bracing herself and trying to hold it all in, but it was impossible. "You are an arrogant jerk that doesn't care about anyone or anything. All you want to do...is be right.

Well, newsflash...you aren't right. You are conceited and if it wasn't for the fact that I need this job, I would...I would..."

He stood up from his desk, "You would what?"

"I would quit, because I didn't apply to be a doormat or a slave and in the few days I have worked with you...that is exactly what I am."

"Are you finished?" He asked, when she took time to breathe. She nodded. "For the way you just talked to me, I could fire you and you wouldn't have to worry about quitting."

She looked away. At that point she didn't think her life could get worse anyway. "I will willingly go," she mumbled.

She reached the door, but he cleared his throat. "Don't go...I'm not through talking." She casually looked up at him, waiting for him to continue. "I could easily let you go and not turn back, but I'm not going to."

Her jaw dropped, "You're not?"

He shook his head, "No. In fact, I appreciate when someone can speak their mind and not back down. Not everyone does that and it's a trait that I admire."

She was not the least bit surprised to learn that. She felt a twinge of hope. "So, you'll give me the advance?"

Their eyes met, but he finally shook his head. "I can't. I know that you think that I'm a hard-nose and maybe you're right, but the fact is that companies have rules for a reason and one of the rules that I stand by is you need to work for everything you receive. It may seem tough, but it seems to always work."

She groaned, nodding her understanding. "Then, I guess it is what it is. Thank you for your time."

"Unless you would like to tell me what you want the money for and perhaps we could work out a loan agreement."

She paused at the door. Every thought she was hearing was telling her to swallow her pride and just tell him, but she sadly felt she couldn't. She felt like a failure and she didn't want him judging her. "Not that important," she said and then walked out of his office. She headed back to her office and sat down at her desk. She was thankful she still had a job, but the realization that she was about to lose her home...was a tough pill to swallow.

***

Jeffrey sunk back in his oversized desk chair. His eyes fell to the picture of his family. He picked it up and looked at it, running his fingers over the picture of his daughter. "He closed his eyes," I love you, Jasmine." He replaced the picture and went back to his work.

His mind drifted away to the feisty blonde. He saw the pain in her eyes and part of him considered just giving her the advance, but he was a stubborn man and not too proud to admit that.

He looked at his notes that he had taken on Troy Houser and began reading them out loud, "Nervous, edgy, argumentative, anxious..." each thing he wrote down was a trait that he saw coming from his client. He didn't know why, but he suddenly had a strange feeling about the whole situation.

He thought back to Marisa's doubts at the very beginning, but then shook off the nagging feeling that he was getting. "I have to trust him," he whispered, putting the notes away.

He stood up and moved to his sports jacket. He headed out of his office. On the way out of the building, he passed her office.

He looked inside to see that she was still at her desk, tapping her pencil on the computer and staring aimlessly at the screen. He wondered what was so interesting. "Are you leaving?" He asked.

She looked up, shrugging. "Why? Do you have a time that I have to be out of the office if you're not here?" She asked, sarcastically.

The way she was aggressive toward him, he noticed how it affected him. He had never seen anything like it. Jordan had left the job because she wasn't able to keep up with his sarcastic antics, but he could see that he was meeting his match. "No...no curfew." He tapped the wall and nodded, "Have a good evening."

He heard her snickering, as he left the office. He knew that there was something she was hiding and he hoped to be the one to crack her code. He smiled, walking out of the building. It would be fun trying.

***

She grabbed her last box and headed out of her apartment. "Thanks for helping me move, Chad. I didn't know who else to call."

He shrugged, "What about your new boss?"

She thought about that and rolled her eyes. "I doubt Mr. Bradley would be the moving kind of man. Besides..." her face fell, "I don't want him to know where I'm staying."

"I wish you would change your mind, Marisa." He spoke, while putting the boxes in the back of his truck. "I have plenty of room."

She knew that it was a generous offer, but she couldn't take him up on that. "I appreciate it, Chad, but I'll be fine. This is only until I start getting regular checks."

They got into his truck and as he pulled away, she turned to him, "Have you decided what you're going to do when the restaurant is closed?"

"Probably collect unemployment until I find something else." He shrugged, "Not really worried about it."

"I miss everyone," she replied, quietly.

He turned and looked at her, when they stopped at a red light. "Everyone misses you, too."

She knew part of her reasons of missing them, was the fact that Jeffrey Bradley just wasn't them. He turned into the hotel that was next to the office. They got out and grabbed her few boxes. They walked into the lobby and she went up to the reception desk. She hoped that they could strike up a deal and not charge her the whole fee up front. She explained the situation and was relieved when they agreed to bill her at the end of each week.

"Thank you!" she replied, gratefully.

She turned to Chad and they walked to the elevator. "You have one more chance to change your mind. A hotel is not a place for someone to live."

She laughed, "I will be fine. At least I'm close to the office." They reached the floor and she got off, walking to the door. She opened the door and entered the room. It wasn't big, but she could make it work. They put the boxes down and she walked to the window.

She peered outside and she laughed, "I even have a view of the office...what more could I ask for?"

He laughed, walking over to look outside. "Not bad," he spoke, but sounding a tad sarcastic. "I'll call you later and we'll go out. You could use a night out."

"You'll have to use my number here. I got rid of my cellphone."

"Okay," she walked over and wrote down the number on a piece of paper. She handed it to him and he put it in his pocket. "Take care, Marisa."

"You, too." She pulled him into a hug. "Thank you for helping pack."

"When you move out of here, I'll be back."

She smiled, nodding. "I will keep that in mind."

He headed to the door and they said their goodbyes. When he was gone, she looked out the window. She noticed that the office building was opening and Jeffrey was leaving. She glanced down at the clock to find that it was seven o'clock on a Friday night and he was just now leaving. She shook her head.

She wondered if his wife ever questioned his later nights. She closed the blinds and fell back against her bed, plopping down on the comforter. Her eyes closed and she drifted off to sleep, not wasting any time.

***

The next morning, she arrived to work on another Saturday. She didn't anticipate having to work the extra weekends at a job that clearly stood for Monday to Friday. However, she kept thinking about the salary and it suddenly became alright.

She hurried into the office, this time beating him. She put her stuff away and logged into her computer. She was busy looking up the information about various prospective clients that he asked her to research, when she saw him looking in her office. "Good Morning!"

He cocked his head, "You're here early."

"I wanted to get working on the research. Is that a crime?" She asked.

She had quickly discovered the best way to get to him, was by acting like him. While she didn't like to perceive herself as rude and arrogant, she would do anything to stand up to him.

"Not at all, I'm impressed," he admitted.

She looked up, as he was walking out of her office. She was confused by some of his attitude shifts. She went back to looking up the research. She jotted down notes of things that he might find beneficial.

When she was done with his list, she got up and went to his office. She put the packet down on his desk and turned away. "Wait a minute, Marisa."

She turned around, "You need me to do something else?" She asked.

He looked through her notes and placed them on his desk. Their eyes met and he shifted in his seat. "Is everything alright? Something seems different."

"Everything's fine," she spoke. "Anything else?"

He shook his head, "I don't mean to be abrasive...at least not all the time," he laughed, but she didn't crack a smile. "You just seem to be a little upset about something." He paused, "If this is about the advance, maybe I was a little stern. You don't get paid for another week and I suppose I could get you part of your first paycheck." He pulled out his checkbook and she stared at him. He appeared to be using his own personal checks. "Would five hundred cover it?"

"Mr. Bradley, forget about it." She looked away, but he remained with his pen poised.

"No, I'm prepared to do this." He argued.

She didn't understand the sudden change. "That's nice, but you might as well give it up. The reason I requested the advance is no longer prevalent. Thank you, though."

She turned away and headed out of the office. She didn't want him to see her flustered, but she felt dizzy. She went back in her office and sat down. She nervously began drumming her fingers on her desk.

She tried to get focused on the next tasks on her list, but she was still struggling at his immense change of heart. It didn't add up. She began typing on her computer and getting her mind on other projects, that she didn't realize how late it had become. She heard the buzzing of her phone. She looked down at the phone, like it had grown a head.

She pushed the button, "Hello?"

"Jamison, will you please come into my office?"

Please? She thought. "Yes, sir." She replied, getting up and heading back to the office. She glanced at her watch and saw that it was past lunchtime.

She knocked on his closed door. "Come in!" His voice wasn't gruff, but instead inviting.

She opened the door and hesitated, before pushing through the door. When he looked up, it was definitely a smile on his face. "Yes?"

He stood up and moved closer to her, "I just wanted to invite you out for lunch. You have been working so hard and I thought we could both use a break."

She fought the urge to check his forehead to see if he was running a fever. "Well, I was planning on just going home."

"Home? That's several blocks away. This way you can get something to eat right away and it's my treat. What do you say?" She hesitated, but finally nodded. "Good," he spoke and it came out enthusiastically. He grabbed his sports jacket and followed her out the door. She stopped at her office and grabbed her purse and then they were off. She was confused, but she was hungry and figured that it wouldn't hurt to just go out for a bite to eat. At least she hoped not.

***

He waited for her to place her order and then he placed his. The waiter left and he turned to her. He didn't know why he was suddenly nervous. He didn't remember ever feeling this way about a woman or anyone else. "So, tell me about yourself, Marisa." He replied, taking a drink of his coffee.

"Marisa?" She asked. Her face turned red. "I don't think you have ever called me that."

"That's your name, isn't it?"

She laughed. "Yes, but I didn't think you knew that. You usually call me Jamison."

He hadn't really thought about that, but he knew that his way of keeping distance between him and someone was to call them by their last name. "Which do you prefer?" He asked, feeling his throat getting dry.

She seemed to contemplate that, "Either."

He smiled, "So, whatever I'm in the mood for?"

"Something like that," she replied with a chuckle. He hadn't noticed her laugh before, but it filled a room and he was drawn to it. There was a long pause, before she spoke. "There's something that I have been wanting to ask you. It's just something that I was interested in."

He took another drink, preparing himself. "Okay. What's that?"

"Well, at the interview I was told that there were several applicants. Yet, you hired me right away. Why?"

He hadn't expected her to be so bold to ask the question. Yet, he really didn't expect her to be so bold about anything. He was wrong about that. "I suppose there was something about you that I felt would be the perfect match to the job."

"That seems vague," she replied laughing.

"Yeah, I suppose it is. It's like when you go out looking for a pair of shoes and you know the exact style you're looking for. You just know and there's no point in waiting for another pair of shoes to come along, when you have the perfect pair right in front of you. Make sense?" He asked.

"Yes, you're comparing me to shoes."

He laughed, this time feeling a blush brushing across his face. "It's just an analogy. When you walked through the door...I just knew."

He hoped it didn't come across as corny, but he knew that it was the truth. By the look on her face, it definitely appeared that she was not thinking it was corny. "Okay, then if that's how you feel...why have things been tense between us?"

The food came and he paused, giving him time to think. When the waiter was gone, he looked back in her direction. "They say opposites attract, so it's obvious you and I would repel. We're a lot alike." She opened her mouth, but he placed his hand up, halting her.

"I know you think that I'm arrogant and rude and any other name in the book. You have been very vocal about that, but I speak my mind and so do you. We are bound to butt heads, but that doesn't mean that at the end of the day I'm not thankful you walked through my door."

He realized the way that came out, but he wasn't about to apologize for it. "I think that we could in essence make a great team, because even though you don't see it...I do value your opinion."

"That makes me feel good. Thank you!"

He smiled, "Now, let's enjoy the food." He took a bite of his salad and saw that she was finally getting comfortable and he breathed a sigh of relief. Everything he had said to her was the truth. None of it was lines that he was just feeding her and he hoped that she understood that.

***

Marisa stared down at the picture of Troy's ex dancing with the other man. Her mind kept going back to lunch with Jeffrey. He definitely surprised her by the easy tone. She had expected everything to be awkward and then when he told her why he chose her for the job, she found herself distracted. There was a heat in his eyes when he spoke the words and she didn't know if it was because she was attracted to him or lonely, but she suddenly felt like doing more than going to lunch with him.

She shook her head, removing the vision from her mind. She looked back down at the picture, tracing the outline of the couple. As she was doing that, she picked up the picture and stared at an image that she hadn't seen before.

She got up and moved to the window light. In the corner there was a faint image of a man staring in the direction of the couple. It was definitely Troy. She was sure of it.

She got up and hurried to his office. She stopped when she heard his voice echoing through the door that was a crack. "You can't do this to me, Janelle. Haven't I lost enough?" She paused, leaning in toward his door. "Please, don't...Dammit..." she heard the sound of a slamming phone and she cautiously proceeded. She considered leaving, but she had come this far. She knocked and heard the faint sound of his voice, "Come in!"

She opened the door and saw that he was sitting at his desk, looking drugged. "I can leave," she stammered.

He shook his head, "Don't bother." He sat up in his chair. "Find something?"

She proceeded to his desk, awkwardly. She held the picture, but before putting it in front of him she said, "tell me about you."

He looked up and confusion was evident. "Pardon me?"

She took the seat in front of me. "Well, it seems that I did most of the talking at lunch. I think you have a story to tell. What is it?"

He shook his head, "Not worth telling."

"Come on, Mr. Bradley. I'm sure there's something. You have a beautiful family. Start there."

When he looked up, she sat back. There was agony on his face and she regretted saying anything. He reached for the picture and stared at it. "Do you know why this picture is on my desk?"

She shook her head, "Probably because it's your family and you want to show them off."

"Well, at one time that was true. However, now it just holds bad memories." She watched as he traced the picture of his daughter. "Her name was Jasmine."

"Was?"

He nodded slowly, looking up. "She drowned last year. She was just five years old." He smiled, "Believe it or not, I used to be a very charismatic gentleman and a family man. However, one weekend we had decided to go camping and I was going to have to work late on Friday night.

So, I told them to go up without me and I would come up Saturday. My wife and daughter were in a boat when a storm came through. She tried everything she could, but the boat capsized and Jasmine went under. She was wearing a lifejacket, but the boat pinned her under.

My wife couldn't find her until it was too late." She could tell that the memories were painful and tears were forming on his eyes. "I never blamed her, but she didn't know how to swim and she blamed me for not being there."

"I'm so sorry, Mr. Bradley."

He nodded, "Please, call me Jeffrey." She nodded, as he continued. "She called me and I rushed to the hospital, but it was too late. Right after the funeral she said she wanted a divorce. It was an amicable one. We didn't have a prenuptial, but I didn't worry about her taking me to the cleaners. It finalized and I thought things were done.

My dad died last month." She covered her mouth, realizing the hurt he was feeling. "I was left a hefty sum of money. My ex is suing me for damages from the loss of her daughter."

"Can she do that?" She asked in disbelief.

He nodded, "Unfortunately, people sue for all types of reasons."

"It's your daughter, too." She argued.

"I know, but her heart is still healing." He frowned, "My heart is still healing."

"My feelings exactly." Marisa stated. She was irritated by the news, but she wanted him to know that she appreciated him telling her the story. "Thank you for opening up to me, but I just think that you're getting the raw end of the deal."

He smiled, "Yeah, you and me both." He shrugged, "It is what it is and I will just have to fight through. Justice will win out, right?"

"I suppose," she mumbled, staring down at the picture.

"You did want to show me something. What is it?" she got up and walked around his desk. She put the picture down in front of him and pointed out the image. She was so close to him, that she was sure her breath was tickling his skin.

Their eyes met and she saw a fury in his eyes. She looked down at the picture. "I think it's Troy."

He looked back to the picture and slowly nodded. "I'll be damned."

"If he was there and saw the affair happening before his eyes, he could have gotten jealous. There is just something about him that..."

"Doesn't feel right," he finished her sentence.

"You feel it, too?"

He nodded, "I just don't want to jump to conclusions, but this is a very good start." She stepped back from him, needing a breather. He stood up and turned to her, "Thank you for listening today and Monday we'll try to dig deeper into figuring out the truth." He moved closer to her and she thought she saw that his eyes moved to her lips briefly.

"I think I'm going to head out for the day. You alright with that?"

He started to nod, but then his lips went down to hers and he kissed her. She pulled away, not knowing what she wanted. His eyes remained connected to hers. "I'm messed up, no good..." he started.

"I know...me too," she whispered.

However, that didn't stop the notion that she wanted to feel his body against hers. "Sexual encounters at work are never a good idea."

She nodded, "I know..." before she could get anything else out, she felt his hand snake around her neck and he was pulling her back into another kiss. "Hm..." she moaned. "Wait..." she breathlessly spoke, breaking from the passionate embrace. "Are we even thinking this over?"

He shook his head moving closer to her and putting his hands on her blouse. "We're being irrational. Just go for it. He ripped the shirt from her body and it fell to the floor. His lips went to her neck, while her hands went to his shirt, removing it from the confinement of his dress pants. She started off tediously undoing button after button, but then knew that she needed to move the show on the road. She busted open his shirt, the way that he had busted open hers. Her hands trailed down his chest, while he continued to kiss her neck.

As his tongue slowly weaved its way out of her, she dropped her hands from his head. She closed her eyes and took in deep and slow breaths. She felt him easing his way back up her. Her eyes opened and she stared at him. She only saw desire and nothing else.

Monday morning, Jeffery walked into the office and as he passed Marisa's office, he couldn't even look up. When he had time to think about it, he realized that it wasn't right. He took advantage of the situation.

He looked down at his desk, where the picture that started everything was still lying in a heap of papers. He smelled her sweet perfume and instinctively kissed her, but it should have stopped at that.

He picked up the picture, clearly seeing Troy Houser as he watched his wife dance with the other man. There was a glare in his eyes and it wasn't able to be refuted. He had the strange feeling he did, similar to the one that he felt when Troy left their meeting.

As he was looking at the picture, he heard a knock on his door. He glanced up to see Marisa in his doorway. "I'm sorry to bother you, but can we talk?" She didn't give him a chance to answer her, as she entered his office and closed his door behind her. When she turned around, he tried to read her mind, yet he saw that it wouldn't be an easy task.

"What's on your mind?" He asked, putting the picture down and looking back up at her.

She was hesitant, glancing around his office and he wondered if she saw the visuals, too. "I want to talk about Saturday," she walked over and sat down in his chair.

He wanted to avoid it at all costs, but he could see that she was not having that in mind. "Okay."

"It wasn't planned..." she began.

"No...it wasn't," he concurred.

"I guess that I was wondering how you felt about it?"

He thought about that. He would be lying if he said that it wasn't what occupied every moment of his mind. He would be denying everything if he said that he didn't want to rip her clothes off and enjoy another day of sex with her.

He bit back the thought and just looked at her. "You are a very passionate woman, Jamison." He groaned, knowing what words he would speak next. "I'm not looking for a relationship."

"I'm not neither," she whispered.

"What we did on the floor of this office, needs to stay between us." She nodded, proving that she was aware of that. His eyes wandered to her lips, the same lips that he could have remained kissing all night, but he looked away.

"We let impulses take over and I'm too much of a stickler to make sure that never happens again."

Her face fell and she looked down at his desk. He knew that he saw hurt in her eyes, but she stood up and nodded. "I am glad that we're on the same page. It was something that we both needed in the moment, we claimed it, seized it, and that was it. Thank you for your time."

She turned from him and left his office. He hadn't expected her to be so casual about it, but he supposed he should have been glad. Instead, he was trying to figure out how he could forget it.

**

Marisa sank down in her chair, after leaving his office. She didn't know what she had expected him to say, but she didn't think he would resort to his abrupt attitude. As she was contemplating how to forget about him, her phone rang. She picked it up, "Hello?"

"Hey honey, I was just seeing how things were going?"

She groaned, hearing her mom's voice. She had given the phone number, because she didn't have her cell anymore.

Now she regretted it. "Things are going great. I absolutely love my job." She wanted to be as enthusiastic as she possibly could. She hadn't told her about the apartment, because she knew she would worry and that wasn't good for anyone involved.

"Good...good..." her mother was saying. "I was wondering if you had time to think about this weekend."

"I don't know, Mom. He has me working weekends and I might not be able to get away." She looked up and saw that he was entering her office, "I have to go. I'll try," she quickly hung up the phone and stood up. "I'm sorry, I..."

"Please, you don't have to apologize. Everything alright?" He asked, a look of concern etched on his face.

She smiled so show that everything was fine. "Yes, it's fine, but I did want to ask you something."

"Sure," he replied, taking a seat.

"Well, every Fourth of July my family has a big barbeque. The whole town comes and it's something pretty cool, but I haven't been back for it since I left home.

I was wondering if maybe you didn't need me this weekend and I could go back to Pennsylvania."

"Well..." he replied slowly, "you'll be in Ohio this weekend, for business."

Her eyes got big, "What?"

He pushed the folder toward her. "I forgot to mention that every year there's a two day lawyer's conference in Columbus, Ohio. Your ticket and itinerary is inside."

She nodded, knowing that she couldn't change that. "Okay."

"I am sorry, Marisa," he spoke as he stood up. She saw that he appeared to be genuine.

"I understand," she replied, looking through the paperwork. She didn't see him as he left her office, but she pushed the folder away. She picked up the phone and called her mom back to give her the news. It couldn't be helped and she would just make her see that.

**

Jeffrey sat in another boring meeting. He didn't like coming to this conference, but it was necessary to keep face. As he was drowning out the topic at hand, about the quality of lawyer care, he glanced to Marisa, who was sitting next to him.

He wished things could have been different, but there was no way to go back. Every minute he spent with her, he grew more enamored with her beauty. Yet, it wasn't enough to make him throw out all worries and just let what happened...happen.

He shifted in his seat, to the growing erection in his pants. His leg slid along hers and she shot a look in his direction. "Sorry!" he whispered, turning his attention back to the speaker.

The speech lasted for another thirty minutes and when it was done and they were walking out of the room, he turned to her. "That...was interesting," she replied.

He laughed, "Well, you really don't have to lie."

She looked at him and they laughed together. She looked away and shrugged, "Yeah, it was pretty boring."

They headed out of the building and the warm air blew past him. "At least it was the last meeting for the day." He glanced at his watch and saw that it was five o'clock. "Want to grab a bite to eat before going back to the hotel?"

She paused. He saw her bite her lower lip. It was a trait he found endearing. "I don't know."

"Please, at least let me do that. It's the least I could do from dragging you to these boring meetings."

She slowly nodded, "Okay." She followed him to his car and he opened the door for her. She looked up at him and cocked her head. She shook her head and snickered, then got into the car.

He came around, but before starting the car he gave her an inquisitive look. "What's so funny?"

"I suppose that I am just thinking back to the first few days of working with you. You were anything but gentlemanly."

He nodded, thinking back to all the arrogance he portrayed. "I suppose I have changed...a little." He also knew that a big part of that was due to her.

"You have changed, but more than a little." She spoke, sitting back in her seat.

He started the rental and pulled from the parking lot. He saw her staring out the window, as if she was thinking. "Any preference of where to go?" He asked, breaking into the silence.

She shook her head, "Whatever!"

He continued to drive, until he was pulling into a Pizzeria. She opened the door, not giving him a chance to. He held back while she walked ahead of him. His eyes sauntered down her frame and then he cursed himself. This wasn't helping the fact that he didn't want to mix business with pleasure.

As he rushed to the door to open it up for her, their eyes met. Her smile was pure and sweet. She entered the restaurant and he knew that what he was doing to get her out of his mind wasn't working and it would require an adjustment...a big one.

***

Marisa tossed and turned in the bed. She didn't know what her problem was. It wasn't like she wasn't used to sleeping on a hard bed. She sat up in her bed and turned on the television. She flipped through the channels and landed on an old movie.

As she watched she began to imagine herself and Jeffrey portraying the characters. She groaned, when the leading male and leading female began kissing. It was like Jeffrey's hands were all over her body and his tongue was dipping into her mouth.

She quickly changed the channel. She didn't have time to have thoughts like that running through her mind.

She started watching a classic sitcom episode of *I Love Lucy*. She was laughing along with the television audience, when she heard the phone in her room ringing. She glanced at the clock to read eleven o'clock. She reached across the bed and answered the phone. "Hello?"

"Hello, Marisa...I'm sorry to call so late." There was a hesitation on his end. "Is that the television I hear?"

"Yeah, I couldn't sleep."

"Me neither," he admitted to her. "A lot on my mind."

"Right. There's been a lot of information thrown at you...I mean us, today. So, it makes sense that our minds are reeling."

There was a brief pause, before she heard him chuckling. "Yeah, that isn't exactly why I can't sleep." For a moment she wondered if it was because of her, but she didn't want to think foolish thoughts. "I actually am calling to tell you that the meetings for tomorrow have been cancelled. I just received an email, something about a water main break at the building they were using."

"Oh...that's too bad," she spoke, but she was really thrilled to know that they didn't have to sit through another boring meeting.

"Yeah, that's what I thought, too." He laughed, clearly seeing her sarcasm. "So, I was wondering...if you would want, that is...would you like to go visit your family tomorrow?"

Her jaw dropped. She processed his words, but wasn't sure if he truly meant them. "That's a three hour trip."

"I realize that. I actually know the Pittsburgh area well. Our plane doesn't leave until eight o'clock. We could get up early, you could visit them, and still be back in plenty of time to catch the plane to New York."

"You're going, too?" She asked, trying to catch her thoughts.

His light breathing was echoing through the phone. "I suppose that I could stay here and you could take the rental. I guess that I never really thought about that." She heard disappointment on his end. "Is that what you want?"

She shook her head, despite the fact that he couldn't see her. She knew that she wanted him to go, but she just was surprised to learn that she hand that in his mind. "You are more than welcome to meet me family."

"Well then...it's settled. Tomorrow we can get up at seven o'clock, get dressed, and head out. I'm sorry that you missed the barbeque."

"That's fine," she quickly spoke. She was still going to see her loved ones. "Thank you, Jeffrey."

"You are welcome." They disconnected the call but she began to reach for the phone again to call her mother. She then decided to leave it as a surprise and she knew that her family would definitely be surprised.

***

They were about fifteen minutes from her house and Jeffrey began to question her about her family. He figured that he should have some idea of where she came from. "So, give me the lowdown about your family. How you grew up and what kind of upbringing did you have?"

She seemed to think about it and he noticed a slight hesitation before she replied. "Well, my mom used to be a nurse. Then she had me and decided that she needed to take some time off to raise me. She was going to go back when I was starting Kindergarten. However, she had my sister before getting that chance. She never went back." She looked out the window and he saw a smile on her face. "She is a great mom and I have truly been blessed."

"So, your sister...were you close?" He asked, generally interested.

She nodded, "She is my best friend." She then turned back to him and spoke, "How about you? Do you have any siblings?"

He shook his head; he wanted to have someone to grow up, with but he wasn't blessed like that. "Nope, only child."

She scrunched her nose, "You must have been spoiled."

He laughed, "You would be absolutely...wrong. I was given money when I needed it, but there was a lot I was lacking."

She showed signs of concern and empathy. "I know exactly what you mean."

He could see that she meant that and it felt good to find someone he could talk to. "Well, I know about your mom and your sister...tell me about your dad."

Her face turned grim and she faced the window. "We don't really talk about him." He could see that he struck an emotional chord. Yet, even though he saw pain in her eyes, she looked back at him and shrugged, "I suppose you might as well know. My dad is at the state prison. He was a drunk most of my life and would take it out on all of us. He left bruises on my sister and me for a good portion of our childhood."

He couldn't believe the truth that was coming out. He reached across the car and grabbed her hand. Their eyes met and he shook his head, "I am so sorry, Marisa. Any guy that does that to his kids and wife, deserves to be locked up."

He saw tears in her eyes as she nodded, "That's why I left right after graduation. I couldn't stand being in the same town with all the bad memories."

He squeezed her hand and her eyes wandered down to the hold. They remained holding hands while going the rest of the way. She pointed to several different streets to turn down, before they made their way to a cul-de-sac.

She pointed to a white house on the end and he pulled in front of the house. He reluctantly pulled his hand away as they got out of the car.

"Thank you!" she said, before they headed up the driveway. "This is exactly what I needed."

"It's my pleasure," he smiled, trying to ignore the fact that he would have given her the moon.

They headed up the steps and she knocked on the door. After a couple of minutes, an older woman opened the door. Her eyes got big and she covered her mouth. "Marisa?"

"Mom..." Marisa spoke. Her voice was shaky. Her mom opened the screen door and threw her arms around her. They held each other in an emotional embrace, while he stayed back. When they pulled away, she turned to Jeffrey. "Mom, this is Jeffrey Bradley...my boss."

Her mother turned to him, "Hello, sir."

"Please, call me Jeffrey." He replied, shaking her hand. "It's a pleasure to meet you."

She smiled, then turned back to her daughter. "I don't understand. I thought you said that you couldn't come this weekend." She held the door open, as they entered.

"I couldn't, but we had our meetings yesterday and they were cancelled for today. So, Jeffrey said that we could come here today." She was beaming and he was thankful that he had made the suggestion.

"Jeffrey, thank you so much."

He shrugged, "I am glad that I could make it work."

"Hillary is going to be so excited to see you." Her mother was saying. "Hillary...come down here."

"What is..." a voice from upstairs yelled. He looked up to see that Hillary was standing at the top of the stairs. "Marisa?" She ran down the stairs and jumped into her arms, they hugged for what felt like an eternity. "I don't understand." She pulled away and he saw that she was just as emotional. She glanced toward him and then back at Marisa. "Who is the guy?"

"This is my boss Jeffrey Bradley."

He shook her hand, "Hello, Hillary. Nice to meet you."

"Likewise," she smiled.

"Tell me everything that you have been up to," Hillary said, grabbing onto Marisa's arm and carrying her away into another room. He didn't know if he should follow or give them space.

"Would you like some coffee, Jeffrey?" Her mother asked him.

He smiled, "No thank you."

She nodded, "Make yourself at home," she then walked away. He awkwardly hung out in the foyer, leaning against the banister. He knew that Hillary and Marisa would want their space and he didn't want to be an intruder.

***

"Girl, you didn't tell me what a fine piece of specimen you were working for," Hillary spoke, as they took a seat on the couch.

Marisa rolled her eyes, "He's not bad."

"Not bad?" Hillary shook her head, "You are either blind or in denial."

Marisa knew that she definitely wasn't blind. She shrugged, trying to forget about it. "Tell me about you. Did I see something on your left hand?"

Hillary laughed, "If I would have known you were going to be here then I would have hidden it from you." She produced her hand and Marisa stared down at the shiny ring. "I'm engaged."

"Mom said you had news, but I had no idea."

"It just kind of happened. I met him two months ago when I was getting my car worked on. We instantly had a connection and then he asked me to marry him. We haven't even had sex...he wants to wait. Can you believe that?"

Marisa slowly shook her head, knowing that she was already one step ahead of that with Jeffrey. "I am happy for you."

"Thank you," she replied, staring down at her ring. Her eyes got big, "Maybe you could get one of these things if you make nice with the lawyer." She winked at her and Marisa playfully hit her on the arm. "Ouch," she laughed.

Marisa looked around the living room, "Speaking of...I wonder where he is."

"You know Mom. She's probably talking his ear off."

"I hope not," Marisa replied, feeling scared. She laughed, thinking of the things her mother could tell him about her.

She started to get up, but Hillary reached out for her hand, pulling her back down. She looked at her and she smiled. "He'll be fine. I want to hear everything that has been going on with you."

Marisa told her the things that she felt she could, conveniently leaving out the fact that she was technically homeless. About an hour later, her mother was calling them in the kitchen for lunch. They headed out of the living room, where she saw Jeffrey standing at the banister.

She caught his eyes and started to laugh. "What are you doing? You could have come in."

He smiled, "I figured you wanted some alone time. I thought about sitting out in the car."

She rolled her eyes, "Not necessary."

"I didn't know what deep secrets you were going to share and I thought if you wanted to talk about me...it would be easier while I wasn't around." He was smiling to show that he was teasing, but she blushed. She hoped that he didn't hear anything. "Did you?"

"Did I what?" she asked.

"Did you talk about me?" He asked with a wink.

She looked away from him, searching for what she could say to him, then decided that she would play along. "Wouldn't you like to know?" She winked, brushing past him and heading toward the kitchen. She was suddenly feeling pretty good about their relationship and wanted the easiness to continue.

***

Marisa didn't want the day to end. Her time with the family was going so well. She looked at Jeffrey as they were saying their goodbyes. He seemed to fit into the family and it was like they were a true couple. "Goodbye, Hillary." I hugged her tightly. "I'll be back soon."

She nodded, then turned to Jeffrey and shook his hand. "It was nice meeting you, Hillary." He then turned to her mother and shook her hand. "Thank you for being so hospitable."

"You are welcome back anytime."

He nodded, "I'll keep that in mind. Thank you." Marisa wondered if they would ever have another reason to bring him back to Pennsylvania.

"Goodbye, Mom," she hugged her mom. "I love you!"

"I love you, too." When she parted, she saw that there were tears in her eyes. She brushed away her own and then turned to Jeffrey.

They headed to the front door. He held the door open for her as she exited the house. She waved as they got to the car. Once inside, she felt the tears take over. She looked at him and he reached out and grabbed her hand. "Are you alright?" He asked.

She nodded, but she still felt the heaviness in her heart. "This meant a lot to me. You have no idea how much."

"I meant it, Marisa. I am glad I was able to do this." She turned back to the window and waved to them, as he pulled away. As the house faded from her view, she let out a sigh. "I better stop and get gas, before we get too far down the road. She silently nodded, as she leaned back in the seat and just let him drive. A few minutes later he was turning into a gas station. When he stopped the car, he turned to her. "Marissa..." he started.

"Yes?" she asked, giving him her attention.

"There's something I have been wanting to do." He leaned in and landed a kiss on her lips. His tongue swooped in, gently massaging her tongue. When he pulled away, she just stared at him. "Now, I'm going to get gas," he said, getting out of the car and leaving her there to think about his lips.

What the hell? She thought. She didn't know what it meant, only that her lips were on fire and her heart was racing. She watched him getting gas and he was looking away from the car. She shook her head, trying to regain her senses.

When he got back in the car, she didn't know if she should look at him or look away. She saw the smile on his lips, causing her to look at him. "What was that?" she asked, still stunned.

"What? I just wanted to do it. Is it a crime?"

She covered her eyes and slowly tried to forget the moment, but she couldn't. She didn't want a casual fling...a simple kiss here to just confuse her even more. She wanted the real thing and something that was lasting. "Don't do that again." She spoke, feeling a sense of nausea in her stomach.

"Marisa...I..." he began, but she didn't want to hear excuses.

"Jeffrey, don't do that again. Understand?"

He slowly nodded, "Loud and clear." He pulled out of the gas station and headed back to Columbus. She didn't care what he thought, but she was not going to be the person that screwed someone to get ahead in life. She deserved better than that.

***

Jeffrey had hoped things would lighten up between them on the airplane. However, he was left to kick himself for kissing her like that. He didn't mean for it to upset her the way that it did.

When she walked to her car in the airport parking lot, she didn't even allow him to walk with her. It was like nothing they had been through meant anything.

As he worked on Monday, he had hoped that she would need to talk to him about work stuff, but she never came to him. He had thought about calling her into his office and lying about needing her help with something, but he knew that would come across as wrong.

He left the office and found himself heading in the opposite direction of his car. He went into the bar to where he ordered a beer. He didn't drink much, but he knew that he needed something to take off the edge.

He slowly drank the beer and thought about the way the previous day ended. As he thought about it, he found his mind drifting to her scent, the way her body felt against his, the way her breath felt against his skin, and the way that he felt when he was with her. He took a drink of his beer and reached for his phone.

He searched for her cellphone number and then called it. It was a recording that came on. "We're sorry, the number you are trying to reach has been disconnected or changed." He disconnected the call and frowned, dialing it again and receiving the same message.

He put his phone away and took another drink, before throwing a tip of the tip jar and leaving the bar. He knew that he needed to tell her the truth, but he wouldn't be able to reach her if her number had changed. As he was walking back to his car, his eyes looked up and he saw Marisa and a man entering a hotel.

Her arm was linked through his and they were laughing. He paused, staring up at the hotel. It all made sense...Marisa was seeing someone else.

***

Marisa was getting good at avoiding him. She knew that the key was to not make eye contact and so far it was working. However, when she came back from lunch and found a note that there was a meeting with Troy Houser, she knew that that was coming to an end. At two o'clock, she headed to the boardroom. He looked up, as she entered. Then he looked back down at the notes.

"Am I just taking notes?" She asked, sitting down in a chair.

"That would be fine," he mumbled. It appeared that they were both avoiding each other. She flipped her notebook open to the page after her previous notes. "If you have anything to add, you can throw it in."

She gawked at him, unsure what to say. "Well, the last time we even really talked about this case was that night I showed you the picture.

That was about a week ago. Any new developments?"

He shrugged, "Just wing it." The way he was being casual, surprised her. She couldn't believe she upset him that much.

She nodded, looking down at her notebook. When Troy walked into the room, she felt nervous. She tried to smile as he took a seat. "Mr. Houser, thank you for coming back in. We have a couple of questions. For starters, can you explain this?" He pushed the picture in front of Troy.

He looked at it and then looked up.

"Yeah, that's my ex and her boyfriend. That was taken while we were still married."

Marisa watched Jeffrey as he grabbed a marker and walked over to the picture, circling the spot where he was standing. "What about this?"

Troy looked down at the picture and his face turned red. "Uh..."

"You were spying on her yourself, you found her with this guy, and you became jealous. Is this all correct?"

"No..." he argued.

Jeffrey chuckled, then looked back his way. "You weren't jealous?"

"I was jealous, but this has nothing to do with why I'm here."

"Is that so?" Jeffrey asked, "The way I see it is you hired a PI. Then you realized that you didn't trust the PI's work, so you went on a hunt. You came across her and her lover at the same time that the PI did. You grew jealous, instantly filed for divorce and would have completely been satisfied with letting it go. However, you discovered that she was going to marry the guy she cheated on you with. So, that angered you and you vowed to do anything you could to make sure that she paid. How close am I?"

He looked between Marisa and Jeffrey. Marisa couldn't believe how much information he was throwing out there about Troy. "I am not on trial," he argued.

Marisa glanced at him, "Did she abuse the children?" She asked, softly. "Or, did you?"

She saw Jeffrey looking at her, but she didn't turn away from Troy's glare. "What?" He asked, but Marisa saw that he was not denying it.

Jeffrey turned to him, "Did you?"

Troy's mouth dropped open, but he did not deny the accusations. "I'm apparently going to need a lawyer." He spoke, looking at Jeffrey.

"You are and you won't find one here." He nodded, standing up and walking out of the office. Jeffrey reached for his phone and dialed a number. "Hey, Troy Houser is about to walk out of the building.

Detain him and call the cops. I'll be out in a minute." He disconnected the call. Jeffrey turned to Marisa, as she was standing up. She started to move past him, "How did you know?" He asked.

"I lived it, remember?" She shrugged, "It's all the same." She left the boardroom and headed back to her office. She closed her door and watched through the window as Jeffrey walked to the security station. She started to cry, feeling the pain from the years of abuse and knowing exactly what his kids had gone through.

***

Jeffrey waited until he knew that Marisa was leaving. He followed her out of the building and watched as she entered the hotel. He knew that it wasn't any of his business. If she was having sex with ten different men, he wouldn't be able to say anything. Although, that didn't stop him from heading to the hotel.

He entered cautiously and saw her get into the elevator. He watched as the numbers went up, stopping on floor three. He got in the other elevator and pushed the button to floor three. He prayed that when the door opened, he wasn't greeted by her. When the door opened, he peeked outside and saw her putting a key into the lock.

He held back, waiting for her to go in. He didn't know what he would say to her, but he knew that he was interested to confront her. He walked up to the door and knocked lightly. It wasn't long, before she was opening the door. She stared at him, "How did you know I would be here?"

"I saw you yesterday come into the hotel and today I followed you."

"Followed me?" She asked, anger taking over.

"I'm not proud of it, Marisa, but I was a little surprised. I know that I have no right to be jealous, but—"

"Jealous?" She asked, frowning.

"Yes...jealous. I know that I don't have any right to be jealous that you are having sex with someone else. I don't own any right to you. We aren't dating, but I do have strong feelings for you and I was going to tell you that yesterday if I could have gotten ahold of you.

Your phone has been disconnected and then I saw you with the guy yesterday...." He heard the sound of laughter, so he stopped talking. She was laughing so hard that she had to go back into the room and sink down on the bed. "What's so funny?"

"You're jealous..."

He rolled his eyes. He should have known that would be the only thing she would focus on. "Move past that and listen to the rest."

"You have it all wrong, Jeffrey. You have no idea just how much."

"Really, then explain it to me." The words came out brash and he regretted that.

Her face turned red and she stood up from the bed. "I don't owe you an explanation. Like you said...I can sleep with anyone I want." She crossed her arms, as if to wager him.

"I know you can." He glanced around the room, noticing the boxes lying around the room.

He looked at her. "I shouldn't have come." He stepped back, as her eyes wandered down to the boxes and then looked back at him.

"Aren't you going to question the boxes?"

"You don't have to tell me anything," he said, reaching for the door.

"Jeffrey, you didn't get ahold of my cellphone, because I cancelled it. The guy you saw is my best friend, Chad. He's been the only friend that I have had and that has supported me." He felt a pang of guilt hit him.

"Those boxes are here because I have been living here. I was evicted from my apartment exactly a week after I got this job."

"Marisa, I had no idea." He spoke, thinking back to when she asked for an advance and he shot her down. "Why didn't you tell me?"

"Pride, stupidity, because I didn't want to play the sympathy card."

"You should have told me," he spoke, softly.

She nodded, "In hindsight...maybe I should have, but it's over and done with and hopefully in a couple of weeks I will be back on my feet...thanks to you and your job."

His hand fell from the door handle and he moved closer to her. "I'm sorry that you have had to go through this."

She moved in closer to him, "It hasn't all been bad."

He brushed her hair behind her shoulder and moved in closer to her, bringing his lips to hers. He would move slowly, if she would just give him the chance. He parted from the kiss and rested his head against hers, "I'm sorry Marisa that I just wasn't honest with you," he whispered, feeling her breath against his skin.

"I have strong feelings for you, too," she admitted. She closed her eyes, as they stood with their heads together and his hands caressing her neck. "Make love to me," she spoke, opening her eyes.

He hadn't thought she would speak the words, but he slowly began to remove her clothes. Her hands went to his outfit and she was removing them from his body. He flicked her bra off with his wrist and then lowered her panties, while she grabbed onto his boxers and pulled them to the ground.

His hand wrapped around her neck and passionately held onto a kiss. She parted from the kiss, to push him down to the bed. Once he was lying on the bed, she straddled him. He slowly entered her, as her lips went down to his.

His hands massaged her large breasts, while their tantalizing kiss took over. She gyrated her hips against his, moving him in and out of her. He pulled from the kiss, because of the intensity of his gyrations. "Ugh...ugh...oh God...ugh..." he moaned, moving his arm around her body and pulling her down to his thrusts.

"Ugh...ugh..." she moaned, moving on top of him with comfort. Her gentle whimpering was breathlessly encompassing him. She crashed down on top of him, as he slowly retracted from her. They kissed, while she wrapped her arm around him.

He was relieved that everything was working out and that all the confusion was gone, because he had no doubt in his mind that they would spend many days and nights exploring the possibilities and he was excited for it to begin.

Unexpected Romance

The blaring alarm clock on the nightstand jolted Jennifer awake. Too groggy to function after a late night at the lab looking over patient case files, she clumsily banged her hand around until she found the annoying culprit and slammed her palm onto the snooze button. Even after years of being lectured that it was better to get up the first time the thing went off, she never could. Only after two snoozes would she allow her eyes to crack open. Not a good habit for a doctor. There were patients to see and research to perform. Who was she kidding? After banging snooze buttons for twenty years, this was one habit she would never break.

After eighteen more luxurious minutes in her cozy warm bed, Jennifer couldn't deny the fact anymore. She had to get up and get going. Waiting any longer and she wouldn't have time for her morning run. No morning run meant a cranky woman—a cranky doctor at that. Not that she enjoyed running but it was the only time she could clear her head completely in order to focus throughout the rest of the day. Caffeine could only help so much so running had become her go-to activity. As much as Jennifer despised the bitter cold of a February morning in the nation's capital, she threw back the covers to begin her day.

It would take at least a mile before the fog of exhaustion began to lift from her mind. The first mile was always the most torturous. After that though, Jennifer could run forever. Adrenaline finally pumping through her petite, 5' 2" frame, she could take on the world. This morning in particular she needed the respite.

Being a pediatric oncologist was her life's dream. That is, after Hannah, her best friend from elementary school suffered horribly and died from a brain tumor. It was the reason she became a doctor in the first place. No child should have to suffer like that, ever. And no parent should have to endure such a loss. But cancer was indiscriminate and unforgiving. Last night she suffered yet another battle with her childhood demon. A three year old child with lymphoma. Jennifer had been so sure her latest protocol would work. She had spent the rest of the night beating herself up for failing yet another patient, another distraught family. Sometimes her life's dream was actually her life's nightmare. This morning she welcomed the punishment of the frigid air filling her lungs as she near sprinted the remaining blocks from her small condominium on K Street to the National Mall. Her destination – the reflecting pond overlooking the Lincoln Memorial.

Once she reached the ice-speckled pond, she allowed herself a moment to rest and take in the beauty of the landscape. Still too early for the onslaught of commuters and tourists who flood the city daily. All was quiet except the occasional rumble of jets overhead as they were taking off from Reagan National. Whether from the freezing temperatures and wind assailing her eyes or from sorrow and frustration at her failure last night, tears ran down her freckled face. Jennifer didn't know what was worse. Losing the patient or the fact that after so many years she still had not toughened up enough to make that pain any less.

Not wishing to dwell on the matter anymore, Jennifer raced back home. Shutting out all thoughts and allowing her body to operate on autopilot. New day, new challenge! She wouldn't allow self-pity to stop her. After many battles lost, and a few won, her determination was greater than ever.

After a quick, scalding hot shower Jennifer towel-dried her short strawberry-blonde locks and made a beeline for the coffee pot. No breakfast. She couldn't remember the last time she actually ate breakfast. Probably before leaving home for college when her overbearing mom would force her to eat before she could leave for school, even if it meant she was late. Her shift didn't start until 10 AM so there was plenty of time to either tidy up her small,

640 square foot condo or aimlessly peruse the internet. Without a second thought, she plopped down in her oversized khaki arm chair with her laptop.

Not obsessed about politics and news like everyone else in this town, Jennifer decided on lighter fare. How long had it been since she'd been on Facebook? Probably since her high school reunion that had been organized via the website, forcing her to get an account. Surprised that she actually remembered her password, the site loaded. Wow! Fifty-two "Friend" requests?! Jennifer was surprised she knew that many people. The newsfeed was filled with funny pictures of cats and babies. Quickly scanning through all the miscellaneous vanities, she noticed a posting from one of her best friends from her days at the University of Colorado. It was a picture of her tall, slender, runway model friend Jacy Standish with her college beau Ethan Davis III. The posting showed the couple with Ethan on one knee and Jacy with the biggest smile ever. Yes, it was the couple's engagement announcement. "Well, it's about time!" Jennifer thought. They have only been together since forever, it seemed.

The posting was a few days old so thankfully Jennifer still had time to send them a congratulatory message. The announcement declared that the wedding was to be at the end of May in Cocoa Beach, Florida. The couple had been living there since Ethan graduated with an advanced degree in aeronautics and went to work with NASA. In lieu of formal invitations, since there was nothing formal about Jacy nor Ethan, the Facebook announcement was also serving as the wedding invitation. Any friends and family that could make it should reply to the posting. "Well, that's certainly a modern approach." Jennifer grinned as she knew it was typical of the couple to be that nonchalant about their own wedding.

After clicking the "Like" icon and commenting a quick "Congrats!" Jennifer noticed she had messages. There were five messages from Jacy. The bride-to-be was curious why Jennifer never answered her home phone and why didn't she have voicemail. The next message scolded her for not keeping in touch and providing her friends current contact information as she was desperate to talk to her sorority big sister and best friend. Another message instructed Jennifer to call her STAT because she had a very important question to ask her. Looking at the clock, she realized it probably wasn't too early to call so she picked up her phone to dial the number listed in the last message.

A groggy Ethan answered the phone but was more than delighted to disturb his soon-to-be wife who was already awake and had just returned from walking the dogs. Jacy's squeal of delight nearly ruptured Jennifer's eardrum. After letting Jacy run on for several minutes about the upcoming wedding and lecturing her friend on her lack of manners for not staying in touch, she excitedly asked the burning question... "Jennifer, will you be my maid of honor?" This was followed by more declarations that she HAD to be her maid of honor and she was NOT taking no for an answer. Typical Jacy.

Promising to check her schedule and to get back to her later that day, Jennifer ended the call hoping she would not have to disappoint Jacy but uneasy with the thought of attending a wedding. Her own personal life was, well lacking the personal part. She was not a big socialite, even though the Chief of Pediatric Oncology enjoyed forcing her to attend fund raisers to benefit the hospital whenever he saw fit. Social settings were just not her thing.

Jennifer noticed another message in her inbox. This time from a blast from the past male friend, also from college, Lorenzo Esposito. Now what could he want? They hadn't spoken to each other since graduation. Despite being close friends in those days, she realized she didn't even know what his post-grad plans entailed. Although they had hung out quite often, going to sporting events together and the occasional party, Jennifer had been too busy trying to get into medical school and Lorenzo chasing skirts around campus for anything more to ever develop between them. Friends had teased that they should stop trying to fool everyone because they obviously belonged together. She and Lorenzo would just laugh it off with a mischievous wink at each other. Never had anything other than a platonic "just friends" relationship ever entered their minds.

Curious what Lorenzo had to say after so many years, Jennifer clicked on the message. It was short and sweet. The usual, "Hi, how are you? I'm fine. Long time, no see." He had heard about the wedding and Ethan had asked him to be the best man but he was lacking a date to the event. Even though they had not kept in touch he was hopeful she would save him from having to RSVP as "1". He went on to explain that he was uncomfortable taking a "date" since weddings were seen as either the kiss of death for a relationship or as getting in line to be the next sucker down the aisle. He could do without the hassle either way. Lorenzo went on to note that he noticed her scant profile on Facebook as showing she was still unattached so he was pleading once again for her help, just like the good ole days in college. He needed a no-frills, no-strings attached wedding date and was hoping she would agree. "Wow! What a romantic?!" she thought sarcastically. He ended the message with his contact information if she was interested in helping him out.

Signing out of Facebook without responding, Jennifer took up her now tepid coffee and thought back to the outgoing, charismatic, undeniably handsome man Lorenzo had been in college. Tall, dark, and handsome didn't come close to describing him then. For a moment she allowed herself to imagine what he might look like now years later. She had to admit, the picture in her head was nice...very nice, indeed. Throughout college Lorenzo had always attracted the ladies, in droves. At one point their group of friends had taken to calling him "Casanova" because of his love'em and leave'em attitude.

After college the gang had all gone their separate ways. Jennifer had been horrible about keeping in contact with anyone. However, she did remotely recall Jacy mentioning that Lorenzo had married a woman he met at his first job after graduation. Jennifer had been surprised the mighty Casanova had fallen so soon. It must not have worked out if he was hitting her up for a wedding date.

While heading out the door to the hospital, she promised herself to clear her schedule at work so she could attend her friend's wedding. Besides she had not taken time off from the hospital in all her years working there. Not even for holidays to go visit her folks in Denver. She was due some R&R and this was the perfect excuse. As soon as she cleared the time off with her boss, she would contact Lorenzo.

After making her rounds at the hospital later that day, Jennifer sought out the Chief of Pediatric Oncology, Jacob Mallory, to discuss her "vacation". She found him where she expected to find him...on the phone in his office attempting to drum up more money for the department from a donor. He motioned for her to take a seat while he wrapped up the call. Jacob was not just the chief of her department but she also considered him a friend. He was of average height but built like a linebacker. His physique was always displayed at its best in Armani or other designer suits with his dark blonde hair cut short and always clean-shaven. Outside of the hospital environment he could easily be mistaken for one of the bigwigs up on Capitol Hill. He was equally suited to the political life. After all, wining and dining for cash from the elites was his specialty.

Ending his call, he turned his piercing aqua blue eyes on her with a charming grin meant to make her melt but somehow she never felt the impact of his bedroom eyes. They briefly discussed her current case load and results of some tests she was running on a new patient. She hoped the prescribed protocol would work since the cancer seemed to be caught in the early stages. The results were still being validated but Jennifer was optimistic. After a few minutes she got up the courage to voice her request. Looking somewhat shocked, but pleasantly surprised, Jacob reassured her that vacation time was much overdue for the workaholic doctor. However, he added that he would be delighted to go with her. Jennifer knew that was a danger area. She had attended some hospital fundraising functions with Jacob and knew he was attracted to her but she had no desire to complicate their relationship. Declining with the excuse of spending time with old friends, she thanked him as she rose from the uncomfortable office armchair to attend to the remainder of her day.

Later that evening, Jennifer returned to her snug condo with a large brown paper bag filled with several containers from the corner Chinese restaurant. Not realizing until much too late that she had not eaten at all during the day, she was ravenous by the time she headed home. Not even bothering to transfer the food from the take-out containers to a plate, she dove into the combination fried rice first. After satiating her hunger and fixing a cup of jasmine tea, she sat back down in her favorite armchair and pulled her computer onto her lap.

First, she notified Jacy that she would indeed attend the wedding and be her maid of honor. Luckily, Jacy was so laid back that she allowed Jennifer to pick out her own dress, as long as it was lavender in color. "Terrific," she thought, "purple does nothing for my Irish freckled complexion." Next, she composed a short message to Lorenzo stating she would attend the wedding and would also appreciate a "no strings" date. They could arrange to meet up once they both got to Cocoa Beach. Before signing off the computer, Jennifer booked her flight, a rental car, and her suite at the resort where Jacy and Ethan would be married.

Following a hot shower and veg'ing out to some reality television show for an hour, Jennifer retired for the night. The wedding had given her something else to think about aside from her young patients awaiting a miracle cure. Jennifer briefly entertained the hope that tonight her sleep would not be interrupted by nightmares. Maybe there would instead be images of warm sands and the sound of relaxing waves and a tall, dark, and handsome man.

The wedding approached quickly and Jennifer left a muggy Washington, DC over Memorial Day weekend for the hot and humid climate of the Central Atlantic Florida coast. In the last few months she had managed to grow her strawberry-blonde locks out just past her shoulders, and had even gone in for a professional mani-pedi a couple hours before her flight. A friend from the hospital had taken her shopping for a dress suitable for the occasion. Despite the lavender not being her best shade, Jennifer was surprised she was actually happy with the selection. She was not happy with the 2 inch high heels they had selected though. She hadn't worn heels since medical school graduation. However, they were necessary as her dress was long and her legs were short.

After a short plane ride and an even shorter drive from Orlando to Cocoa Beach, Jennifer arrived at The Cocoa Sands Resort and Spa shortly before the wedding rehearsal. If she was lucky, she would have a chance to stroll on the beach before meeting everyone in the ballroom. Luck was not to be had as Jacy spotted her friend in the lobby and rushed over to hug and greet her. Jacy was still the same as in college. Super model gorgeous with long legs and shining long blonde hair. She took charge of the situation and sent the bell hop to the room with Jennifer's luggage while she dragged the weary traveler to the outdoor bar area where everyone else had already congregated.

Seeing some familiar faces and some not-so familiar faces, Jennifer was handed a drink while making introductions and greeting old friends. Not all of the old gang was here, it seemed. She would have to ask Jacy about that later since she was being reprimanded for being the last to arrive by Jacy's mom. Through the crowd, at the other end of the bar, sat a very familiar handsome face – Lorenzo. The groom immediately piped up that he was just glad his buddy's date had finally shown up because it was a shame for such a man to be all alone. "Oh no!" Jennifer thought. She had heard this line of discussion before quite a number of times during college. Anytime Lorenzo had been girlfriend-free for more than five minutes, Ethan and Jacy had pushed them to get together. Maybe agreeing to this wedding date was a mistake.

There wasn't a lot of time for conversation as the wedding planner came out to the bar to escort the wedding party into the ballroom for rehearsal. Jennifer could tell this lady ran a tight ship and thrived on the stress of producing the perfect wedding for her clients. Considering how laid back Jacy and Ethan were about such thing, they had waited several years to tie the knot officially after all, Jennifer was surprised in their pick for a wedding planner. Guess it was better for someone else to stress about the wedding because the bride and groom weren't going to do so. As they were walking back into the hotel, Jennifer felt a soft touch on her elbow. Turning around she gazed up at her incredibly tall, incredibly attractive, wedding date. Lorenzo always had the most amazing smile and it was in full force as he linked their arms together to usher her into the ballroom. The warmth from his touch was reassuring and familiar as he had escorted her to a dozen or more functions in college. "Yes," she thought, "This was a good idea."

Wordlessly they entered the ballroom with the rest of the party and took their respective places.

The rehearsal, thankfully, was short and sweet. Jennifer was ravenous since once again she had forgotten to eat that day. A full seven course meal awaited everyone in the main banquet hall of the resort. The tables were littered with place cards with centerpieces of fragrant candles and rose petals. She was looking forward to the meal and getting reacquainted with Lorenzo, as well as other long lost friends from the good ole days. Engaged in conversation with Janice, another former college friend who had always been known as the "mother" of the group, Jennifer felt someone staring at her. Looking around she discovered two of the darkest, most gorgeous chocolate brown eyes gazing at her from across the room. Lorenzo had already found their designated places and had her chair pulled out for her. Mumbling an excuse to Janice, Jennifer began to walk over to him realizing she was being way too self-conscious about herself as she neared him, with her head slightly bowed but looking up through her lush brown eye lashes shielding brilliant emerald green eyes. "Why am I so nervous?" she thought with some frustration.

The dinner was superb and the conversation flowed easily around the table full of college pals. Janice was married with a passel of kids, all under the age of eight which were at home in Pennsylvania with her husband. Kyle had his own architectural firm in Dallas and had just become engaged to his assistant Sarah. He assured everyone that they were invited to the nuptials next winter. Candace was a divorced nurse and single mom but was hoping her boyfriend of the last three years would finally pop the question. He responded with a flamboyant roll of his eyes. Everyone was in good health and good spirits. It truly was fantastic to be back with her group of friends. Until now Jennifer had not realized just how much she had missed them. Her world now consisted of work, work, and more work. No friends really outside of the hospital and definitely no boyfriend.

Lorenzo, however, remained quiet as everyone else discussed their lives since college and plans for the future. Jennifer didn't remember him being the quiet one. He was always the jovial, fun all the time, type of guy. He would offer a small smile or laugh as appropriate, but seemed to be staying outside the conversation instead of a part of it. His silence unnerved her but she didn't wish to ask unwanted questions but made a mental note to ask Jacy about the alteration in Lorenzo later.

With dinner over, the wedding party moved back to the outdoor bar area where they could enjoy the cool ocean breeze and their drinks. Not realizing just how tired she was, and there wasn't nearly enough food in her stomach to combat much more alcohol, Jennifer chose a lounge chair by the pool to relax in. At least she could kick off her strappy high heel sandals she had been in all day. Her feet were going to really hurt tomorrow. Jennifer had worn nothing but sneakers and crocs since graduating medical school. She was not cut out for heels, despite the need for added height, as she barely topped out at 5'2". Everyone else gathered around the pool deck, sipping mai tai's and other fruity umbrella drinks. Ethan started the group on something he called zombie brain shots. She didn't know what was in it but it looked disgusting. Jennifer declined. With that the party was in full swing. Good thing the wedding ceremony wasn't until late afternoon tomorrow as this particular group was going to need some hangover recovery time in the morning.

The party lasted well into the evening but most began to file away to their respective rooms shortly after midnight. Jennifer had nearly fallen asleep in her lounge chair. It wasn't until the last of the chattering died away that she noticed she was alone except for Lorenzo who had taken up a perch along the side of the pool, splashing his feet around. Throughout the after-dinner party, he had still remained quiet. This was not the man she remembered from college. The larger-than-life sexy, fun-loving Casanova. This made her sad and want to find out what was bothering her friend. Yes, they had been out of touch for many years. However, she found that she still cared about his well-being and had missed his presence in her life all this time. She got up from her lounge chair and walked over to the pool to sit down beside him. For several moments, they just sat there without saying a word.

Lorenzo was the first to break the awkward silence between them by remarking about being proud she had realized her dream of being a prominent pediatric doctor in a renowned hospital. It was a vague attempt at small talk. She thanked him and then they sat in silence for a while longer until Jennifer couldn't bare it anymore. Turning to him and looking up into his eyes, she saw sorrow reflected in their dark pools. There was an overwhelming desire to just hug him tightly as if he needed a shoulder to cry on. The urge was so strong that she did timidly reach up to stroke his cheek, which was prickly from a day or two old growth of beard. Instead of withdrawing from her as she feared, he placed his hand over hers and held it for what seemed many moments with his eyes closed. "La mia bella amica," he uttered softly.

After sitting a few more moments in silence, Lorenzo turned to Jennifer with that old familiar smile she was accustomed to seeing. "I'm so sorry for being such a poor date. It wasn't what I planned at all. I thought the wedding would be a good distraction for me and instead I've only been sad since arriving here. That's no way to treat such a beautiful lady," he said with sincerity. She could tell he was sad but didn't understand why.

Jennifer gazed up into his eyes and said softly, "I'll forgive you but you have to tell me why you are so sad. I was expecting this larger than life happy-go-lucky dude from my youth. Seeing you this way makes me sad and worried. This 'date' as you call it can only get better but you have to be straight with me."

With that he sighed and let the tale spill out. He had married several years ago to a wonderful woman, Lisa. They were happy and even happier when they became a family with the birth of their son Raphael. A spirited five year old that was a miniature version of himself with his wife's quirky sense of humor. Their happiness was cut short a couple years back when Lisa was killed in a horrific accident on I-66 coming home from work one day. She wasn't even supposed to be on the roads but had offered to deliver company documents to the Senate sub-planning committee chairman since he and his business partner were overwhelmed completing a project for another client.

Lorenzo continued his story about how he was struggling as a single dad. Business was fine but he worried about his son growing up without his mom. If he had to admit it, he was also lonely and missed his wife very much. He thought he'd brave it out for Ethan and Jacy by coming to the wedding but it was taking more of a toll on him than he had imagined. That was why he had sent her the Facebook message. He knew if anyone could see him through this weekend, it would be Jennifer. "Guess I should've been more upfront and explained all that beforehand. Quite frankly I never thought you'd say yes. Figured you had some hot shot doctor boyfriend to escort you here." With that last statement he actually conjured up a small teasing half-smile.

Jennifer continued to hold his hand and listen for hours as he told stories about his wife and his son. He took out his iPhone to show her a picture and the boy was indeed a copy of his handsome dad. Their conversation flowed to other topics such as her career and lack of a personal life, what they had been up to since college, and reminiscing about their time together in school. Before they realized it the sun was coming up over the ocean horizon and they were still seated on the pool deck with their feet dangling in the water.

As the hotel staff was starting about their day, Lorenzo and Jennifer went to their own rooms for much needed rest. Despite no sleep since the day before, her head was spinning with everything he had told her. After getting through all the sadness, they had reconnected during the course of the night. Felt like she had her friend back and with that thought she was able to close her eyes and sleep.

A few hours later a loud banging awoke her. She had overslept. It was Jacy with the brilliant smile of a happy bride. The two women exchanged stories as Jennifer jumped in the shower and got ready for the day. Thankfully, the wedding planner had arranged for someone to do their make-up and hair. All she had to do was make herself presentable. While waiting on her friend, Jacy took pleasure teasing Jennifer about her late night sojourn with Lorenzo. Jacy had always hoped the two would end up together, ever since their freshman days. They had thwarted every attempt by herself and Ethan to make the transition from friends to lovers. Secretly, Jacy wished that her wedding might light a fire in their direction but she kept that information to herself.

A few hours later, after a quick brunch, getting dolled up by the resort's spa staff, and getting the bride squeezed into her lacy, halter-top styled wedding gown, it was time. Jacy didn't seem nervous at all. She and Ethan had been together so long the wedding was just a formality. Jennifer, on the other hand, felt shaky as she proceeded down the carpeted aisle from the pool area to a spot on the beach where the groom and his handsome best man awaited. Traversing the terrain in high heels had been a bad idea after all. She nervously glanced up as she approached them and saw Lorenzo smiling at her with a gleam in his eyes. She gave him a quick wink and stepped aside for the bride's arrival, trying her best not to trip.

The wedding was short and simple. No frills but still sweet and romantic. Within minutes Jacy and Ethan were pronounced husband and wife, kissed, and everyone cheered. Jennifer glanced over to see how Lorenzo was handling the situation. She needn't have worried. He was all smiles and staring straight at her. Her stomach experienced an unfamiliar butterfly sensation, but she dismissed it in her mind as needing to eat something. "It couldn't be more than that," she thought.

The reception was held in the ballroom with French doors that opened out to the beach area. During dinner Lorenzo gave a sincere, yet hilarious toast to the bride and groom as he regaled the wedding guests with the story of how the two had met, had instantly despised each other, but within a week were caught making out in the chem lab. Everyone laughed, except Jacy's parents. It was her turn. Jennifer had forgotten she needed to make a toast so she tried to wing it. After stumbling around for the right words, she went with the traditional congratulatory message to the groom with best wishes for the bride. Then reversed herself saying "Knowing Jacy as well as I do, maybe the best wishes part belongs to the groom. Hope you have a big enough closet for all her shoes and that you don't live near an animal shelter since Jacy will bring home every single dog, cat, bird, mouse, whatever."

Music began shortly afterwards and the dance party ensued. Jacy and Ethan had always been big dancers and had dragged Jennifer and Lorenzo to all the clubs around campus. Jennifer was never comfortable in that environment, but Lorenzo always seemed to make it okay. Just like old times, he stayed by her side the entire night and didn't pull her out onto the dance floor until a Frank Sinatra ballad began to play. He didn't even ask. Just took her arm and led her out to dance. She recognized the strains of

"The Way You Look Tonight". Lorenzo was the only person who understood her preference for Frank Sinatra over Nirvana. It had been a running joke that Jennifer had arrived at campus in a time capsule from the 1950s because she never liked the typical "alternative" music most co-eds did.

They danced closely. For some reason Jennifer couldn't find the courage to look up into his eyes. All she could focus on was the feel of his hand stroking the small of her back through the flimsy dress material as they danced and listening to the beat of his heart as she laid her head on his chest. If they were back in school they would be bantering back and forth about who was the better dancer or just joking around in general.

Too soon the song ended to be replaced by "The Chicken Dance". Hoping to escape, Jennifer pulled away to walk back to the sidelines but Lorenzo had other ideas. Yes, she was going to have to endure this most ridiculous wedding ritual. She was sure the "Electric Slide" would follow soon enough, but hoped they had seen fit to exclude "The Macarena". Before realizing it, it had been several upbeat dance numbers and she was still on the dance floor. Sweaty and thirsty, she motioned to Lorenzo that she was getting a drink. He followed closely behind as they grabbed a couple champagne flutes off a nearby waiter's tray and strolled outside for a breath of fresh air.

Removing her shoes on the sand, they walked out to the edge of the Atlantic Ocean. The sun was setting over the horizon. Jennifer plopped down on the sand to take in the beauty of the scene as she rarely saw the sunset anymore since she was always at the hospital or in the lab. Lorenzo joined her as they silently watched the glowing orange orb seemingly descend into the water. It was the first time in years that either of them had felt peaceful. This weekend had done wonders for them both, whether they realized it or not.

Unaware of the passage of time, the bride and groom came searching for them an hour later for the bouquet and garter throwing tradition. Jennifer always tried to make herself scarce during this particular portion of any wedding but decided to humor Jacy this once. Luckily, one of the groom's sisters was intent on being the next to get hitched and knocked everyone out of the way. Lorenzo stood stock still as Ethan threw the garter right at him and let the item fall to the floor where the pre-teen ring bearer grabbed it up. With all the wedding traditions complete, the bride and groom quickly made their exit so they could start the real celebrations in the honeymoon suite. The rest of the wedding party meandered around the ballroom for a while longer but started to disperse for their own rooms. Jennifer looked over at Lorenzo with a coy smile and motioned for him to follow her.

Earlier that day Jennifer had spotted a billiards room down the hall from the spa area. In college they had played pool against each other relentlessly. A few times they had partnered up to swindle money from unsuspecting underclassmen. With a wink, she began to rack up the balls and selected her cue stick. "How about a friendly wager? For old times' sake," she challenged.

Laughing, Lorenzo accepted her dare. After requesting a couple drinks from the bartender, he asked, "So what are we betting this time? It's not like I have a research paper I need your help on anymore and I don't think they will allow me on the plane with a case of scotch. What's it gonna be, little girl?"

"Alright there, jolly green giant," she teased back with the pet name she had given him freshman year, "We're both relatively successful people. We could actually bet real money this time."

With a frown, he replied, "No. No. That's no fun. Let's make it interesting. Whoever wins gets to make the other either tell a truth or take a dare." This proposal had potential but Jennifer was a little wary recalling past dares from him but decided to just go with it.

"You're on, big guy," she retorted with a smirk. Even though she hadn't played pool in years she was confidant it would come back to her. However, the strategy didn't work quite as she had planned. After thoroughly whipping his opponent, not once but three separate times, Jennifer admitted defeat and pleaded for mercy.

Appearing deep in thought Lorenzo issued his ultimatum. Truth or dare? Always uncomfortable with the truth category, she chose "dare". His dark eyes sparkled at the prospect as he contemplated his request. "Okay, I dare you to skinny dip in the pool or ocean right now."

Thankfully the alcohol that had flowed all night helped her find courage to do so but she was still not happy about it. After trying several times to convince Lorenzo to go "Best 5 out of 7 games", she resigned herself to her fate. Even the bartender snickered as she headed out to the door to the pool. After seeing that the pool was a bit too well lit for her liking, she chose the darker, more concealing ocean. Jennifer timidly approached the edge of the surf to test the water temperature before shedding any clothes. Being the Atlantic Ocean, it was chilly no matter what time of year.

Looking back to see Lorenzo standing smugly a few yards back, Jennifer instructed him to turn around and close his eyes. Despite it being nighttime, the moon was full and cast too much light on the beach for her liking. Grumbling under her breath that she should have known not to accept a dare from that man in particular, she tried the zipper at the back of the dress. It wouldn't budge. After a number of failed attempts she gave up and called for Lorenzo to help. The look on his face said that he was enjoying this a bit too much. He unhooked the clasp at the top, which she had completely forgotten about, and then slowly slid the zipper down to the small of her back. Her skin was chilled from the cool breeze coming off the ocean but where his fingers barely grazed her back as he worked the zipper almost seemed on fire. She shook her head slightly to clear her head. "Must be the alcohol affecting me," she reasoned.

With the zipper situation remedied, Lorenzo retreated to his spot on the sand a few yards away. Being a gentleman, he turned away as she undressed. Still in her undies, Jennifer started to enter the water when she heard, "Skinny dipping means skin only, little girl," followed by a smug chuckle. Wincing at being caught trying to cheat, she shed the rest of her garments and plunged into the waves.

Resurfacing quickly she looked over to see Lorenzo doubled over laughing. Wishing to get out of the frigid water and avoid any ocean inhabitants, she tersely instructed him to get a towel or at least turn around while she put her clothes back on. He turned away still laughing. As she came onshore she couldn't find her undies. In her haste she had discarded them too close to the edge of the water and they had floated away with the tide. Reaching for her dress, Jennifer realized that due to being thoroughly drenched, she had difficulty getting it back on. After a few minutes struggling, Lorenzo had finally ceased laughing and questioned what was taking so long. Embarrassed she admitted the truth causing more laughter to erupt. After a few seconds, she started laughing too at the ridiculousness of a thirty-something year old doctor childishly taking a silly dare to strip off her clothes and run into the ocean. Her present predicament with the dress just highlighted the hilarity of the situation.

Finally regaining his composure, Lorenzo backed over to her so as not to see her clinging to the flimsy dress. He had left his suit jacket in the billiard room so he unbuttoned his dress shirt and handed it to her. Being so tall and Jennifer being so short, the shirt covered her almost to her knees. Playfully hitting him in the chest with the crumbled up dress, they made their way back to the hotel.

Luckily, due to the lateness of the hour, the lobby and hallways were relatively empty. Lorenzo escorted her back to her room. They were both still giggling when they arrived at her door. As she turned to open the door, Jennifer found herself wanting to invite him in for a drink but thought better of it. Instead she thanked him for a memorable "date" and gave him a quick kiss on cheek before retreating into her suite and closing the door behind her. She stood with her back against the door for several moments contemplating why she had gotten so nervous just now. It was just Lorenzo after all.

Jennifer practically snuck out of the hotel the next morning to leave for the airport. Not sure why she didn't want to run into anyone, particularly Lorenzo, she was packed and driving away almost before the resort starting serving breakfast. Apparently she wasn't the only one attempting to escape unnoticed. As she entered the airport lobby she spotted his tall, dark head of hair at the check-in counter. The silly, flirty looks the airline attendant was giving him made Jennifer roll her eyes. Lorenzo could always turn seemingly normal women into acting like gaga teenagers drooling over him. In college it had been entertaining to watch. Now, she was just annoyed.

Momentarily he turned around and caught her staring at him. Flashing that swoon-worthy smile he walked over on the pretense of helping with her luggage. "Hope you remembered my shirt when you packed this morning," he joked. They compared airline itineraries and discovered they were on the same flight to Reagan National. Appearing happy about the situation, Lorenzo proceeded through the line with her to the check-in counter where he requested a seat change for her so they could sit together in first class. The same attendant as before did not seem thrilled to fulfill his request. Jennifer stifled a giggle as the woman banged away on her computer terminal to make the switch.

They had plenty of time to stroll to the concourse as the flight wasn't for another two hours. Lorenzo suggested stopping for coffee and muffins. Jennifer agreed to the coffee. "Are you still not eating breakfast? No wonder you are so tiny," he remarked. Two tall vanilla lattes later, they were seated in the terminal with nothing to say. In silence they sipped their coffees and stared out the window waiting on their flight to arrive.

Finally, Lorenzo broke the silence by saying, "Listen. You know my situation and I know yours. Neither of us is looking for a relationship, but I really do miss your friendship. I was kind of hoping we could keep in touch more, especially now that we know we live in the same metro area. Also, we could help each other out of awkward situations, like going to weddings or events without the stress of someone thinking it was a real date." Jennifer nodded her head in agreement and looked up into his chocolate eyes. Having a sexy standby, go-to date was the perfect solution. She stuck her hand out to shake his to seal the agreement, but he leaned in and gave her a quick peck on the cheek.

The return flight went quickly as they discussed a myriad of topics. He spoke mostly about his son and his genetically-inherited love of soccer. She discussed her work at the hospital and how she wished she had more time for research since she felt a big breakthrough was just around the corner. Before they knew it, the fasten seatbelts sign lit up and the airplane descended. Having the window seat, Jennifer always enjoyed the arrival into this particular airport as it gave the illusion that the plane was about to crash into the Potomac River right before landing safely on the thin strip of land.

After retrieving their luggage, Jennifer made to give him a swift goodbye hug. Instead she found herself in a giant bear hug. Neither really wanted to let go. Saying goodbye, they headed their separate ways. Lorenzo to the parking garage to drive back to the DC suburb of Warrenton, VA. Jennifer to the Metro station to take the train into the District.

Jennifer's thoughts remained on Lorenzo the entire ride back to the station closest to her Georgetown condo. It was a long walk from there in the humid weather with the clouds overhead, threatening rain. She didn't notice though. Her mind ran over the events of the past couple days. Never in the last few years had she allowed herself to daydream. She was just too busy for that. Nevertheless, as a spattering of rain drops began to fall Jennifer didn't even notice as she replayed the Sinatra song dance over and over in her mind. She blushed at the memory of her skinny dipping escapade. But the image that kept asserting itself was of Lorenzo smiling wickedly at her as they played pool. Her skin still felt the faint trace of where his fingers had brushed against her back unzipping her dress. Perhaps agreeing to be each other's go-to wedding date had not been the greatest idea.

Jennifer resumed her normal schedule and didn't hear from Lorenzo for a couple of weeks. Trying to justify her increased interest in Facebook, she lied to herself that she wasn't really just seeing if there were any messages from him. She was genuinely interested in everyone's pet pictures and what they had for dinner. Then one stormy evening as she was relaxing after a long day at the hospital with a cup of herbal tea and a bowl of sugary kids' cereal, her Facebook page finally indicated she had a message. Surprisingly, she could feel her heart beating faster in her chest when she saw that it was indeed from Lorenzo with an apology for not contacting her sooner. He indicated that he wasn't really comfortable communicating via social media and requested her number instead, or at least a viable email account. He included his full contact information in the message so she took out her cell phone and plugged in his information after sending a quick reply with her own information.

Later that night as she was just getting out of the shower the phone rang. No one ever called her except the hospital so she assumed it was the dreaded "There's a patient in distress" or worse call. Without glancing at the caller id, she answered and was delighted to hear the deep, husky voice of Lorenzo. Jennifer was surprised he called her so soon after she sent her contact information. Still wearing a towel and her hair dripping wet, she sat down on her bed to chat.

Hours later she was still wearing a towel with her hair dried naturally wavy and tousled. They had talked about everything and nothing, it seemed. When Jennifer happened to glance over at the clock she was shocked to see it was well past midnight. As she tried to say goodbye, Lorenzo surprised her again by stating there was a particular reason for his call. He needed a date. His son's teacher was getting married. His son really wanted to go to the wedding, but Lorenzo dreaded the matchmaking that would go on if he showed up without a female companion. Every one of Raphael's teachers and room moms seemed to make setting him up with any available female in the school district as their personal goal in life. He hated it! "Please, please, pretty please," he begged, "save me from this impending disaster!" Laughing at his predicament, she tried to play coy with her answer just to tease him. Ultimately showing pity, Jennifer agreed. She wrote down the date and time on her whiteboard in the kitchen and made a mental note to double check her schedule at work. Jokingly thanking her for saving his life, he said good night. Once she hung up the phone, doubt set in. Not only was she going to another wedding with him. She was also going there with his son. Jennifer wished she had thought of that before saying "yes".

As it turned out, she wasn't scheduled to work the day in question so no backing out that way. Her supervisor, Jacob, was somewhat taken aback when he later asked her to attend a hospital fundraising event at the Mayflower Hotel that same evening. Teasing her about finally getting a social life, he mildly suggested that he hoped she still had time for her research. The comment was completely uncalled for but had its intended effect by making Jennifer doubt herself. "Was it really necessary that she spend her time helping out an old friend, who quite frankly should be getting set up on dates in order to meet someone and provide a mother-figure for Raphael," she thought. "Perhaps it was selfish of her to want to spend time away from the hospital or anything benefitting the hospital when saving children's lives with her research was the most important thing in the world." After mulling it over, she had almost convinced herself to cancel with Lorenzo. However, when she tried to call him to tell him so, he sounded so excited and grateful she was going to be there with him that Jennifer didn't have the heart to turn him down.

Not having a car since living in DC, on the date of the teacher's wedding, she took the Metro to the subway station farthest west of the city. Lorenzo would pick her up there. To avoid walking the many blocks to the Metro station in painful high heels, she slipped her comfy sneakers on and packed the heels away in an oversized designer purse her mother had given her for Christmas. The vision of a petite woman in a pale green sundress and sneakers must have been amusing because Lorenzo starting chuckling as soon as he saw her emerge from the station. "Cut it out, meathead, or I'm turning around and getting back on that train," she threatened.

"Hey, Dad! You going to let her get away with calling you that?" said a robust little boy voice. Lorenzo was so tall she hadn't even seen the little boy behind him. He was a perfect miniature of his father with dark olive skin and jet black hair that was a little too long and kept falling over his large, almond-shaped eyes. He was dressed in a khaki pants, with a button-down shirt and even a clip on tie. The perfect little man, except for the dirt-smudged sneakers on his feet. "My kind of kid," she thought. She wondered how much Lorenzo had argued with the boy to get him in the dress clothes.

Lorenzo laughed and replied, "Yes, I will let it slip this once since she is a lady and we should always show them respect." With that he introduced his son and the little man reached out to shake her hand. Being a little Casanova himself, the boy adeptly turned her hand so he could bend over to kiss the top. Jennifer thanked him and complimented him on his attire and manners. He, in turn, commented on her brand of sneakers since apparently they were not the "in" brand of his generation. As the two continued to debate the finer aspects of various sneaker brands, Lorenzo escorted them back to the car.

To say Raphael was charming was indeed an understatement. He entertained Jennifer the entire ride to the church where the wedding was to take place. She was so captivated by him she forgot to change her shoes in the car. As she stepped out of Lorenzo's white Chevy SUV, he made a little "hmm hmm" noise. When she looked up at him oblivious to the problem, he started laughing. This time Raphael jumped in to scold his father for laughing at a lady. After thanking her little hero, she finally noticed the issue and started laughing herself. This seemed to confuse the boy. After his brave defense of the pretty lady, she was now laughing. When she sat back down in the car and pulled out her high heels to change he was even more shocked. How could one explain to a five year old boy that he could get away with wearing sneakers to a wedding but a lady could not? Raphael just rolled his eyes and said "Whatever".

As they walked arm in arm towards the church, Jennifer admired her escort out of the corner of her eye. Lorenzo looked dapper in a light grey suit and plum colored silk tie. His hair had grown longer since the wedding in Cocoa Beach and fell over his right eye hiding a small scar just below his eye brow. Jennifer recalled him explaining the scar to her one night. When he was ten years old, an opposing team player was angry at losing a game and in the last second of the game kicked the ball as hard as he could right at Lorenzo's face, splitting the skin above his eye. Just before walking into the church, she reached up to brush the hair away from his eyes and unconsciously allowed her finger to lightly trace the scar.

As soon as they entered Jennifer felt that all eyes were on them. At least all the females in the room were looking at Lorenzo and sizing her up. He may not realize it but she could tell some of those females weren't too happy to see another woman on his arm. Lorenzo, on the other hand, saw more than a few envious stares from the attending men. He knew he had a hottie on his arm and he enjoyed the satisfaction of knowing that this fetching beauty was with him. Just friends or not, he was still proud to be seen with Jennifer whether she was in sneakers, a formal dress, or just his shirt. The image of her wearing his shirt coming off the beach had haunted him ever since that night. Attempting to shake off the vision, as they were in a church and that could only lead to "un-churchly" thoughts, he moved to shake hands with some of the gentlemen in the foyer and to introduce his date.

They were ushered into the crowded sanctuary by an elderly gentlemen and took their places in a middle row. Luckily the ceremony started soon after their arrival as Jennifer was feeling awkward having so many people looking her over She knew they were evaluating in their minds if she was good enough for the handsome man next to her. Some, she noticed, frowned. Others gave a small grin of approval. However, there was more than one that gave her an outright evil look. The buxom blonde in the third row was obviously not happy with her presence. Sweet-natured Raphael kept leaning over to point out and whisper the names of everyone he knew. The blonde in question was the teacher's assistant in his class.

The ceremony was beautiful and much longer and formal than Jacy's wedding had been. Raphael was well-mannered and remained quiet and observant the entire time. Too bad the three preteens in the back row weren't so well-mannered. When the ceremony was over, they went back to the car to drive to the local country club for the reception. Raphael resumed his constant chatter with Jennifer. He pointed out his school and his team's soccer practice field. He described, in detail, his last game where he scored the winning goal against his arch rival Landon. The boy definitely had spunk and character. Jennifer already loved him and they had only been together for an hour or more.

The reception was held at an antebellum-looking house overlooking a pristine golf course. There were tennis courts adjacent to the building and a pool with colorful winding slides behind it. After dinner the children were taken to another room in the building where they could play arcade games or use the indoor basketball courts while the adults stayed in the banquet hall for dancing and drinks. Several people came over to introduce themselves, including the teacher/bride. One sweet middle-aged woman, who had already had a bit too much wine with dinner, commented that Raphael's dad had outdone himself with his date and that she shouldn't mind the other women there giving her jealous stares. Laughing, Jennifer agreed wholeheartedly. However, she was shocked when the blonde teacher assistant strutted over, and without acknowledging Jennifer's presence, asked Lorenzo to dance. He was stunned as well and indicated he already promised his date a dance. With that, he led Jennifer to the small dance floor as the music changed from some hip-hop number to a more subdued soft rock ballad. Trying not to giggle, Jennifer glanced over at the blonde woman who had stormed off.

The rest of the evening, Lorenzo and Jennifer kept mostly to themselves. Dancing when it was a slow tune and sitting out the club dance music. Raphael came bounding into the room again when he tired of the game room. Deciding it was time to leave, they again congratulated the bride and groom and made a beeline out the door. Once outside, Lorenzo issued a genuine sigh of relief it was over. Jennifer now understood why he had needed her tonight – to fend off the hordes of women wanting to throw themselves at him. "Must be a tough life," she thought as she started to giggle. Raphael just looked confused. He was so cute at that moment, Jennifer had to resist the urge to pinch his little cheeks. She was pretty sure he would not appreciate that.

The little boy seemed genuinely upset when they arrived back at the Metro station for Jennifer to catch her ride home. Looking into his sad face, so much like his father's, she promised it would not be the last time they would see each other. Surprising even herself, she asked him for a hug which he gladly provided. The look on Lorenzo's face as she shyly glanced up through her eye lashes, was a mixture of sadness and pride. Jennifer imagined he would give anything to have Raphael's mother here to give him hugs. Standing on tiptoe, as she had quickly reclaimed the sneakers when they had left the reception so was lacking the added height from the heels, she gave Lorenzo a quick kiss on the cheek while holding onto his hand so as not to topple from the effort. Being so tall, she was truly on the tips of her toes. He, in turn, held the tips of her fingers a little than necessary as if not wanting to let go. With a reassuring smile, Jennifer turned towards the Metro station to leave.

Lorenzo sent a thank you message to her via Facebook the next day with an emoticon of flowers. After that Jennifer didn't hear from him for over a week. She tried to convince herself she wasn't disappointed and refocused all her energies on her patients.

A new protocol she had designed was showing positive results for a couple of her younger patients in the earlier cancer stages. Unfortunately, it had been too little too late for one young boy in the more advanced stages of lymphoma. It had been an incredibly difficult day as she dealt with his loss. Jennifer kept chastising herself for not developing the protocol sooner so she could've saved him. Jacob, after seeing her distress, ordered her to take the rest of the day off. Several hours were spent running to rid herself of her demons. The ones that tormented her every time she lost a patient.

She heard her phone ringing as she approached the door to her condo. Unable to unlock the door fast enough, she missed the call. Checking caller id, she recognized Lorenzo's number. The voicemail indicator came on and she pushed the button to listen. He had just heard from their mutual friend Kyle in Dallas. His wedding date was set for the first week in December. The official invitations would be in the mail soon but he suggested booking the flight and hotel sooner rather than later. His fiancé had just discovered there was a convention of certified public accountants in the same hotel as the wedding. He ended by jokingly asking if she was up for yet another wedding.

Not in the mood to think happy thoughts that should always go along with weddings, Jennifer postponed calling him back until later that night. Despite trying to sound cheerful, Lorenzo sensed something was off. Changing his manner of voice from jovial to concerned, he asked what was wrong. She didn't mean to have a meltdown but was unable to say the words without her voice shaking and tears springing to her eyes again. She hadn't lost a patient in months and this time it really hit her hard. He listened sympathetically and tried say reassuring words of comfort. His heart ached for her as the agonizing pain in her voice was clearly evident.

Feeling exhausted from her emotional ordeal, Jennifer apologized for making him listen to her pathetic troubles. He assured her that it was no trouble and he was happy to be there for her anytime. Suddenly he asked her address. "Oh, great!" she thought. "Now he thinks he needs to send me a sympathy card or something." After giving him the information, Lorenzo did the strangest thing. He abruptly said he had to go but would contact her soon. Surprised by the change, she muttered a goodbye and hauled herself up off the sofa to get a much needed shower.

A couple of hours later her home phone rang with the tone indicating someone was buzzing her from the front entrance to her building. Alarmed, she asked who was there and was startled to hear Lorenzo's deep voice announcing himself. After hitting the button to unlock the door to the building, she ran to the bathroom and was dismayed at what she saw looking back at her in the mirror. Her eyes were puffy and her nose a bright shade of pink after all the crying she had done that day. "Oh no. I'm a total mess," she scolded herself. Splashing some cold water on her face didn't seem to help either. Too late. Lorenzo was already knocking on her door.

Taking a deep breath she opened the door. Without a word, Lorenzo reached out and drew her into an embrace. They moved inside the condo without breaking apart. As the door closed behind them, her tears started again. He held her as she sobbed. It wasn't until her body relaxed against his and her tears were spent that he gently pulled away just a little to look into her eyes. She saw his sympathy for what she was going through but she also saw something else. Almost as if it pained him to see her like this.

Realizing she must look a mess, Jennifer made to move away to get some tissues. Instead, Lorenzo tenderly stroked her cheek to wipe away a stray tear. His large hand cupped her face tenderly as he continued to gaze into her watery eyes. Not even realizing what she was doing, Jennifer leaned towards him and put her arms around his neck. Slowly, as if afraid to break away but also afraid to move closer, he tilted his head so they were eye to eye, nose to nose. Moments passed where Jennifer could only feel her heart thudding in her chest. Finally he closed the final distance and softly touched his lips to hers.

Tenderly at first and then with more urgency as long pent-up desire welled in them both, they kissed. His soft, sensual lips covering hers. As the kiss intensified his tongue parted her lips with a light stroke. The movement sent thrilling shivers through her body that left her hungry for more of him. Their tongues explored one another as if dancing to their own soft ballad. Deep inside her, Jennifer felt heat waves of passion surging throughout the body. From her very core to her limbs, long denied feelings bubbled up numbing her mind to anything else but the luscious feel of his body pressed against hers.

Lorenzo deftly guided them towards the oversized chair which was the first piece of furniture he could find. He settled her into the chair and knelt in front of her without breaking their connection. His hands caressed her face and neck as he deepened the kiss. Desperate to have him even closer her hands found the open collar on his shirt which she used to tug him closer to her. All thoughts had vacated her mind as soon as his lips had touched hers. There was nothing but sensation and the fire scorching through her veins.

Breathless, he pulled away to look into her blazing emerald eyes. There was a question in his eyes that remained unasked. Jennifer answered, without hesitation, as she pulled his head back towards hers. The intensity of their mutual need for each other was unable to be denied any longer. Had it always been there? Lorenzo gently scooped her up in his arms and moved them towards her bedroom.

Hours later, as the sun began to shine through her bedroom window, Jennifer stretched like a satiated cat as she ran her hand over Lorenzo's muscular sleeping form. The light streaming between the blinds only accentuated the perfection that was the man. Despite knowing him for years and seeing him in everything from a tuxedo to swim trunks, never would she have dared imagined him like this. Naked, in her bed, with his tousled hair covering his eyes as he continued to slumber. Jennifer reached up to move the hair away from his beautiful face so she could get a better look. Seeing him asleep it was hard to believe this angel was the same man that had taken her to such dizzying heights of ecstasy last night. She blushed at the memories.

Then realization struck. If he was here, who was with Raphael? How had she not thought of him before? She shook Lorenzo awake. He groggily sat up and reached for her as if to replay the events of last night, but she stopped him by the distraught look on her face. "Hey, I thought we got rid of that facial expression last night. What happened while I was asleep?" he asked.

She couldn't believe he didn't know. "Raphael. What about your son? Please tell me you didn't leave him alone just to come all this way to console me," she begged. With a huge sigh and laugh, he told her that the reason it had taken him so long to get here last night was because he packed up Raphael and sent him to a sleepover at a friend's house. Jennifer nearly collapsed back on the bed in relief. Of course he had taken care of his son first. Seeing her concern for the boy, Lorenzo smiled up at her and pulled her close. First he kissed her eyelids, then trailed light kisses down her face and neck before coming back to her mouth. They fell back on the bed together and spent the rest of the early morning enjoying each other.

A couple hours later, they had both showered and dressed. He needed to get back to coach his son's soccer game that afternoon. She had rounds to complete at the hospital and she was already late. As Lorenzo kissed her goodbye he asked her to come out to the game and spend time with him and Raphael for the weekend. Maybe she could even pack an overnight bag, he suggested. An offer like that was too good to refuse so she agreed to text him when she reached the Metro station closest to Warrenton. With a final longing kiss, they parted ways for the day. Both anticipating seeing each other again in just a few hours. Both exhilarated by their realized passion for each other and both nervous about where that left them as friends.

Jennifer found herself smiling like a silly lovesick girl as she made her rounds at the hospital. A couple nurses read the signs and were happy for the beautiful workaholic doctor. They commented, "It's about time that girl got a man!" Even the fretful parents of her patients picked up on her improved demeanor. This was a side to their child's doctor they had never witnessed. It was refreshing. The only person not happy about Jennifer's improved mood was Jacob. Although he had never officially made a move on her, he still thought of her as the one he would eventually captivate and marry. She had all the attributes of the perfect wife – gorgeous, highly intelligent, career-centric, and most importantly, she could charm the bigwigs in Washington out of their money for the hospital with just a bat of her eye lashes. Yes, Jennifer was his ideal candidate for the job of Mrs. Jacob Mallory. She, of course, was completely unaware of his plans.

As she finished with her files and put them back at the nurse's desk with specific instructions for each patient, Jacob approached her. As she turned to leave, she nearly bumped into him. "Sorry, Jacob. Didn't realize you were there," she apologized and made to go around him as she was anxious to get out to Warrenton for Raphael's game. He blocked her way and instead took her arm and led her to his office on the pretense of needing to consult about a patient. Reluctantly, Jennifer followed.

As they sat down in his office, he coolly commented on her changed behavior. Jennifer could tell he was not happy about something but was not in the mood to wait around to find out why. He continued, "Normally, I would be ecstatic seeing you so smiling and downright jovial with the staff and patients." His tone indicated he was not ecstatic at all. Quite the opposite. "However, it seems after you lost your patient just yesterday that perhaps you would become less distracted and refocus on saving the others instead of happily humming as you complete paperwork." His objective was clear – make her doubt herself and refocus the blame on the patient's death on her to guilt her into leaving behind whoever was diverting her attention from her work even for a second.

At first she was bewildered that he considered her to be unfocused on her patients and her work. After a few moments thought, she realized he could be right. Even she was astutely aware that ever since she had reconnected with Lorenzo, she found her mind drifting to him. Jennifer had convinced herself it was only when she was away from the hospital and not that often. After last night's events, maybe it had been more than that and she just hadn't realized it. Observing the look of doubt cross her face, Jacob went in for the kill. "Perhaps you need something to fire your motivation for your research. There's a fundraiser tonight at Smithsonian. Why don't you come with me? You can redouble your efforts if more money is flowing in for research." Sadly defeated, she shook her yes and left the office. Jacob sat back in his chair with a smug smile.

Her new found pep vanished as she exited the hospital. "He was right," she chided herself, "I could've saved that suffering child if I had just spent more time at the hospital, more time researching the new protocol so it could've been used before it was too late. This was all my fault. What was I thinking that I could have a personal life now? I've done without one for years. Obviously I don't need a man or love, and certainly not a family. My life's work is at a crucial stage. I can't allow myself to be diverted any longer. I owe it to the other children in that ward. Despite her heart and body screaming their need for Lorenzo, she resolved to end things with him before she lost the will to do so.

Tears rolled down her freckled face as she dialed Lorenzo's number. It went straight to voicemail so she left a short message saying there had been some complications at work and she would be unable to make Raphael's game. Unable to hold herself together when he called back just a few moments later, she turned off her phone and headed back home. The condo seemed so much lonelier without him. She thought, "Has it really only been a few hours since Lorenzo was here holding her, kissing her, making love to her?" It seemed like a lifetime ago now.

Without feeling much like going to a party, much less a charity event with Jacob, she dressed in a subdued gray chiffon number that fell off one shoulder. She may look dazzling but she didn't feel the part. Jennifer just went through the motions that evening. Smiling when talking with potential donors. Allowing Jacob to usher her around the room as his own personal property. She was even caught unawares when he introduced her to a high-ranking senator as his girlfriend. It jolted her out of her reverie like being struck by lightning. Unwilling to make a scene or embarrass him in front of the party guests, she continued to smile even when the senator made a remark to Jacob about not letting such a beauty get away. Jacob, of course, was in agreement with the suggestion.

Later that night, his car dropped Jennifer off at her condominium building. Jacob tried to convince her to invite him upstairs for nightcap and perhaps more. The entire ride back he had spent making allusions to how they made such a great "power couple". Not in the mood to deal with him and not wanting to risk her job at the hospital by giving him a piece of her mind, she bolted from the car without as much as a goodbye. "How could she have allowed him to manipulate her like that?" she wondered. It took his antics tonight to reveal the creep underneath. He wasn't worried about her neglecting her patients or research. He was only concerned about alienating her from everyone else so she would be vulnerable to him. How could she not have seen it before? Racking her brain for signs that she had missed, she recalled overhearing some nurses commenting about "poor sweet doctor" being preyed upon by "the big guy" and being completely oblivious. They had been talking about her, hadn't they? Honestly, Jennifer didn't know who she was more angry with...Jacob for pushing doubt into her mind that she was not a good doctor because she wasn't focused enough on her work and making her believe it was her fault patients died or herself for believing him. She had denied herself any life for years due to her own self-doubts. He had merely amplified that doubt and handicapped her emotionally so she wouldn't stray from her work, stray from his sight and control. Perhaps the best place to lay her anger was at her own feet for allowing it to happen.

She was so caught up in her inner rage that she didn't see the tall shadow come up behind her as she opened the front door to the building. It wasn't until she moved into the building and saw a muscular arm reach out to hold the door open that she turned around in fright. She was shocked to see Lorenzo standing in the doorway with an anguished look. What he was thinking she couldn't guess. They had made plans to be together that day and she had wimped out by leaving him a message with no explanation. Now here she was dolled up from her night on the town with her boss. They stood in the vacant foyer staring at each other in the dark for several moments before Lorenzo turned to leave without saying a word. Desperate to explain, she reached for him but he flung her arm back.

As he brusquely walked out the door, a pouring rain had just started. Jennifer rushed out to stop him, but he continued briskly walking to wherever he had parked his SUV. Unable to keep up in her 2 inch heels, she stopped only long enough to pull them from her feet. The shoes were left there as she raced after him. Even though she was a fast runner and had placed in the last Marine Corps marathon, Jennifer found it difficult to keep up. As he neared his car, she dashed across the street unaware of an approaching taxi. The last thing she saw was Lorenzo's look of horror as he turned to see the collision. Then everything went dark.

Jennifer awoke to a throbbing in her head and the incessant beeping of heart rate monitor. Placing her hand to her head and feeling the large lump, she moaned in pain. The sound awakened the sleeping giant beside her bed. Despite everything, Lorenzo had stayed with her. Her mind was still too fuzzy from the accident that she couldn't begin to understand why after she had ditched him and his son last night. Perhaps he could forgive her not showing up for him, but letting Raphael down – she doubted anyone could forgive that. She certainly didn't forgive herself.

Lorenzo took her hand and asked how she felt. Instead of saying the expected response like "fine" or "horrible" or any derivative of the two, she simply said "stupid". Thinking she meant stupid for running out into the street in front an oncoming car, he nodded agreement. "Haven't you heard of looking both ways before you cross the road?" he challenged.

Her head still groggy and her thoughts jumbled, she tried to explain that it wasn't being hit by the car that was stupid. It was how she had convinced herself that she was a horrible person for wanting a life, wanting him and his son in her life instead of spending every waking moment under Jacob's thumb at the hospital. She tried explaining how he had manipulated her into doubting her dedication to her patients and guilted her into going to a hospital fundraiser instead of where she belonged at Raphael's game. It was stupid to believe she couldn't be a good doctor if she allowed herself to have anything or anyone else in her life. It was stupid not to realize that she wanted, that she needed love too. And it was stupid of her not to realize all this time that she needed and loved him.

By the time she finished speaking, they were both in tears. The nurse came in to check on her patient to find the doctor and her hot looking companion holding each other as if for dear life. She recognized the signs, so she quickly and quietly left in order to disturb the lovebirds.

As she was signing her release papers, Jacob stopped by her room. Lorenzo recognized him as the gentleman that had dropped Jennifer off the night before. He certainly didn't like the way the man was looking at her. By the expression on her face, Jennifer wasn't happy to see him but she motioned for Lorenzo to wait outside.

Jacob tried apologizing for not walking her in, as if that would have prevented the accident. Unable to contain her emotions any longer she let into him for all the years he had spent parading her around like an ornament at charity events. All the while belittling her work and making her doubt her own dedication and ability to saving children's lives. It had all been for his benefit. With her by his side he could raise money supposedly for her research, but she never saw a dime of that money. She was always scrapping by with used equipment and no personnel. Despite the odds, she still made significant progress. Exhausted from her long overdue rant against him, she verbally gave him her notice of resignation. She would take her research and skills to another hospital.

After he left, Lorenzo returned awestruck by what he had heard through the thin glass doors. Apparently, the entire floor had heard her accusations as there was applause from the nurse's station as Jacob stormed off to his office. With a look of admiration, he shook his head. "Well, does this mean you have some time to hang out with a young man who is desperately waiting to hear the news that you are okay, and with his old man?"

"After all this, do you really still want me around? It's not like we can just go back to the other night and pretend none of this happened," she replied.

"Yes, WE," he emphasized, "want you around. And not just for a soccer game. Not just as an overnight guest. Not as just a convenient date for weddings." Holding her bruised face in his hands, he looked into her eyes and confessed, "I want you, need you in my life. Ever since college, I've been in mad love with you but knew you didn't feel the same. For years I hid behind the status of friend. Too afraid to speak up even when you took off for medical school." He continued as she stared at him in disbelief, "Seeing you again brought all those feelings rushing back but you still showed no signs of wanting anything other than a platonic friendship. You were only focused on your work. I understand your need to help save lives. I understand your desire to find the cure so other children don't have to suffer like your friend Hannah. I understand all that and love you for all that and more. You've just been too blind to see it," he confessed.

Whoa! Jennifer didn't trust her ears on that last part. "Did he just say 'love'?" she questioned herself. With new tears rolling down her face, she nearly punched him. "Love? You've been in love with me and never said a word? Are you sure you don't want to take that back? Better do it quickly before I hold you to that." In reply, he pulled her close. The kiss that followed was soft, yet deep and all-consuming.

The pounding in her head was no more. The only pounding she felt was her own heart. She pulled back for just a moment to ask, "And how does Raphael feel about all this?"

A few months later in Dallas, Lorenzo and Raphael escorted Jennifer into the wedding ceremony for Kyle and his bride. Ever since that day in the hospital they had been together. She had been true to her word and resigned from Georgetown University Hospital. After taking some much needed and deserved time off, she had just accepted a job offer at a private research facility and hospital being built on the outskirts of the DC metropolitan area as their director of pediatric cancer research. The condo in Georgetown sold quickly, as the district never suffered from the housing market bust like the rest of the country. Presently, she was renting a townhouse in Warrenton so she could be close to "her boys".

Her relationship with Raphael had bloomed quickly. They were completely attached to each other. Even the blonde teacher's assistant that had been so rude to her at the other wedding admitted that Jennifer was devoted and loving to the boy. The soccer team adopted her as the team "mom" as she always brought them healthy snacks and tended to their bumps and bruises. There had been one instance where Raphael had been hit in the head with the ball so hard that he was knocked out for a few moments. Jennifer hadn't realized until then just how much she had grown to love him as she begged and pleaded with God for Raphael to wake up and be okay. He was, of course, but she could no longer deny she wanted to be a mother to him.

As for her relationship with Lorenzo...Jennifer wanted to kick herself every day for being blind to his feeling for her for so long, and blind to her feelings for him. He didn't allow her to wallow in regret though. The time was much better spent making up for lost time, which happen to include making lots and lots of love. Despite their need to be together, she insisted on keeping her own apartment. She didn't want Raphael to be upset having another woman sleeping his dad's bed. If they have bothered to ask, Raphael would have gladly told them otherwise.

Jennifer could not believe how blessed she was having Lorenzo and Raphael in her life. As she sat in the church pew flanked on both sides by the men she loved and listening to the words being said by the priest about love and family, she finally realized just how important those things were. Nearly missing her opportunity for true love gave her a greater appreciation for the words being spoken for the bride and groom. Lorenzo wasn't just her wedding date. He wasn't just her boyfriend. He and his sweet son were her life.

After the lovely ceremony, the wedding party adjourned to the large, heated tent erected on the local minor league baseball field. Turns out Kyle's company did considerable business with the team's owner who had loaned them the location for the reception. After dinner and dancing, Raphael was showing signed of fatigue so they decided to return to their hotel. Lorenzo seemed reluctant to leave and then excused himself for a moment. Confused, she stayed with Raphael as they waited for their coats.

A few moments later the strands of Frank Sinatra's "The Way You Look Tonight" began to play. Lorenzo returned and without a word ushered Jennifer out onto the dance floor for one final dance. Raphael stood just to the side of the dance floor watching them intently. As she leaned her head against his chest and listened to his heart thumping she became concerned it was beating so quickly. Towards the end of the song, Lorenzo dropped to one knee and gazed up at her with such a mixed expression of fear and longing. She didn't immediately notice the small box he had pulled out of his suit jacket. Confused, she stared in disbelief as the music faded away and Lorenzo uttered the words he had been waiting years to say to her. "Jennifer, my love, you are my heart and soul. I can no longer live without you. I want, I need you as my wife and my partner in life. Raphael wants and needs you as his mother." With that the boy ran over to the couple looking up at her with the most beautiful expectant expression. Lorenzo continued, "Jennifer, will you marry me?"

There it was. The question she hadn't realized she had wanted to hear so badly. Almost unable to speak, she looked into Raphael's face and then Lorenzo's and she knew that she was home. With happy tears streaming down her face, "Yes," she whispered, "yes."

For Keeps

Scott Mitchell and Tiffany Reynolds have been best friends since grade school. Although Scott knew that he and Tiffany would never end up being a "couple," he always hoped that they would end up together one day. He was disheartened when Tiffany chose to move three thousand miles away to New York City to pursue a career in advertising. When Tiffany graduated two years earlier, Scott hoped she would have moved back home to the small California town in which they both grew up in.

However, that didn't happen, and because of this, Scott was only able to see Tiffany when she returned home during the holidays. This always put him in a sad mood because he wasn't able to see his best friend as much as he would have like to. While he had lots of guy friends, Scott never felt close enough to any of them to share his inner feelings in the same way he was able to do with Tiffany.

As the years dragged on, Scott slowly began realizing that it wasn't their best friend status that left him wanting Tiffany closer, it was the fact that he had true feelings for her and he never felt at ease to tell her.

That was all going to change and soon. He flipped open his cellphone and replayed her message:

"Hey, Scott. It's your BFF. I just wanted to let you know that I am heading back in town and I have some news for you...actually two pieces of news for you. I'm sorry that I missed you, but I will call you as soon as the plane touches down. Love you Scott. Talk to you soon!"

He disconnected the call. He didn't know why he saved it, but he just felt compelled to. That call came in twelve hours, four minutes, and thirty-three seconds ago. He couldn't wait to have her call back. "I am such a loser," he moaned to himself. "Here I am pining away for a girl that I wanted nothing to do with when we were ten years old. If I would have known then, what I know now." He said, shaking his head. He grabbed a change of clothes and went into the bathroom. He started the shower and got undressed.

As the water washed over him, he could hear the sound of his cell phone. He quickly stepped out of the shower, not caring that the water was still running. He wrapped a towel around his body and headed back into his bedroom, reaching the phone before it hung up. "Hello?"

"Scott?"

His heart skipped a beat, hearing her voice. "Tiff? I wasn't expecting your call so soon."

"Did I wake you?" She asked.

"No," he replied, sinking down on the bed. "I was just taking a shower." He cursed himself for being so vocal, when he heard the hesitation. "It's good to hear your voice, Tiff."

She chuckled. He loved the sound of her laughing. "You hear my voice all the time. I call you more than I call my mother."

"You know what I mean. It's great to hear your voice, knowing that you're back in California." He replied, crossing his fingers. "You are in California, right?"

"Yes, I am. The plane touched down about ten minutes ago. I told you that I would call you right away."

Scott smiled to himself. It made him feel good that he was the first call she made. "Do you need a ride somewhere? I could come get you and be there in less than twenty minutes." He looked down at his wet body and shrugged. He would take the fastest shower anyone has ever taken if he had to.

"That's sweet, Scott, but I'm going to get a rental. Thanks for the offer though."

"Sure, no problem," he states, a little disappointed.

The awkward silence builds and he fights the urge to talk too much, but he can sense something is on her mind. "So, what's new?" He asks, hoping it didn't come across as a strange question.

"A lot," she confesses. "In fact, I was hoping that maybe we could talk this evening for supper. If you're not busy."

He thought about his busy work schedule, but he could move some things around. "Tonight would be perfect."

"Great! I will plan on meeting at our place about 6:30."

He smiled, knowing that she meant *Uncle Tony's Pizzeria*. "I will see you then." He replied, disconnecting. He went back to his shower, feeling excited about the evening. He was ready to tell her the truth and hope for the best, or at least hope that she wouldn't choose to discontinue their friendship.

***

Tiffany wrung her hands together. She could feel her heart thumping in her chest and she didn't know why she was so nervous. She glanced around the restaurant and saw that he was still not there. He was her best friend and the fact that she felt like she was getting ready to see a stranger was weird. They didn't see each other often, but when they did it was like they had never been apart.

She looked up and saw him rushing into the restaurant. She took a deep breath and stood up. He hurried to her. "I am so sorry for being late." He kissed her cheek, "It was a busy day at work."

"No problem. I wasn't worried. I knew you would show." She smiled at him. He looked at her and grinned. For a moment she was reminded how she grew up having the biggest crush on him and he never seemed to notice. She cleared her throat, "I figured we didn't need to look in the menu."

He smiled, "You would be correct." He looked at her, "You're looking good, Tiff."

She blushed, "Thanks. You don't look half bad yourself." Their easy banter would pick up. It always did. The waitress walked over and they ordered their usual Pineapple and Pepperoni pizza, something only the two of them would enjoy. She then turned back to him. "So, how have you been? Any new girlfriends I should know about?" She took a drink of her soda and he laughed.

"Not quite. You know me...I'm involved with my job. Isn't that enough?"

She thought about that. It was true that he did seem to be a workaholic, but he always found time to make for her. "I have a feeling when you find that someone special then that will all change."

He smiled, "Think so, huh?"

She nodded, confidently. "I actually have some things that I want to discuss with you."

"Hm..." he replied. "I thought this impromptu supper was because you missed me."

She shrugged, "Well, that's true too."

"Okay, I feel a little bit better," he spoke with a laugh. "I actually have some things that I want to discuss with you too."

"You do?" She asked, surprised.

"I do, but I thought maybe we could wait a little bit before I delve into that. So, feel free to begin."

She waited for a moment, trying to figure out how she wanted to proceed. She had been rehearsing the way she was going to tell him for several weeks now, but it all seemed to go out of her mind. "It can wait. How's your family been?"

He raised his eyebrows. "That's changing the subject, but they have been doing really well. Sid just started at the University and Bryce is a senior this year."

"Wow. That's hard to believe. I remember when they were just—"

"Pests...bothering us relentlessly?"

She laughed, "I was going to say that I remember when they weren't even in school yet. I feel old."

"Tell me about it," he replied, chuckling.

The waitress came with their food and they fell into an easy silence as they started to eat. "I really am excited that you're here."

She smiled, "Me too." She took another bite and figured she would wait until they were done eating, before bringing up the reason she was in town. "Has work been going okay?" She asked, stopping to take a drink.

"Busy as ever, but loving every minute of it. I should ask you how your jobs going? After all, working at a big time ad agency must have some perks."

She nodded, but barely made eye contact. "It's been great, but I actually quit there two weeks ago."

His jaw dropped, "Must not be that great. Why did you do that?"

She shrugged, "Had my reasons."

He put down his slice of pizza. "We have known each other for almost twenty years and have been best friends for fourteen of those years. You aren't going to get away with that. What happened?"

She groaned, taking her last bite of pizza. "I'm moving back to California."

"What? Are you serious? When were you going to tell me that?"

"Tonight," she replied nonchalantly. "I was waiting for the perfect moment. Are you surprised?"

"Um...yeah, I'm surprised." A smile is on his face, but then he starts to frown. "May I ask why? I mean you seemed so happy when you made the decision to stay there. What changed?"

She knew that it was the moment she had been practicing for. "Well...my fiancé is getting transferred." That wasn't exactly how she envisioned telling him, but it got the point across.

He stared at her and then shook his head, "I'm sorry, I thought you just said that your fiancé is getting transferred."

"That's exactly what I said. Surprise...I'm getting married."

She couldn't read his mind to see how he felt about the news. She knew that he wasn't expecting it, when she had only been dating Erick for a month. She hadn't even told her family or Scott that she was seeing someone. "When did this happen?" He asked.

"He proposed a couple days ago, but he asked me to move to California with him two weeks ago."

"I'm sorry that I am finding this a little hard to believe. I mean, up until about five seconds ago I didn't even know you were dating anyone. Now, to hear that you are moving to California with your fiancé? It's a lot to take in."

"I know," she replied quietly. "I didn't plan it. One day I was meeting him, the next day he was telling me that he loved me, then he was saying that he was getting transferred to California, and asking me to go with him. It just all happened so quickly, but I do love him."

"You do?" He replied softly.

She didn't need time to consider it. She knew that in her heart she felt love for him. "He gets me in ways that not too many people do." She looked down at her empty plate, "Similar to ways that you get me."

He nodded, taking another bite of his pizza. "Wow...I am just in shock."

She knew he would be, because outside of the occasional dating she never really was too involved with boys. She never seemed to have time for them, when she was too preoccupied with other things going on in her life. "Are you happy for me?" She asked, carefully considering the question.

He slowly nodded, but then added a smile. "Of course I'm happy for you. It's just going to take some time to get used to." He hesitated, looking down at the table, "When am I going to meet him?"

"He'll be in town in a few days." She said. "I wanted to prepare my family...and you, before you met him." She replied, but part of her still wondered why she was worried about what they would thing...especially Scott. She couldn't explain it, but she was most worried how Scott would react to him.

***

Scott had to process the news. The minute Tiffany told him she was getting married, he found himself sick. They went on with their meal, like nothing was happening inside of him, but he was finding it difficult to concentrate. He wanted to be happy for her, but the thought of losing her to another guy was too much to bear.

"I am so relieved that you took the news this way." She was saying.

"Oh...why's that?" He asked, taking a drink.

She shrugs, "I don't know. I guess you're opinion matters to me." It was a simple response, but he questioned if that was all. "It was actually more difficult telling you, than it will be to tell my parents."

Scott slowly nodded and then glanced down at her finger. He didn't even want to bother asking why she wasn't wearing the ring. He figured she did that so that she could tell people, without having them see the ring first. "Maybe it's because I was your first husband." He frowned, "Come to think of it...did we ever officially get divorced? You might want to check into that, before you say you'll marry this guy."

Her eyes got big, but then she smiled and started to laugh. "The playground marriage, who could forget that?" She shrugged, "I'm pretty sure the marriage was dissolved the day that you carried Sissy Baker's books to her class in ninth grade." She shook her head and acted like she was crying, "It broke my heart."

He smiled, "She was a tough girl. She threatened to beat me up if I didn't carry her books." He winked at her and she laughed. "I was only trying to save my life." He thought on what he wanted to say next and his mind drifted back to his dream that he woke up to. "I have actually been thinking about that marriage." He admitted.

She smirked, "You have?"

He nodded, "Yep and it occurred to me that I don't even remember how it came about." He shrugged, "I guess it really doesn't matter, but it's something that I have wondered."

"You mean...you don't remember the undying love you had for me?" She took a piece of her pizza and shook her head, "I am hurt." She took a bite and he could see her smiling.

"I have to admit, I did have a thing for girls in pigtails." He replied, laughing.

She snickered and nodded, "I figured." She looked down at her plate and he could see that she was thinking about that day. "Don't you remember? You wanted to play on the monkey bars and I told you that I would only let you do that if we got married." She smiled, "I was pretty tough back then."

He thought about that and then the realization snuck in. He laughed, "That's right. The monkey bars get me all the time." He turned quiet and then looked at her, "You know, that was really the start of our friendship."

She raised her eyebrows and then nodded. "We've been close ever since."

He could see that there was something on her mind and he decided to try to find out what was going on. "I can tell something's bothering you."

"This won't change anything, Scott. We'll still be friends."

The way she said that, caused a knot in his chest. "I know we will. Just not best friends, because that will be reserved for your husband. I get that." He told her everything that he needed to tell her, but in his mind he was fumbling with the words. He was going to have a hard time getting over this.

*****

Tiffany laid in bed, her eyes were focused on a picture of Scott and her that they had taken in a mall photo booth. She wanted to believe that everything was going to be alright when it came to their friendship, but her head was telling her that nothing was going to ever be the same. Things at her parent's house went fine. They were happy for them and no doubts were left behind.

She heard her cellphone ringing and she reached it from the bed. She glanced at the caller ID and saw that it was Erick. She answered the call. "Hello?"

"Hey, babe." He said. "How was your first day back?"

She looked at the picture and then placed it on the hotel nightstand. "It went well." She smiled to herself, "When does your plane arrive?"

"Well, that's one of the reasons I was calling." He said. His voice sounded apologetic.

"Yes?" She asked.

"I just found out that the transfer isn't going to be finalized for two more weeks."

The phone nearly fell from her hands. "Are you serious?"

"I'm sorry Babe, but I have to stay here until that becomes definite."

She couldn't believe this was happening. "I came here now, because I thought that you would be following shortly behind." She looked around her hotel room, "What should I do here while I wait for you to arrive?"

"Well...maybe you could start looking for a house for us to live in. Plus, you still have to find a job."

She nodded slowly, "Fine," she said, knowing that the disappointment was there.

"Babe, don't be like that." He says. His voice held concern, but she wasn't at the point of worrying about that. "We will be together soon and it will be like we were never apart."

"I know," she sadly replied. "I will see what I can do without you here."

"I love you," he replied.

She let out a breath, "I love you, too. Goodbye." She hung up the phone and turned to the picture of Scott. She dialed up his number, hoping it wasn't too late. He answered quickly, showing that it wasn't a problem. "Hey, Scott."

"Hello...miss me already?"

She smiled to herself, "Not quite."

"Ouch, I'm hurt," he teased.

She rolled her eyes, "I was just calling to see what you were doing this weekend."

There was a hesitation on his end and she wondered if maybe she was too quick to jump to the conclusion that he wouldn't be busy. "Well, I..." he started, but she quickly broke in.

"I am sure you are busy. I didn't mean to be insensitive. You have a life. We can get together later."

"Tiffany, are you through?" He asked. She closed her mouth and didn't say anything else. "I have a lunch meeting with a client, but after that I have no plans. Did you want me to meet your fiancé? I hope," he replied, laughing.

"Well, not exactly. It turns out that he won't be coming back for a couple more weeks." She paused, "long story. I just thought that maybe we could go to some of the old places we used to go."

"Well, I think that that would be a fabulous idea." He replied. "I could pick you up at the hotel about two o'clock. If that works for you?"

"That would be great," she agreed. "See you in a few days. Goodnight."

"Goodnight," he said, as they disconnected the call. She put the phone back on the nightstand. She knew that beginning the following week she would need to start looking for that perfect job. She laid back in bed and closed her eyes. She would have plenty of things to do to keep herself busy, until Erick was arriving in California.

***

Scott picked her up at two o'clock sharp. He didn't want to question why her fiancé wasn't going to be there until later. He didn't really care. He was happy to step in and show her a good time. He walked up to her hotel room door and knocked. She opened up the door instantly. Her smile always caught him off guard. She left the hotel room and glanced up at me. "Thank you for wanting to get together."

"Of course." They fell into an easy stride with one another.

"How did your meeting go today?" She asked.

He was always surprised with how much she seemed interested in what he was doing. "It went well. I signed him on with a contract." They left the hotel and walked to his car. He stood at the passenger side, opening the door for her.

"Thank you!" She replied, getting into his car. He hurried around to the other side. "Where are we going first?" She asked.

"I have my preferences, but I suppose it can be your choice." He said, hoping she would choose their favorite ice cream shop.

"You want dessert?" She asked.

He laughed, "You read my mind." He put the vehicle into motion and they headed toward their destination. "So, you were rather vague on the phone. Why isn't your fiancé coming to California yet?"

She looked out the window, like she didn't want to make eye contact. "His work put a delay on his transfer." She shrugged, turning to face him. "I guess that it gives me time to sort out of my life here. I have to find a job and I can start looking for houses."

"Alone?" He asked, trying not to butt in.

She nodded, "It might not be the best scenario, but I can always send him pics of what I find and get his opinion. Right?"

He could tell that she was trying to be stronger about it than she was letting on, but he couldn't make her feel worse. "Of course."

She smiled, turning back and glancing out the window. He felt for her and couldn't believe how her fiancé would be willing to wait this long to meet up with her. He had a hard time being that far away from her and they weren't even dating. He pulled into the ice cream shop and her demeanor instantly changed. She seemed happy. "This is exactly what I need. Marla's famous double scoop fudge—"

"Peanut butter ice cream sundae," he finished for her.

She nodded, "I can taste it already." They got out of the car and headed into the small building. The minute they were seated, the teenaged girl approached them.

"Hello, my name is Noelle. Would you like a menu?"

They both shook their heads, "That won't be necessary," Tiffany responded, ordering the two desserts. "Thank you!" She said, watching the girl walk away. "Remember when I worked here?" She asked, turning back to Scott. "The outfits haven't changed."

He laughed, "This place was hopping on Friday nights after football games, but you seemed to love it."

She nodded, "I did." As her words came out, he spotted Marla heading their way. Tiffany looked up and jumped to her feet. "Marla..." she pulled her into a hug. "I have missed you." When she parted, it looked like she had tears in her eyes.

"We have missed you too, When I saw the order, I just knew that it would be my two favorite customers." Marla spoke with a smile. She turned to Scott and nodded. "Scott, good to see you too."

"Thank you Marla...likewise."

"So, what brings you back to California?" Marla asked, focusing back on Tiffany.

"Well, I am moving back to town."

"Her fiancé will be joining her shortly," Scott said. When Tiffany looked at him, he wasn't sure if it was anger or shock that he said anything. He was leaning more toward anger.

"Fiancé?" Marla asked, looking down and noticing the ring on her left hand. Her jaw dropped. "Holy cow...what does he do for a living?"

"He's a lawyer and he is transferring the branch in town." She held out her hand and Scott caught himself looking at it again. Each time he thought about the fact that she was getting married, he cringed. He looked up, forcing himself not to look at her engagement ring. There was a smile on her face, but there was also sadness in her eyes. He could feel it.

"Well, congratulations." Marla turned back to me and smiled, "I must admit, I always thought maybe the two of you would end up together." She laughed, "Apparently, I am not destined to be a psychic." She grinned, "Glad to have you home."

She walked away and Tiffany took her seat. Her face was red and I watched her for a second, before clearing my throat and trying to lighten the mood. "It must be that darn wedding when we were ten. It has people all confused."

She looked up and laughed, "Is that it?"

He shrugged, "Makes perfect sense." He looked up and saw the ice cream heading to their table. "Perfect timing." The girl put the ice creams down. "Thank you," he said, handing Tiffany a spoon. "Dig in."

They each took a bite as Tiffany sighed. "Heavenly."

He took a bite and nodded in agreement. This was something that would take away all worries and doubts and nothing was going to change that.

***

Tiffany waited by the car, as Scott disappeared. He gave no explanation, but said he had a surprise for her. They had just finished at the ice cream shop and it definitely took her mind off of the fact that Scott wasn't going to be there.

She saw Scott heading back to the car. He was on the phone as he approached her. "We'll be there. Thank you Veronica." He disconnected the call, "Get in."

"Who was on the phone?" She asked, inquisitively.

"We are going to pick you out the perfect home." He replied with a smile. "I'll explain on the way." Tiffany wasn't sure about that, but got in anyway. He began to explain immediately. "Veronica Baylor is one of my clients and one of the top notch realtors in the area. I called her and asked her to put together a list of houses and we're going to meet her at one of them."

Her jaw dropped, "We're what?"

He glanced at her, "You heard me."

"Yeah, I heard you, but I don't feel like this is such a great idea. I mean...this is something that I am supposed to be doing with my future husband." She shrugged, "Seems strange."

He shook his head, "It's not strange. He isn't here and I am. It's better than going out alone. Besides, maybe I can help you get the perfect price." He turned back to the road. She was still apprehensive, but decided to go with it. He continued driving, until he turned onto a secluded street. He pulled up in front of a house that had a sale sign in front of it.

She looked at the house and imagined living there. It was fairly good size, but she would have to check the inside out. She got out of the car and they headed up to the door. From the car in the driveway, she knew that the realtor was already there.

He opened the door and called out, "Veronica?"

A tall woman came out of a room, wearing a smile. "Hello," she held out her hand and Tiffany shook it.

"Hello," Tiffany spoke. She was looking around the entrance of the house.

"Thank you for meeting us on such short notice," Scott was saying.

"Not a problem. Let me give you both the guided tour."

They followed her, through another room where she introduced the living room. It was a nice size room and Tiffany could picture the type of furniture they would get and where it would go. "This is a nice room," Scott was saying and she nodded.

"I'll show you the kitchen." As she led the way, she looked back at them. "When are you both getting married?" She asked.

"Um..." she glanced at Scott, looking for some help to explain it to her, but he was just smiling. "We're not." She finally spoke. The realtor looked away and she playfully hit him. He laughed.

"Tiffany is getting married. We're just friends."

"Oh..." Veronica said, seeming unfazed. "This is a nice kitchen. Do you like to cook?"

She opened her mouth to speak, but Scott was speaking instead. "She makes great peanut butter and jelly sandwiches." He replied. She glared at him and she could see that he was having a wonderful time on her behalf.

Veronica glanced back at her and Tiffany snickered, "I do alright in the kitchen." She turned and snared in his direction. "You are dead," she whispered.

He raised his eyebrows, but brushed past her as they entered the kitchen. "The best part of the house is the majority of appliances are staying."

"Why is the seller selling?" She asked, glancing at the nicely decorated room.

"She is getting older and her daughter lives out of town, so she decided to move closer to her daughter. She doesn't want a lot of her stuff."

"This is a nice kitchen," Tiffany mumbled, looking at the appliances. They each seemed fairly new. The tiled floor was also something that she liked.

"We can go upstairs where you will see the two bedrooms and a bathroom." They followed her out of the kitchen. When they reached the staircase, she pointed to another door. "There is a half bath right there." She led the way up the stairs and they reached the floor. She opened the door and they entered the room. "This is the master bedroom. It has a bathroom attached." She looked all over the bedroom. It was bigger than her New York bedroom, at least by three times.

"This is nice," she replied, opening up closets and stepping inside. In the bathroom, she could see the sink was completely made of ceramic and also looked brand new.

"Wow..." Scott mumbled, stepping in behind her.

She looked at him and nodded, "Nice, huh?" She whispered.

He nodded, "Definitely nicer than my apartment."

She smiled, as they stepped out of the bathroom. They exited the bedroom and looked at the other two. They were about the same, just smaller. "This is nice. Really it is," she started. They headed down the stairs and Veronica turned to her when they reached the foyer. "I am almost too afraid to ask the asking price."

Veronica held up her finger and disappeared back into the kitchen. "This is nice, but it's going to be way too expensive," she whispered to Scott.

Veronica came back into the foyer and looked over the paper. "You are looking at $115,000."

Tiffany gasped, figuring that it would be something like that. She opened her mouth, but again Scott was interrupting. "I'm sure that is just the asking price."

Veronica nodded, "I am sure that the owner would negotiate."

Tiffany tried to smile, "I appreciate the offer, but in order for us to be able to afford it...we would have to agree to way less than that. I am sure that she won't agree to negotiate that much. Thank you, but we'll have to keep looking." She headed out of the house, not wanting to think about it for another minute.

Scott joined her and they got into the car. "Don't you want to at least try?"

She thought about that, but then shook her head. "We have only looked at one house. I am sure there will be much more to look at. Thank you!" He turned from her and they waited until Veronica's car pulled out of the driveway and they followed her. She had no doubt that there would be plenty of houses that they could look into.

***

Scott dropped Tiffany back off at her hotel. He had one of the best times he could have even imagined just looking at houses with her. It felt like they were a couple that were getting ready to get married. He still didn't know how Erick could stand being away from her.

He got back home and threw his wallet and keys on the coffee table and crashed on the couch. He didn't know how he would pull it off, but he knew that he wouldn't feel right if he didn't try to win her heart. He couldn't give up without a fight.

He got off the couch and thought about ways to a woman's heart. He grabbed a notebook from the kitchen drawer and took a seat at the table. He began writing her a letter:

Dearest Tiffany:

I have tried numerous times to tell you what's in my heart, yet the words always fail me or you are with someone else. While this might not be the most opportune time, I feel that I have to be honest with you and myself. Since the first day I laid eyes on you, I knew that you were something special. It was after our fake marriage at the age of 10, that I began to realize that there was more to you.

You are beautiful inside and out and I have been blessed to call you my best friend, but over the years I have struggled with what's right and wrong. I have wanted to be happy for you and I am, to an extent. I have watched you pursue your dreams and I couldn't be more proud of that. I stood back and didn't say a word, when you chose to stay in New York City, even though my heart was being ripped from my chest. I hear news that you are getting married and I am left wondering how I could be so stupid.

I am asking you not to walk down that aisle, because what you need is and has always been right before your eyes. I love you, Tiffany and nothing is going to stop me from saying that. I have been too scared to admit it, but I am running out of time and this is my last hope. Please, give us a chance. You are everything I could ever want and I have to tell you that. I will remain by your side no matter what

happens, but I am hoping that you can find it in your heart to say that
you love me too.

Love,

Scott

He looks at the letter and almost crumples it up, but he can't.
He spoke from the heart and that's all he could do. He did know
that he couldn't give her the letter so soon. He would focus on
other ways to get through to her and use the letter has a final piece.
He closed the notebook up and left the kitchen. He needed to take
a cold shower and try to put her out of his mind. It wouldn't be
easy, but it was what needed to be done.

***

Tiffany yawned as she filled out her third application online. She
hoped that one of the employers called her. She was just about to
hit submit, when she heard a knock on her hotel room door. She
quickly hit submit and then went to the door. She peered outside
to find a man holding a bouquet of flowers at her door. She opened
the door and smiled. "Hello."

"Hello. Are you Tiffany Reynolds?"

"Yes," she replied, staring at the bouquet of pink roses. They
were her favorite color of roses.

He handed the flowers to her. "Enjoy!" He smiled, turning and
walking away from her.

She looked down at the flowers and carried them back into
the room. She placed them on the table and leafed through the
bouquet, until she found the car. She removed it and read what it
said:

Tiffany –
You are more beautiful now than the first day I saw you.
I hope these brighten your day.

She flipped the card over. It wasn't signed. "They have to be from Erick," she assured herself. She smelled the bouquet and smiled. "They sure are gorgeous," she mumbled, placing them on the table to brighten up the room. She heard her cellphone ringing and looked down to see that Scott was calling her. "Hey, Scott."

"Hey...what are you doing?"

She looked back at her computer and groaned, then looked at the flowers. "Staring at the most beautiful bouquet of roses. Erick knew the pick me up I needed." There was silence on the other end that she thought she had gotten disconnected. "Are you there?"

"Uh yeah...I'm here."

"So...what's up?" She asked, getting back to the reason he called.

"I thought maybe we could go out for lunch. I have some extra time, before having a meeting this afternoon."

"Sure, that would be great."

"Okay, meet you at my work at noon?"

"I'll be there," she replied. "See ya then," she hung up the call and looked back at the roses. She dialed up Erick's number. It went straight to his voicemail. She waited for the beep and then spoke, "Hey, babe...I just wanted to call you and tell you how much I love you and I miss you. I'm sure you're busy getting things finished up for work, but I can't wait to talk to you. Goodbye." She hung up the call. She wanted to hear his voice and thank him for the beautiful flowers, but it could wait. She walked back to the computer and closed it up. She would give it some time before applying for any more positions. She needed to get ready for lunch.

***

Scott couldn't concentrate. He should have known that she would assume the roses were from Erick. He groaned in frustration, tossing his pen. "What did this pen do to you?" He looked up to see Heather, his receptionist, standing in the door.

"Oh...thanks." He said, taking the pen from her. He hesitated, before looking up at her. "You're a woman."

"Thanks for the brilliant deduction," she replied with a laugh.

He smiled, "I just meant, out of curiosity what do women like to receive as gifts?"

"Flowers," she stated, with conviction.

"Been there...done that," he replied. "What else?"

She seemed to ponder on that. "Well, you can't go wrong with candy...chocolate especially." He had thought about that, but he was trying to get away from the usual gifts. He chose flowers, because he knew how much she loved pink roses. "Jewelry is always a plus." She replied, smiling. "I guess that most women really just go for something that comes from the heart." She shrugged, "Doesn't have to take a lot of thought, but it needs to be real."

He nodded, trying to think about that. Some ideas entered his mind and he thought that he would have to try them out. "Thank you. Now, did you need something?"

"I was going to let you know that I was going out for lunch. Do you need anything?"

"Nope, I will be heading out soon. Enjoy."

She smiled. She turned around, nearly running into Tiffany. "Hey, Heather." They hugged one another, but when they parted Heather turned back to me. A look of recognition in her eyes. I tried to ignore her, turning to Tiffany.

"Tiffany, I hear that congratulations is in order." She stuck her hand out, showing Heather. I had to roll my eyes, because I was getting tired of dwelling on it. "That is a beauty." She glanced back at Scott, "It's a beauty, isn't it Scott?"

Scott nodded, "It sure is." He stood up and walked to the door. "Are you ready to go?"

"I better get going," Heather said.

"Goodbye, Heather." He called, as she left the office. "Where do you want to go?"

She shook her head, "I don't care."

They headed to the door and left the building. As they walked down the street to the corner restaurant, she began talking about the flowers. He wanted to ask if she was trying to make him jealous, but decided against it. He opened the door for her and she entered. "How did he sign it?" He asked.

She turned to him, "That's kind of private, don't you think?"

"Oh excuse me," he replied, sarcastically. He walked up to the podium and the hostess had them follow her. When they sat down, he looked at the menu. "If you have some cute name for each other and you don't want to tell me how he signed it, then more power to you." He looked through the menu, hoping she would see that he wasn't bothered by her words; even though he was.

"It's not that. In fact he didn't even sign his name. It was the words that meant the most. That's all."

He looked up at her, "If he didn't sign his name, how do you know that he sent them?"

She laughed, "Who else would send them?"

He shrugged, "I don't know. I was just curious." He looked back at the menu, knowing that he needed the conversation to be dropped. "I'm starving," he said, changing the subject.

She looked in the menu and he casually glanced at her from the corner of his eye. He hoped that the next attempt went more smoothly, because he was bombing out.

***

Tiffany received a call, right after she got out of the shower. She didn't recognize the number, but since she had submitted so many applications she knew she needed to answer it. "Hello?"

"Hello, is this Tiffany Reynolds?"

"Yes, this is she." She said, crossing her fingers.

"Hello, Ms. Reynolds. This is Matthew Riley from Riley advertising. How are you doing?"

She could barely find the words. She couldn't believe the owner was actually calling her. "I...I'm doing great." She replied, trying not to sound too eager.

"Good to hear. I was hoping you could come in today so we could talk. I have received your application and I am very impressed." She could have squealed with pleasure, but she held back.

"That would be great. What time works best for you?"

"How about coming by at eleven o'clock. Do you know where we're located?"

She nodded, realizing that he wouldn't be able to see the gesture. "I do. I will be there. Thank you!"

"You're welcome. See you soon!" The call was disconnected and she stared at the phone. She twirled around her hotel room. She was hoping that this was the break she was looking for. She glanced at the clock, she had two hours to get ready and be there. She knew that it was about thirty minutes away, so she would have plenty of time. She grabbed her classiest outfit she had packed and got dressed. She spent more time on her hair and makeup. She wanted it to be perfect.

She was putting her earrings in, when she heard a knock
. She rushed to the door and peeked outside. A guy was standing at her door. She frowned, but then flung the door open. "Hello?"

"Ms. Reynolds?" He asked. She nodded, "Please sign here." He handed her a clipboard. She signed her name and then he handed her a small box. "Have a nice day."

"You too," she replied, absentmindedly. She looked at the package and saw that there was no return address. Her name and the hotel address was handwritten on the front. She recognized the writing, but couldn't immediately place it. She opened up the box and found another box inside. This time it was a velvet box. She opened it up and stared at the necklace. Her eyes got big, finding the gold cross inside. Wrapped around the cross was rubies that alternated with topazes. She pulled it from the box. "It's gorgeous," she spoke, putting it around her neck and going to the mirror. "Perfect to complete the ensemble." She couldn't believe how thoughtful Erick was. His birthday was in November, representing the topaz birthstone and her birthday was in April, representing the ruby. She ran her hand over the cross.

She had yet to hear back from him when she received the flowers a few days earlier. She picked up the phone and dialed his number again. Again it went straight to his voicemail. "Hey, Erick. I am starting to worry a bit. I haven't heard back from you in a few days. Thank you so much for the necklace. It's gorgeous. Also, the flowers were perfect. I love you." She hung up and glanced one more time in the mirror. She was ready to go land the job.

She called a cab and fifteen minutes she was out the door and heading to Riley Advertising. She was relieved to see that she wasn't nervous. She was anxious though. She paid the cab driver and hurried up the front steps. She was glad that she had brought her portfolio along. She felt professional and ready to make her move.

She approached the desk with confidence. "My name is Tiffany Reynolds. I am here to meet with Matthew Riley."

"Of course, Ms. Reynolds. He will be out in a few minutes. You may have a seat."

She sat down and waited for him to arrive. Like clockwork, it was only a couple of minutes. He walked out with swag, offering his hand to her. "Ms. Reynolds, it is very nice to meet you."

"Likewise," she spoke, standing up. She followed him, past the reception desk.

"Please hold my calls," he stated to the receptionist. They entered a room and he held back for her to go before him. "Please, have a seat."

She took a seat and placed her portfolio down. "I want to thank you for taking the time out to meet with me."

He smiled, "I have made some calls and you have come highly recommended." He stated. "Your previous employer was sorry to see you go."

She blushed, "I had to make a tough decision. I enjoyed working there."

"May I ask why you chose to leave?"

She thought about that, letting out a slow breath. "My fiancé is getting transferred here. So, I had no choice."

He nodded, "It's a good reason." He looked down at her application. "I am very impressed with your resume. I am assuming you have samples of your work."

"Of course," she said, reaching down and opening her briefcase. She took out her campaigns and handed them to him. It was the first step of letting herself out there and she hoped that he liked it.

***

Scott looked up to find Tiffany entering his office. A smile was present on her lips. He stood up. "This is a pleasant surprise." His eyes instantly went to her necklace. He could definitely see that she wore it well.

"I got a job," she said, throwing her arms around him.

He held her close, feeling how much he wanted that to be an everyday occurrence. "That is wonderful news, Tiff." She pulled away and there was so much happiness in her eyes. "I bet Erick is ecstatic."

Her eyes fell to the ground, "He probably would be if I could get ahold of him." She shrugged, "I knew that I would be able to see you."

He tried not to show how much those words meant to him. He pointed to her necklace, "Nice necklace. Is it new?" He wanted to fish to see what she would say. "I see it has rubies and topazes in it."

She smiled, holding the necklace. "Yes, I just got it today. As you know my birthday is in April and Erick's is in November." His face fell. He couldn't believe his luck. Her eyes lit up and she laughed, "I didn't think about that, but so is yours."

He nodded, "The eighteenth. How about him?"

"The twelfth." She replied. She seemed to think about that, "What a coincidence."

"I'll say," He mumbled. "Well, I think that's amazing news about the job. We should celebrate tonight. I can pick you up when I get off work today. It will be about six o'clock. Does that work?"

"That would be great," she smiled. "I'll see you later."

"See you," He called, as she left his office.

He sunk down in his chair and opened up his desk drawer. He pulled the letter out from the corner of his desk. He read through it. It was time to make the next move. He was sure of it. He folded the letter and put it into his jacket pocket. He got up and left his office for another meeting. By the end of the evening she would know exactly how he felt and he could hope that she felt the same.

***

Tiffany tried one more time to call Erick. She groaned in frustration, disconnecting the call. She didn't know why she couldn't get ahold of him. She heard a knock and she went to answer it. "I will be with you in a minute." She called, heading back to get her purse.

"I thought we could have a picnic today. If that's alright with you?"

She frowned, "It's been pretty cold. Are you sure about that?"

He snickered, "Where we're going it won't be cold. I promise."

She thought that was strange, but shrugged. "Whatever. I'm game if you are." She shut her hotel room door and headed with him down the elevator and out the hotel. They got to his car and she saw the picnic basket in the backseat. "It's been awhile since I've been on a picnic," I admitted.

"I think you'll be surprised by the location," he replied. Their eyes connected and he was smiling. She got into the car and he went around to the other side. The drive was quiet, but in a good way. When they turned the corner, she remembered how they had come down this same road a few days ago. She glanced at him and he was just smiling. She didn't bother mentioning it. When they pulled into the driveway, she knew that something was going on.

"What are we doing here?" She asked, staring up at the first house they had visited. A *Sold* sign was in front of it. "What's going on?"

He laughed, "You'll see."

They got out of the car and he grabbed the picnic basket. They then headed up to the front door. She watched as he unlocked the door with a set of keys. "What in the world?" She asked, entering the house.

He turned around, "I bought it."

Her jaw dropped, "Are you serious?"

He laughed, "I knew you would say that. I just fell in love with this house and decided that it was time to make the move. What do you think?"

"I think you are out of your mind." She replied, smacking him on the arm. "This is pretty cool, but sad. You got a house before me and I was the one looking."

He laughed, "I'm sorry, but I didn't want to pass it up."

She had to admit she was a little jealous, but she was also thrilled for him. "Congrats Scott," she leaned up to kiss his cheek, but he turned his head so that her lips were touching his. The kiss lingered for a moment, until she realized what was happening. "Scott..." she said, touching her lips.

"Tiffany, listen to me." He said. He took his hand to her waist and she slowly pulled away.

"I'm getting married," she quickly said, moving backwards.

"He hasn't even called you." He argued.

She glared at him. "He's sent me flowers and a necklace to show me that he is thinking about me. That's all I need."

He moved to her, "Tiffany, I bought you those things." He said.

She opened her mouth, but no words came out. She shook her head, "You're lying. His birthstone..."

"Is my birthstone. You said it yourself. I know your favorite flower. Go with your heart. Do you honestly think I'm making this up?"

She didn't know what to believe. She was going to be Erick's wife and this wasn't supposed to happen like this. "I am getting married," she spoke again.

"To the wrong man," he replied.

"Stop it!" She yelled. "You are my best friend and nothing will ever happen between us."

"Why not? Are you that scared?" He asked, intently staring at her.

"Why are you doing this? I know those gifts came from Erick." She looked away from him, feeling tears stinging the back of her eyes. "Take me home."

"Tiffany, don't....talk to me."

She shook her head, "Take me home." She spoke again. She turned from him and ran from the house. She couldn't let him get to her. She knew the truth and that's what mattered.

***

"Tiffany, won't you please hear me out." Scott said for the hundredth time. "I wouldn't lie to you."

She couldn't stay in that car and listen to him. Nothing seemed real. She reached for her door handle. "Don't call me," she said, with anger in her voice.

Pain was etched on his face. He pulled something from his jacket pocket and placed it in her hand. "Just read it. Please."

She closed her hand on the letter. She anticipated, she would just throw it away, but she didn't say that. "Goodnight," she replied, jumping out of the car and heading into the hotel.

The moment she got inside, she felt the tears fall. She got into the elevator, feeling her body shaking from the tears. When she got out of the elevator, she walked to her room. She opened the door and fell to the bed.

She looked at the folded piece of paper and thought about just throwing it away. Instead, she opened it up and started to read. The more she read the worse she felt. She covered her mouth. The fact that he felt that was shocking to her, but it didn't change the fact that she wasn't available. As she got up, she threw the note into the wastebasket. She heard her cellphone ringing and she grabbed it from her pocket. She sighed with relief, seeing Erick's name across the screen.

"Hello."

"Hey, babe. It's been awhile."

She wanted to argue that that was his fault, but she didn't have the energy. "You have no idea how much I needed to hear your voice." She said, falling back down on the bed.

"I'm sorry I have been out of touch. It's been crazy, but I did get your messages." She held onto his words. It would be a relief to hear him talk about the gifts that he got her. "I must admit, I'm a little confused. What flowers and necklace are you referring to?"

A gasp escaped her lips. This couldn't be. "Um...never mind, I was mistaken." She said, dumbfounded.

"Oh..." he snickered.

She felt a weight in her chest, but tried to get over it. "I got a job today."

There was a long pause, before he spoke again. "You did? There's actually something that I need to tell you."

"I'm listening."

"There has been a change of plans. I was offered a better position if I stay here. It equals more money and more responsibilities. In the long run I can't pass it up."

"You didn't call me. This would be news that you should have told me before I went and got another job."

"I know, baby, but I just found out and I couldn't let you know earlier. It wasn't finalized. Just tell the place that hired you that you're fiancé is staying in New York. They'll understand."

She couldn't find the words to express how upset she was. "I won't understand. This job is giving me opportunities that I don't want to pass up. I love you, but..." her words dropped off.

"What are you trying to say?"

"We barely know each other. You are obviously more wrapped up in your job than I could ever compete with."

"That's not true," he argued.

"Yes...it is." She continued, "It would never work out."

"But..."

"I will mail you the ring back. Good luck and I wish you every bit of happiness."

"Tiffany, don't..." he started, saying the same words that Scott had spoken. She hung up the phone, feeling relief.

She looked at her ring and pulled it off her finger. She placed it on the dresser and went back to the wastebasket. She picked up the letter and reread it. She knew that Scott was someone that could handle a mixture of being with her and working. She grabbed her purse and headed to the door. She needed to talk to him and she hoped there was a cab around. When she opened the door, she nearly ran right into him. "I, couldn't just leave..." he began, before he could go on she wrapped her hand around his neck and pulled him close to her. Their lips connected and she melted into him. His tongue ran along hers and she pulled from him.

"I'm sorry," she spoke, grabbing his hand and pulling him into the hotel room. "I love you," she spoke, pulling him back to her and wrapping her arms around him. They could talk later. The only thing that mattered to her was showing him how much she cared for him and she would show him that the rest of her life.

Lost Love

Although Chase had broken up with her 2 years earlier, Liv hoped for a reconciliation. Chase had long since moved on, while Liv, a hair stylist, never went out on a single date. When they first broke up, Chase wasn't sure that he made the right decision.

As time wore on, however, his feelings for Liv were quickly fading. Conversely, Liv's feelings were getting stronger for Chase, despite his snubs.

Liv, a seasoned employee at Salon54, first laid eyes on Chase when he came in to get his haircut. Liv and her friends were swooning over this six-foot-two brunette who walked in with a confident smirk. He knew he was hot.

Liv thought he was the hottest guy she has ever seen but felt that he was "out of her league." Chase was a partner in a large law firm who played polo, was a member of a posh country club, and who traveled all over the world. Of course she didn't know that at the time, but his appearance and attitude ended up perfectly matching his background. No surprise there.

Liv came from a blue-collar family, whose father was a construction worker. Her mother was a stay-at-home mom, but worked part-time as a manicurist in the basement of their modest Seattle home.

While in high school, Liv excelled in math and science, but her family was unable to afford sending her to college. She wanted to become an engineer, but her dreams were dashed when her father lost his job.

Liv had to go to work to help support the family, and in her spare time, she decided to go to cosmetology school. She paid for her beauty school tuition out of the money she made from working at the local pet shop, and after about a year, she passed the state boards to become a licensed cosmetologist.

On Liv's 30th birthday, her friends took her out to a popular nightclub to celebrate. Although she met a few guys that sparked her interest, all she could think about was Chase. She was hoping that he would make a second appointment for a haircut and return to the salon.

As luck would have it, Chase returned to the salon a couple months later, and to Liv's complete surprise, he asked her out. Their first date took them to Chase's country club, where Liv met his friends.

Chase was 10 years older than Liv, although he acted and looked much younger. Even though he acted youthful and vibrant, his friends seemed boring and arrogant. Despite her dislike for his friends, Liv quickly fell in love with Chase. He treated her well, and even offered to pay for her to go back to college.

The couple soon settled into a mundane dating routine, and although Liv was still happy, she could sense that Chase was losing interest in her. He seemed irritated and distant with her, and started going out a few times a week.

Most of Chase's family members liked Liv, however, his mother never warmed up to her. She never thought that Liv was good enough for her son, but remained cordial to her.

Chase's mother, Vera, on more than one occasion, tried introducing her son to various women. These women were all professionals, and a few were attorneys, just like her son.

Chase's father, Jack, also an attorney, stayed out of his wife's matchmaking schemes, as he was in his own little world, with a mistress of his own and a huge drinking problem.

Chase didn't invite Liv to his grandmother's birthday party, and when he arrived, he was greeted at the door by one of the most beautiful women he'd ever seen. He never saw her before, and wondered who she was there with. Little did he know, his mother invited her in an attempt to get him interested in someone other than Liv.

Her plan worked. Chase and the other women, whose name was Chelsea, hit it off almost instantly. He couldn't stop looking at her, and was intrigued by her New York accent.

Chelsea worked as an entertainment attorney, who represented a number of big name sports and music personalities. She even invited Chase to a sporting event which had been sold out for weeks.

Even though Chase had no intentions of breaking up with Liv, he could no longer ignore his feelings for Chelsea. They soon started having lunch dates at 5 star hotels, and even managed to plan a getaway weekend to the Poconos.

When Chase started becoming increasingly distant from Liv, she started to suspect the worst. By this time, Chelsea was pressuring Chase for a commitment. Although they've only been seeing each other for about a month, their relationship was growing more and more intense.

The sex was amazing, and Chase never experienced anything like it before. Chelsea was willing to try new things in bed, and seemed to want sex multiple times a day. Liv, by contrast, was rather modest, and her sexual appetite was diminished by her escalating depression, and the side effects from the medication she was taking.

As the months passed, Liv was getting ready to go to Florida for a hair show. She and Chase were drifting further and further apart, but they still managed to maintain a dim spark of excitement between them. On the evening before she was schedule to leave for her trip, Liv and Chase went out for a romantic dinner, and then came home and spent the next three hours making love.

After their love fest, Chase turned over and went to sleep. Liv, the eternal romantic, want to cuddle, but Chase rebuffed her advances. The next morning, Chase drove Liv to the airport, and he couldn't help but feel profound relief. He would now be able to spend the next week with his new "friend," Chelsea, and called her as soon as Liv boarded the plane.

For almost the entire week that Liv was on her business trip, Chase stayed with Chelsea at her downtown apartment. The couple enjoyed cooking dinner together and waking up next to each other. Chase didn't know how he would tell Liv that he no longer loved her, and he even wished that she would stay in Florida for the long-term.

He was not responsive to her text messages, and only took her phone calls sporadically during that entire week. The week flew by quickly, and before he knew it, Chase found himself at the airport once again, but only this time, he was picking Liv up. She was elated to see him, but he cringed when they hugged.

Liv sensed that something was wrong, and was starting to worry. Chase told her that he was tired because he spent the entire week working on a brief for an upcoming legal case.

The couple trudged through the holidays together, but as Valentine's Day approached, Chase could no longer suppress he desire to be with Chelsea. Although he knew that Valentine's week was not the most appropriate time to break up with Liv, he felt it was necessary, because he wanted to spend Valentine's Day with Chelsea.

He didn't bother with formalities, and simply blurted it out. He told Liv that he was no longer happy with her, but didn't volunteer any information about his other woman. He further explained that he just needed time to be "by himself," and that "maybe" he would come to his senses and come back home to be with her. After Liv pressed him for answers, he finally came clean about Chelsea.

After hearing the news, Liv broke down, and didn't think she would be able to function at work the next day. Of course, Chase told her that he didn't mean for it to happen, but when he met Chelsea, an instant connection was made. He didn't really want to divulge so much information about how he felt about Chelsea, but he felt that unless he "drove his point home," Liv wouldn't take him seriously.

Liv was blindsided by the breakup. She tried to keep busy with work and going out with friends, but she couldn't shake the despair she felt. Although she was asked out on dates, she always declined.

In Liv's eyes, nobody would ever hold a candle to Chase, and she had no desire to date anyone because she knew it would never progress into anything further. In the meantime, Chase and Chelsea were seen around town at various restaurants and social events.

On one occasion, Liv caught a glimpse of the couple getting out of a cab. This almost pushed her over the edge, but she managed to hold onto her dignity. After three years passed, Liv's feelings for Chase were still as intense as they were when they first started dated. Chase's feelings for Liv, on the other hand, were almost non-existent. Sure he had fond memories of their time together, but never really felt as though Liv was his soul mate.

Liv eventually started seeing a counselor because she was not bouncing back from the breakup. Her sleep pattern was disrupted, her diet was poor, and she stopped socializing altogether. The only social stimulation she got was when she went to work, and even there, her social interactions were severely limited.

The counselor was worried for his patient's safety, and feared that she was spiraling into a deep, dark depression. Liv was eventually referred to a psychiatrist, who adjusted her medication and sent her on her way. When the medication kicked in after a few weeks, Liv's mood brightened, and she started considering dating again.

Liv met a nice guy at the gym, and when he asked her out for coffee, she felt flattered. Like Chase, Jason was older, distinguished and well-educated. Their coffee date was pleasant, but according to Liv, there was no spark.

When Jason asked her out for dinner, Liv hesitated, but decided to give him another chance. She was very critical of other men, but hoped that she would once again, find love. Jason took Liv to dinner and a play, and as the date was coming to a close, Jason leaned in for a kiss.

Liv had no intentions of kissing him, and in fact, she had no intentions of ever seeing him again. All she could think about was Chase. Three years have passed, and still, her love was as strong as ever. Liv's co-workers were worried about her, and when she had too much to drink one night and drunk dialed Chase, they really became concerned. Fortunately she hung up before he answered the phone, but her number showed up on his caller ID.

Chase was curious to find out what Liv wanted. His relationship with Chelsea was starting to cool, and lately, he started thinking about how much Liv loved him when they were together. He hesitated at first, but after a couple days, Chase returned Liv's call.

You could have knocked her over with a feather when she saw Chase's number come up on her caller ID. She was shaking as she answered the phone, and as soon as she heard his voice, she broke down sobbing.

Something stirred in Chase's heart, because he too, felt tears welling up in his eyes. Their phone call was brief, and in fact, it lasted only seconds, because Chelsea walked into the room just as Liv answered. Chase took this as a sign.

Liv knew that Chase still felt a connection to her. She quickly put that phone call out of her mind, and tried to focus on her job.

She went on a few more dates, and much to her surprise, Liv found a guy with whom she clicked with.

Her friend introduced her to an accountant who was from the same town that Liv was from. In fact, they lived within a few blocks of each other when they were teenagers, but they went to different schools. He went to a private, all-boys school, and Liv went to a public school.

At first, the relationship progressed slowly, but after a few months, Liv started developing strong feelings for her new friend, whose name was Ben. He took Liv to meet his family in Florida, and they absolutely loved her. Unlike Chase's mother, Vera, Ben's mother, Patty, felt that they were the perfect couple.

As their relationship grew stronger, Liv's feelings for Chase were becoming distant memories. In fact, days went by where she didn't even think about Chase at all. Chase, on the other hand, couldn't get Liv out of his mind. His relationship with Chelsea was hanging by a thread, and he yearned for the relationship he once shared with Liv.

He was starting to realize that breaking up with her was a mistake, and he hoped that she was not involved with another man. Chase finally raised enough courage to call Liv back, and when she answered, his heart stopped. He almost hung up, but was able to whisper out a weak, "Hi Liv, how are you?" Liv was gracious and warm, and replied, "Hi, Chase, it's nice to hear from you."

The conversation was strained and awkward, but in Chase's mind, the ice had been broken. He was certain that he could get back into Liv's good graces once again, so that they could pick up where they left off. Their conversation consisted solely of small talk, and neither one asked about the other's personal life.

Liv almost felt sick to her stomach when she heard Chase's voice, because it brought back the painful memories of their breakup. She was grateful that she had Ben, because he filled the void that Chase left. When she told Ben that Chase called, he became suspicious. Why would Chase call Liv after three years apart? Did Liv initiate the first call, he wondered? Liv finally confessed to Ben that she did, indeed, "drunk dial" Chase days before.

It seemed that now, the tables were turned. Chase was the one who was pining away for Liv, while Liv, on the other hand, was blissfully "in like" with someone else. It never occurred to Chase that Liv would move on and start a new life with someone else. He also felt that Liv was his "ace in the hole," in case his relationship with Chelsea didn't work out. Would he and Liv ever reconcile, he wondered?

Even though Liv was happy with Ben, she couldn't get Chase out of her mind, and wanted to connect with him again, just to find out more about his relationship status with Chelsea.

Liv felt a twinge of guilt for thinking about calling Chase because Ben had been so good to her. She didn't want to be shady or go behind his back, so she talked to him about her intentions.

Liv felt that she needed to get Chase out of her system once and for all before she would be able to move forward with her relationship with Ben. A total commitment to Ben was out of the question, in Liv's mind, unless she was completely over Chase.

Ben agreed that Liv needed to get Chase out of her system before they could take the next step in their relationship, so he encouraged Liv to make the phone call. Feeling better now that she confessed her feelings to Ben about Chase, Liv picked up her phone and dialed Chase's number.

He answered on the first ring, and couldn't believe his good fortune that Liv was calling him. "I want to see you," Liv said, as soon as Chase answered the phone.

Chase was shocked, but elated. By this time, he and Chelsea were barely speaking, and she was spending more and more time away from the apartment that they shared since the beginning of their relationship.

Liv and Chase planned to go out for dinner so that could talk. Both were excited, anxious, but uncertain about a future together. When Liv saw Chase for the first time in three years, she was surprised that her heart wasn't racing, and that she did not have butterflies in her stomach.

Although it was nice to see Chase, that intense spark of passion and love was not there. Chase, on the other hand, could barely contain his emotions, and started to cry when they hugged.

He apologized to Liv for hurting her, but she was unfazed. The cold and uncaring manner in which he "dumped" Liv always bothered Chase, but he never had the opportunity to tell Liv how he felt. They talked about Chase's relationship with Chelsea, and how it started out so intensely, but then, over time, seemed to have burned itself out.

Liv listened quietly as Chase spoke about how Chelsea was a workaholic, and how she never cooked a meal for him in three years. Not only didn't she cook, she never cleaned either. Chase finally hired a cleaning service to come in twice a month to tidy up, but he wished that Chelsea was a little more domesticated.

She wasn't into the "housewife" thing, and she certainly didn't have any maternal instincts either. Liv couldn't help but feel a twinge of satisfaction while Chase was droning on about his faltering relationship with Chelsea. Chase was the type of guy who enjoyed home-cooked meals, who liked a clean home, and who wanted to start a family someday.

Liv wanted to start a family too, but it was becoming more apparent to Liv, that instead of wanting to start a family with Chase, she wanted to start one with Ben. Throughout the entire dinner, Chase talked about himself and his relationship with

Chelsea. He didn't ask Liv what was going on in her life until it was almost time for them to leave.

Chase was certain that Liv had been waiting around for him to come back all this time, and was profoundly disappointed when Liv told him that she had met someone else. What made Chase feel even worse was when Liv told him that she was falling in love with Ben. Chase asked, "how could you have fallen out of love with me?" Liv replied, "It took a long time, but I finally found someone who appreciates me, embraces me for who I am, and whose family loves me." On one hand, Chase was happy for Liv, but on the other hand, he was jealous, hurt and angry.

How could he have let Liv go? He knew what a great woman she was, but he let his mother's silly opinion of Liv get in the way. Chase now realizes that Liv was the "one that got away," and his hopes of finding his one true love have been dashed.

As their dinner date was ending, Chase felt that he had lost Liv forever. He decided to swallow his pride and beg Liv for another chance. He realized the error of his ways, and vowed that if she would give him another chance, he would do everything in his power to make her the happiest women alive.

Although tempting, Liv gently declined. Her feelings for Chase had changed, and she knew that she would never be able to love him like she once had. Chase wouldn't let up on his request for another chance, and Liv, who kept politely turning him down, was getting increasingly aggravated by his persistence. Liv once thought that the sun rose and set on Chase, but now, she was beginning to see his true colors emerge.

Chase had always been on the arrogant side, and was accustomed to getting his way all the time. He was spoiled as a child, and always seemed to have the upper hand when it came to relationships. If he didn't get what he wanted, he became pushy, overbearing and selfish.

Chase was sure that if he kissed Liv, that old spark would re-ignite in her soul. Not only did Liv turn away from Chase's attempt at a kiss, she was repelled by it. He no longer had the same effect on her, and in fact, she wished that she could have snapped her fingers to bring her back home to Ben. She felt safe with Ben because he was so genuine and kind. There was not an arrogant or selfish bone in his body.

Liv always lived on the edge with Chase, and always questioned his feelings for her. She knows that Ben is in love with her, and only her. He is not on the lookout for someone better, or for someone who is on the same level as he is educationally. Even though Liv doesn't have a college education, she is extremely bright, quick witted, wise and perceptive. Qualities that Chase never saw in her.

He criticized Liv because of the way she spoke and because she never attended college. He wanted to pay for her college education so that she could "better herself," however, Liv believes that he only wanted her to go to college because he was concerned that she wasn't "scholarly" enough, and that it didn't look good for him to be with an "uneducated" woman.

Just to make sure that Chase was completely out of her system, Liv relented and kissed him. The kiss soon became more intense, and Liv could sense that Chase was getting overly enthusiastic. Since she wasn't feeling the same way, she retreated. She now knew, for sure, that Chase wasn't the man for her. When she kissed Ben, passion stirs inside her, but when she kissed Chase, she felt nothing.

Although Liv felt guilty about kissing Chase, because she knew it would hurt Ben, she just had to know for sure if the excitement, love and passion were still there. They were for Chase, but not for Liv. It was then and there, that she decided to say good-bye, once and for all. Liv would never turn back, and would finally close that chapter in her life.

After a year had gone by, Liv and Ben started planning their wedding. They were now totally committed to each other, and were living together. Liv quit her job as a hair stylist, and was now working for Ben. This allowed them to spend all day together, which they cherished. Some couples enjoy the time they spend away from each other while they are both at their respective jobs, but for Liv and Ben, working together in the same office works well for them. In addition to being soul mates, they are best friends, and can let their respective guards down when they are together. Although Ben is technically Liv's boss, he never plays that card. He is also careful to never show favoritism to Liv in front of his other employees. He treats everyone with respect, and no one is treated better than anyone else. Many of Ben's employees have been with his for years, which is a true testament to his character. Liv is proud to be his life partner, both personally and professionally.

Liv was getting excited for her wedding, and before the big day, members of her bridal party gave her a bachelorette party. Liv almost forgot what it was like to have a good time with her friends, because the last time they all went out together, Liv was in a funk over Chase. She is grateful that her friends saw her through her ordeal, and is honored to have them be a part of her wedding day. The celebration started off at a neighborhood bar where the ladies indulged in a few tropical drinks, then it was off to Liv's favorite restaurant. The night was exciting and fun, and Liv couldn't remember when she had such a fun time with her friends. The merriment came to a screeching halt in the blink of an eye, however. While the ladies were enjoying their dinner and each other's company, a familiar figure walked through the door. It was none other than Chase. He was accompanied by an older woman, who Liv later recognized as his mother, Vera. The two looked solemn as they were seated at their table, and barely spoke to one another while they dined.

Chase and his mother hadn't yet noticed that Liv was at the restaurant, and Liv wanted it to stay that way. She didn't want anything casting a pall over her special evening, but when she had to go to the bathroom, she wondered how she'd sneak past their table without her cover being blown. After thinking about it, she realized that she didn't care if they saw her or not. She didn't owe either one of them anything and didn't even feel obligated to greet them. Liv and her entourage made a beeline for the bathroom, but not before Chase's mother noticed them. "Isn't that Liv?" she asked.

Chase was stunned and took this as another opportunity to try and win her back. It's fate, he thought. Yes, it was fate, but not in the way that Chase had hoped for. He stalked the bathroom door and waiting for Liv to come out. When she did, he greeted her with a hug. Liv tried to be personable, but again, she couldn't hide her disdain for Chase.

Liv and Chase ended up having a brief conversation. Liv was more than happy to tell Chase about her impending nuptials to Ben. She then learned why Chase and his mother looked so stone-faced when they walked into the restaurant.

It turned out that Chase was the one who was now battling severe depression ever since Liv didn't return his affections the last time they had dinner together. In fact, his depression got so bad that he had to give up his law practice and move in with his mother.

This was the first night he had been out in public in months. His relationship with Chelsea had long since fell apart, and he was having a hard time re-building his life. Liv felt bad for Chase, and now wondered if his mother felt any remorse for sticking her nose in their business by setting him up with Chelsea.

Liv and Ben were married in a beautiful ceremony, and now have an adorable baby girl. Chase is still living with his mother, and has let his law license expire. He did get a job working as a handyman in the neighborhood, however, and Liv has since shown pity on him and hired him to install a white picket fence around her and Ben's sprawling new home.

Second Chance Romance

Ruthless pig Justin dumped devoted Jodi after he hooked up with a younger, more attractive woman. While Jodi tried moving on with her life, she couldn't shake the paralyzing depression she felt.

She craved Justin's love more then ever, even though it had been three years since he left her. She begged him to take her back but this only turned him off more.

Jodi met charismatic Justin when he came into the hair salon where she worked. She fell in love with him at first sight even though she found him arrogant, cocky and brazen. Everything about him was thrilling to her. He was a champion polo player who belonged to an exclusive country club and he traveled all over the world.

Jodi grew up poor, and while she did well in high school, she was unable to attend college because of financial constraints and responsibilities at home. After her father got fired from his job, Jodi had to work full-time to help pay the bills.

Justin was 12 years older than Jodi, although he acted much younger. She found his friends to be boring, stodgy, and arrogant. Despite her disdain for his friends, she quickly fell in love with him. He treated her like a queen, and even offered to pay for her to go back to college. At first, they were blissfully happy.

The couple soon settled into a mundane dating routine, and although Jodi was still jubilant about their relationship, she sensed that Justin was becoming restless and bored with her. He seemed irritated and distant, and even stopped coming home after work. When he began hurling cruel comments to her, she felt hopeless and vulnerable.

Most of Justin's family members liked Jodi but his mother never warmed up to her. She never thought that Jodi was good enough for her son, but remained cordial to her.

Justin's mother, Caroline, on more than one occasion, tried introducing her son to various women. These women were all professionals, and a few were lawyers, just like her son.

Justin's father, Peter, also an attorney, stayed out of his wife's shameless matchmaking schemes. He was in his own little world, with a mistress of his own and a huge drinking problem.

Justin didn't invite Jodi to his grandmother's birthday party, and when he arrived, he was greeted at the door by one of the most beautiful women he'd ever seen. He never saw her before, and wondered who she was there with. Little did he know, his mother invited her in an attempt to get him interested in someone other than Jodi.

Her plan worked. Justin and the other women, whose name was Christine, hit it off almost instantly. He couldn't stop looking at her, and was intrigued by her New York accent.

Christine worked as an entertainment attorney, who represented a number of big name sports and music personalities. She even invited Justine to a sporting event which had been sold out for weeks.

Even though Justin had no intentions of breaking up with Jodi, he could no longer ignore his feelings for Christine. They soon started having lunch dates at 5 star hotels, and even managed to plan a getaway weekend to the Poconos.

When Justin started becoming increasingly distant from Jodi, she started to suspect the worst. By this time, Christine was pressuring Justine for a commitment. Although they've only been seeing each other for about a month, their relationship was growing more and more intense.

The sex was amazing, and Justin never experienced anything like it before. Christine was willing to try new things in bed, and seemed to want sex multiple times a day. Jodi, by contrast, was rather modest, and her sexual appetite was diminished by her escalating depression, and the side effects from the medication she was taking.

As the months passed, Jodi was getting ready to go to Florida for a hair show. She and Justin were drifting further and further apart, but they still managed to maintain a dim spark of excitement between them. On the evening before she was schedule to leave for her trip, Jodi and Justin went out for a romantic dinner, and then came home and spent the next three hours making love.

After their love fest, Justin turned over and went to sleep. Jodi, the eternal romantic, want to cuddle, but Justin rebuffed her advances. The next morning, Justin drove Jodi to the airport, and he couldn't help but feel profound relief. He would now be able to spend the next week with his new "friend," Christine, and called her as soon as Jodi boarded the plane.

For almost the entire week that Jodi was on her business trip, Justin stayed with Christine at her downtown apartment. The couple enjoyed cooking dinner together and waking up next to each other. Justin didn't know how he would tell Jodi that he no longer loved her, and he even wished that she would stay in Florida for the long-term.

He was not responsive to her text messages, and only took her phone calls sporadically during that entire week. The week flew by quickly, and before he knew it, Justin found himself at the airport once again, but only this time, he was picking Jodi up. She was elated to see him, but he cringed when they hugged.

Jodi sensed that something was wrong, and was starting to worry. Justin told her that he was tired because he spent the entire week working on a brief for an upcoming legal case.

The couple trudged through the holidays together, but as Valentine's Day approached, Justin could no longer suppress he desire to be with Christine. Although he knew that Valentine's week was not the most appropriate time to break up with Jodi, he felt it was necessary, because he wanted to spend Valentine's Day with Christine.

He didn't bother with formalities, and simply blurted it out. He told Jodi that he was no longer happy with her, but didn't volunteer any information about his other woman. He further explained that he just needed time to be "by himself," and that "maybe" he would come to his senses and come back home to be with her. After Jodi pressed him for answers, he finally came clean about Christine.

After hearing the news, Jodi broke down, and didn't think she would be able to function at work the next day. Of course, Justin told her that he didn't mean for it to happen, but when he met Christine, an instant connection was made. He didn't really want to divulge so much information about how he felt about Christine, but he felt that unless he "drove his point home," Jodi wouldn't take him seriously.

Jodi was blindsided by the breakup. She tried to keep busy with work and going out with friends, but she couldn't shake the despair she felt. Although she was asked out on dates, she always declined.

In Jodi's eyes, nobody would ever hold a candle to Justin, and she had no desire to date anyone because she knew it would never progress into anything further. In the meantime, Justin and Christine were seen around town at various restaurants and social events.

On one occasion, Jodi caught a glimpse of the couple getting out of a cab. This almost pushed her over the edge, but she managed to hold onto her dignity. After three years passed, Jodi's feelings for Justin were still as intense as they were when they first started dated. Justin's feelings for Jodi, on the other hand, were almost non-existent. Sure, he had fond memories of their time together, but never really felt as though Jodi was his soul mate.

Jodi eventually started seeing a counselor because she was not bouncing back from the breakup. Her sleep pattern was disrupted, her diet was poor, and she stopped socializing altogether. The only social stimulation she got was when she went to work, and even there, her social interactions were severely limited.

The counselor was worried for his patient's safety, and feared that she was spiraling into a deep, dark depression. Jodi was eventually referred to a psychiatrist, who adjusted her medication and sent her on her way. When the medication kicked in after a few weeks, Jodi's mood brightened, and she started considering dating again.

Jodi met a nice guy at the gym, and when he asked her out for coffee, she felt flattered. Like Justin, Brandon was older, distinguished and well-educated. Their coffee date was pleasant, but according to Jodi, there was no spark.

When Brandon asked her out for dinner, Jodi hesitated, but decided to give him another chance. She was very critical of other men, but hoped that she would once again, find love. Brandon took Jodi to dinner and a play, and as the date was coming to a close, Brandon leaned in for a kiss.

Jodi had no intentions of kissing him, and in fact, she had no intentions of ever seeing him again. All she could think about was Justin. Three years have passed, and still, her love was as strong as ever. Jodi's co-workers were worried about her, and when she had too much to drink one night and drunk dialed Justin, they really became concerned. Fortunately she hung up before he answered the phone, but her number showed up on his caller ID.

Justin was curious to find out what Jodi wanted. His relationship with Christine was starting to cool, and lately, he started thinking about how much Jodi loved him when they were together. He hesitated at first, but after a couple days, Justin returned Jodi's call.

You could have knocked her over with a feather when she saw Justin's number come up on her caller ID. She was shaking as she answered the phone, and as soon as she heard his voice, she broke down sobbing.

Something stirred in Justin's heart, because he too, felt tears welling up in his eyes. Their phone call was brief, and in fact, it lasted only seconds, because Christine walked into the room just as Jodi answered. Justin took this as a sign.

Jodi knew that Justin still felt a connection to her. She quickly put that phone call out of her mind, and tried to focus on her job. She went on a few more dates, and much to her surprise, Jodi found a guy with whom she clicked with.

Her friend introduced her to an accountant who was from the same town that she was from. In fact, they lived within a few blocks of each other when they were teenagers, but they went to different schools. He went to a private, all-boys school, and Jodi went to a public school.

At first, the relationship progressed slowly, but after a few months, Jodi started developing strong feelings for her new friend, whose name was Nathan. He took Jodi to meet his family in New Hampshire, and they absolutely loved her. Unlike Justin's mother, Caroline, Nathan's mother, Kerry, felt that they were the perfect couple.

As their relationship grew stronger, Jodi's feelings for Justin were becoming distant memories. In fact, days went by where she didn't even think about Justin at all. Justin, on the other hand, couldn't get Jodi out of his mind. His relationship with Christine was hanging by a thread, and he yearned for the relationship he once shared with Jodi.

He was starting to realize that breaking up with her was a mistake, and he hoped that she was not involved with another man. Justin finally raised enough courage to call Jodi back, and when she answered, his heart stopped. He almost hung up, but was able to whisper out a weak, "Hi Jodi, how are you?" Jodi was gracious and warm, and replied, "Hi, Justin, it's nice to hear from you."

The conversation was strained and awkward, but in Justin's mind, the ice had been broken. He was certain that he could get back into Jodi's good graces once again, so that they could pick up where they left off. Their conversation consisted solely of small talk, and neither one asked about the other's personal life.

Jodi almost felt sick to her stomach when she heard Justin's voice, because it brought back the painful memories of their breakup. She was grateful that she had Nathan, because he filled the void that Justin left. When she told Nathan that Justin called, he became suspicious. Why, he thought, would Justin call Jodi, out of the blue, after three years apart. Did Jodi initiate the first call, he wondered? Jodi finally confessed to Nathan that she did, indeed, "drunk dial" Justin days before.

It seemed that now, the tables were turned. Justin was the one who was pining away for Jodi, while Jodi, on the other hand, was blissfully "in like" with someone else. It never occurred to Justin that Jodi would move on and start a new life with someone else. He also felt that Jodi was his "ace in the hole," in case his relationship with Christine didn't work out. Would he and Jodi ever reconcile, he wondered?

Even though Jodi was happy with Nathan, she couldn't get Justin out of her mind, and wanted to connect with him again, just to find out more about his relationship status with Christine.

Jodi felt a twinge of guilt for thinking about calling Justin because Nathan had been so good to her. She didn't want to be shady or go behind his back, so she talked to him about her intentions.

Jodi felt that she needed to get Justin out of her system once and for all before she would be able to move forward with her relationship with Nathan. A total commitment to Nathan was out of the question, in Jodi's mind, unless she was completely over Justin.

Nathan agreed that Jodi needed to get Justin out of her system before they could take the next step in their relationship, so he encouraged Jodi to make the phone call. Feeling better now that she confessed her feelings to Nathan about Justin, Jodi picked up the phone and dialed his number.

He answered on the first ring, and couldn't believe his good fortune that Jodi was calling him. "I want to see you," Jodi said, as soon as Justin answered the phone.

Justin was shocked, but elated. By this time, he and Chistine were barely speaking, and she was spending more and more time away from the apartment that they shared since the beginning of their relationship.

Jodi and Justin planned to go out for dinner so that could talk. Both were excited, anxious, but uncertain about a future together. When Jodi saw Justin for the first time in three years, she was surprised that her heart wasn't racing, and that she did not have butterflies in her stomach.

Although it was nice to see Justin, that intense spark of passion and love was not there. Justin, on the other hand, could barely contain his emotions, and started to cry when they hugged.

He apologized to Jodi for hurting her, but she was unfazed. The cold and uncaring manner in which he "dumped" Jodi always bothered Justin, but he never had the opportunity to tell Jodi how he felt. They talked about Justin's relationship with Christine, and how it started out so intensely, but then, over time, seemed to have burned itself out.

Jodi listened quietly as Justin spoke about how Christine was a workaholic, and how she never cooked a meal for him in three years. Not only didn't she cook, she never cleaned either. Justin finally hired a cleaning service to come in twice a month to tidy up, but he wished that Christine was a little more domesticated. She wasn't into the "housewife" thing, and she certainly didn't have any maternal instincts either. Jodi couldn't help but feel a twinge of satisfaction while Justin was droning on about his faltering relationship with Christine.

Justin was the type of guy who enjoyed home-cooked meals, who liked a clean home, and who wanted to start a family some day. Jodi wanted to start a family too, but it was becoming more apparent to Jodi, that instead of wanting to start a family with Justin, she wanted to start one with Nathan.

Throughout the entire dinner, Justin talked about himself and his relationship with Christine. He didn't ask Jod what was going on in her life until it was almost time for them to leave.

Justin was certain that Jodi had been waiting around for him to come back all this time, and was profoundly disappointed when Jodi told him that she had met someone else. What made Justin feel even worse was when Jodi told him that she was falling in love with Nathan. Justin asked, "how could you have fallen out of love with me?" Jodi replied, " It took a long time, but I finally found someone who appreciates me, embraces me for who I am, and whose family loves me." On one hand, Justin was happy for Jodi, but on the other hand, he was jealous, hurt and angry.

How could he have let Jodi go? He knew what a great woman she was, but he let his mother's silly opinion of Jodi get in the way. Justin now realizes that Jodi was the "one that got away," and his hopes of finding his one true love have been dashed.

As their dinner date was ending, Justin felt that he had lost Jodi forever. He decided to swallow his pride and beg Jodi for another chance. He realized the error of his ways, and vowed that if she would give him another chance, he would do everything in his power to make her the happiest women alive.

Although tempting, Jodi gently declined. Her feelings for Justin had changed, and she knew that she would never be able to love him like she once had. Justin wouldn't let up on his request for another chance, and Jodi, who kept politely turning him down, was getting increasingly aggravated by his persistence. Jodi once thought that the sun rose and set on Justin, but now, she was beginning to see his true colors emerge.

Justin had always been on the arrogant side, and was accustomed to getting his way all the time. He was spoiled as a child, and always seemed to have the upper hand when it came to relationships. If he didn't get what he wanted, he became pushy, overbearing and selfish.

Justin was sure that if he kissed Jodi, that old spark would re-ignite in her soul. Not only did Jodi turn away from Justin's attempt at a kiss, she was repelled by it. He no longer had the same effect on her, and in fact, she wished that she could have snapped her fingers to bring her back home to Nathan. She felt safe with him because he was so genuine and kind. There was not an arrogant or selfish bone in his body.

Jodi always lived on the edge with Justin, and always questioned his feelings for her. She knows that Nathan is in love with her, and only her. He is not on the lookout for someone better, or for someone who is on the same level as he is educationally. Even though Jodi doesn't have a college education, she is extremely bright, quick witted, wise and perceptive. Qualities that Justin never saw in her.

He criticized Jodi because of the way she spoke and because she never attended college. He wanted to pay for her college education so that she could "better herself," however, Jodi believes that he only wanted her to go to college because he was concerned that she wasn't "scholarly" enough, and that it didn't look good for him to be with an "uneducated" woman.

Just to make sure that Justin was completely out of her system, Jodi relented an kissed him. The kiss soon became more intense, and Jod could sense that Justin was getting overly enthusiastic. Since she wasn't feeling the same way, she retreated. She now knew, for sure, that Justin wasn't the man for her. When she kissed Nathan, passion stirred inside her, but when she kissed Justin, she felt nothing.

Although Jodi felt guilty about kissing Justin because she knew it would hurt Nathan, she just had to know for sure if the excitement, love and passion were still there. They were for Justin, but not for Jodi. It was then and there, that she decided to say good-bye, once and for all. Jodi would never turn back, and would finally close that chapter in her life.

After a year had gone by, Jody and Nathan started planning their wedding. They were now totally committed to each other, and were living together. Jodi quit her job as a hair stylist, and was now working for Nathan. This allowed them to spend all day together, which they cherished. Some couples enjoy the time they spend away from each other while they are both at their respective jobs, but for Jodi and Nathan, working together in the same office works well for them. In addition to being soul mates, they are best friends, and can let their respective guards down when they are together.

Although Nathan is technically Jodi's boss, he never plays that card. He is also careful, however, to never show favoritism to Jodi in front of his other employees. He treats everyone with respect, and no one is treated better than anyone else. Many of Nathan's employees have been with his for years, which is a true testament to his character. Jodi is proud to be his life partner, both personally and professionally.

Jodi was getting excited for her wedding, and before the big day, members of her bridal party gave her a bachelorette party. Jodi almost forgot what it was like to have a good time with her friends, because the last time they all went out together, Jodi was in a funk over Justin.

She is grateful that her friends saw her through her ordeal, and is honored to have them be a part of her wedding day. The celebration started off at a neighborhood bar where the ladies indulged in a few tropical drinks, then it was off to Jodi's favorite restaurant. The night was exciting and fun, and Jodi couldn't remember when she had such a fun time with her friends.

The merriment came to a screeching halt in the blink of an eye, however. While the ladies were enjoying their dinner and each other's company, a familiar figure walked through the door. It was none other than Justin. He was accompanied by an older woman, who Jodi later recognized as his mother, Caroline. The two looked solemn as they were seated at their table, and barely spoke to one another while they dined.

Justin and his mother hadn't yet noticed that Jodi was at the restaurant, and Jodi wanted it to stay that way. She didn't want anything casting a pall over her special evening, but when she had to go to the bathroom, she wondered how she'd sneak past their table without her cover being blown.

After thinking about it, she realized that she didn't care if they saw her or not. She didn't owe either one of them anything and didn't even feel obligated to greet them. Jodi and her entourage made a beeline for the bathroom, but not before Justin's mother noticed them. "Isn't that Jodi?" she asked.

Justin was stunned and took this as another opportunity to try and win her back. It's fate, he thought. Yes, it was fate, but not in the way that Justin had hoped for. He stalked the bathroom door and waiting for Jodi to come out. When she did, he greeted her with a hug. Jodi tried to be personable, but again, she couldn't hide her disdain for Justin.

Jodi and Justin ended up having a brief conversation. Jodi was more than happy to tell Justin about her impending nuptials to Nathan. She then learned why Justin and his mother looked so stone-faced when they walked into the restaurant.

It turned out that Justin was the one who was now battling severe depression ever since Jodi didn't return his affections the last time they had dinner together. In fact, his depression got so bad that he had to give up his law practice and move in with his mother.

This was the first night he had been out in public in months. His relationship with Christine had long since fell apart, and he was having a hard time re-building his life. Jodi felt bad for Justin, and now wondered if his mother felt any remorse for sticking her nose in their business by setting him up with Christine.

Jodi and Nathan were married in a beautiful ceremony, and now have an adorable baby girl. Justin is still living with his mother, and has let his law license expire. He did get a job working as a handyman in the neighborhood, however, and Jodi has since shown pity on him and hired him to install a white picket fence around her and Nathan's sprawling new home. Karma at its best...

Second Chances

Brooke felt an immediate attraction to charismatic Sean the moment she first saw him at her best friend, Lisa's wedding. Although he was there with a date, Brooke couldn't help but stare at him.

Sean was stunningly handsome and sensual, and he had the most dazzling smile she'd ever seen.

When Lisa returned from her honeymoon, she called Brooke and asked her what she thought about Sean.

"I thought he was gorgeous! Too bad he was with a date," Brooke said.

"She's not his girlfriend, and in fact, he seems to be interested in you," Lisa explained.

"You have my permission to give him my phone number," Brooke told Lisa.

"I already did," Lisa replied.

When Sean finally called her, Brooke was jubilant, but she was so nervous that she couldn't think of a thing to say. She felt that their conversation was strained and awkward at first, but as it progressed, the couple's banter flowed freely and effortlessly.

Brooke learned that Sean was a wealthy investment banker who grew up only minutes away from Brooke's hometown.

"I'm sure that we know some of the same people," Sean said.

"Where did you go to high school," Brooke asked.

"Central, how about you?"

"Riverwoods," she replied.

The couple continued on with their small talk for what seemed like an eternity to Brooke, but after a while, Sean finally asked her out.

"What are you doing Saturday night?"

"I don't have plans yet," Brooke said.

Sean asked, "Have you ever been to that new restaurant on Mayfair Street yet?"

"Not yet, but I've been wanting to check it out for the longest time. I've heard that they have the best pub food around and that it has live entertainment on the weekends," Brooke replied.

Brooke didn't want to say anything to Sean, but her ex-boyfriend, Levi was the restaurant's manager.

She and Levi had broken up about a year ago after she found out that he was cheating on her with one of the waitresses he worked with.

Brooke was devastated by the break-up, and was convinced that she would never find love again.

"I'll pick you up at 7," Sean told Brooke.

"Great! I'm looking forward to seeing you."

While Brooke really didn't want to bump into her ex-boyfriend at the restaurant, she hoped that he would see her with Sean.

Levi wasn't the jealous type, but Brooke hoped that if he saw her with another guy, he might regret leaving her.

She recently heard that he and his waitress girlfriend were no longer together, and as far as Brooke knew, he was single once again.

Levi worked long hours at the restaurant and didn't have a lot of time for a social life.

When Sean arrived to pick her up, Brooke was dazzled by his rugged good looks. He was impeccably dressed and smelled delicious. She shamelessly stared at his perfectly toned body, and was starting to get excited at the thought of his touch.

"You look absolutely gorgeous," Sean told Brooke.

"Thank you. You don't look so bad, yourself!"

As the couple drove into the restaurant's parking lot, Brooke starting feeling anxious. What would she do if she saw Levi?

She thought about telling Sean that her ex-boyfriend was the manager, but decided against it, at least for now.

The restaurant was dark and cozy, which gave Brooke a sense of peaceful comfort. Even if Levi was working, she didn't think that he could possible see her, unless he walked up to her table.

Brooke finally started to relax, knowing that she wouldn't have to encounter an uncomfortable meeting with her ex-boyfriend.

The conversation between she and Sean was flowing nicely until he asked her about her past relationships.

"How long did your last relationship last?"

"About two years," Brooke replied.

"What happened, if you don't mind me asking?"

"Things just didn't work out between us, and we decided to go our separate ways."

Sean continued to press Brooke for answers about her relationship with Levi. Feeling uncomfortable by his intrusive questions, Brooke finally told him that she didn't want to talk about it anymore. Embarrassed by his boldness, Sean apologized.

After only a couple of hours, Brooke determined that Sean would make a good boyfriend.

She liked the fact that he was considerate of her feelings, had the same job for ten years, was close to his family, and had tons of friends.

While Brooke didn't enjoy talking about her past relationships, Sean had no problem doing so.

"My last relationship lasted for about five years, and even though we were in love, we both knew that it wouldn't last."

Sean further explained, "She was quite a bit older than I was and wasn't interested in having a family, which is something that I've always dreamed of."

He also commented that her family wasn't too fond of him because he wasn't established in his career yet.

From the side of her eye, Brooke saw someone resembling Levi. Her initial reaction was to quickly leave the restaurant, but after thinking about it, she decided to stay.

The person who looked like Levi was stopping at each table conversing with the customers. As it turned out, it was him.

Brooke's heart was literally beating out of her chest because Levi, the restaurant manager, was making his way to her and Sean's table.

"Oh my God, here he comes," Brooke said to herself.

Sean sensed that something was wrong, and asked Brooke what it was. At first, she didn't want to volunteer any information about Levi, but she knew that she had to.

"That guy over there, the restaurant manager, is my ex-boyfriend, Levi."

"Do you want to leave?" he asked.

"No, it's okay. I don't care if he sees me."

Before she knew it, Levi was standing at their table and asked, "Hi guys, is everything alright?

At first, Levi didn't notice that it was Brooke sitting at the table because he was looking at Sean when he greeted them.

As soon as he discovered it was her, he exclaimed, "Brooke, it's good to see you again!"

"Nice to see you too, Levi."

Brooke introduced Levi to Sean, and she could tell that they both felt uncomfortable when they shook hands.

Sean as was classy as ever during the introduction and he even engaged Levi in a conversation about the restaurant.

"This is such a great place. How long have you been working here?"

Levi answered, "I really enjoy it here. I've been with the restaurant for about three years."

He further added, "management is great and my co-workers are cool."

For some reason, Brooke was starting to get annoyed at how well the two guys were getting along.

After a few more minutes of small talk, Levi excused himself so that he could get back to work.

Before he left the table, however, he slipped a note into Brooke's purse, which was hanging off the back of her chair.

She didn't discover the note until the next morning when she was looking for some gum.

The note read: "Brooke, you took my breath away when I saw you tonight. After seeing you, I realized that I made a terrible mistake in letting you go. I know that you've moved on with your life, and I'm really happy for you, but sad at the same time."

Levi went on to say, "I am so sorry for hurting you and for turning your life upside down. If you could find it in your heart to forgive me, I'd be forever grateful. Please, Brooke, I'm begging for another chance. I've been constantly thinking about you for months, and I can't get you out of my mind. I feel powerless and helpless without you in my life. I'm in agony. Please call me. I love you, Brooke."

Brooke was stunned. Even in her wildest dream, she would have never guessed that Levi was still in love with her.

In fact, she assumed that she was simply a distant memory in his mind.

While she was flattered to learn that he still had strong feelings for her, she had no desire to reconnect with him.

Brooke finally told Sean about what happened between her and Levi and how he ruthlessly cheated on her with one of the waitresses he works with.

Sean seemed to sympathize with Levi and even went so far as to say, "well you guys weren't engaged or anything, so I really don't see a problem with it." This comment infuriated Brooke and made her reconsider her relationship with Sean.

While it was true that Brooke and Levi weren't engaged, they had a mutually exclusive relationship with an understanding that neither one of them would see other people.

After Sean's snarky comment, Brooke's entire impression of him changed for the worst.

This wasn't the only rude comment he made either. He also mentioned that he really didn't blame Levi for cheating on her because the temptation of being surrounded by so many beautiful cocktail waitresses would make any man stray.

Brooke couldn't believe what she was hearing, and she vowed that if Sean made one more snotty remark, she was going to stop seeing him.

In fact, the better Brooke got to know him, the more appealing Levi became.

While Levi did cheat on her, he always treated with her with the utmost respect and kindness throughout the duration of their relationship. She even feels partially responsible for their break up.

Brooke always pressured Levi into getting a better paying job and furthering his education.

She also demanded all of his time. Levi worked long hours, and he sometimes didn't get home until after midnight.

Brooke didn't care. She would often demand that he come over after work, even if it was late. Levi always complied, and never gave her a hard time about it.

This doesn't justify his cheating, but Brooke was now starting to realize that she may have driven him right into the arms of another women. One who was understanding, patient and not so demanding. Brooke craved his attention all the time and he felt smothered by it.

One of Brooke's co-workers told her that Levi's relationship with the cocktail waitress was staring to heat up again. She thought they broke up, but maybe not.

Brooke found this disturbing, especially since he recently professed his love for her through his letter.

Sean's behavior toward Brooke was starting to turn her off more and more. He always wanted to talk about her relationship with Levi, and even started pressuring her into revealing the most intimate details of their sex life.

Sean often asked, "Did you enjoy having sex with him?"

He further inquired, "Who was better in bed, Levi or me?"

Brooke replied, "You're being so intrusive and I resent all the questions." She also told him, "I'm starting to think that we should take a break from each other.

We used to be so happy and always had fun together. Now, there's always conflict."

"The reason there's so much conflict is because you don't want to share anything with me.

When I ask you for details about your relationship with Levi, I expect you to be forthcoming. You're so secretive about everything. I don't understand it," Sean remarked.

Brooke's responded, "I'm hesitant to talk about my former relationships because it's really none of your business. I don't ask you about the intimate details of your past relationships."

Sean was starting to fall in love with Brooke, but he didn't know how to tell her.

After all, they've only been dating for a short time, and he didn't want to come on too strong.

He knew that his prying would be a turn-off, but for some reason, he couldn't help it.

He didn't want to lose Brooke by being too possessive because he considered her his "dream girl."

The couple eventually decided to take a break from one another, and stopped dating for about a month.

During this time, Brooke re-evaluated her feelings for Levi. His note made her feel special, and deep down, she knew that he loved her.

The question was, however, did she still love him?

While she often thought about Levi, Brooke was staring to miss Sean.

She wondered if he felt the same way, so one night, after having a few drinks with some friends, she decided to call him.

"Remember me?" she coyly asked.

"I thought I'd never hear from you again," Sean answered.

"I really miss you, and came to realize just how much I care for you," Brooke said. "Can we meet for dinner next week to talk."

"Next week isn't good for me because I'm going to New York to visit my parents," Sean answered.

Brooke's heart sank. She was now convinced that Sean was no longer interested in her.

"How about Friday of next week?" he asked.

Excited, Brooke responded, "That sounds great, Sean. I can't wait to see you."

Brooke was anticipating her date with Sean and she hoped that they would be able to patch things up between them.

Even though he started acting like a jerk at the end, Brooke knew that he had a good heart, and that he genuinely cared about her.

When Sean picked her up, Brooke could barely catch her breath. He looked amazingly handsome and sexy.

They hugged for what seemed like an eternity, and being with him felt natural and right to Brooke.

The restaurant was romantic and the talk was sweet. By the time they got back to Brooke's house, they could hardly keep their hands off one another.

"Would you like to come in for a cup of coffee?" Brooke asked.

"I would love to."

They sat on the couch and starting kissing. Sean gently put his hands on Brooke's blouse. "I know I said I wanted to take things slow, but I'm not so sure now, so just go for it," she said.

He quickly ripped the blouse from her toned body and it fell to the floor.

His eager lips kissed her neck, while her hands unbuttoned his shirt, removing it from the waistband of his pants.

Brooke started out slowly, but then decided to bust open his shirt in the same manner in which Sean busted opened her blouse.

Her quivering hands found their way down his muscular chest, while he hungrily continued to kiss her.

Brooke arched her back, moaning each time he kissed her.

His strong hands rubbed her back, as he slowly took off her bra. Her ample breasts pressed firmly against his waiting chest.

Her hands unzipped his pants and she quickly removed them. Sean's hands went to his underwear while Brooke tugged on them to get them off.

He kissed her breasts while she eyed his ample erection. She was getting more and more excited with every glance, and when he undid the zipper on her dress, she was consumed with desire.

His hands went to her panties, looping his slender fingers through them, gently pulling them off her body.

Before Brooke had time to anticipate Sean's next move, she felt him pick her up, laying her down on the bed.

Their lips finally met, his eager tongue darting inside her mouth. As their tongues intertwined, his hands massaged her ample breasts, savoring the softness of her supple skin.

As Sean was ready to make love to Brooke, he hesitated. "Damn it, I don't have a condom," pulling back in disappointment.

She pulled him even closer. "Don't worry, I'm on the pill," she soothed, as they kissed and he penetrated her.

"It feels so good" she softly said, arching her back, but never breaking away from his kiss. His thrusts are deliberate and intense, which forces her to lose contact with his lips. It felt like a dream.

While one of Brooke's arms was holding onto Sean, she tried to grasp onto anything she could to hold onto as her body bucked up against his, finally choosing the side of the nightstand.

He had a hunger that she never experienced before. "Damn...yes...yes" he groaned, holding her even tighter to his body.

She could feel him pulsating within her, "God, yes..." she cried. She sighed deeply, almost unable to move, while his rhythmic grinding came to a halt. "That was amazing," she whispered.

As Brooke was basking in the afterglow, she felt Sean's hands moving up her legs, gingerly caressing her.

She wasn't sure what he was going to do, but when she felt his finger gently penetrate her, she moaned, savoring his every move.

In addition to using his finger, he began using his tongue to tease her.

As his tongue glided in and out of her, she reached down and grabbed his head to pull him in even closer to her.

After the interlude was over, Brooke was surprised at her lack of emotion towards Sean.

In fact, during the entire lovemaking session, she was thinking about Levi. She knew that it wasn't fair to Sean, but she couldn't help how she felt.

Had Levi never left that note in her purse, she feels she would have been better off. All these months, she barely thought of Levi. She was moving on with her life and socializing more than ever.

"Sean, I enjoyed our time together, but I can't help but feel that we're not right for each other."

"What about last night," he questioned.

"Last night was great, but there was something missing," Brooke replied.

She further explained, "I don't know how to explain it. I feel as though I should have been into it more, but I wasn't."

"Were you thinking about that jerk, Levi while we were making love?" he asked.

"Sean, I don't want to lie to you. Ever since I saw Levi at the restaurant, I can't get him out of my mind. He and I shared years together, and it's hard to forget about him. I thought I was starting to get him out of my mind once and for all, but seeing him again sparked some old feelings inside me."

"Brooke, please give me a chance to make you happy. I know I can make you forget all about Levi. You're just confused because you saw him again after all those months. The feelings you have for him aren't love. You're just confused."

"Maybe you're right, Sean," Brooke said. She further remarked, "Thank you for being so patient with me. I guess I am confused."

Brooke ended up giving Sean another chance, but as the weeks went by, she still couldn't stop thinking about Levi. She knew that she wanted to call him to talk about a reconciliation.

As she dialed his number, Brooke was shaking. She was hoping that his voicemail would pick up so that she could leave a message. It didn't.

"Hello?"

"Hi Levi, it's Brooke."

Levi's voice cracked as though he were starting to cry.

"Hi baby, I miss you so much. We should still be together. I really screwed things up between us."

"What have you been up to, and how serious are you with that guy I saw you with at the restaurant?"

"We've been dating for a while, and while we're semi-serious, our relationship can't compare with the one we had," Brooke said.

"Does this mean that I have a chance?" Levi asked.

"A very good chance," she said.

Brooke and Levi decided to meet at a neighborhood coffee shop, and when they first saw each other, they hugged and cried.

They both commented on how being together felt so right, and that neither one of them had found true happiness since the break up.

The couple decided that they wanted to spend the rest of their lives together, but they would first have to break the news to their current partners.

Brooke knew that Sean would take it hard, but he was a strong enough person that he would bounce back quickly and get on with his life.

Levi's current girlfriend, on the other hand, might not take it so well. She had been pressuring him for an engagement ring because she wanted to settle down and have a family with him.

"Let's go away for the weekend," Levi suggested.

While Brooke normally would have jumped at the chance to have Levi all to herself for an entire weekend, she didn't feel right about it. She wanted to end things with Sean before taking Levi up on his offer.

It disturbed her that Levi would suggest going away together before ending it with his current girlfriend.

"You'll have to end your relationship before I'll go away with you."

Levi reasoned, "I'll have a talk with her when I get back."

It was right then and there that Brooke decided she didn't want anything more to do with Levi.

He planned on cheating on his girlfriend just like he cheated on her. This brought back so many negative memories, and she really sympathized with the other woman.

"I see that you haven't changed much. You don't have a moral compass," Brooke said.

"Come on, Brooke, give me a break. I've been under a lot of stress lately. The restaurant is crazy busy, and I've been working 80 hours a week."

Levi further explained, "All I ask is that you give me another week to end the relationship. You'll see, Brooke. I'll do right by you."

"I'm sorry Levi. This isn't going to work out." I can't be with someone who seems like a serial cheater. You cheated on me, and now you're scheming to cheat on her."

"Brooke, you don't understand," Levi argued.

"Unfortunately, Levi, I do."

"I'd never be able to trust you. How do you expect me to love you when I can't trust you?"

"Goodbye, Levi."

Surprisingly, Brooke wasn't too upset about how it all played out. She felt worse thinking about how she hurt Sean when she broke up with him.

She even wondered if Sean would take her back. She hated the dating scene, and always preferred to be in a relationship, even if it did have some ups and downs.

Brooke was looking forward to reconnecting with Sean. She had a feeling that he was thinking about her, and would welcome her back with open arms.

They were always so connected to each other, and they both assumed that they would end up getting married one day.

Brooke couldn't decide on whether to text Sean or to call him. She longed to hear his voice, and hoped he would feel the same.

She dialed his cell, but he didn't answer. She didn't leave a message, but instead, decided to call him on the home phone.

After the phone rang about three times, someone answered it. "Hello?"

Brooke was confused, because the person who answered the phone was a woman. She must have dialed the wrong number.

"I'm sorry, I think I have the wrong number," Brooke said.

"Who were you trying to reach?" the woman asked.

"A friend of mine named Sean," Brooke replied.

"You have the right number. This is his wife. Who can I say is calling?"

"Never mind. I'm sorry to have bothered you."

Badly shaken, Brooke trembled as she disconnected the call. How could Sean have met someone and gotten himself married in such a short period of time?

She felt that her dreams were shattered. She lost two men that she loved to other women. Maybe it was time for a change of pace, she thought.

Brooke decided to pack up and move to Florida, where she had family. She took a job in retail until she could find something in her field. While her new life wasn't exciting by any stretch of the imagination, it was quiet and serene.

If she met someone, it would be great. If not, she wasn't going to stress out about it. As the week turned into months, Brooke started feeling depressed.

Her social life was almost non-existent, and her job bored her to tears. While she had family in Florida, they were much older than she was, and they lived hundreds of miles away.

On a whim, Brooke decided to enroll in a cooking class at the local park district. She always loved to cook, but never considered herself a gourmet. Not only would the class give her the opportunity to brush up on her culinary skills, but she also might meet some new friends.

Brooke had so much fun on the first night of the class. The people were outgoing and welcoming, and the group was very diverse. Although Brooke was happy to meet the women the class, she was more intrigued by the tall, handsome stockbroker who also signed up to learn how to cook.

"Hi, I'm Jack. What's your name?"

"Brooke. It's nice to meet you, Jack."

She couldn't believe her luck. Not only was she engaged in an activity that she enjoyed, but she also met a guy. While she never met Jack before, he looked so familiar. In fact, he looked a lot like Levi, much to her dismay.

During the fourth cooking class, Jack asked Brooke out for coffee. She eagerly said "yes," but was shocked to discover who he was.

"Have you always lived in Florida," Brooke asked.

"No, I actually just moved here to manage a restaurant. My brother, with whom I'm estranged from, used to manage it, but ran it into the ground. The restaurant is owned by our grandparents, and when they discovered that he had been fooling around with all the waitresses and stealing money from the business, they fired him and sort of disowned him."

Jack further explained, "My brother has since moved out of state, and from what I hear, he's managing another restaurant."

A chill ran down Brooke's spine. Right then and there, she knew that Jack was Levi's brother.

"What's your brother's name?"

"Levi," Jack replied.

Brooke didn't let on that she was in a relationship with Levi. If things between them were to get serious, she would tell him. But for now, she didn't see a reason to.

Both Brooke and Jack enjoyed each other's company so much that they decided to go out on a real date. One date led to another, and before she knew it, the couple was engaged.

Through the grapevine, both Sean and Levi got wind of Brooke's upcoming wedding. By this time, Sean was already divorced from his wife, and Levi had broken up with his girlfriend. They each sent Brooke congratulatory emails, professed their love for her and revealed that she was truly "the one who got away."

****

About the Author

J.L. Ryan is a bestselling author who has written over 50 books, including the wildly popular Billionaire Boys Club, Billionaire Games, Billionaire Bachelors, and Adventures In Romance. Ryan has also attended numerous book signings and writer's conventions including Romance Writers Of America Conferences. Living in New York, J.L. enjoys spending time with family and friends, volunteering at a large metropolitan homeless shelter, and working in the dog rescue community.

www.ingramcontent.com/pod-product-compliance
Lightning Source LLC
Chambersburg PA
CBHW060242030726
47493CB00025B/1560